fred
Carter

THE
LAST
ACT

THE
LAST
ACT

A NOVEL

BRAD PARKS

DUTTON

DUTTON

An imprint of Penguin Random House LLC
penguinrandomhouse.com

Quote from *Pippin*, "Corner of the Sky," by Stephen Schwartz
Quote from *Wicked*, "Defying Gravity," by Stephen Schwartz
Quote from *Hamilton*, "Wait for It," by Lin-Manuel Miranda

DUTTON and the D colophon are registered trademarks of Penguin Random House LLC.

LIBRARY OF CONGRESS CATALOGING-IN-PUBLICATION DATA
Names: Parks, Brad, 1974– author.
Title: The last act : a novel / Brad Parks.
Description: New York, New York : Dutton, [2019]
Identifiers: LCCN 2018024578| ISBN 9781524743536 (hardcover) | ISBN 9781524743550 (ebook)
Classification: LCC PS3616.A7553 L37 2019 | DDC 813/.6—dc23
LC record available at https://lccn.loc.gov/2018024578

Printed in the United States of America
1   3   5   7   9   10   8   6   4   2

Book design by George Towne

This is dedicated to my former colleagues at
The Star-Ledger and *The Washington Post*,
who nurtured me as a young writer, and to
all the journalists across the world
who have the courage to find and tell the truth.

THE
LAST
ACT

AUTHOR'S NOTE

T his is a work of fiction.
However.

It is inspired—and loosely informed—by the real-life case of Wachovia Bank. Between 2004 and 2007, the bank failed to apply proper money-laundering controls to at least 378 billion dollars' worth of transfers to and from Mexican *casas de cambio,* currency exchange houses.

In doing so, Wachovia created what federal authorities later described as an open channel between Mexican drug cartels and the US banking system. Wachovia, which has since been acquired by Wells Fargo, collected billions of dollars in fees for this service.

It is unknown what portion of the *casas de cambio* money was legitimate and what was illicit drug profits. The US Drug Enforcement Administration discovered the arrangement only by following the paper trail relating to the Sinaloa drug cartel's purchase of a DC-9 plane that had been seized in Mexico, laden with cocaine. Wachovia eventually paid 160 million dollars to settle a federal investigation into what was then the largest violation of the US Bank Secrecy Act ever uncovered.

As significant as the fine was, it was only a fraction of what Wachovia made off its *casas de cambio* business. Then there is the larger context: the so-called war on drugs, which the United States has waged since the 1970s.

Largely because of this war, a country founded on principles of freedom and democracy now incarcerates its citizens at a higher rate than Russia and China combined. The vast majority of those offenses are petty, street-level crimes that are, monetarily, many orders of magnitude less than the one committed by Wachovia.

And yet no Wachovia executive faced criminal charges, nor served a single day in prison.

That's why this is a work of fiction.

Because who could believe something so preposterous?

ACT ONE

Gotta find my corner of the sky.

—Pippin, from *Pippin*

CHAPTER 1

They confronted him shortly after dark, maybe thirty feet from the safety of his car.

Kris Langetieg—husband, father, affable redhead—had just emerged from a school-board meeting. He was walking head down alongside the lightly trafficked side street where he had parked, eager to get home to his family, distracted enough that he didn't notice the two men until they were already bracketing him on the narrow sidewalk. One in front, one behind.

Langetieg recognized them immediately. The guys from the cartel. His loafers skidded on a fine layer of West Virginia grit as he came to a halt. A thin summer sweat covered his upper lip.

"Hello again," one of them said.

The one in front. The one with the gun.

"What do you want?" Langetieg asked, sweat now popping on his brow. "I already told you no."

"Exactly," the other one said.

The one behind. The one closing fast.

Langetieg braced himself. He was a big man. Big and soft. Panic seized him.

A man in front. A man behind. A fence to his right. A truck to his left. All the cardinal points blocked, and his car might as well have been in Ohio. Still, if he could get his legs under him, if he could get his arms up, if he could get some breath in his lungs . . .

Then the current entered him: twelve hundred volts of brain-jarring juice, delivered through the wispy tendrils of a police-grade Taser. Langetieg dropped to the ground, his muscles locked in contraction.

The doors of a nearby panel van opened, and two more men emerged. Both were Mexican and built like wrestlers, low to the ground and practical. They picked up Langetieg's helpless bulk and dumped it in the back of the van.

As the van got under way, the wrestlers blindfolded him, bound his wrists and ankles, and stuffed his mouth with a dish towel, securing it in place with another binding. Each task was accomplished with the ruthless efficiency of men who had done this before.

Langetieg's only sustaining hope was that someone saw what had happened; someone who might even recognize that an assistant US Attorney for the Northern District of West Virginia was being taken against his will.

He strained to listen for the blare of sirens, the thump of helicopter rotors, some reassuring sound to tell him his captors hadn't gotten away clean.

But it was a hot summer evening, the kind of night when folks in Martinsburg, West Virginia, were still inside, savoring their air-conditioning. So there was nothing. Just the hum of tires on asphalt, the whoosh of air around molded steel, the churn of pistons taking him farther from any chance of rescue.

For twenty-five minutes, they drove. The ropes bit his skin. The blindfold pressed his eyes. A small corner of the dish towel worked its way farther back in his throat, nauseating him. He willed himself not to puke. He already couldn't breathe through his mouth; if the vomit plugged his nose, he'd suffocate.

Lying on the floor of the van, he felt every bounce, jolt, and jerk of the vehicle's suspension. He could guess where they were traveling, albeit only in vague terms: first city streets, then highway, then country roads.

Soon the ride got rougher. The relative hush of the asphalt was replaced by the cacophony of gravel, of tires crunching on small stones, spinning them up to ping off the underside of the vehicle. Next came dirt, which was bumpier than gravel or asphalt, but quieter. The loudest sound was the occasional brushing of weeds against the chassis.

Finally, they stopped. When the doors swung open, Langetieg smelled pine. The wrestlers grabbed him again. No longer paralyzed, Langetieg bucked and thrashed, howling into his muzzle like the wounded animal he was.

It didn't accomplish much.

"You want to get tased again, homie?" one of the men asked in Spanish-accented English.

Langetieg sagged. They carried him twenty more feet, then up a small set of steps. He was inside now. The pine scent vanished. Mildew and black mold replaced it.

He was untied one limb at a time, then just as quickly retied, this time to a chair.

Only then did they remove the blindfold. The lead cartel guy stood in front of him, holding a knife.

The gag came off next.

"Wait, wait," Langetieg said the moment his mouth was free. "I've changed my mind. I'll do whatever you want. I'll do—"

"Sorry," the man said. "Too late."

CHAPTER 2

I went to the theater that day telling myself this was it.

The last rush from hearing the seats fill up before the show. The last time striding out into the lights and losing myself in a character. The last opportunity to romance an audience.

I had been doing this, at venues both grand and grim, since I was seven years old. It had been a good run. No, a great one: probably better than ninety-nine point nine percent of people who had ever entertained the conceit that they could entertain; certainly better than an undersize, plain-looking, lower-middle-class kid from Hackensack, New Jersey, had a right to hope for.

But it is the one immortal truth of both life and theater that all runs come to an end. Usually before the actor wants them to. Whereas I had once been prized for my precocity and small stature and ability to play child roles as a teenager and teenage roles as a young adult, I was now just a cautionary tale: the former child Broadway star who had finally grown up.

At twenty-seven, I was too old for kid roles (not to mention too broad in the chest and, lately, too thin in the hairline). At the same time, I was too young to play most character roles. And I was definitely too short to be a leading man.

I could also acknowledge, albeit painfully, that I had taken my talent as far as it could go. Being the pipsqueak who sang his heart out was nice, but it wasn't the same as possessing the kind of once-in-a-generation gift—Mandy Patinkin's range, Leslie Odom Jr.'s pipes, Ben Vereen's feet—that might have kept me perpetually employed on the Great White Way.

Then there were other professional realities. My legendary agent, Al Martelowitz, had finally died this past spring. A week after his funeral, his agency dropped me, citing my paucity of recent revenue production and dim prospects for improving it.

From my inquiries elsewhere, I had learned that the number of elite agents willing to represent me was exactly zero. That effectively consigned me to cattle-call auditions, a process as brutal as it was pointless. Every sign seemed to be pointing toward the exit.

One of my favorite Broadway standards is "Corner of the Sky" from *Pippin*. It's about a young prince who laments, "Why do I feel I don't fit in anywhere I go?" While I had landed the part several times—Pippin is short—I had never truly felt his anxiety before now.

My corner of the sky had always been under stage lights. I wasn't sure where I was going to fit in anymore.

So far, my search for a real job had been limited to one cover letter, sent to a former castmate who was now running a nonprofit theater in Arkansas and needed an assistant managing director. But I knew I was soon going to have to stop rubbernecking at the wreckage of my acting career and start adulting. Amanda, my fiancée, was a painter, and a damn good one. She was angling toward a show at the Van Buren Gallery—yes, *that* Van Buren Gallery.

In the meantime, one of us needed to have a job with a steady paycheck and healthcare. And Amanda couldn't swing that and stay as productive as she needed to be. It was on me to finally put my college degree, paid for by the spoils of a more lucrative time in my life, to some remunerative use.

So this was it. The final curtain. The last act.

The Sunday matinee of Labor Day weekend was, for reasons both historical and practical, the end of the season for the Morgenthau

Playhouse, a summer stock theater in the Catskills that had been surviving primarily on nostalgia for at least a quarter century. I was one of two Actors' Equity members in the company, which meant the Morgenthau had splashed ". . . also featuring Tommy Jump!" across its promotional materials.

Like our geriatric audiences would remember that Tommy Jump had played Gavroche in the first Broadway revival of *Les Misérables;* or that he had been nominated for a Tony Award for his role as smart-mouthed Jackson in the short-lived but critically acclaimed *Cherokee Purples,* which had the misfortune of debuting in the depths of the Great Recession, when the last thing anyone wanted to see was a show about a family who had left the rat race in order to farm and sell the ultimate organic heirloom tomato.

(Go ahead and laugh. Then remember that the biggest hit of the last decade was a musical about America's first secretary of the treasury.)

The irony that my swan song was coming in the Morgenthau's production of *Man of La Mancha* was not lost on me. I wasn't Don Quixote. That would have been a little too on the nose. I was Sancho Panza, because the short guy always gets cast as Sancho. I had been tilting at windmills all the same.

Once the overture began, the performance seemed to pass in an eyeblink. Time onstage always went that way for me. I was soon peeling away my costume, scraping off my makeup, and saying good-bye to fast friends I might never see again. Before I knew it, the stage manager, eager to strike the set, was shooing us out. It was time to confront the rest of my life.

I had just exited the back of the theater, into an afternoon that felt like dog's breath—the last febrile exhale of a steamy summer—when I heard a man say, "Hey, Tommy."

Thinking it was someone who wanted me to sign his *Playbill,* I turned toward the voice, shielding my eyes from the glare of the setting sun. Through my squint, I realized I recognized his face. It was one I hadn't seen in a long time, one I certainly didn't expect to be grinning at me outside the Morgenthau Playhouse.

"Danny?" I said. "Danny Ruiz, is that you? Holy crap, Danny Danger!"

His nickname back in the day. Entirely tongue in cheek.

He chortled. "Long time since anyone's called me that. I bet no one calls you Slugbomb anymore."

His pet name for me, also a hundred percent facetious. We had been on the same Little League team, or at least we were when my acting schedule allowed me to play. I hit like a Broadway phenom, which is to say I don't think I ever got the ball out of the infield.

"No," I confirmed. "Definitely not."

"Though I don't know, maybe they should," Danny said, shaking my hand and squeezing my biceps at the same time. "You got pretty jacked. What happened to little Tommy Jump?"

"He found the weight room," I said.

"Damn. What are you benching these days? Like two-fifty?"

"No, no. I try not to get too big. No one wants to hire an actor who can't put his arms down."

"Still, you look great."

"Thanks. You too," I said. "Damn. How long has it been?"

"If I'm not mistaken, nine years."

Which is when we graduated high school. I was so surprised by his mere presence, it hadn't yet struck me how out of place it was that he was wearing a suit. On a Sunday. When it was at least ninety degrees.

There was another guy lingering nearby, similarly clad.

"You're right, you're right," I said. "Geez, I can't believe it. Danny Danger. What are you up to these days?"

"Working for the FBI."

He delivered the line so straight I laughed. The Danny Ruiz I knew was a slacker who did his homework the period before it was due. He was at least three time zones removed from whatever preconceived notions I had about an FBI agent.

Then I realized he wasn't joking. In a practiced motion, he drew a wallet out of his back pocket and opened it up, displaying a gold shield.

"Wait, you're serious?" I asked.

"Gotta grow up sometime," he said with a small shrug, returning his badge to his pocket. "I am now Special Agent Daniel Ruiz. This is Special Agent Rick Gilmartin."

The other man nodded. He was taller than Danny, over six feet. He had blue eyes and a reserved, disapproving air about him—like I had done something wrong, but regulations forbade him from explaining it to me. Which probably made him just about perfect for the federal government. In his right hand, he clutched a metal briefcase.

"You want to get some coffee or something?" Danny said. "There's something we'd like to discuss with you."

At that moment, I got my first shot of nerves. This wasn't Danny Ruiz, my onetime classmate, who happened to catch me in a show and now wanted to gab. He was acting as a representative of the United States government's primary law enforcement agency.

"What's this all about?" I asked in a faltering voice.

"Let's just get some coffee. There's a diner up the street."

He said it in an open, friendly way. He was still smiling.

His partner wasn't. The man hadn't spoken a single word.

I knew the diner well because it was the cheapest place in town.

As we walked, Danny filled me in on his life since high school. After graduation, he went into the army—I vaguely remembered as much—where he was quickly disabused of his slacker ways. Then he used the GI Bill to attend John Jay College of Criminal Justice. As a senior, he scored high on some test and was soon being recruited by the FBI. He was now with the unit that investigated money laundering, which was considered highly prestigious.

I listened with half an ear, distracted, nervous, trying to guess which federal statutes I had broken. Had I inadvertently laundered money? What *was* money laundering anyway?

Danny was yammering on like we were talking over pigs in a blanket at a class reunion. But I imagined this was what FBI agents did. Lured you in. Relaxed you. Then sprang the trap.

When we arrived at the diner, it was mostly empty. The theater crowd had gone elsewhere for its evening meal, to places that didn't have paper place mats containing coupons for oil changes. The waitress signaled for us to sit anywhere we liked, and Danny selected a corner booth, several tables away from any other customers.

"So if I've done the math right, you've been with the FBI, what, three years now?" I said as we sat down.

"Three years, yeah. Hard to believe. It's been a good ride, though. You've been acting this whole time?"

I trotted out my usual line: "Beats having a real job."

Danny smiled again. "That's good. Real good. That's actually why we wanted to talk to you."

And then he said the last thing I expected to fall out of an FBI agent's mouth: "We have an acting job for you."

"An acting job?" I repeated. "So I haven't done anything wrong?"

Danny laughed. Gilmartin didn't.

"No, no," Danny said. "We'd like to hire you."

"I'm not sure I understand."

"First of all, you need to keep this quiet," Danny said. "If you choose to move forward with this, we're going to ask you to sign a nondisclosure agreement. But for now a verbal agreement will do fine. Is that okay? Can you promise not to tell anyone about this conversation?"

"Uh, yeah, sure."

He leaned in closer. "Okay. Good. So this isn't something we advertise, for obvious reasons, but the FBI sometimes hires actors.

Our agents can only go undercover so often before they're compromised. And then there are cases like this one, where we need . . . someone whose dramatic abilities exceed those of your typical FBI agent."

"What's the role?" I asked, wondering if this was part of an elaborate joke.

Danny sat back and nodded at Gilmartin, who opened his briefcase and extracted a mug shot of a middle-aged white man with receded brown hair and a fastidious goatee. His face was fleshy and pallid. His eyes had bruise-dark bags under them. I needed only one glance to see this was one sad character.

Agent Rick Gilmartin cleared his throat and spoke for the first time.

"This is Mitchell Dupree, a former executive for Union South Bank," he said in a nondescript, TV-news-anchor, anywhere-in-America accent. "USB is the fifth-largest bank in America, just behind Citigroup. Dupree worked for the division that dealt with international business in Latin America. To his friends and neighbors, even to his family, he appeared to be very ordinary. But all the while he was leading a double life, working for the New Colima cartel."

"New Colima is the latest bad flavor to come out of Mexico," Danny explained. "Around the time you and I were lining up senior prom dates, they split off from the Sinaloa cartel. Their first big moment was when they killed thirty-eight Zetas and dumped their dismembered bodies in the middle of the Mexican equivalent of I-10 at rush hour. It was like, 'You think these guys are tough? You don't know what tough is.'

"Basically, New Colima is to Mexico what ISIS is to the Middle East. You know how we had Saddam, and we thought he was a pretty bad guy until we got ISIS, which was far worse? It's the same thing here. The US government went all in to break up Sinaloa and arrest El Chapo. All it did was create a power vacuum that New Colima has only been too happy to fill."

Gilmartin took over: "They're militarized to an extent no cartel has ever been, and they've been hugely aggressive when it comes to taking territory, establishing supply lines, bribing officials, and recruiting manpower. Their drug of choice is crystal meth, and they were smart enough to concentrate on markets in Europe and Asia first, so they were able to get strong without the US authorities bothering them too much. Then they made their move here. There are some estimates that a third of all crystal meth in America is produced by New Colima.

"But the drugs are only part of the story," Gilmartin continued. "Money is the gas for a cartel's engine. It's what allows them to buy guns, men, and planes, the things they need to keep growing. The DEA likes to seize a few kilos of product, hold a press conference, and declare it's winning the war on drugs. At the FBI, we realize we're never going to be able to stop the inflow of drugs. This country is just too huge. It makes more sense to go after the money. One of the biggest logistical issues for cartels is that they're in a cash business. Cash is big and bulky and vulnerable to seizure, especially when you're talking about the huge sums the cartels deal with. In the new global economy, cartels want to be able to move money safely and conveniently with the push of a button. But they need people like Mitchell Dupree to do it for them. Dupree laundered more than a billion dollars of cartel money over the course of about four years or so."

He paused as the waitress came over and placed waters in front of us. At Danny's insistence, I ordered a cheeseburger. The agents stuck with black coffee.

Gilmartin waited until she was gone, then said, "Dupree eventually got sloppy. By the time we caught him, we were able to tie him to an offshore account that had several million dollars in it. We think there might be others, but we never could find them. The US Attorneys Office convicted him for money laundering, racketeering, wire fraud, pretty much everything it could get to stick on him. He's now six months into a nine-year sentence at FCI Morgantown in West Virginia."

"FCI stands for Federal Correctional Institution, but don't let that scare you," Danny interjected. "It's minimum security, mostly white-collar types, strictly nonviolent offenders. The place looks like a college campus—no bars, no razor wire. We're talking about Club Fed here, not some hard-ass place where you have to become someone's bitch if you want to survive."

Gilmartin went on: "For our purposes, Dupree is now a small means to a much bigger end. We have him on wiretaps talking about a trove of documents that he secretly kept as insurance. We believe he's told the cartel that if anything happens to him or his family, he'll release the documents. They could be used to prosecute the entire top echelon of New Colima, including El Vio himself."

"That's the boss of New Colima," Danny said. "It translates loosely as 'the seer,' because supposedly he's the guy who sees everything. It's kind of an ironic name, because he's only got one good eye. The other is all weird and white. So the seer is actually half-blind."

"When we confronted Dupree about the documents and offered him a deal, he refused to tell us where they were," Gilmartin said. "No matter how much pressure we applied, he kept his mouth shut, which was great for the cartel but very frustrating for us."

Danny's turn: "We looked everywhere for those damn documents. We executed warrants on his home, his office, his social club. We had agents follow him to see if he had a hidden storage unit. We plowed through his financials looking for signs he was renting another office or house. We got nothing."

Back to Gilmartin: "Dupree made an offhand comment on one of the wiretaps about a remote cabin he or someone in his family owns. It's his getaway. But we couldn't find any record of it. We think that's where he stashed the documents. So, really, it's pretty simple. We want you to go into the prison under an alias, posing as an inmate. You'll become friendly with Dupree, earn his trust, and then get him to tell you where that cabin is."

"And how am I going to do that?" I asked.

"That's the challenge, Slugbomb," Danny said. "If we thought this was easy, we wouldn't need to hire you. Obviously, you can't let on you know about him, the bank, or the cartel. It would make him suspicious. You're just another inmate, there to serve your time. If he wants to confide in you about what he's done, great. But we're not looking to prosecute Dupree for anything else. All we want is the location of those documents."

"What if he won't tell me anything?"

"We think he will," Gilmartin said. "We've talked to some counselors at the BOP, the Bureau of Prisons, and they tell us that their minimum-security facilities allow for quite a bit of inmate interaction. Friendships form quickly. Based on this, our SAC—sorry, special agent in charge—has approved a six-month operation, starting from when you enter Morgantown. Obviously, if we're able to secure the documents, we'll pull you out immediately. But if after the end of six months you still don't have anything, the operation ends all the same. The psychologists say it'll either happen by then or it won't happen at all."

Six months. I'd be out by March. The waitress appeared with the coffee. She slid the check, facedown, on the side of the table with the guys in the suits.

"And what happens to this guy, this Dupree, when I find the documents?" I asked.

"It depends if he cooperates or not," Gilmartin said. "If he doesn't, there's nothing we can do for him. If he does, he and his family get WITSEC—federal witness protection. We've offered it before. He's refused, because he thinks he can't trust us. Once we have the documents, he won't have a choice."

I looked back and forth between the two agents for a moment. Danny was taking a tentative sip of his coffee. Gilmartin hadn't touched his.

"I don't know," I said. "I . . . I do musical theater. We can't go more than three sentences without bursting into song, and even then we follow a score. What you're talking about here is more like improv. I took a class on that once, but this is . . . This is improv on steroids."

"Don't sell yourself short," Danny said. "You're smart, likeable. You're from Hackensack—the Sack, baby! You got the gift of gab. You're also a guy he won't see coming. FBI agents, we're cut from the same cloth. The way you talk, the way you think, you're a creative type. He'll never suspect you're working for us. And, no offense, you're, what, five-two?"

"Five-four," I said defensively.

"Whatever. Point is, you're no one's image of an FBI agent. You'll probably crack him in three days."

Before I could think to voice any of the other myriad questions that were starting to form, Danny leaned in again.

"Plus, we'll pay you a hundred grand, minimum."

"Seriously?"

"Fifty when you go in. Fifty when you come out, whether you succeed or not. Plus, there's a hundred-thousand-dollar bonus if we're able to secure indictments based on information you provide us."

Two hundred thousand dollars. It was a dizzying amount of money. A sleep-better-at-night amount of money. A look-at-yourself-differently-in-the-mirror amount of money. And for six months' work. I couldn't imagine the job in Arkansas was going to pay more than thirty a year.

"We'll put this all in writing, of course," Danny continued. "It'll be in a contract you'll sign with the bureau where you agree to be an informant for us and you understand there are inherent risks and blah-blah-blah. Right now all you have to do is say yes."

Say yes. The word would come a lot easier if he wasn't talking about prison.

"I have to talk it over with my fiancée," I said. "You said I can't tell anyone, but—"

"Of course, of course," Danny said. "The nondisclosure agreement is really for things like social media or press interviews. You can definitely talk it over with your fiancée. I think I saw her on Facebook. Amanda, right?"

"Right."

"Our offices are technically closed for the holiday anyway. Take tonight and tomorrow, talk it over, think about it. Come Tuesday, our SAC is going to want an answer. If it's not you, we need to hire someone else. But you were my first choice. I vouched for you."

"Thanks," I said.

"I know we've given you a lot to think about. Once you sign the agreement, we can help you craft a backstory and talk you through some of the other details."

He reached for his wallet and produced a twenty, placing it on the table as he pocketed the check. Then he pulled out a business card, which he handed to me.

"This has my office number and cell number," he said. "Don't bother with the office number. You'll just get shunted to my voice mail. Call the cell if you have any questions."

"Right," I said.

Danny nodded at Gilmartin, who stood. Danny slid out of the booth behind him.

"We'll let you eat in peace," he said. "Good seeing you, Tommy."

"You too, Danny."

Gilmartin nodded curtly. Danny knocked twice on the table, then led their exit.

I ran my fingers across the embossed lettering on the business card. My erstwhile Little League teammate Danny was now Daniel R. Ruiz, Special Agent, Federal Bureau of Investigation, New York Field Office.

The waitress set down my cheeseburger just as a Chevy Caprice whipped past the diner. It was, technically, unmarked. But only to someone who didn't recognize those classic law enforcement specifications: the dual exhaust pipes, the reinforced suspension, the souped-up engine.

Danny was driving. He had taken off his suit jacket. His service weapon was in a holster, snug against his left shoulder.

I stared at the top of the burger like the answers to all of life's riddles were hidden amidst the sesame seeds.

A hundred thousand dollars. Maybe two hundred, depending on how persuasive I could be. And I could be, if it mattered that much. Right?

I went to the theater that day telling myself this was it.

But maybe the Morgenthau wasn't the last act after all.

CHAPTER 3

Herrera saw them from a distance, three Range Rovers, all black and bulletproof, ripping along in a lopsided V formation, kicking up plumes of dust that stretched for half a mile behind them like long, billowing snakes.

El Vio might have been in any of the three. Or none. You never knew for sure.

You never knew anything with El Vio.

As the vehicles closed in, their windshields glinting in the bright sun, Herrera could already hear the General's voice barking orders in excited, high-pitched Spanish. The General was chief of security for the cartel. He did not sound very secure.

These inspections were never announced. Nor did they conform to any pattern, at least not that Herrera was aware of. There might be three in one month, nothing for an entire year, then two on consecutive days.

Be unpredictable. That was El Vio's first rule, both for his generals and for himself. Change everything, all the time: the places you stay, the restaurants you frequent, the women you sleep with. It was impossible to ambush a man who never kept a set schedule.

Rule number two: Don't drink, take drugs, or do anything to dull your wits. Even for a moment. Because that could be the moment you'd miss something that could cost you your life—whether it was the drone flying overhead, the snick of a safety coming off a gun, or the subtle shift in a man's eyes as he lied to you.

Three, be daring—*atrevido,* in Spanish. *Atrevido* was one of El Vio's favorite words. Timidity was for shy woodland creatures. Running a cartel required bold action. Hit your enemies hard enough, fast enough, and they'll be too stunned to hit back.

Four, and most important, make sure the Americans never had anything concrete on you. Mexican police could be bribed or intimidated into not arresting you. Mexican judges could be bribed or intimidated into not convicting you. Mexican jailors could be bribed or intimidated into letting you go free. Not so with the United States. Therefore, extradition was the worst of all possible outcomes. El Vio dreaded extradition more than death.

Four rules. Followed with unerring constancy. Herrera had been told El Vio developed them by studying those who had come before him, from El Patrón to El Padrino, from El Lazca to El Chapo. He had learned from their rise and, more important, their fall.

Herrera had heard the General say that El Vio needed to relax more. Surely, El Vio—who had become the richest, most feared man in Mexico, the master of an empire forged by his cunning and brutality—could relax and enjoy what his labors had brought him.

But as far Herrera knew, El Vio never let up. That was part of his legend. El Vio, the fifth son of a poor avocado farmer. El Vio, who spent his teens learning the trade from the original Colima cartel. El Vio, who taught himself three languages by watching foreign television shows. El Vio, who rose to become chief enforcer for the Sinaloa cartel before deciding he could do better on his own.

And now look at him. As Sinaloa stumbled, he surged. He commanded an army of five thousand, roughly equal to the entire US Drug Enforcement Administration. He had entrenched supply lines to the wealthiest markets in North America, Europe, and Asia.

All this, and the Americans still had virtually nothing on him.

They couldn't directly tie him to a single ounce of methamphet-amine, much less the tons he shipped across their border every year.

El Vio had only one vulnerability, and that was the banker.

Herrera had heard all about this from the General, usually when he was drunk. There was a banker in America who had helped laun-der a portion of El Vio's vast fortune. He was caught, but before El Vio could get rid of him, the banker made it known he had hidden documents. They could be used to implicate at least a dozen top leaders, including El Vio himself. He would be extradited for sure.

If anything happened to the banker or his family, these docu-ments would be turned over to American authorities. It was a gaping liability. The General, as chief of security, had not yet found a way to close it.

Which was the main reason Herrera heard panic in the General's voice when those speeding vehicles were spotted.

The compound the General commanded was known as Rosario No. 2. There was no point in giving it a more clever or inspiring name. There were others like it. El Vio would insist it be dismantled and moved elsewhere soon enough. It consisted of seven buildings, surrounded by a twelve-foot razor-wire fence that kept workers in as much as it kept intruders out.

Five of the buildings were flimsy metal warehouses with ventila-tion fans on both ends. They were spaced out, because methamphet-amine had an unfortunate propensity to explode during production. But that was really the only downside of it. Whereas cocaine and heroin required huge acreage for growing plants—which could be spotted by the Americans with their satellites—meth was easy to hide.

The sixth building was a barracks for the General and his lieuten-ants, who were expected to watch over Rosario No. 2 and protect it from attacks by the Mexican authorities or, just as likely, rival cartels.

Still, it was the seventh building that mattered most. They called it "the bunker," because it was made of double-reinforced concrete. It contained a stockpile of weapons and enough ammunition to hold off a Mexican Army battalion for a month. It also served as a nerve center for monitoring a number of highly sensitive security operations.

Including the one watching the banker.

The General was outside the bunker when the Range Rovers arrived. He had ordered several of the lieutenants, Herrera among them, to join him.

"Stand up straight," the General barked. "El Vio doesn't like slouching."

Herrera straightened. The vehicles stopped.

El Vio climbed out of the first one. He was five foot seven and built like a welterweight. His thick dark hair was combed back from his forehead and held in place by gel. His face was partially covered by mirrored sunglasses, which he kept on even when indoors, so people wouldn't be able to stare at his right eye, the one that was said to have been injured in a childhood accident.

He wore black cargo pants with a gray T-shirt made of some kind of breathable material. His utility belt contained, among other things, a knife and a pistol.

"Vio," the General said, taking a few tentative steps forward. "How good to see you."

El Vio froze the General's momentum with one glance. There was no exchange of handshakes. Herrera had never actually seen El Vio touch anyone.

"Do you have news for me regarding our friend in West Virginia?" El Vio asked.

"Our friend." That's how they referred to the banker.

"Not yet," the General said. "We're working on it."

"That's what you told me last time."

"Soon. Very soon. I am confident. We have an excellent operation in place."

"Also what you told me last time."

"I'm doing everything I can," the General said. His voice trembled.

"Are you?" El Vio said.

The way he posed the question did not invite an answer.

"I just need more time," the General pleaded. "This will soon be resolved."

El Vio received this promise with little emotion.

"Come closer," he said softly.

The General took a few steps.

"Closer," El Vio said again.

The General complied. Now the rest of him was trembling.

"Closer."

The General took another step. Behind him, Herrera had also moved forward. But without fear. Something in him wanted to be nearer to El Vio.

"That's good," El Vio said.

"The Americans are having no more success than I am," the General said. "They are—"

The words stopped when, in one swift motion, El Vio removed his knife from its sheath and plunged it into the General's eye. The right one.

The General crumpled, bringing both hands to his ruined face, howling as the blood gushed. El Vio watched his agony with mild interest, like he was considering a beetle that had landed on its back and was struggling to right itself. Herrera could see a smaller version of the General's prostrate shape reflected in the mirrors of El Vio's sunglasses.

Then El Vio turned to the uneven line of lieutenants.

"Who will finish this?" he said.

None of them moved. Not even Herrera. He wasn't sure what El Vio meant. Finish the banker? Or finish—

Then El Vio spoke louder: "Who will finish this?"

That's when Herrera understood. And he was ready. *Atrevido. Be daring.* He straightened. El Vio didn't like slouching.

The General had grasped the knife handle. He was trying to remove the blade, which had gotten stuck in his eye socket. Herrera walked up, drew his weapon, and shot the General behind the ear. The General collapsed. Herrera fired three more rounds.

He was repulsed yet thrilled.

El Vio walked up to the corpse, turning the body over and pressing his boot against what was left of the General's skull to get the leverage needed to extract the blade. El Vio wiped each side of the knife on his pants, resheathed it, and then looked at Herrera.

"Congratulations," El Vio said. "You've just been promoted."

CHAPTER 4

For at least the tenth time in the last twenty minutes, Amanda Porter looked at the clock that hung on the wall of the kitchen—which was also the living room, her studio, and the only room in this shabby, stifling, non-air-conditioned second-floor apartment that wasn't a bedroom or a bathroom.

Five fifty-two. Were this an ordinary matinee, Tommy would have been back by now. He was obviously still saying his good-byes.

The ceiling fan took another spin through the same hot air it had been futilely recycling all afternoon. She sighed, appraising the painting she had been halfheartedly jabbing at, knowing she was too distracted to give it the kind of attention it demanded.

Was this one headed for the trash? She tossed way more than she kept. For months now she had been sending photos of her completed work to Hudson van Buren, the proprietor of the Van Buren Gallery and one of the most influential voices in the business. He didn't need to see the bottom ninety-eight percent of her work. Only the top two, thank you very much.

When people met Amanda Porter, they immediately underestimated her, because she had this cute southern twang; because she was five foot two, blue-eyed, and adorable, with her wavy strawberry-blond hair, her button nose, her freckles; because she was twenty-seven but could get carded buying a lottery ticket.

Those looks belied the fierceness with which she attacked her work. No one looked at her and thought *scrappy,* but that's how she thought of herself. She was the scrappy girl who had made it from this little nowhere town in Mississippi to a scholarship at Cooper Union—and now to the brink of artistic stardom—by outworking everyone and refusing to compromise. She poured her drive for perfection into her art. It was excellence or nothing.

And this piece in front of her was . . . maybe okay? She was in no state of mind to decide. She put down her brush, ran the back of her hand across her damp brow, and then subconsciously tucked a curl behind her left ear.

She thought about Tommy, about this next step in their lives. Her concern for at least the last year—if not the entire time they had known each other—was that their relationship had never really been tested. It had all been too easy, like a canvas that practically painted itself. And what good was that? What was art without struggle? What was life without struggle? If she had learned anything during her escape from Plantersville, Mississippi, it was that anything worth having needed to be earned.

They had met at one of those strange New York parties for the rich, beautiful, and eclectic, all of whom had been haphazardly tossed together in some rich guy's Park Avenue penthouse.

Amanda was there because the host had discovered one of her paintings. She felt very much alone and conspicuously southern, afraid to open her mouth. Her accent marked her as some kind of exotic mutant. She didn't dare tell anyone she grew up in a small town in Mississippi; or that the biggest, most cosmopolitan place she ever got to visit was Tupelo, where the Elvis Presley Birthplace and Museum was considered the pinnacle of culture.

Tommy, the former Broadway star, had found Amanda in the corner, her preferred location in a large crowd. As the youngest, poorest, and least-connected guests, they had bonded over how out of place they felt. They had both been raised by single mothers, not quite hand to mouth but also pretty far from the summer-in-the-Hamptons set.

She liked him immediately. He was a little short, sure. But he had a nice smile and a nicer ass. He was clearly in great shape. And smart. And interesting. And interested. And . . . well, who could ever really put their finger on human attraction? Amanda later told a friend that the moment she got around Tommy, it was like there was a bowl of Rice Krispies somewhere nearby: Everything went *snap, crackle, pop.*

He kept asking her questions, and before she knew it, she was the one dominating the conversation. Even though she frequently chose not to, Amanda Porter *could* talk. She even liked to talk, especially about art, and especially when she felt like the guy listening was (a) actually listening and (b) understanding what she was saying. Oh, and (c) not just trying to get her into bed.

At the hostess's insistence, Tommy sang "Love Changes Everything" from *Aspects of Love,* which was cheesy and wonderful and brought the house down. His voice was rich, warm, full of life and character.

Before long, they were discussing the similarities between their seemingly disparate passions.

"We're both performers," he told her at one point. "You just perform on canvas."

They talked until two A.M., and then he started walking her home when they couldn't find a cab. By that point, she had moved onto hoping he *was* trying to get her into bed. Her deepest concern was that this gorgeous, talented guy—who worked out a lot and sang beautifully—had to be gay. Her friends always teased her that growing up in the Bible Belt had endowed her with a deficient gaydar (her defense being that no one was *allowed* to be gay in Plantersville, Mississippi). Had she spent the evening flirting with a guy who would be more interested in her brother?

Then she decided not to wait until they reached her place to find out. They ended up making out for two hours on a park bench.

No, not gay.

Subsequent explorations of his ardor and stamina only confirmed it.

They quickly became inseparable. He would spend long hours just watching her paint—"This is better than any show on Broadway," he insisted—and she became a de facto member of whatever cast he was in.

Each of them had other friends, but they quickly fell away. Tommy's were constantly being scattered to the acting winds. Amanda's came in two groups: her fellow scholarship kids, who had mostly retreated back to their respective Mississippis, Missouris, or Maines to teach art and attempt to sell their paintings locally; and the rich kids who could afford to stay in the New York area but whom Amanda had never felt especially close to.

So, really, it was just the two of them. Which was fine as far as both were concerned.

He proposed after three months, just as he was about to hit the road with a touring company. She made all kinds of rational arguments about why it was too soon. He swatted them away by borrowing a line from one of her favorite movies, *When Harry Met Sally:* "When you realize you want to spend the rest of your life with somebody, you want the rest of your life to start as soon as possible."

She said yes. He suggested they trek down to city hall the next day. She resisted.

Wait, she said. Just wait. Until the time was right. Until she was more established as an artist. Until they passed over the line—and, surely, it would be a bright, white one—that demarcated the end of extended postcollegiate adolescence and the beginning of stable, stolid, sensible adulthood.

That was two years ago. Every now and then, he would ask her about setting a date. She always demurred. Her go-to line became, "Honey, if it's 'til death do us part, what's the hurry?"

She couldn't bring herself to tell him she still had her doubts about them. She wanted to know what they would be like as a couple when the newness wore off, when the real relationship began. It was just difficult to discern because, with Tommy, there was always something new. A new show. A new role. A new city.

It was like a perpetual honeymoon. They had never even gotten in a serious fight, as ridiculous as that sounded. Even when she was despondent from her failure with another painting or just plain crabby, Tommy was nothing but sweet, thoughtful, and impossibly good to her. He insisted he had never found it so easy to be nice to someone.

And in some ways, it was great. A dream. It certainly occurred to her that maybe, just possibly, it always would be like this.

Except there was that unanswered question about whether Tommy would be like her own father, a man she barely knew because he bolted the second things got difficult.

And make no mistake: Things were about to get difficult.

A t quarter after six, the door downstairs opened. Then she heard the stairs creaking gently, which immediately told her something was up.

When Tommy was being Tommy—flush from a great performance, filled with the energetic joy that gave him—he charged up the steps and burst through the door, primed to share his triumph; or to see the progress she had made on her latest attempt at a painting; or, if nothing else, to lure her into bed.

When he was off for some reason, he didn't charge. He crept.

He once told her that one of the reasons he fell in love with her was that, unlike other women he had dated, he couldn't hide his feelings from her with his acting ability.

"You read me like a book," he always told her.

It's not that hard, she often thought.

Something must have happened during the last show. He flubbed a line. The audience was flat. She'd find out soon enough.

She quickly picked up her brush and pressed it to her painting, like that's what she had been doing the whole time he had been gone. She was still sweating. The ceiling fan may have actually been making the room hotter.

He entered quietly, shutting the door softly behind him.

"Hey," he said.

"Hey. How'd it go?" she asked, already seeing the uncertainty in his eyes.

"Fine," he said. Then: "There's something I need to tell you."

"That's funny, there's something I need to tell you, too."

"You want to go first?" he asked. "Mine's pretty big."

She swirled her brush in a cup of murky liquid, damp-dried it with a rag, and said, "No, you go ahead."

They sat in plastic chairs, bellied up to a circular plastic folding table that had been their one furniture splurge for this apartment. Then Tommy related his bizarre encounter with two FBI agents, one of whom was a childhood friend. Tommy was incapable of telling a story without performing at least a little, though Amanda got the sense he was working very hard to give her the unembellished version of the events.

She didn't say a word as he spoke, letting him continue his presentation, which finished with, "So, what do you think?"

Amanda's hands were folded in front of her. Theirs had been a peripatetic relationship, with Tommy's next gig serving as the driver, deciding where they went next. He would just come home and announce, *It's a regional theater in Cincinnati,* or *It's a touring company for* Phantom of the Opera, or whatever.

She had never said no. As long as they were together, and as long as she didn't have to go back to Plantersville, what did it matter? She could paint anywhere.

This felt immeasurably different.

"So let me get this right," she said. "They're sending you to *prison*."

"Yeah."

"Like an actual prison. With bars and skinheads and guys named Bubba."

"It's minimum security. Bubba Lite."

"But it's still prison."

"For six months, yeah."

She stared down at the hard plastic top of the table, trying to assemble her thoughts.

"But how does it actually work?" she asked, looking back up. "You knock on the door of a prison and say, 'Hey, y'all mind if I bunk up here?' And then after six months, you're like, 'Oh, j/k. See y'all later.'"

"They're the FBI. I'm sure they can pull some strings."

"And they think this guy is going to spill his guts to you? *You*. Some kid he doesn't know."

"Well, obviously, I'm going to have to find a way to get close to him, earn his confidence. I'm sure the FBI can get me assigned to his work detail or whatever. I don't know. Maybe I'll tell him I'm trying to escape and ask him if he knows a place where I can lay low for a while and then he'll tell me about his cabin."

"And if that doesn't work, they come get you after six months. Win or lose."

"Right."

"And this is worth a hundred thousand dollars to them."

"I guess so, yeah. This guy Dupree is big-time. You know how much the government spends fighting drugs? A hundred grand or two is like tip money."

"What if something bad happens? Someone beats you up or, I don't know, something happens to me or . . . or your mom."

"I don't know. I assume they'll just come and get me," Tommy said. "But if it's before six months, I forfeit the second fifty thousand."

"So you could take the fifty, stay for a day, then come home."

"I could, yeah. But then I'd be walking away from a shot at another hundred and fifty thousand dollars."

It was unnecessary to emphasize the point. Amanda's mother cleaned houses. Tommy's mother was a school secretary. They had both worked their entire lives and never seen that number in their bank accounts.

"And this Danny guy, how well do you really know him?"

This was another part of growing up poor: natural suspicion of those in power.

"We go about as far back as you can," Tommy said. "Kindergarten, I guess? We called him 'Danny Danger' because he would blow up Matchbox cars with cherry bombs or wear camo pants. Like that made him a tough guy. But he was basically a good kid, you know?"

"Would you trust him with your life?"

Tommy rocked backward, looking like he had just bitten a lemon. "It seems a little melodramatic when you put it that way. This isn't my life we're talking about."

This made Amanda only more fervent. "Yes, it is. It's your life *and* my life. It's . . . it's this family's life."

Tommy paused. Amanda had never referred to them as a family before.

"Well, yeah, I know him as well as I know anyone," Tommy said. "And I guess, yeah, I trust him."

Amanda let out a long, slow breath. "So you really want to do this?"

"It's not that I *want* to, believe me. I can think of things I'd rather do for the next six months than worrying about what's going to happen every time I bend over to pick up the soap. But think of it as an acting job that happens to be in, I don't know, Botswana or something. Someplace you can't go with me. An acting job that's really, really lucrative."

"I'm not with you because I want to be rich," Amanda said. "I'm with you because I want to be *with you*."

"Of course. But this . . . This could be a short-term inconvenience that could really set us up long term. If nothing else, it'll give us some breathing room. You'll be able to keep painting—"

"And you'll be able to keep acting," she said.

Busted, she thought. The yearning that immediately came to his face when she said it had been unmistakable. It was like telling a man who had been fasting that there was an all-you-can-eat buffet next door.

"Don't tell me that didn't cross your mind," she said.

But it clearly was now. The Amanda Porter who could read Tommy like a book was now seeing whole chapters springing off the page. They could rent an inexpensive place in Jersey, something near his mother. He could keep auditioning. He could do a real agent search instead of just making phone calls. He could find people who remembered him in *Cherokee Purples* or one of his other triumphs and felt he deserved another shot.

For that matter, with a hundred grand or more in the bank, he could take a stab at what had always been his most audacious dream: take a year or two off and write his own musical—one where a short guy played the lead.

"Look, let's just take this one step at a time," he said. "Is this something you think I should pursue or not? I've got until Tuesday, but I can always call him and say, 'Thanks but no thanks, go find someone else.'"

"And lose out on a hundred grand," Amanda said.

"Right. Though now you're arguing out of both sides of your mouth."

"I'm not fixin' to argue either side, honey. I just . . . Going to prison on a wild-goose chase for six months sounds utterly insane. But passing up on all that money is pretty nuts too."

She stopped there. They spent a moment just looking at each other, doing one of those couple checks, where you stare at each other for a few quiet seconds and decide everything or nothing—but either way, it happens together.

The moment lasted longer than usual.

Finally, he broke the silence. "What do you say we sleep on it and see how we feel in the morning? If we both think it's something I should pursue, I'll call Danny and tell him we at least want to see the contract. There's no harm in looking. Nothing is going to happen until I sign it."

"Okay," she said, releasing a big breath. "I guess that makes sense."

"Good," he said. "Anyhow, you said there was something you wanted to tell me?"

"Yeah. I'm pregnant."

CHAPTER 5

For a protracted moment, I gaped at her, stupefied.

Two words, neither longer than two syllables, and yet I still couldn't resolve them. *I'm pregnant.* Preg-nant. That's . . . As in . . . *Hang on, I know I can work this out—*

Then? Boom.

Like a happy grenade went off.

Clasping both hands to the sides of my face, I yipped, "You're pregnant?"

Suddenly, I was out of my seat. The chair had spilled behind me, and my feet were no longer attached to the ground. I was jumping up and down in the middle of the kitchen, yelling, "We're pregnant! We're pregnant! Oh my God, we're pregnant!"

This news was so incredible it simply had to be shared. Immediately. With someone. There was a guy trudging along the street outside. I ran over to the open window and shouted, "Hey! We're pregnant!"

He gave me a thumbs-up and a hearty, "Good job, buddy."

Then I started racing around the apartment and—apropos of absolutely nothing—started singing John Philip Sousa's "Stars and Stripes Forever," undeterred by its lack of lyrics. I was the brass section. I kept time by banging my hands together.

On the second lap, I grabbed Amanda from out of her chair and led her in this sloppy promenade that was a mash-up of a waltz and square dancing. Tommy Jump wasn't a triple threat for nothing. She was laughing—I may have been coming off as a bit of a lunatic—which just made me want to twirl her more.

Then, abruptly, I stopped.

She wasn't on the pill. And there had been a night not long ago when her diaphragm slipped. But still—

"Wait," I said, "are you sure?"

Never one for an excess of exposition, Amanda led me into our cramped bathroom, where she had stashed the three at-home pregnancy tests she had taken.

Still dazed and a little light-headed from my frenetic celebration, I was soon looking at the evidence our lives were about to change drastically, and it came in the form of three pen-size plastic dipsticks, lined up next to the sink. One had a plus sign on it. Another displayed this thick pink line. The third, the most unambiguous of all, simply read, YES.

Yes.

Yes!

I could feel my love for Amanda doubling and tripling. I could feel my love for the baby, this human being I didn't even know yet, this thing that was no more than a lump of cells in my fiancée's uterus but suddenly represented everything I ever really wanted from life. Forget the theater. Forget pretending to be someone else.

Being a dad. Being the father to this child that neither of us ever had. Now *that* was the role of a lifetime.

My heart was jackhammering, but it was also growing, expanding to make room for a new person in our family. *Our family.* We weren't merely a couple anymore. We had become something infinitely greater, something as big as love itself.

I was about to strike up the band for another stirring rendition of Mr. Sousa's march when Amanda said, "We don't have to keep it."

Bewildered, I looked at her, standing before me, vulnerable and filled with doubt. I had never fully convinced Amanda to see herself as I did: gorgeous, brilliant, and on a fast track toward artistic greatness. Part of her was always this poor girl from Mississippi, the daughter of a woman who cleaned other people's houses—like that even mattered—who believed anything good that happened to her today was likely to be taken away tomorrow.

"What do you mean we don't have to keep it? I thought we wanted kids."

"We do. But the timing is awful."

I gently grasped her by the shoulders and spoke with more passion than I had ever summoned in twenty years onstage.

"The timing is always awful. It was awful when we met. It was awful when I proposed to you. It was awful when you made me the happiest man ever and said yes. But you know what's not awful? You and me together. And you know what's even less awful? You and me bringing a baby into this world. She'll be a little girl and she'll look just like you and we're going to love her and hold her and teach her everything we know, and she's going to blossom into an incredible woman and we're going to grow old together watching her and it's going to be the most wonderful, most awe-inspiring, most magical thing we've ever seen."

I was looking straight into her eyes, which were so clear and blue they still sometimes startled me. I pulled her a little closer and kept going.

"And I'm not saying it's going to be easy, because you're always the one who tells me that nothing easy can be worthwhile. But you're going to be an incredible mother. And I'm going to be the best goddamn father I can be. And you're going to paint, and I'm going to do whatever I have to do, and we're going to look back on this moment in this crappy little apartment, in this crappy little town, and someday we're going to say that slipped diaphragm was the best thing that ever happened to us."

There was this moment of stillness, when everything in the room— every sound, every movement, even our breathing—seemed to stop.

Then, in relatively short order, three things happened.

One, she burst into tears.

Two, I burst into tears.

And, three, we ended up making love. It was a deeper, more meaningful experience than all the other times we had made love, like we were rewriting the history of our baby's conception. This was no sloppy accident. This was an intentional act by two devoted parents who wanted nothing more than to bring forth new life.

As I lay there afterward, watching the late-summer afternoon shadows creep along the scuffed wooden floors of our tiny bedroom, I found myself gaining fresh clarity on my circumstances. Gone were all the existential questions—the why-am-I-here, what-does-it-all-mean kind of hand-wringing that sometimes troubles actors and other people who have too much time on their hands. Transcendentalism has no place in the contemplations of a man whose fiancée has just informed him she's knocked up.

My thoughts and priorities were now much more concrete. I wasn't the most important person in my own life anymore. I wasn't even in second place. The baby mattered more than anything. And the baby's mother mattered more than anything besides the baby.

Supporting them. Making sure their needs were met. That was the reason I was taking up space on this hot, crowded planet.

Amanda could humbly insist we didn't need to be rich, and it was true to a certain extent. I had hung out with some stupidly wealthy people in the theater world, and there was nothing self-actualizing about owning four houses. On some level, it was just more toilets that might someday require you to call a plumber.

But the fact remained that—beyond the basics of food and shelter—this child would need piano lessons. I simply couldn't abide my daughter laboring under the same handicap as her father, who went into musical theater and never learned to do anything more than plunk out a single-line melody.

And there was no question piano lessons would be a lot more attainable with a hundred grand or two in the bank.

I turned my head toward Amanda, who was nestled against my side, her unruly blond hair spilled across my chest. She was tracing her fingers across my biceps. I took in a deep breath and then said what I now knew to be true:

"I think I have to do this FBI thing."

Her caresses didn't stop. She just said, "I know."

CHAPTER 6

The next morning, we were back at the diner: Danny, Rick Gilmartin, and I.

Different waitress. Same place mats.

The agents were again wearing suits, the government kind, bought on sale from a place that was never not having a sale. We small-talked until after we ordered breakfast, at which point I was antsy enough that I moved us on to the business at hand.

"So how does this work exactly?" I asked.

Danny looked at Gilmartin, who reached down for his briefcase and produced roughly six stapled legal-size pages. He slid them across the table.

"AGREEMENT, made between Thomas Henry Jump (the 'Informant'), whose address is"—and there was a blank where I, the itinerant actor, would have to figure out something to fill in—"and the Federal Bureau of Investigation (the 'Employer'), whose offices are at 935 Pennsylvania Avenue NW, Washington, DC . . ."

And so on. I picked it up and skimmed, slowing down on the part that dealt with the money. It was "fifty thousand United States dollars" on going in, and "fifty thousand United States dollars" on getting out. It was even tax-free "per Attorney General's directive in consultation with the Internal Revenue Service"—whatever that meant. Plus there was another "one hundred thousand United States dollars" if information I provided led to further indictments.

I looked up from the paper. Amanda and I had agreed that if anything seemed off about the agreement, I'd walk away. This was the first thing to give me pause.

"You guys need to be able to get an indictment before I get paid the bonus?" I said.

"That's right," Danny replied.

"What if I tell you where that cabin is, you get the documents, but you can't get an indictment for some unforeseen reason? That hardly seems fair."

"Oh, we'll get the indictments," Danny said. "We have a saying that you can indict a ham sandwich. If we find those documents, we'll have more indictments than we'll know what to do with. Plus, I'd argue the more open-ended wording is in your favor. Say you don't get the location of the cabin or any documents but Dupree tells you something else we can use. Even if all he does is implicate his secretary—which, believe me, is *not* what we're hoping for out of this operation—you still get the hundred g's."

"Yeah, but why can't it say 'arrest'? I shouldn't lose out on my bonus because some prosecutor messes up."

"Again, I'd tell you that's not in your favor," he said patiently. "We don't always arrest someone. Sometimes they turn themselves in. Sometimes we indict them but never catch them, so there's no arrest. The way we have it worded now is better for you, trust me."

Trust me. Already I was hearing the echo of Amanda's voice asking, *Would you trust him with your life?*

I returned my attention to the agreement. Paragraph after paragraph passed under my gaze. The final page was embossed with the FBI seal and signed "Jeff Ayers, Federal Bureau of Investigation."

"Who is Jeff Ayers?" I asked.

"He's a deputy director," Danny said.

"Why am I not just signing this with one of you guys?"

"Because we're not high-enough level," Gilmartin said. "Confidential informant agreements at this dollar amount need to be blessed by someone deputy-director level or higher. Chances are excellent you'll never meet Jeff Ayers."

"Don't worry," Danny assured me. "You're not missing much."

Gilmartin was again reaching into his briefcase.

"We also have these two," he said, procuring a pair of documents, both of them thinner than the main agreement.

The first one read "Nondisclosure Agreement." Its words were prickly, basically saying that if I revealed the nature of my work for the FBI, I would forfeit any payments due to me and would be liable for any damages that might arise out of my carelessness.

The next one read "Exoneration Agreement."

"What's this for?" I asked.

"This is probably the most important thing we'll sign," Danny said. "It's your Get Out of Jail Free card."

"I don't understand. Why would I have to be exonerated when I didn't actually do anything?"

"That's not going to be *exactly* true for a little while," Danny said, his voice modulating higher on "exactly."

I felt my eyes narrow. My mouth had become some fractional amount drier.

"It is vitally important for the operation—for your safety, really—that we maintain the appearance that you really have committed a crime," Gilmartin explained. "If anyone starts getting suspicious, you have to look legitimate. Your fellow inmates, including Dupree, will have access to their lawyers, and their lawyers have access to Westlaw, LexisNexis, things that allow them to look up cases. We have to lay down a paper trail that appears to be genuine.

"You will plead guilty to a federal crime, likely bank robbery, because that's clearly under FBI jurisdiction. You'll then be sentenced by a federal judge, just like anyone else. The assistant US Attorney we deal with will know the real story, but no one else will. For six months, you will technically be a convicted felon. You need this piece of paper that says we acknowledge you didn't actually do what you were convicted of. That's how you know we can get you out after six months."

Which answered Amanda's question about how I got into and out of prison. It was the FBI pulling strings, as I thought. They were just heavier strings than I anticipated. More like ropes.

Or chains.

"So no one at FCI Morgantown will know I'm not really a crook?" I asked.

"Not even the warden," Danny confirmed. "We've had problems in the past where someone who works at the prison tells someone else on staff, who tells someone else, and the next thing you know . . . Well, I'm sure you've heard the phrase 'snitches get stitches.' It wouldn't be quite that literal at a minimum-security facility, because everyone there is keeping their nose clean. But, believe me, even there, you *do not* want anyone knowing you're with us. We have a liaison with the Bureau of Prisons who works with us, but he's in Washington. Everyone on-site is what we call operationally dark. That's why we give you that toll-free helpline number. In case you need to get out in a hurry, you know we have your back."

Gilmartin amplified this: "As far as the bureau is concerned, if you're working for us, you're one of ours. We'll treat you like we would treat any agent. We don't hang our people out to dry."

I nodded. Amanda was right. I really was putting my life in Danny Ruiz's hands. I looked at him, sitting there in his FBI suit, with his FBI shield in his pocket. He had grown up a lot since the days of Danny Danger.

We both had, I guess.

"So talk to me about the timeline here. If I agree to all this, how soon can we get started?" I asked, thinking about Amanda's pregnancy. I wasn't thrilled about the prospect of being absent for a large portion of it, but I damn sure was not going to miss the big event at the end.

"Immediately," Gilmartin said. "Once you sign the paperwork, we'll take you to West Virginia, where we'll introduce you to the assistant US Attorney we work with down there. He'll get you in front of a magistrate, where you'll plead guilty. We can ask for the sentencing to happen as quickly as possible, but we don't have total control there, because we're at the mercy of a federal judge's calendar. Plus, the judge needs a presentencing report from the probation office, and those take a few weeks. In total, you're looking at a month or two."

"How soon after I go in front of the judge do I start serving my time?"

"Again, immediately," Danny said. "Part of the deal you'll strike with the US Attorneys Office is that you'll be serving your time at FCI Morgantown. Those kinds of requests are not unusual in plea deals. Morgantown is close by, and we double-checked with the Bureau of Prisons: It has empty beds. You'd be processed in the same day you're sentenced."

Meaning the clock would start ticking when Amanda was, at most, two months pregnant. I'd be out in time, even if she ended up delivering a little early.

"What if I want a lawyer to look this over?" I asked.

"I'd encourage you to. But that would be at your own expense," Gilmartin said. "My guess is you could probably find someone who would look at this for a thousand or two."

Money I didn't have. Not yet anyway.

"And when would I get paid?"

"As soon as you sign these documents, we'll put the requisition in," Gilmartin said. "We wouldn't be able to get it today, because of the holiday. But usually they do twenty-four-hour turnaround. You'd probably have the money by Wednesday."

So it was a catch-22. I couldn't afford a lawyer until after I signed the agreement.

I'd simply have to serve as my own. I had signed numerous contracts during my years in the theater. This one wasn't as dissimilar as you might think.

"Okay, you guys mind if I do some reading here?" I asked.

"Only if you don't mind that we eat while you do it," Danny said. "I'm starving."

W e fell silent as I tucked into both the pancakes and the documents in front of me. Now that I was no longer skimming, I saw they were relatively straightforward. I could leave at any time I wanted, though I would forfeit any monies not yet paid to me. In the event of emergency, I was to contact the agent assigned to me, but the FBI also had a toll-free helpline that was staffed at all times. After six months, the parties could extend the agreement until such time as the work was finished, but only by mutual consent.

Most of the verbiage was dedicated to the notion that if I got hurt or killed, it wasn't their fault, and neither I nor my heirs or assignees could sue them.

I had gotten through the main agreement and was moving onto the exoneration agreement when Gilmartin excused himself and disappeared around the corner, toward the men's room.

As soon as Gilmartin was out of earshot, Danny leaned in and said, "Hey."

I looked up.

"Ask for more money," he whispered.

"Really?" I whispered back.

It didn't occur to me I could do that. This perhaps explains why I became an actor and not a business tycoon.

"Definitely. The asset seizure fund is like Monopoly money to my bosses. It's easy come, easy go. But it's real money to you, am I right?"

"Yeah, sure," I said.

He continued talking fast and low. "There was an operation in Houston a few months back where the actor got paid one-fifty, plus a one-fifty bonus for indictments. And the targets weren't nearly as high-level as the ones we're gunning for here. When Rick comes back, tell him you want twice as much. He'll push back, because he can't increase the payout without approval from higher up. Just hold your ground. Worst thing that happens is our boss says no."

"All right," I said. Then I added, "Thanks."

"Just looking out for you, Slugbomb. Now do me a favor and wait a little bit before you hit him with the request. If you do it right when he gets back from the bathroom, he'll know it was my idea."

"Got it."

I went back to the documents. When Gilmartin returned, I kept reading, like nothing had happened. I waited until I finished the exoneration agreement and the nondisclosure agreement, and then I got myself in character.

No longer was I Tommy, the easygoing actor. I was now Mr. Jump, the shrewd negotiator. I gathered the papers, butted them together, and placed them in a neat pile in front of me.

Then I fixed Gilmartin with a steely look.

"Well, this all seems to be in order except for one thing," I said.

"What's that?"

"The money," I said. "It's not high enough to account for the risk I'm taking, going to prison for you guys. I want a hundred when I go in, a hundred after six months, and two hundred if you get any indictments."

I snuck a glance at Danny, who remained impassive. Then I swung my gaze back to Gilmartin, who looked ruffled for the first time since I met him.

"You want the money *doubled*?" he said. "That's outrageous."

"It's a big ask, Tommy," Danny said, pretending to pile on.

"I don't think so," I said. "If you want me to sign something saying the FBI isn't liable for my death or dismemberment, I want to be paid accordingly."

Gilmartin had crossed his arms and was scowling at me.

"Well, I can't . . . I can't authorize that," he said.

"Then why don't you talk to the person who can?" I said.

Gilmartin grimaced. "I hate bothering our SAC on a holiday weekend. Can I at least tell him that you're in if he says yes?"

"Why don't we just see how the phone call goes," I said.

Gilmartin's grimace had turned into a full-on frown. "All right," he said. "I'll call him. Hang on."

He slid out of the booth and walked outside. At the moment he disappeared from our view, Danny shot me a wink. Then we saw Gilmartin pacing near the Chevy Caprice, talking in an animated fashion.

The phone call lasted two or three minutes. Toward the end, Gilmartin seemed to be doing more listening than talking. Then he slipped back into the diner, calmer than before.

"Our SAC said he can't double it, because if word got out that would create problems for him with some other operations," Gilmartin said. "But he's willing to meet you halfway. Seventy-five and seventy-five, plus one-fifty for indictments. *However*, he wants me to stress that this is the best he's willing to do, *and* he says the offer expires at high noon today. He either wants you in, or he wants us to move on. This is now take-it-or-leave-it time. What's it going to be? You in or not?"

I looked out the window, down the hill toward where my pregnant fiancée was right now starting to pack our meager belongings into boxes.

High noon. It was very spaghetti western of them. It meant there wasn't time to get a lawyer, which I hadn't really wanted to do anyway. I simply had to make a decision here.

If I said no, I didn't know what we were going to do next. I could hope for Arkansas to come through. Amanda could hope to sell a painting or two. We'd be barely scraping by.

If I said yes, my six-month sacrifice would support our family for years to come.

"Okay," I said. "I'm in."

CHAPTER 7

N atalie Dupree didn't have a lot of time for revenge fantasies.

She was the mother of two kids who needed regular feeding, chauffeuring, attention, affection, homework help, reminders about practicing the saxophone, and other parental services she delivered lovingly—and alone, now that her husband was in prison.

Her parents? She loved them, too, but they also came with a formidable set of challenges. Her father suffered from dementia *and* cancer, which were having the slowest race ever to decide which would kill him first. Her mother's macular degeneration had recently resulted in two minor fender benders, the loss of her license, and a burgeoning set of logistical issues. Natalie had heard people use the term "sandwich years" to describe this phase of life, when you were caring for both your children and your aging parents. That still didn't seem to adequately describe how squeezed she felt.

On top of that, she was the solo head of a household that was a study in entropy, one that suffered from spasmodic eruptions of dust bunnies, dirty laundry, and leaky faucets even as it settled into greater states of disorder, chaos, and decay.

She was also a part-time sales associate at Fancy Pants, a boutique that catered to women who desired overpriced clothing precisely because it was overpriced. Natalie could barely contain her resentment toward certain customers—these women who acted like having to hire a new housekeeper was life's greatest inconvenience—but when she was forced to reenter the job market, Fancy Pants was the only employer that offered flexible hours and didn't stumble over the fourteen-year gap in her résumé that child-rearing had created.

Natalie had read articles about how incarceration didn't just punish inmates; it punished their families, too. And then some. Not only had she been deprived of her husband's contributions—financially, emotionally, physically—she now had another person dependent on her.

So, no, she didn't really have time for this.

And yet there she was, back in Buckhead—the tony Atlanta neighborhood where they used to live before Mitch's legal fees and their imminent bankruptcy had forced a move—parked outside the kind of house she couldn't afford anymore.

It was a neoclassical monstrosity with white columns, a three-car garage, and, most ostentatiously, a pair of stone lions guarding the front door.

Natalie hated those lions.

Almost as much as she hated the man who lived there, Thad Reiner.

It being Labor Day, she wasn't even sure if Reiner was there. He could well have been off at Tybee Island, frolicking with all the other rich families who had second homes there.

She had taken the usual precautions all the same. She was wearing dark sunglasses and driving a used Kia that was unrecognizable to anyone who knew her when she lived around here. Her hair was a different color too: Now that she could no longer afford going to the salon every two weeks for highlights, she was dyeing herself straight blond out of a bottle from the drugstore.

Still, it was absurd. All of it. Absurd that a suburban housewife would be staked out in front of someone's house. Absurd that she daydreamed about confronting the man who lived there. Absurd she thought hurting him would in any way improve the daily battle with resource depletion that was now her life.

But, really, imagine there was a man who had taken nearly everything from you. He had taken your husband—the father of your children, your best friend and lover—and left you with an empty bed at night. He had taken most of your money and any hope you might ever achieve financial security and left you with anxiety about what would happen if the car's head gasket crapped out. He had taken an existence of yoga classes, salon visits, and volunteer work and left you with Fancy Pants and aching feet. He had taken your dignity, your standing in the community, and many of the people you once counted as friends and left you ostracized, with people who treated you as either a pity case or like you were bathed in radioactive material.

Imagine he had done all that and not suffered so much as a moment of retribution. He had gotten to go on living his comfortable life, in his massive house, with his stupid lions and his endless pretentions, while you and your family were relegated to shame, infamy, and impoverishment.

Natalie Dupree didn't have to imagine any of this.

That's what Thad Reiner had done to her.

And that's why she kept finding herself back here, parked in front of his house, imagining scenarios where she finally delivered the reckoning he so richly deserved.

CHAPTER 8

With two FBI agents schlepping boxes, Amanda and I needed less than an hour to empty our apartment and cram everything into our Ford Explorer.

It probably wouldn't have taken much longer had it been only the two of us. This was a trick we had performed many times. We knew which objects fit where, right down to the houseplants that rode buckled into the back seats.

As we finished the job, it felt like the end of an era. Before too much longer, everything we owned would no longer be contained by one SUV. Couples could do that. Families could not. What I knew about babies could fit inside a napkin holder, but I had a dim understanding that they came with a lot of bulky accessories.

Our last act in the old apartment was also the official first act of our next chapter. Rick Gilmartin presented me with the three documents I needed to sign, including the updated agreement, which now had 75,000 dollars and 150,000 dollars in the appropriate spots.

I let Amanda read them over, then signed everything on the kitchen counter.

We departed for points south shortly thereafter. I drove. Amanda was in nervous good spirits, doing her best to tamp down her natural pessimism and let my optimism have a moment to frolic. This was our new adventure.

Danny and Rick followed behind us as we started down the New York State Thruway. They let us set the pace but had warned me not to go too fast: Unless it was an emergency, they weren't allowed to use their FBI badges to evade speeding tickets.

My mother was expecting us that afternoon, so I called and alerted her we were on our way. Then I told her we would have company and that she needed to be on her best behavior. I didn't want her subjecting Danny or Rick to the Barb Jump Inquisition, an interrogation that lasted half as long as the Spanish version but was at least twice as painful.

Our plan was that we'd stop in Jersey for the night and dump most of our stuff in her basement. Then we'd continue to West Virginia the next morning.

Now that I had signed the documents, everything during our journey—gas, meals, hotels, whatever—would be paid for by Danny and Rick, in cash, courtesy of the asset seizure fund. We just had to remember to grab receipts to keep the FBI's accountants happy.

Already, we had filled our gas tank and bought sandwiches. It was a little strange to think my roast beef was being funded by drug money. But it was probably better than what it would be buying if the FBI hadn't seized it.

On the way down, Amanda exercised her phone, both finding an obstetrician and confirming that my Actors' Equity insurance, which she qualified for as a domestic partner, wouldn't lapse while I was out of work.

Then we talked for a while, agreeing it was too early to start telling people we were pregnant. Including my mother. Especially my mother. One of her nicknames was BBC, the joke being that if you wanted to know what was happening in Hackensack, all you had to do was listen to the Barb Broadcasting Corporation. The bigger the news, the wider she spread it.

It was midafternoon as we crossed over the Jersey border and merged onto Interstate 80, toward Hackensack. Traffic was almost nonexistent. Everyone was either "down the shore," as Jersey folks said, or barbecuing.

We slowed as we entered my neighborhood, a grid of small, tightly packed houses just south of Route 4.

My mother—full name Barbara, though everyone calls her Barb or, at school, Ms. Jump—moved here when I was a toddler. I have no memory of living anywhere else, nor with anyone else. My father, to whom she was not married, left us before my first birthday, under circumstances she has never discussed. It never occurred to me to feel deprived by his absence. You can't miss what you don't know.

Before I was born, Mom had tried to make it as a stand-up comedienne, waiting tables during the day so she could be free to book gigs at night. From what I know of it now, it's a brutal line of work— doubly so if you're a woman. I can only imagine what it was like for her in the eighties and early nineties, with even more sexist attitudes holding sway and even fewer women trying to hack it. When she started showing with me, there were several club managers who absolutely refused to book a pregnant woman, especially one without a wedding ring.

I want people laughing, not feeling sorry for you, one of them told her.

Once I was born, that was it. She never explicitly said she chose me over stand-up. It hadn't occurred to me that's what she had done until later in my teenage years, when I was already deep into my own acting career and it finally started dawning on me my mother had once been—and still was—a human being with drives and desires that went beyond merely raising her son. But while her attempts to become a successful comedienne ended with my arrival, her love for the stage did not. When I demonstrated a proclivity for performing as a four- and five-year-old, she was the first to encourage it, signing me up for local kids' theater productions, doing all she could to nurture my talent. Her experience in comedy made her the toughest stage mom on the block. Woe to the director who tried to give us crap.

Mom buried her own aspirations deep, seldom even acknowledging what she had once wanted to be. Though there was one time when I was sixteen and, in retrospect, at the pinnacle of my run on Broadway. I had just gotten a rave from Ben Brantley in the *Times* for my work in *Cherokee Purples*. We were all dreaming of the show becoming a hit. We were at a party after opening night, and Mom had drunk too much wine, which was unusual for her. With her tongue loosened, she admitted she had once dreamed of having a one-woman show on Broadway, of seeing STARRING BARB JUMP on a marquee on Forty-Second Street.

"I never made it," she said with tears rimming her eyes. "But now my son has."

If there was one thing that really killed me about giving up acting, it was that I felt like I was failing for both of us.

This is not to portray my mother as some kind of tragic figure living in wistful remembrance of the past. For the last twenty-five years, she's been a secretary at Hackensack High School. It might sound strange to say she's become famous for it, but in her own way, she's much more legendary as a school secretary than she ever could have been as a struggling comic. *Everyone* in Hackensack knows Ms. Jump, who is not quite five feet tall but cuts a larger-than-life figure.

Her job is to run the main office, but she treats it more like she's emceeing a cabaret. The Barb Jump Show at Hackensack High is one of the longest-running acts in American theater, and no one—not the students, not the parents, not even the principal—is safe. If anyone gives her a hard time, she treats them like they're a heckler at Carolines.

She is also notoriously impatient, which is why she was waiting for us in the short driveway that fronted her tidy, two-bedroom, postwar ranch as we pulled up.

I don't want to say I was shocked by her appearance. Maybe just mildly surprised my forever-young mother was starting to show her age. In a few weeks, she'd turn fifty-three. Her mostly dark brown hair was gaining more gray strands, and they refused to lie down as politely as the others did. Her crow's-feet had spread a little farther away from her soft brown eyes. The skin around her neck was loosening.

"My babies!" she called as we got out of the car, assaulting Amanda with a big hug.

Mom plainly didn't like Amanda when we first starting dating. I think a Jersey girl didn't know what to make of someone from Mississippi, like Amanda was going to burn a cross on our lawn because Mom was half-Jewish. Early on, I had the suspicion my mother would have been thrilled if we broke up and I wound up dating some girl from Hackensack, someone more in my mother's immediate realm of comprehension.

She had since warmed to Amanda and was now always cooing over her hair, her clothes, whatever. Mom could coo with the best of them.

Once she was done with Amanda, Mom grabbed me, wrapping her tiny arms as far around me as she could. I don't care what age you are. A hug from your mom always feels good.

"My God, Tommy, you're like squeezing a two-by-four," she said, poking my shoulder. "You're lucky I don't have a pin on me. I'd prick you and I swear all those muscles would pop."

"Hi, Mom," I said.

The Chevy Caprice had pulled up at the curb. Danny was already out, lingering on the sidewalk. Mom broke away from me.

"Danny Ruiz!" she called. "What's this I hear about you joining the FBI? Does the FBI know you used to try to sneak candy out of my jar at work? Did that come up in your background check? Because if anyone asks, I'm diming you out."

"Hey, Ms. Jump," he said. "Nice to see you."

He had stuffed his hands in his pockets. His shoulders had slumped a little. Only my mother could instantly turn an FBI agent into a high school sophomore who was sheepish about forgetting his hall pass.

"Look at you, in your suit. You look like you're coming out of a penguin factory," she said. "Don't worry. If you're staying for dinner I think I've got some sardines in the cupboard."

Then she turned to Gilmartin, instantly measured his nonexistent sense of humor, and thrust out her right hand.

"Hi, Barb Jump," she said crisply.

"Rick Gilmartin," he said.

"Very nice to meet you."

"Likewise."

"So can you stay for dinner?" my mother asked Danny. "If you don't want the sardines, I've got potato salad and burgers. I'd love to have you both."

I held my breath for a moment. It was one thing for my mother to resist her natural urge to ask fifty-seven thousand questions of Rick and Danny while we were out in the driveway. I doubted she could keep her resolve throughout an entire dinner.

But Danny saved all of us by saying, "That's very kind, Ms. Jump. But we're going to help Tommy and Amanda get their things stored, then we're going to take off."

"You sure?"

"Yes, ma'am."

Gilmartin had already moved to the back of our Explorer, trying to get as far from my mother as possible.

Mom had cleared out a corner in the basement for our stuff. Once we had it stowed, the agents announced their departure. Danny said they'd be back by nine the next morning so we could continue toward West Virginia.

Before long, I was out in the backyard, a fenced-in enclosure that was just barely longer than the house and perhaps twenty feet deep.

A portion of it was dedicated to a tiny deck that had held the same metal-and-plastic Kmart patio set for the last quarter century. Mom had already opened the sun-faded umbrella. Amanda was in the house, showering off the grit from the move, so it was just the two of us.

I could tell from the way my mother was hovering around me that she was dying to know what was going on. I was fiddling around with the charcoal—Mom inexplicably stored it outside, in a small shed that contained her gardening supplies and was something short of waterproof—which was my excuse for being evasive with her.

It didn't take long for Mom to get fed up. And not with the charcoal.

"Tommy, stop messing with the fire and talk to me. I'm your mother. Sit."

I sat. As a rule, Barb Jump was where nondisclosure agreements went to be broken. But there would be no keeping this from her. So after swearing her to secrecy, I filled her in on my interactions with the FBI.

When I was through, she didn't bother hiding her feelings. She simply demanded, "Okay, *why* are you doing this?"

"It's a lot of money, Mom."

"I know, but I don't like it. It feels like *Damn Yankees*. You're Joe Hardy and you're making a bargain with the devil."

"It's not the devil. It's Danny Ruiz."

"You know what I mean. Since when do we do things for the money in this family?"

"Since I'm twenty-seven years old and it's time I grow up and face reality. I'm not hacking it as an actor, and this will go a long way toward helping us transition to whatever comes next."

"You're hacking it just fine. You've been in a rough patch since Mr. Martelowitz died, that's all. You've got too much talent to walk away."

"I was in a rough patch *before* Mr. Martelowitz died. Him being alive just covered it up. We've talked about this, Mom."

"I know, I know. But I thought . . . I thought you would come to your senses. I thought this summer thing would end and you'd rededicate yourself, or maybe something else would shake loose and . . . I don't know, I just don't think you should quit on yourself, that's all. You were an eyelash away from a Tony, for God's sake."

"Mom, I was only nominated."

"Yes, but you should have won. That guy from *Billy Elliot* wasn't nearly as good as you."

"Even if I had won it wouldn't matter. Do you know how many Tony winners are out of work?"

"I know," she said, pouting a little. "But what if . . . what if you gave yourself a year? Just a year. It could be your present to yourself. Or to me. You could live here and take the bus into the city for auditions. Would you do that for your mother?"

"Mom, no. I appreciate what you're saying. But it's over. This FBI thing is going to pay me a lot of money, and it's what I'm going to do."

She leaned back, now studying me, her son, who wasn't as young as he used to be, either.

"Is this coming from Amanda? Is something going on with you guys?"

"No," I said.

"You think that if you come home with all this money, she's finally going to marry you. Is that it?"

I almost said no. But I didn't want to lie to my mother. So I said, "Well, yeah, that's crossed my mind."

And then, like she could smell it on me, my mother pulled the truth out of thin air: "She's pregnant."

My face must have fallen by half a foot. My mother required no further confirmation.

"Oh my goodness! She's pregnant! Oh, Tommy, honey," she said, putting both hands to her mouth and sucking in sharply.

I still hadn't said anything.

"I knew it," my mother continued. "I knew the moment I looked at her. Her ass was bigger."

"Mom, stop," I said. "That's not even possible. She *just* found out."

"It doesn't matter. It's first-trimester ass. Everyone gets it. Even your walking stick of a mother. One moment, I was the same scrawny little girl I had always been. The next moment, I was Kim Kardashian."

Ladies and gentlemen, the Barb Jump Show.

"You can't tell anyone," I said.

"Okay."

"I'm serious. I can't have you going all BBC on this one."

"Okay, okay," she said, then heaved an outsize sigh. "You realize this is exactly why you shouldn't do this . . . this prison thing. Amanda is young and pregnant and unmarried and scared. Believe me, I've been there. She needs *you,* Tommy. Not a pile of cash."

"And she'll have me. In six months."

She grabbed my hand. "Tommy, can you please think about this? If not for you or Amanda, for me? Prison is dangerous. They don't send people there as a reward for saintly behavior. You're my sweet, gentle, loving boy. I don't care how many muscles you have now. You don't belong in a place like that."

"I'll be fine, Mom," I said.

Then, because there were tears starting to form in her eyes, and because I didn't want to have to deal with her emotions on top of everything else, I took my hand away and stood up.

"The fire is probably hot enough by now," I said. "I'm going to start the burgers."

CHAPTER 9

Amanda stepped out of the shower, finished drying herself, and wrapped the towel around her head.

For a few moments, she stopped to examine herself in the mirror, looking for some external confirmation of what was happening inside. Was her skin glowing yet? Had her breasts begun to swell? Were her hips broadening?

It was like waiting for puberty all over again. And, much like the first time, when she began the first anxious search for changes in her nine-year-old self, nothing much was happening.

She briefly drummed her still-flat stomach, then walked out of the en suite bathroom and into the bedroom. It had been Tommy's when he was a boy, and his mother had since turned it into a museum to her only child. Framed *Playbill* covers lined the walls, as did pictures of Tommy's adolescence.

There was Tommy as a ten-year-old, appearing in a regional production of *Oliver!* There was Tommy at the barricades in *Les Miz*. There was Tommy, stage left for a big company number in *Wicked*. There was Tommy with Michael Crawford at a benefit.

As much as it was a shrine to a boy's achievement, it was also a testament to a mother's devotion.

While Amanda dressed, she peeked out the blinds toward the

porch, where Tommy and his mother were having what appeared to be an intense conversation.

Amanda loved Barb. From a distance. Barb was just a little . . . overwhelming at times. So high-energy. So constantly putting on a show. So garrulous. Her habit of saying whatever came to her mind whenever it arrived there was fundamentally at odds with Amanda's southern upbringing, where politeness was prized above honesty.

But then again, what did she expect from a woman whose name was a sharp object combined with an action verb?

Amanda was just stepping away from the window when Tommy's phone, which he had tossed on the bed, began to blare out "Corner of the Sky" from *Pippin*. The caller ID showed a 501 area code. A girl from northern Mississippi didn't need to be told that was Arkansas.

Without a second thought, she answered the call.

"Hello?"

The man on the other end said his name so quickly Amanda missed it. But she didn't miss the end part: ". . . from the Arkansas Repertory Theatre."

"Oh, yes, hello."

"Is this Amanda?"

"It is."

"Tommy brags about you all the time. He says you're quite an artist."

"Depends on the day," she said.

He laughed. She hadn't been trying to make a joke.

"Anyhow, is Tommy around?"

Amanda again glanced outside, where Tommy was still in a serious-seeming conversation with Barb.

"Actually, he's busy at the moment."

"Oh. Well, I was actually calling to offer him a job. I know he was in the middle of a run up until yesterday so I wasn't going to bother him. But now that it's over I didn't want to wait too much longer.

His cover letter was amazing. I read it to the board, and they were like, 'We've *got* to get this guy.' We'd love to have him join us."

Amanda squeezed the phone. It might as well have been fate calling, telling them to ditch this FBI foolishness. Forget the instant riches. Forget the New York galleries. Move to Little Rock—a lovely town with its own galleries—and join the ranks of the other artists who couldn't quite make it in New York.

Wow. That last part just hopped into Amanda's brain, bypassing the usual filters of kindness or fairness.

Yet she couldn't deny it, either.

Then there was something else, even more spontaneous: Whatever Arkansas was paying him, it sure wasn't three hundred thousand dollars.

Still. Forget it. Money wasn't everything.

Except her mother cleaned houses. Three hundred thousand dollars was more than she made in a decade.

For six months' work.

And then he could keep acting. Which, whatever he might say about it, was what he really wanted. In some ways, so did she. Amanda hadn't fallen in love with an assistant managing director. She had fallen in love with a man whose passion was being *on*stage, not near it.

She worried being deprived of that great joy would change him. She worried he'd come to resent the baby if the knowledge of the child's conception and the formal capitulation of his dreams were so intimately entwined. She worried he'd resent her, as the person who made the baby.

And then they'd split, and she'd end up raising the child by herself, brave and lonely in Mississippi, just like her own mother.

Her brain urged her to stop having these destructive thoughts, to recognize that they were being offered one last chance to take a graceful exit ramp off this insane FBI highway.

That's very exciting. Hang on. Let me see if I can interrupt him.

She knew that's what she should have said.

What came out instead was: "Oh, I'm so sorry. He accepted another job earlier today."

Which was true.

"Uhh, oh. Okay. Well, I'm sorry to hear that, obviously. But tell him I said congratulations. That's . . . that's great."

"I'll do that," she said. "Thanks so much for calling."

She finished dressing, then walked out onto the deck, where Tommy was flipping burgers and ignoring his mother.

He looked up, faked a smile.

"Hey," he said. "Did I hear my phone ring?"

"Yeah," Amanda said. "Telemarketer."

CHAPTER 10

My mother dealt with her peevishness toward me in typical fashion: giving me the iceberg treatment that night, then melting
all over me when we went to leave the next morning.

Single moms and their sons. Don't try to figure us out.

We continued our journey south, crossing into the rolling hills of
Pennsylvania, then dropping down on Interstate 81 through a narrow slice of Maryland, then into West Virginia's verdant panhandle.

I followed Danny and Rick to exit 13, which offered the weary
highway traveler a rich assortment of franchised restaurants and chain
hotels. We passed by lesser accommodations on our way to the pinnacle of near-highway lodging, a Holiday Inn.

As I got out and stretched, Danny greeted me with: "Welcome to
Martinsburg, West Virginia. This is home for the next month or so."

I scrutinized the hotel with renewed interest. It was newish. The
plantings were fresh and cheerful. I had definitely stayed in worse.

Gilmartin went inside, dealt with the paperwork, was soon handing me a key card.

"We'll let you freshen up a bit, and then we're going to come see
you, if that's okay," Danny said. "We need to talk a little strategy
before the prosecutor drops by."

"The prosecutor," I repeated.

"Yeah. He's the one guy who's in on this whole thing, remember?"

Oh. Right.

"Don't worry. He'll be discreet," Danny said in response to what must have been a questioning look on my face. "That's why we're meeting at the hotel, not his office. The last thing we want is for one of your future fellow inmates to see you palling around with an assistant US Attorney."

I nodded like I fully understood and approved of this decision. Then I grabbed as many bags as I could carry and took the elevator to the second floor.

We unpacked, then Amanda spent a little time in the bathroom. She was making noises about taking a nap.

For some reason, she hadn't slept well the night before.

The knock on our door came about half an hour later. Gilmartin was carrying the ubiquitous metal briefcase. Danny had a manila folder under his arm.

"This is your Mitchell Dupree briefing," he said, handing me the folder. "It's everything we have in our dossier on him, condensed and with the boring parts taken out. We had to let the interns do something."

"If there's anything you feel is missing, just ask and we'll see what we can do," Gilmartin added.

I went over to the small desk against the wall and took a seat. The folder had a sticker attached that informed me the contents were TOP SECRET and that if I wasn't the intended recipient I could be punished by up to ten years in prison and a five-hundred-thousand-dollar fine.

Before I opened it, I looked up and said, "I *am* the intended recipient, right?"

"That stupid sticker," Danny said. "I swear, the bureau puts it on toilet paper."

Taking that as permission to proceed, I was soon looking at a series of eight-by-ten glossies of Mitchell Dupree. It started with that hangdog mug shot, but there were others: Mitchell Dupree, in a dark suit, getting out of a gray Lexus sedan; Mitchell Dupree mowing the lawn outside a boxy McMansion; Mitchell Dupree walking through a parking lot with two kids and an adult I assumed was his wife, a petite woman with highlighted blond hair, tasteful clothing, and Pilates-toned legs.

And so on. And so on. They were shot from a distance, with the use of a zoom lens, capturing the subject unawares. And they created a different impression of the man than I had anticipated.

I thought Mitchell Dupree would be more of an evil-genius, master-manipulator type. But he looked ordinary. Or, perhaps more accurately, unextraordinary: the average-height, pudgy, goateed, balding white guy you've passed in the bread aisle of the grocery store a thousand times. It made it difficult to cast him as the unconscionable sociopath who did the bidding of the ruthless cartel, unconcerned about the human wreckage he might be helping to create. He struck me as a guy who had gotten in over his head.

Or maybe that was what I needed to tell myself if I was ever going to be able to stomach being near him.

"We had quite a surveillance operation, as you can see," Gilmartin said.

I nodded, then started reading. Mitchell Dupree was born in the suburbs of Atlanta, the son of a stay-at-home mom and an IBM-executive dad. He went to Georgia Tech, where he double-majored in international relations and Spanish. He worked for Coca-Cola's South American operation for a few years, then returned to school, earning his MBA in finance and accounting from Emory.

From there, he hooked on at Union South Bank, earning promotions as the bank made its own rapid rise during the wild, lightly regulated days of the early 2000s. Dupree's language skills, education, and professional background eventually made it a natural fit that he should join the bank's Latin America division. I didn't really understand any of his job titles and couldn't fathom what those people—those men and women who hid behind the tinted glass of big-city skyscrapers—actually did all day long. Maybe someday he'd explain it to me.

I got into the criminal part of the story next, though that wasn't much more transparent to me than the banking part had been. The jargon of the federal judiciary was just elliptical enough that even when you thought you understood the individual strands—indictment, arraignment, sentencing—it was difficult for the uninitiated to weave it into whole cloth. The short version is he went to prison.

Just like what was about to happen to me.

"Okay," I said. "I'll study this more later."

"No, you won't. You don't have the security clearance to possess these," Gilmartin said. "The only way you can review these materials is if we're with you."

"Besides, you don't want to get too familiar with this stuff," Danny said. "I think it's valuable for you to get some sense of his background, because we want you to be able to prepare for this role. But you're not supposed to actually know any of it, remember? When you meet him, he's just another stranger in prison."

"Right. Of course."

"Now, would you like to meet the new you?"

"Sure," I said.

Danny nodded at Gilmartin, who went to his metal briefcase, which he had set on one of the two queen beds in our room. Amanda was sitting on the other one, an introvert in full observation mode.

Gilmartin extracted an envelope and was soon pulling out a birth certificate, passport, and driver's license, which he handed to me.

"Here you are," Gilmartin said. "This is everything you need to be a new man. If you think they're excellent forgeries, you're wrong. These are the real deal."

"Right," I said, looking at the driver's license. The FBI had taken one of my headshots and digitally altered the background so it looked like a DMV photo.

"Peter Lenfest Goodrich," I said. "What kind of a name is Lenfest?"

"It's a family name," Gilmartin said. "Our experience indicates the key to a good fake name is to have two common names and one unusual one that you can then talk about. It's always good to have a conversation piece."

"People call you Pete," Danny said. "Pete Goodrich. A good name for a good guy. You were a high school history teacher. Everyone liked you. You had a beautiful wife named Kelly and three lovely kids: Louisa, Gus, and Ellis."

"We ran a number of possibilities past the profiling unit in Quantico," Gilmartin said. "They thought it was vital you have a white-collar background, like Dupree, and that you have children. Dupree has two kids. According to the psychologist's report at FCI Morgantown, being away from his children is the greatest hardship of his incarceration. This will give you something to bond over."

"Will it be a problem when my wife and kids never visit me?" I asked.

The agents looked at each other uncertainly. This was something they hadn't considered.

Danny started with, "Well, Amanda *could* pretend to be Kelly and—"

"No way," I said immediately. "You're hiring me, not her. Leave her out of it."

I knew I had Amanda's support in this. The room fell into uncomfortable silence.

Then it came to me: "While I'm in jail, Kelly and the kids had to move back in with her parents, and they live in California. It'll probably be at least a year until they're able to visit."

Danny cracked the kind of mischievous smile I hadn't seen since his Danny Danger days and looked at his partner. "See? Told you my boy was good."

Gilmartin nodded and continued his briefing. "As you can read on your license, you lived in Shepherdstown, West Virginia, not far from here. It's a nice town, upscale for West Virginia, a tourist destination—"

"Yeah, I actually appeared in a theater festival there once," I said. "At Shepherd University."

"Perfect. We don't think Dupree has ever been there, so you can take some liberties with your story. But we still suggest you spend some time there over the next few weeks and refamiliarize yourself with it. Visit the school where you worked. Imagine the life you had there."

"West Virginia. So I'd have a touch of a southern accent," I said, already trying one out. Not like I was auditioning for *Porgy and Bess*. Just a little mountain lilt.

Danny picked up the narrative: "Like we told you before, your crime has to be federal. What we were thinking is that you had a mortgage that was a bit of a stretch and then your wife got hurt on the job but was screwed out of her disability. You were a schoolteacher in West Virginia, so you didn't make much to start with. You fell behind on your payments. You got a second job. Then a third. It still wasn't enough. You got even further in the hole until the bank decided to foreclose. You pleaded with them to give you another chance. Couldn't they work with you a little? But the bank took a hard line.

"So there you were. You were going to lose the house you worked so hard for. You were angry. You were humiliated. You were desperate. So one day you lost your mind and decided to show that bank who was boss. You told them you had a gun and demanded they give you everything in the vault. You were going to make yourself right financially *and* get your revenge against the bank, all at once."

"I just snapped," I said. "I blamed the bank for everything."

Gilmartin took back over. "This will be another point of cohesion for you and Dupree. The profilers tell us Dupree likely had antipathy toward the bank he worked for. They theorize he had been denied an important promotion. They think it explains how he could have gotten into money laundering in the first place. He wanted the extra money he would have gotten from the promotion, *and* he wanted to stick it to the bank. Just like Pete Goodrich."

"How did I get caught?" I asked.

"Because you were an amateur," Danny said. "You didn't know the FBI gives banks tracking devices to throw in with the money. You were just getting down to counting the cash when suddenly you had a dozen agents swarming your hideout."

I nodded, my imagination already starting to fill in the gaps of my new story. I was Pete Goodrich. Noble husband. Trying hard as a father. Louisa was my little darling. Gus was a bit of a mama's boy. Ellis, while only a baby, was showing signs of being a complete hellion.

At school, I gave my everything for my students, even though the damn state tests were ruining education. My second job was tutoring. My third job was tending bar at an Applebee's by the highway.

That meant I closed down the restaurant at twelve thirty A.M., crawled into bed around one. Too amped to sleep, I tossed and turned until at least two. And then at six thirty, the alarm clock jerked me awake, at which point I rushed myself into the shower so I didn't smell like stale Budweiser at school.

But even though I was working myself beyond exhaustion, I still couldn't appease that damn bank. So, sleep deprived and in the darkest place of my thirty-three years, I pulled pantyhose over my head, walked into the lobby, and made like Jesse James, whom I used to teach a unit on in my US history classes.

There was more to come. A lot more. But, yes, I could sink my teeth into this role.

J ust as I was beginning to inhabit Pete Goodrich's world, there were three sharp raps on the door.

"That must be Drayer," Gilmartin said.

After a brief check of the peephole, Gilmartin welcomed an older man with fine white hair that he combed forward in an attempt to cover more forehead. He wore rimless glasses, wrinkle-free cotton khakis, a blue blazer, and a tie that hadn't been fashionable since the nineties. That was probably the last time he had worried about trying to impress anyone.

I rose to greet him. So did Amanda.

"Pete Goodrich, meet David Drayer, assistant US Attorney for the Northern District of West Virginia," Gilmartin said. "And this is Pete's wife, Kelly."

Without smiling, Drayer stuck out a hand, which I shook. He did the same with Amanda, adding a polite "ma'am" when he did so. I got the sense he didn't want to be there.

"Hi, Pete Goodrich," I said, practicing both the name and the slight accent. "Nice to meet you."

Drayer nodded. Amanda returned to the bed. I remained standing.

"We wanted you two to have the chance to get acquainted," Danny said, like he was setting us up on a date. "Maybe you can tell Pete here how everything is going to work, set his mind at ease a little bit?"

"Sure," Drayer said. "My office has you scheduled to go before the magistrate at one o'clock tomorrow. You should probably arrive at the courthouse around eleven or so. When you get to the metal detectors up front, tell the court security officers you're a self-surrender. They'll call the marshals, who will take you downstairs and get you finger-printed. Then they'll bring you in front of the magistrate. He'll ask you questions about whether you understand what you're doing and whether you're doing it willingly and without coercion. All you have to do is say yes. You'll have an attorney present. He's a member of the local defense bar who doesn't know anything about your, uh, your circumstances. He'll be told you're taking a sweetheart of a deal and that there's nothing he has to do and that he can bill whatever he thinks is reasonable and it will be taken care of."

Drayer glanced toward the agents like he was checking to see if he had gotten it right. Neither said anything.

"Will there be any evidence presented or anything like that?" I asked.

"No," Drayer said. "Tomorrow is just the arraignment, where you're formally answering the charge against you. Once that's settled, the magistrate will decide whether you need a bond. Because you're a self-surrender and because my office will be recommending you be released without bond, you should be in good shape there. You'll be released on personal recognizance. Really, everything that's going to happen to you is pretty routine. We do it all day, every day, and no one is going to kick up too much of a fuss about someone who wants to save us time by pleading guilty. Does that make sense?"

I found myself doing the same thing: Looking at Gilmartin and Danny, like they could tell me whether I had any questions. They stared back, offering no guidance.

Finally, I just shrugged. "Yes, sounds pretty straightforward."

"Good," Drayer said. "Well, then, unless you need me for anything else . . ."

Drayer was already leaning toward the door.

"Actually, there is one more thing. It's something I wanted to show both of you," Danny said. Then he turned to Amanda. "What I'm about to show these guys is highly, highly classified. I'm afraid I'm going to have to ask you to leave for just a few minutes, Mrs. Goodrich."

"Sure," Amanda said, hoisting herself off the bed.

Danny waited until she was out of the room to resume: "This is a reminder of . . . of what this is all about. At least for me it is. Take a seat, if you don't mind."

He nodded toward the queen bed Amanda was no longer occupying. Drayer and I sat on the end of it.

"There can be this belief that money laundering is a victimless crime, because there's no blood involved," he said, as he went to the seemingly bottomless metal briefcase and sifted through its contents. "In this day and age, it's just some guy in a tie, sitting in an office, fiddling with his computer keyboard. What's the big deal, right?"

Danny had found the envelope he was looking for and withdrew its contents.

"But the fact is, the money is the whole point of this thing. It's why the cartels do what they do in the first place: to make lots and lots of money. And they can only use that money for the things they want if they can clean it. So what Mitchell Dupree was doing was an absolutely essential part of the whole operation. The cartel wouldn't bother selling all those drugs, killing all those people, or ruining all those lives if they didn't have the Mitchell Duprees of the world to make it worthwhile for them."

He handed me another eight-by-ten glossy. It was an official-looking portrait of a husky man smiling in front of a United States flag. He had a poof of reddish hair atop his head and a wide, freckled face. He looked like a fraternity brother who excelled at keg stands.

"This is Kris Langetieg," Danny said, then corrected himself: "Was Kris Langetieg. He was a good man. Had a wife. Two boys. He was dedicated to the cause of justice. Very, very dedicated. I'm saying this for your benefit, Pete. David knew him. He can tell you: Kris Langetieg was the best kind of person, am I right?"

I looked over toward Drayer. His face had gone hard. He was staring down at the floor.

"But then Kris . . . Well, obviously, his zeal for justice made him a threat to New Colima," Danny said. "And New Colima doesn't like threats. So this is what they did to him."

Danny dropped another photo in between us. It was a close-up of a face that had been so thoroughly butchered it took me a moment to recognize it was the same person. The eye sockets were empty. There were bloody holes in the sides of the head where the ears should have been. The mouth hung down in horror, exposing gums covered in pockmarks, from where the teeth had been ripped out. The red hair had this bulge in it, and I realized it was because a large chunk of the skin underneath had been picked up and then put back down again.

Scalped. In addition to everything else, he had been partially scalped.

I turned away from the photo. Too late. It had already found its way to that part of my brain where things stick.

Drayer rose unsteadily and staggered into the bathroom. The next thing I heard was him retching forcefully into the toilet. I was close to losing it myself.

"This is what the victims look like in this so-called victimless crime," Danny said quietly. "You want to know what keeps me going? This. You want to know why we need you to be successful? This. You want to know why we need to bring down this cartel? *This*."

His eyes were pure fire. His head bobbed lightly up and down, affirming the words as he spoke them. I was struck by how my onetime Little League teammate, the former class clown, had metamorphosed into a serious, focused young man.

"Kris' funeral was something else," Danny said. "Closed casket, obviously. His wife, his children. They were devastated. Devastated. It's something you never forget."

This FBI thing wasn't just a job for Danny Ruiz. It was a calling. Now I understood why.

I was also finally grasping the magnitude of the stakes for me. This wasn't the movies. New Colima wasn't a bunch of dashing Mexican guys in white linen suits, smoking cigars and drinking sangria at a picturesque seaside hacienda. They were brutal, soulless killers who placed zero value on human life. They tortured the soon-to-be dead for the sheer terror it created in the living. They respected no laws, no government, no sense of the desire felt by most decent people to live in peace.

And I was about to dangle myself into their universe—near, if not in, their crosshairs.

I could think of it as an acting job all I wanted to. I could invest myself in the role, like I always did. I could tell myself it was pretend.

The potential consequences were not. They were as real, and as terrifying, as anything I could imagine.

CHAPTER 11

I didn't tell Amanda about the photo. My pregnant fiancée already had enough extra burden.

Since I needed to practice making up stories, I invented one about how Danny had showed us classified documents that related to money laundering, but how to me—and any non-accountant—they were basically impenetrable.

She accepted my lie without question, and then we got on with our evening, which we passed quietly, watching movies and ordering room service. Danny had told us to put whatever we wanted to on our bill. The asset seizure fund could handle it.

It would have felt like a vacation, except I had Kris Langetieg's mauled face gaping at me in my mind all night. I kept having macabre thoughts about what order they had done things in. Had it been ears first, then teeth? Had they waited to do the eyes last so he could see everything that was happening to him? Or had they indiscriminately carved until he finally died of blood loss?

At one point, when Amanda was in the bathroom, I googled "Kris Langetieg." There were two stories in the Martinsburg *Journal* about the assistant US Attorney who had been murdered.

So he was a prosecutor. Like Drayer. No wonder his stomach hadn't been able to handle that photo.

There was nothing in the story about the condition of Langetieg's body. Those details had been withheld from the press. The Martinsburg Police Department professed to have no leads as to who was responsible. Most of the story was about what a beloved school-board member and dedicated father Langetieg was and how he was being mourned by the community. The paper did not speculate as to whether Langetieg's death had anything to do with his profession.

A few days later, there was coverage of the funeral, which was more of the same. After that, there was nothing. To the public, the whole thing looked like a strange, inexplicable, perhaps random homicide.

I had a tough time falling asleep—and I was a guy who could ordinarily sleep anywhere, at any time, for pretty much any duration. My struggles continued in the morning, which was even stranger. Truly, one of the joys of my profession was dozing until noon.

Instead, there I was at 6:23 A.M., listening to the Holiday Inn's air-conditioning rattle, wondering if I should just pull the plug on this whole thing. I was an actor, not a slayer of international crime syndicates. Why was I making myself a combatant in a war that wasn't really mine? What would the cartel do to me if they learned what I was after and whom I worked for?

If my friend from Arkansas had called at that moment, I probably would have leapt into his waiting arms, then gone to Danny's room, apologized profusely, and told him I was out.

After tossing and turning on this for another hour or so, I finally rousted myself, before I woke Amanda, and went downstairs to the Holiday Inn's workout room. For half an hour, I poured nervous energy into a rack full of free weights, working my shoulders, arms, back, and chest until they were trembling. Then I switched to the treadmill, cranked up the incline, and ran up an imaginary mountain for another half an hour. My lungs were searing. Perspiration fell off me in nickel-size drops.

By the time I returned, Amanda was up and dressed. She wore leggings and one of my button-down shirts, a simple outfit that looked amazing on her. More than two years after our first date, and she still sometimes took my breath away more than any treadmill possibly could.

"Good morning," she said, in a way that was less a greeting and more of an appraisal of my sweat-soaked state.

"Just wanted to get a workout in," I said. "All we did yesterday was drive and eat. I was feeling gross."

"Oh," she said.

"How about I clean myself up and then let's get some breakfast?"

She patted her stomach and smiled faux sweetly. "I just threw up twice, darlin'. You're on your own for breakfast."

"Threw up as in . . . morning sickness?"

"I guess," she said.

There was this goofy grin on my face, which was probably not the appropriate reaction to the news that one's partner had hurled. But there was something beautiful about it, this corroboration that life was indeed stirring inside her. I kissed her lightly on the forehead, so as not to get her wet.

"I'm going for a walk," she said. "I think some fresh air would help."

"Good idea," I said.

I ordered some breakfast, then jumped in the shower. I stood under the water for a while, marveling again at this turn in our lives.

She really is pregnant. I really am going to be a father. It was still surreal to me. But it also reminded me why I needed to go through with this.

It was like the workout had purged more toxic thoughts from my mind, and I was now thinking more rationally about the risks involved. As a prosecutor, Kris Langetieg had explicitly identified himself as an enemy of the cartel. His entire career, his very being, was a full frontal assault against New Colima.

I was, at most, coming from the side. Even if I was successful, New Colima would never know Thomas Henry Jump had contributed to their downfall.

They might not even know about Peter Lenfest Goodrich. I couldn't imagine Mitchell Dupree was going to volunteer to his cartel bosses that he had unwittingly told a federal informant about the location of his document stash. Depending on how artful I was, he might not even know he tipped me off or that I was the one who tipped off the feds.

Feeling more optimistic about my situation, I ended my shower. As I got dressed, I replied to a text from Danny, who was looking to come over with Rick.

Before long, they were knocking on the door. Their first order of business was to rather unceremoniously hand me a briefcase filled with cash—seventy-five thousand dollars in bricks of crisp, clean, hundred-dollar bills—that had apparently been brought down from New York by another agent that morning.

One brick of it was more money than I had ever seen in one place. And there were lots of bricks.

Before I could get on with gawking at it, Danny moved onto the next order of business: the toll-free helpline, which I had seen mentioned in the contract. He pulled a slip of paper out of his pocket and handed it to me.

"Your first call is always going to be my cell," he said. "If you haven't memorized that by now, you should. Call it anytime, day or night, and I'll deal with whatever you have going on. However, in the event that I don't answer or I'm unavailable for some reason, you should also memorize those two numbers."

I looked down at the slip of paper. Next to the toll-free number was "211-663."

"All you have to do is dial that number, then say that number," he continued. "You'll be connected to someone who can pull up your case file and dispatch an agent."

"Can I try it now?" I asked.

"Absolutely," Danny said.

I walked over to the hotel phone and dialed. After one ring, a female voice answered with, "How may I help you?"

Not *Federal Bureau of Investigation, how may I help you?* Which made sense. You never knew who was listening.

"Two-one-one, six-six-three," I said.

"Hold please."

The line went silent, but not for more than ten seconds. Then there was an earnest-sounding male voice:

"Hello, Mr. Goodrich. What can we do for you today?"

"Uh, nothing," I said. "Everything's fine. Just testing."

"Very good, sir. Call back anytime. We'll be here."

"Will do," I said.

Then I hung up.

Danny was smiling again. "So, admit it—pretty cool, huh?"

"Not the uncoolest thing ever," I allowed.

"I will tell you from experience, there are definitely worse things than being backstopped by the most powerful government in the world," he said. "Now, there's one more thing, as long as we're dealing with communications."

"Go ahead."

"Once you're on the inside, your phone calls are subject to monitoring by prison staff," Danny said. "There may be things you want to tell us that you want to be absolutely sure they don't know about. If that's the case, ask me to buy some lottery tickets for your wife, your mom, whoever. The numbers you call out correspond to the letters of the alphabet, one through twenty-six. Use twenty-seven through thirty for a space between words. You should also toss in numbers higher than thirty, but that's just to mislead anyone who might be listening. We ignore those and focus on the relevant ones. Make sense?"

"Sure."

"It's not exactly two-hundred-fifty-six-bit encryption, but it'll do," Danny said. "Since you're going to have some time on your hands during the next month while you're waiting to be sentenced, you should memorize what numbers correspond to what letters. I've already done the same thing, so I'll be able to transcribe whatever you tell me quickly."

From the front of the room, there was a whirring noise as the lock on the door released. Amanda was returning from her walk. Danny and Rick went quiet as she entered.

"Sorry," she said. "Am I interrupting?"

"Actually," Rick said, then tapped his left wrist.

"I know," Danny said, nodding toward the bedside clock. "Ten forty-seven. You need to take off."

"Right," I said, looking across the room at my half-eaten breakfast with regret. "Let's go."

"Not us. Just you," Danny said.

"Aren't you guys coming with me?" I said, feeling a spurt of nerves. After just two days of being shepherded around by them, I had grown accustomed to the comfort of the flock.

"Sorry. I don't know if you've noticed, but we look just a little bit like FBI agents," Danny said, jerking a thumb toward Rick. "Especially the stiff white guy over there. If one of your fellow convicts at the courthouse were to see you getting out of our Caprice or walking the hallways with us, and then you showed up at FCI Morgantown a month from now, this game would be over before it even started."

Rick, as usual, reinforced this with a more official-sounding version: "From here on out, it's important you preserve the facade that you are Pete Goodrich. You are guilty. You are contrite. You should not expect special treatment, because you won't be receiving any. Remember: Unless you are deciding to give up on the operation, you don't know us. You don't know *any* FBI agents. Why would you? You're just a history teacher who robbed a bank."

"Got it," I said, then turned to Amanda, who was now next to me. "Well, I guess I'm taking off. I'll be back in a few hours."

Her smile was nervous and lacking in conviction. She gave my hand a squeeze.

"Okay," she said. "Be careful in there."

"There's nothing to worry about," Danny said. "All he has to do is make like a good little boy and admit to being a criminal."

T he W. Craig Broadwater Federal Building and United States Courthouse was a solid four-story rectangle located in the heart of downtown Martinsburg. The ground floor was faced in smooth concrete. The upper floors had been covered in a wan, yellowish tile that looked like it belonged in a 1960s bathroom.

On the front of the building, the official United States seal—that famous eagle clutching the arrows—looked sadly faded.

I couldn't quite summon the nerve to enter right away, so I strolled around the neighborhood a bit. There wasn't much to see: the local paper, the *Journal,* had offices next door. Next to the newspaper was a beauty school. Across the street was a Jamaican restaurant.

Finally, having stalled long enough, I walked in through a pair of glass doors and was confronted by three court security officers, all of them in blue blazers and gray pants.

"Hi," I said. "I'm a self-surrender."

"What's your name?" one of them asked.

"Pete Goodrich," I said smoothly, having rehearsed both the name and the accent during the short drive to the courthouse.

He brought a walkie-talkie to his lips, and I was soon under official escort. As the next hour unfolded, I was shuffled from station to station and called "sir" more times than any actor ever had been or should be. I was fingerprinted, photographed, and, in a turn of events that Danny Ruiz definitely did not mention ahead of time, relieved of my clothes and strip-searched.

I quietly bore the whole process without complaint, because that was the reaction most likely from Pete Goodrich, a beaten man who was ready to accept whatever humiliations awaited him.

When they were through processing me and I had redressed in a faded orange jumpsuit that was too long for me, they led me to the holding area—a cell with a narrow ledge to sit on and not much else. After roughly an hour, one of the marshals returned and shackled me at the ankles and wrists, with the wrists attached to a loop around my waist. Then he led me back up to the first floor. He undid the wrists before we entered the courtroom. My ankles stayed bound.

Pete Goodrich humbly accepted this. Tommy Jump thought it was ridiculous overkill.

As I shuffled into the courtroom, taking small steps, David Drayer was waiting at the prosecution table.

At the defense table, there was a man in a suit who couldn't have been much older than me. He looked up at me blankly as the marshal shunted me to his side, then shook my hand before gesturing for me to sit.

There were no people in the gallery. As Drayer suggested, this was another routine day at the justice mill. No one really cared what happened to one more soon-to-be felon.

The magistrate was a man with a shiny face, a nearly hairless head, and a gray-brown beard.

"Is your name Peter Lenfest Goodrich?" he said.

"Yes, sir."

"How old are you?"

"Thirty-three."

"How far did you go in school?"

"I have a college degree, Your Honor."

"Have you ever been treated for any mental illness or addiction to narcotic drugs?"

He said it quickly, and it took a moment for my brain to catch up. So there was a dumb pause before I said, "No, Your Honor."

"Is there anything in your condition today that would affect your ability to understand and respond to my questions?"

"No, sir."

"Have you received a copy of your indictment?"

"Yes, sir," I said, even though I hadn't.

"You are charged with bank robbery. This is a violation of US Code 18, section 2113(a). Do you understand the charges against you?"

"Yes, Your Honor."

"Do you need any further reading of the indictment?"

"No, Your Honor."

"I see you have an attorney present. Have you had the opportunity to discuss your case with him?"

I looked toward him and said, "Yes."

"And how do you wish to plead, guilty or not guilty?"

Somehow, I thought there would be more questions before we got to this one, the only one that mattered. I wasn't truly in—past the point of no return—until I answered.

I gave it perhaps five more seconds' thought. A hundred and fifty thousand dollars. Maybe more. Enough to get my fiancée over her cold feet. Enough to feed, house, and clothe my child until her mother and I figured things out. Enough to start a new life.

All for six months of my time.

It was a good deal. And now it was time to seal it.

I took a deep breath, stuck out my chest, and said, "Guilty."

ACT TWO

It's time to trust my instincts, close my eyes, and leap.

—Elphaba, from *Wicked*

CHAPTER 12

Three hundred minutes. That's how much monthly phone time the Bureau of Prisons permitted Mitch Dupree and every other inmate at FCI Morgantown who had managed not to lose his privileges.

In Dupree's case, that meant three hundred minutes to stay current with everything in his wife's and kids' lives—all in the desperate hope that when he got out eight-plus years from now, he might still have some shred of a relationship with them.

It worked out to ten minutes a day, and Dupree tried to keep each call at that length, rationing himself so it would last. The Bureau of Prisons called the accounts TRULINCS, an acronym for Trust Fund Limited Inmate Communication System. With a stress on the "limited." Mitch set the timer on his watch to keep track of call length. The kids knew they had but so much time each day, and they prepared for it, like they were readying to make a report.

The fourteen-year-old, Charlie, typically had no problem staying within the limit. Everything that wasn't good was fine. Everything else was "I dunno." Mitch used to worry his son was holding out on him or that the boy resented his father for getting locked up. Then Mitch remembered that most modern fourteen-year-old boys actually don't have that much to say about anything that didn't pertain to video games.

The eleven-year-old, Claire, was more talkative—when she was in the mood and wasn't being a sullen preteen. She talked about her friends, and her ex-friends, and which ex-friends were about to become current friends, and so on. Mitch actually took notes so he could remember who was in, who was out, and who was somewhere in between. When it came to girl politics, Congress had nothing on middle school.

If Claire and Charlie used all ten minutes, Dupree and his wife, Natalie, would postpone whatever they had to talk about until the next day. The children came first. The grown-ups got the table scraps.

The previous three days, the kids had taken up all the time. But on this day, Charlie had mumbled a few unmemorable things about band practice and Claire had been betrayed only once, leaving a full two minutes for the parents.

Mitch knew how lucky he was to still have Natalie. Despite the burdens his incarceration imposed on her, she had stood by her man. Many of the other inmates weren't as fortunate. The ones who weren't in the midst of divorce when they arrived soon found themselves there.

"I miss you, baby," Mitch gushed as soon as the kids were clear of the line. He didn't like them to know how much he was suffering, being away from them.

"We don't have time for that," Natalie said softly. "They're watching me again."

Mitch felt this like a punch. "Who?"

"I don't know. They didn't look Mexican, but . . . They were just sitting across the street in a car, trying to blend in. A man and a woman. I saw them with one of those satellite dish thingies. They started aiming it at us as soon as we got on the phone last night."

This was one of the many downsides of their financial situation. No longer did they live in the gracious home set well back from the road in the tony Garden Hills section of Buckhead. They had cashed it out—after the lawyers had eaten through all their savings—and downsized to a three-bedroom, one-and-a-half-bath, sixteen-hundred-square-foot saltbox with gray siding. The place was being marketed as a teardown. It didn't even have central air.

The only real selling point for the Duprees was that it allowed the kids to keep going to the same schools. So they bought it, even though it meant living in a small house that was practically on top of the street, offering no privacy—auditory or otherwise.

"Then it's probably not the cartel," Mitch said. "If it's a listening device like that, it's the FBI or the DEA. They can't get a warrant to tap the phones anymore so . . ."

And the Bureau of Prisons was possibly listening to him speculating about it. He didn't care. If he was right, he wasn't telling the government anything it didn't already know.

"Are they out there right now?" he asked.

"I don't see them, but . . ."

But that didn't mean anything. They could be hiding anywhere. A crowded neighborhood gave them endless cover.

"I wish they would go away," Natalie said softly. "It's so creepy just to have them . . . *out there*. Listening. And watching. Are you sure we can't . . . I was watching this YouTube video about witness protection. I bet they'd send us someplace warm, someplace—"

"We've talked about this. There's the kids and their school."

"The kids care about their father more than they care about what school they go to."

"All the more reason we can't do WITSEC. The moment I hand over those documents, I'll be as good as dead."

"Yes, but maybe—"

"They'd find us. Guaranteed. This is the only way we stay alive."

She sighed. "I just don't know how much longer I can take it with these people out there. What if it is the cartel and they decide to come after me?"

"They wouldn't dare. They know what I have."

"I need more protection than that."

"I know. I'm sorry. There's nothing I can do."

Like that wasn't already obvious.

"I have to go," Mitch said. "Ten minutes. I love you."

He didn't keep the line open long enough to hear whether she replied.

CHAPTER 13

Perhaps I had watched too many old movies, but I was expecting to be transported to prison in some aging rattrap school bus with caged windows, surrounded by scarred men who would look at me like I was the fresh fish they were about to eat for dinner.

The reality was more comfortable and less interesting. It was just a white SUV with a yellow US Marshals star on the side. I was the only prisoner. And if I could ignore the fact that I was shackled in three places, the ride through the early-fall hills of West Virginia was really quite pleasant.

It was October 9. The thirty-five days between my pleading and my sentencing had been uneventful. I was free on that personal recognizance bond. Agents Ruiz and Gilmartin had gone back to the field office in New York, showing up roughly once a week to collect receipts, pay our tab at the Holiday Inn, and make sure I wasn't getting cold feet.

They had guided me through setting up my commissary account and my TRULINCS account, which would help me survive and communicate. They had also been preparing me mentally for life on the inside. Their main point—and they found various ways to make it—was that I couldn't trust anyone.

"Remember," Gilmartin had told me several times, "everything your fellow inmates tell you will likely be a lie."

Otherwise, Amanda and I had been on our own. I worked out and began a score for a musical, tinkering with an I-want song about an out-of-work actor who aspires to the role of a lifetime. The melody was a struggle. The words came more easily. I have lots of experience at longing.

I had also spent a lot of time browsing the Internet, learning all I could about prison generally and FCI Morgantown specifically.

Amanda painted with more urgency than ever. After months of e-mailing, Hudson van Buren had proposed a face-to-face meeting. Amanda downplayed it, merely deeming it a sign her unofficial apprenticeship was progressing well. But she was a master of never letting her hopes get too high. Why would van Buren propose a meeting if not to offer her a showing?

We eased into a pattern of working during the morning and into the afternoon, then knocking off around four. We had a lot of sex—not having to worry about getting pregnant was sort of awesome that way. But sometimes we just went for a walk, then watched movies.

It was perfectly lovely except for Amanda's morning sickness, which often extended into the afternoon and evening. I wouldn't have been surprised if our baby came out craving Saltines and Gatorade. That was all Amanda could get to stay down some days.

Once or twice—well, okay, more like twice-and-a-half—I broached the issue of marriage, proposing that we run down to the local courthouse and make ourselves official before I went off to the big house. Each time, Amanda hastily swatted the notion aside. She wanted us to be "settled" first.

Like I needed more pressure to get this done.

During our separation, Amanda decided to live with my mother in Hackensack, because it was closer to the New York art scene. I didn't know how that dynamic was going to play—they got along now, right?—but I acted like it was a champion idea. Mostly, I was hoping my mother would quietly sever the Achilles tendon of any guy who made a run at my fiancée.

The trickiest part of those otherwise happy thirty-five days was when my probation officer came around to complete the presentencing report. He wanted to know everything—and I mean *everything*—about Pete Goodrich, forcing me to invent all kinds of details about myself. Who knew I had been in the Peace Corps after college? Or that I coached JV soccer?

Amanda impersonated "Kelly," Pete's wife, for a brief phone interview. We told the probation officer that we had lost our house to foreclosure and that she and our three kids were already in California with Kelly's parents.

Also over the phone, Gilmartin ended up posing as the high school principal who had hired me; Danny Ruiz pretended to be the history department chair *and* my former next-door neighbor, Dave Cola. My mother got to be my mother. At least she didn't have to fake being distraught about her little boy going off to prison.

In what felt like a very West Virginia thing to do, I put Amanda's name down as my "cousin" in the relatives section of my presentencing report questionnaire. I had learned from the FCI Morgantown handbook that if she wasn't in my presentencing report, I couldn't put her on my visitors list. Not that we were planning to have her visit. But it was nice knowing she could. Just in case.

Once completed, the presentencing report said I was a nice guy who made a terrible mistake, and it recommended I get ten years. The number staggered me, even if I wouldn't actually have to serve it. *Ten years.* It sounded like a life sentence.

In his generosity, David Drayer knocked that down to eight years, which was still astonishing. I kept reminding myself I would be out in six months. Otherwise I got a little light-headed. Drayer packaged the sentence reduction with a request that I serve my time at FCI Morgantown, near my alleged "home" in Shepherdstown. The judge generously went along with both recommendations, which is how I ended up in that white van, headed west.

About two hours into our journey, around noontime, we stopped at FCI Hazelton to pick up another inmate. Again, I was braced for the worst: a skinhead with facial tattoos, a gangbanger whose arms were thicker than my neck, a lunatic in a straitjacket drooling from all the drugs the medical unit had force-fed him to keep him sedated.

Instead the first real prisoner I interacted with was a solidly built middle-aged white man with salt-and-pepper hair. He slid into the seat next to me with a smile and a friendly nod.

"Hi," he said. "Rob Masri."

"Pete Goodrich," I replied in my Pete Goodrich voice, which came easily after a month of rehearsing it.

"First day?" he asked.

I was still wearing my civilian clothes, marking me as a rookie, so I said, "Yep."

Pete Goodrich was the kind of guy who said "yep" instead of "yes."

"And what brings you to the Bureau of Prisons?" he asked.

"Thought we weren't supposed to tell each other that sort of thing. The websites say, 'Do your own time, keep your head down,' all that stuff."

"Oh yeah, that," he said. "There's a place for that. But you'll find that gets pretty lonely after a while. My theory is this whole thing sucks, but it'll suck a little less if I have friends. I'm guessing you could use one right now."

"Yep," I allowed.

"So, in that case, I'm Rob Masri, and I'm a lawyer from Charlottesville, Virginia, or at least I was until I decided to buy stocks based on privileged information a client gave me. Now, thanks to a prosecutor who decided to make his career on my back, I'm in the midst of an eleven-year sentence. Not that I'm bitter about that."

He flashed a smile. Everything my fellow inmates would tell me would likely be a lie, according to Gilmartin, but his story seemed plausible enough.

"What's your deal?" he asked.

Here goes nothing. "I was a teacher in Shepherdstown, West

Virginia," I said. "Got desperate one day and robbed a bank. It'll cost me eight years."

"Nice," he said. "And you're heading to Morgantown?"

"Yep."

"Good for you."

"Why good?"

"Because Morgantown is a vacation compared to most places. Certainly compared to that place," he said, then jerked a thumb toward Hazelton, now growing smaller as our van descended the hill it was set on. "That's medium security. Maybe that doesn't sound so different from minimum security, but it's like going backwards about ten thousand years in human evolution. You got all the worst elements in there: the gangs, the sexual predators, the guys who will just as soon fight you as look at you. Whitey Bulger got pummeled to death right inside those walls. I'll spare you the rest of the horror stories. Just, trust me, whatever you do for the next eight years, do *not* get yourself sent to a place like that."

"But why'd you end up there?" I asked. "Insider trading, that's not violent. And I'm assuming you didn't have a record. Shouldn't you have been in minimum all along?"

"Yeah, except you need to have ten years or less on your sentence before you're eligible for a place like Morgantown. They actually made me serve close to two years at Hazelton. They told me the whole time it was because there were no beds in Morgantown. Turns out Morgantown has a capacity of thirteen hundred and they only have about nine hundred guys there right now. Go figure."

He shook his head. "But you'll learn that's the Bureau of Prisons. They'll act like they have all these rules and are doing everything by the book, but there have been so many past edicts and promulgations from on high, there are at least three policies contradicting the policy they're enforcing. The only consistency is inconsistency."

Masri offered this and other pointed observations about the world I was about to enter as we got back on the highway and continued our journey toward Morgantown. He quieted only when we exited the highway. After a few turns, we slowed as we passed a short wire fence that wouldn't have stopped a mildly determined dachshund.

Beyond it lay FCI Morgantown, which I recognized from photos I had seen on the Internet. It was set in a small bowl, surrounded by hills on all sides. A softball field and some low-slung buildings were spread out along paved paths, with plenty of green space in between. A few trees dotted the rolling landscape. A small stream bisected the valley.

Once we made the turn into the facility, the wire fence turned split log, like they had put Abraham Lincoln in charge of security. On the south side of the facility, which backed up against the largest of the hills, there appeared to be no barrier at all other than trees.

There were also no guard towers, no sniper turrets, no defensive structures or prisony looking things of any kind. Dotting the grounds were a few tall light stanchions, but even they weren't the massive floodlights I might have expected.

All in all, it was about as intimidating as your local community college. I recalled from my reading that FCI Morgantown had originally been the Robert F. Kennedy Youth Center, constructed while he was attorney general, then named for him after his assassination. It retained that kid-friendly feel.

"Here we are," Masri said as we passed a small, manned security booth. "Welcome to Camp Cupcake."

During my last briefing from Rick Gilmartin, he told me FCI Morgantown was organized in what they called a unit management system. That meant each prisoner was assigned to a housing unit. Your work detail and any classes you might take were not segregated by unit, but pretty much everything else was. You ate with your unit, slept with your unit, recreated with your unit.

All in all, he made it sound a bit like Hogwarts.

My first job, then, was to make sure the intake officer in the Admission and Orientation Program—the Sorting Hat, as it were—placed me in the same unit as Mitchell Dupree. And the FBI couldn't help. Danny and Rick had reminded me of this a number of times: Their influence stopped at the main gates.

The one thing Rick had been able to tell me was that, according the FBI's Bureau of Prisons liaison, Dupree was housed in Randolph. It was the only one of the five residential cottages with a wheelchair ramp. And that, I had decided, would be my ticket in.

So it was that when Pete Goodrich disembarked from the van, he had developed a slight but persistent limp.

I limped from the photograph station to fingerprinting, then to being strip-searched. I limped as I accepted my new clothing: khaki shirt, khaki pants, a black belt, and black steel-toed boots, an ensemble that was actually quite sharp-looking. If you were color-blind.

My pants were, naturally, too big for me. They gave me safety pins to cinch them and a promise to locate pants that actually fit sometime later.

I didn't complain. I just kept limping as they gave me my operations handbook, which was a few dos and a whole lot of don'ts.

Several times, I was reminded that I wasn't allowed to cross the perimeter road, which ringed the facility. That was the de facto fence. And it was all they needed. They continued hammering the nail Rob Masri had already countersunk: The five years they added to your sentence were only a small piece of the penalty for escaping FCI Morgantown; the larger part was that, when they caught you, you weren't going back to Camp Cupcake.

It was Hazelton. Or worse.

With that fresh in my mind, I limped over to Health Services for my medical screening. No one, it seemed, was much impressed by my hobbling, though I was working hard not to overplay it.

Once in the examining room, I got myself gingerly up on the table and allowed myself to be examined by a diligent nurse practitioner. She made no comment on my lameness as she methodically took my vitals and gave me a general once-over.

Then, finally, she gave me an opening. "You seem to be in excellent health," she said. "Any issues we should be aware of?"

"No, ma'am," I said, because Pete Goodrich was a ma'aming sort of guy. "I'm healthy as can be."

I held my perfect-patient smile for a moment before I let it cloud over. "Only thing is, my knee is acting up. But that's nothin'."

"Your knee?" she asked.

"Messed it up playing soccer a bunch of years back," I explained. "Insurance wouldn't cover surgery, so I've just had to live with it. One of those things, you know."

She looked down at some papers in a folder she was holding. "There's nothing about knee problems in your presentencing report," she said, without raising her head.

"That's because most of the time it's fine. It just flares up now and then," I said, rubbing it as I drew breath through my teeth. "Locked up during the ride here. It was kind of tight in that van."

The nurse wasn't buying it for a second. "If you're trying to get me to write you a scrip for painkillers, you're going to have to try *a lot* harder than—"

"No, ma'am. Wouldn't even want anything like that. Tried them once and they made me feel all fuzzy in the noodle," I said, tapping my skull. "Most of the time it's not even an issue. Especially when it's warmer out. Only gives me trouble when it gets colder. Every once in a while . . . well, like I said, it just flares up. Don't like winter much."

Tommy would have said winters could be a real bitch. Pete didn't use that kind of language around a lady.

"I see," she said cautiously, still wondering what I was driving at.

"Seriously, I *don't* want drugs," I said, fixing her with sincere eye contact. Then I added, "Only time it really bothers me is going up and down stairs. There aren't any rooms on the fourth floor here, are there?"

"No, nothing like that," she said, looking back down at some paperwork. "They have you marked down for one of the cottages. Those are all one floor, though they have steps leading up to them."

"Oh," I said, looking a little downcast, rubbing my knee. "Is there anything with, I don't know, a wheelchair ramp or something? I can handle those, no problem."

"We have an ADA-compliant cottage," she said. "I could put in a recommendation for you to be placed there. It's called Randolph."

Bingo.

I winced, rubbed my knee one more time, and said, "Well, if you think that'd be best."

CHAPTER 14

For all the times she had been to New York City, and all the years she lived there as a student, Amanda always felt like the quintessential country mouse the moment she passed into Manhattan.

It wasn't merely that its city-that-never-sleeps hustle, its tall buildings, or its cultural importance—self- and otherwise—made it feel like the municipal opposite of Plantersville, Mississippi.

No, really, it was its people. The guys hanging out in the parking lot at the Better Buy could scoff at New Yorkers all they wanted. To Amanda Porter, these were the people who had been selected—by dint of their high birth, their elite educations, or their prominent talents—to be in Manhattan, the cultural center of the nation.

They were chosen. And she was not.

Not yet.

Which was the purpose of her long-anticipated visit to the Van Buren Gallery. Located on Madison Avenue, just above Seventy-Eighth Street, the Van Buren Gallery was near the Met, the Guggenheim, and more accumulated capital than she witnessed throughout her entire childhood.

Fittingly, the gallery's proprietor, Hudson van Buren, was so old-money that his fortune was said to go back to the city's Dutch founders. He was named after the explorer, not the river—back when he was born, the river was so polluted you could get cancer from looking at it too long—and he rather resented all the bridge-and-tunnel parents from Park Slope, Maplewood, and Montclair who had made his name so common with their children.

With his money, contacts, and influence, Hudson van Buren had long been a kingmaker on the New York art scene. If Hudson van Buren declared an artist was the next big thing, she became so practically overnight. He'd lift the phone and the artist's work was on the cover of *The New Yorker,* or at MoMA, or wherever else he desired. And, of course, that meant her pieces were for sale at his gallery. He made a fortune selling paintings precisely because everyone knew he didn't need the money.

When van Buren had e-mailed Amanda and suggested that October 9 might be a good day to meet in person, it had felt like fate. That was the day of Tommy's sentencing. It was a time for new beginnings.

After a tearful good-bye with Tommy, she had driven up from West Virginia, then taken the bus in from Hackensack. She was nervous enough during the ride that her hands dampened the magazine she was attempting to read.

There were other galleries and other influencers. But none who could change her life quite as quickly, or quite as completely, as van Buren.

She had donned a shirtdress with the top two buttons undone, black nylons, and low heels she wouldn't have to worry about tripping in. She had pulled her curls away from the sides of her face, gathering them with a simple clasp, but wore it down in back. Tommy always liked it that way.

At precisely four o'clock, the time of her appointment, Amanda entered the glass front door of the gallery and was greeted by a receptionist whose exquisitely styled hair immediately made Amanda feel like a peasant. The receptionist called up to an executive secretary—also impeccably presented, wearing shoes that easily cost more than Amanda's entire outfit—who then led Amanda up a brushed-steel spiral staircase, through a discreet door, and into some offices that looked down on the open gallery space below.

Here the feeling changed. Out were the glass and steel. In were the mahogany and exposed brick. Before long, Amanda was being escorted through a door—again, wood, not glass—into the inner sanctum of Hudson van Buren.

He was tall and wore a linen suit that was perfectly tailored and remarkably unwrinkled given the hour of the day. Amanda knew from articles about him that he was nearing sixty, though his sandy-colored hair and unaged complexion made him look younger. As Amanda shook his hand—hers clammy, his soft and warm—she guessed he never passed more than a few days without a manicure.

"It is *such* a pleasure to meet you," he said with a smooth baritone voice and a sincere smile. "I really have enjoyed getting to know your work, and now I look forward to getting to know you."

"Thank you for meeting with me," Amanda said.

"Oh my, and where is *that* accent from?" he asked.

"Mississippi," she said.

"Wonderful. Mississippi. I spent a weekend in Biloxi a few years back. Beautiful city."

"Yes," she said.

"Hold my calls, Marian," he told the secretary.

"Yes, sir," she said, then exited.

"Come in," Van Buren said with a sweeping gesture.

The square footage alone was intimidating. Amanda was accustomed to a student's Manhattan, where three women crammed into a unit meant for one and every inch had to be maximized. Van Buren's office was bigger than any apartment she had lived in. In Manhattan, as in few other places, space meant power.

Through the office's huge picture window, Central Park's leaves were just beginning to turn. The fresh-cut flowers inside, and the vases they were arrayed in, had been selected to match.

She immediately recognized most of the pieces on the walls around her. They were by the kinds of artists Amanda wanted to be when she grew up, all of whom had been discovered by Hudson van Buren when they were roughly Amanda's age.

Now here she was, perhaps ready to join them.

Van Buren pointed Amanda toward a couch that was part of a tastefully decorated sitting area. Amanda sat on the end closest to the window. There was a bucket of champagne icing on the coffee table in front of her. Van Buren poured them each a flute, pressing the crystal into Amanda's hand before she could consider objecting. In Plantersville, they didn't even serve champagne at weddings.

"I figured we should celebrate," he said.

She wasn't sure what they were celebrating—did this mean he was going to accept her work?—but he touched his glass with hers, then brought it to his lips. She hesitated, thinking about the baby. The websites said a little bit of wine now and then was okay, right? Still . . .

Then she considered how important Hudson van Buren could be to her unborn child's college fund and took a sip.

"Mmm," he declared. "You like it?"

"Yes," she said, even though she had barely tasted it.

"Good. Drink up. There's more where that came from."

He then sat at the opposite end of the couch, crossed his legs casually, and began mansplaining the qualities of her work. He lavishly complimented both her composition and her subject matter. It was so different, so fresh. Compelling in its themes. He had clients—"especially the limousine liberals on the Upper West Side"—who would soon be engaging in bidding wars for her stuff.

"Five figures will be a starting point," he said confidently.

Amanda just nodded along, awestruck. They would split revenues fifty-fifty, as was standard. He was considering giving the entire gallery over to her work for a month—a real statement—then having her share the next two months with other artists. That's *if* there was anything left at the end of the first month. He had at least two dozen specific clients in mind who would probably clean them out.

The room was soon spinning. Partly because of the praise. Mostly because of the champagne. She had been throwing up all morning, pulling off the highway to heave every time she got the urge, emptying her stomach. She hadn't wanted to drink anything beyond the first few sips, but he filled her glass the moment it was anything less than full, and she felt that unshakable southern politeness.

Van Buren had moved toward her on the couch each time he refilled her glass and was closer to her end than his when he said, "You seemed nervous when you came in here. Were you?"

"I was," she allowed.

"Don't be. Don't be," he said. "Look, I know my reputation. Just ignore it. You and I, we're going to be partners in this. But we're also going to be friends. This business, it's so personal. For you, the act of creation is personal. For me, the selling is personal, because I'm not just selling the art, I'm selling myself. So we . . . we have to be in this together. And there can't be any nervousness or hesitation. Do you know what I'm saying?"

"Yes. Yes, of course."

"Here, just relax," he said.

Before she could respond, he had grabbed her by the shoulders, turned her toward the window, and was massaging the base of her neck.

"You're too tense," he said. "We're going to be just fine, you and I. This is the beginning of wonderful things for you and your career."

As he spoke, he worked down to the muscles in her shoulders. It was surreal to Amanda. How had a business meeting turned into a back rub?

Then he reached around and loosened the third button of her dress.

"What are you doing?" she asked.

"Just trying to get to your neck a little better," he replied, his hands already back to work.

Since when is my neck located at the front of my dress? But she was too frozen, too tipsy, too uncertain to react.

"You're really very pretty, you know that?" he said. "A lot of the young women I see, they don't even know what they have. The way you carry yourself, with such confidence, it makes you even more alluring."

She felt heat in her face. He reached around, undid the fourth button, then returned to her shoulders, working the bare skin.

"In the art business, you're what we call the total package," he continued. "Talented. Beautiful. Great personality. And that accent! You are destined for big things, Miss Amanda Porter. All you need to do is let it happen."

Finally, a lucid thought broke through the alcohol: *Wait, let* what *happen?*

She needed to stop this. Immediately. This was totally wrong.

"I'm sorry, I'm married," she lied, turning toward him so he couldn't rub her back anymore.

"So am I," he said smoothly. "My wife and I have an open relationship."

Does she know that?

Amanda looked down with detachment at the pale pink lace of her exposed bra.

"But I'm . . . I'm not interested in . . . in this part," she said.

"Hey, it's okay. We're okay here. Just relax."

His hand went to her thigh, which he began massaging. He started near the knee and worked upward, lifting her dress as he went. She could barely believe it was her own leg. His face was flushed and focused on her crotch, his breathing suddenly raspy. Up close, he didn't look so young anymore. More like a gross old man.

Was this what he really wanted all along? Had it ever been about her art? She felt cheapened, repulsed, manipulated. The country mouse hadn't come all this way to be a meal for a snake.

"Stop, stop," she said.

She stood up, slipping away from his hand. She yanked down the hem of her dress and then began hastily fastening the buttons, the two he had undone plus another.

"Hey, what's the matter?" he said, still smooth as ever.

"I told you. I'm not interested in this."

He sat up a little straighter.

"You know what I can do for you and your career, right?" he asked.

"Yes," she said.

"Then sit back down. There's no hurry. We can take it slow."

"No, we can't," she said firmly.

He rose from the couch, and for a moment Amanda thought he was going to come after her, maybe back her into the corner. He was much bigger than her. She wouldn't be able to fight him off physically. She prepared to scream, to kick him in the groin, to scratch and claw and show him what Mississippi fight looked like.

But he walked past her, to the door of his office, which he opened.

"It's been very nice meeting you, Amanda," he said loudly. "Your work is quite promising, though it needs a little more time to mature. You let me know when you're ready for me to give it another look."

CHAPTER 15

They made me wait in Health Services for a while, for what reason I couldn't say.

It gave me time to parse and overparse the nurse practitioner's words. She'd *recommend* I get housed in Randolph. That didn't mean it was a done deal. Or did it?

Finally, a corrections officer invited me to gather my bedroll and new clothing, then escorted me out.

"Where we goin'?" I asked, pleased with how down-home Pete Goodrich was sounding.

"Your housing unit," he replied, which didn't exactly tell me what I really wanted to know.

I limped onward. We passed a small, human-dug pond ringed with benches that formed the centerpiece of campus. It was maybe forty feet long and twenty feet wide, rectangular in shape, with an oddly greenish hue that wasn't going to get it confused for Walden anytime soon.

"The pond have a name?" I asked.

"People call it 'the pond,'" he said, without a trace of irony.

We passed what was clearly the chapel on our left. Then he walked me inside the largest structure on campus, which he called the education building. It included classrooms—both GED and vocational—and the library, as well as a pair of gyms, one filled with cardio equipment, the other an open space with basketball backboards at either end.

Then we were back outside, moving in the general direction of the large hill that loomed over the southern end of the facility. According to Google Maps, which I had pored over for hours during the previous month, it was known as Dorsey's Knob Park.

"What about the hill?" I said, pointing toward it. "What do people call that?"

"The hill," he said, again with total sincerity.

Then we took a path that angled to the left, and I saw—with considerable relief—we were now pointed toward a squat, tan-brick building that had a wheelchair ramp built onto it.

Hello, Randolph.

I squeezed my fist in triumph. Just a little.

But now, having accomplished my first objective—get into Randolph—I was onto my second.

Find Dupree.

It probably wouldn't be that difficult, assuming Gilmartin's BOP liaison was correct. And, Lord, I hoped he was.

I certainly wasn't going to ask the CO, so I just tried to keep an eye out for Dupree as I limped ahead. Other than the wheelchair ramp, Randolph appeared to be identical to the four other cottages in the layout. It was designed like a lowercase *t*—a sans serif *t*, without the little tail. We had entered at what was essentially the *t*'s armpit.

The interior walls were concrete block, painted white. At my feet, the floor was polished white tile with little dark flecks that I guessed were supposed to imitate marble. Above me was a corkboard drop ceiling with recessed fluorescent lights. In other words, it looked like pretty much every other publicly funded building constructed between approximately 1945 and 1985. Who knew prison and high school had so much in common?

The CO took us down a hallway toward the left wing of the *t*. I could already guess the top and right wings were designed identically. These were the residential portions of the cottage.

The hallway emptied into a common area. In the middle were three bunk beds, all empty. With Morgantown below capacity, they weren't needed. Twelve doors ringed the room.

A few of the doors had people behind them who were now eyeing me, the new guy. But for the most part, the inmates—including, apparently, Dupree—were elsewhere.

We walked to the second room on the left, a nine-foot-by-nine-foot space that was short on both comfort and charm. The walls were the same unadorned cinder block found in the hallway. It had a slender window in the far corner that offered a narrow view of the entrance to the building.

"This one's yours," the CO said.

Shoved against the wall to the left, there was a metal desk with a circular seat welded to it. In front of me were two gray metal lockers, perhaps three feet high, bolted to the wall.

The one on the right was empty. The one on the left had some personal items on top—a brush, some deodorant, a toothbrush and toothpaste. There was also a picture frame that contained a photograph of a smiling dark-skinned woman and an adorable girl, perhaps eight or nine, whose black hair had been tightly braided into pigtails.

On the wall to the right was a metal bunk bed. The top bunk was bare, save for a three-inch mattress set atop a web of rickety bedsprings. The bottom bunk looked like it had been made by a West Point cadet: a white fitted sheet pulled tight across the mattress, a white flat sheet whose top portion was folded crisply down atop a white blanket, which had been neatly tucked with hospital corners.

"You can put your shoes and jacket under the bed," the CO said. "All your other belongings need to fit in that locker. You can get a lock from the commissary, which I'd recommend. We do regular inspections, and you're responsible for making sure you don't have any contraband in there. Don't cover the window. The room has to be clean every morning. Fail an inspection and you'll get a point. Get three points, and you'll end up in the SHU."

He pronounced it like "shoe," and I knew better than to ask what it was. The Special Housing Unit, also known as solitary confinement, had a reputation that preceded it. You spend twenty-three hours a day in a cell by yourself. For an extrovert, no greater punishment could be devised.

"Dinner starts at five. You'll go when your unit is called. After that you have free time until eight thirty or so. That's when you'll be called back to your unit. Last standing count of the day is at nine. Lights-out is ten. In the morning, your unit manager will be able to tell you what your work assignment is. Any questions?"

"No, sir."

"Good," he said. And then, in his most officious voice, he added, "Welcome to Morgantown."

I thought he was going to throw in a salute. But he just turned and departed. Sometime in the next two weeks, I would get a formal daylong orientation program. Otherwise, I was now just another inmate, as righteously deprived of my liberty as anyone else there.

But, unlike the rest of them—whose primary occupation would be counting the days, months, and years until their release dates—I had a mission.

A fter setting down my things, I poked my head back out of my room. For all I had read about the rigors of prison, for all I had attempted to prepare myself mentally for the challenge, this was my first moment being truly on my own.

I wobbled out into the common area and continued back up the hallway, toward the main entrance. The bathroom, which had no door, was on my left. I turned into it. It was covered in yellow tile. There were two sinks with mirrors. The shower stall was curtained.

Out of curiosity, I pulled back the curtain, ready to be horrified by the colonies of mold and fungus. But other than a few decades' worth of soap scum, it was clean enough. Another bonus: There was only one nozzle, so there would be no communal showering, nor worrying about the possibilities thereof. Another prison trope, evaporated.

Most of the voices seemed to be coming from past the entrance, down in the body of the *t*. Hoping to catch sight of Dupree, I exited the bathroom and walked past a guard booth and an administrative office, then into a TV room.

There were six flat-screens affixed to the walls. None had the sound up. Men were listening to them with headphones, tuning into the sound via radio. There were stickers under each screen dictating the frequency—107.5 for news, 104.5 for music and entertainment, 98.1 for sports, and so on.

A few heads turned my way as I entered, but then swiveled back just as fast. I had already read that new guys weren't all that unusual. At a place where there were nine hundred men, many of them serving relatively short stints for nonviolent crimes—eighteen months, two years, whatever—there was a fair amount of churn.

To my immediate left was a room that appeared to be a kitchen. If you could call it that. Really, it was just a stainless steel sink with an icemaker next to it. In the middle of the room was a charging station for the small MP3 players inmates were allowed to purchase. Beyond that, four tables with four chairs each were bolted to the floor.

There was no Dupree. I kept moving through the TV room, walking quickly so I didn't block anyone's view. The final space was a small room where men were playing cards, sitting at tables identical to the ones in the kitchen.

Again, they paid me no particular mind. Again, no Dupree.

Having pushed myself as far as I wanted to go for the moment, I reversed course and returned to my room. There was now a man in there, sifting through the contents of the left-side locker.

And he was a giant.

Six foot seven, at least. Three hundred pounds, at least. The room was nine-by-nine, eighty-one feet square. I swear he filled eighty-two of them.

He was facing away from me, and he was shirtless. There was a tattoo of what appeared to be a family tree etched across his broad back, though it was difficult to make out the names or detail, because it had been scrawled in black ink against skin that was very nearly as dark.

I had paused in the doorway, mostly because there wasn't room for me to enter without violating his personal space. He turned when he became aware of me, and I was soon staring at roughly his navel, the height difference between us was so great. A bit of his belly spilled over his belt, but his arms, neck, and chest were solid, more muscle than fat.

People don't come this size in the theater world. He was, without any exaggeration, one of the largest human beings I had ever found myself in close quarters with.

And apparently he was my roommate. I don't know if this was random or if it was the intake officer's idea of a joke: Put the tallest guy at the prison with the shortest.

"Can I help you?" he said in a slow, fathomless voice. His southern accent was much stronger than Pete Goodrich's, even more pronounced than Amanda's when she was drinking, so it came out as "Kin ah hep you?"

"Yeah, hi," I said. "I've been assigned to this room. I'm Tom—"

I stopped. I had gotten so distracted by his massiveness, I nearly forgot my new name.

Before he noticed (I think), I corrected myself: "I'm Pete Goodrich."

"Frank Thacker," he said.

He reached out his hand, which was the size of a hubcap and, when I shook it, at least as hard. I got the sense he wasn't even trying to squeeze. That was just his grip.

"Where you from?" I asked.

"South Carolina," he said.

The natural follow-up would have been to ask where I was from, and I was ready with my best "Shepherdstown, West Virginia." But he just said, "You mind taking the top bunk, sir? They fixed the bottom one special for me."

He pointed, and I saw that the crossbeam at the foot of the bed had been rewelded to a spot about two feet higher than its original position, thus allowing his feet—and, heck, probably half his calves—to protrude off the end of the sleeping surface.

"Yeah, sure, of course," I said, mostly because the last place I wanted those three-hundred-and-whatever pounds was sleeping directly above me. The bunks were metal, but they didn't look *that* sturdy.

"I'll help make your bed in the morning, if you want," he said. "Don't want to get no points."

"That'd be great, thanks."

I had finally worked my way up to where I was looking at his face. It was as broad as the rest of him, with a nose that may have been twice as wide as mine. He shaved his head. Or at least I think he did. It was a little difficult to see that high. His eyes were coffee-colored and not particularly large, especially given the size of the rest of him.

Maybe it was because so much of the world was beneath him, forcing him to look down all the time, but there was something gloomy about his visage.

"All right, then," he said with a nod.

He turned back toward his locker, extracting a tent-size shirt, which he put on gingerly. He was cognizant of the length of his arms and didn't want to accidentally strike me. He was surprisingly graceful, given his size.

I eased past him and sat on top of the desk. Then I pointed to the picture atop his locker.

"That your daughter?" I asked, in an attempt to start a conversation.

"Yes, sir."

"She's adorable."

"Thank you, sir," he said.

"How old is she?" I asked.

He didn't answer. It was possible he was so intent on buttoning his shirt he hadn't heard me. When he was done dressing, he dipped his head and said, "See you at supper, sir."

Then he walked out. He hadn't exactly been unfriendly. But he was no Rob Masri. We weren't going to instantly trade life stories.

Frank Thacker's secrets were going to stay buried a little deeper.

R andolph continued filling up as dinnertime approached. I made my first foray to the phone in the hallway and called Amanda but got no answer. We had already decided that I wouldn't leave messages for her. Phone minutes were too precious to waste.

Then I called Danny. I had promised him a check-in. He wanted to know I was successfully in place, so he could brief his SAC.

It speaks to the inherent loneliness of incarceration that after even just a few hours, it already felt good to be able to talk to someone who knew me before I got there. I burned minutes yammering at him about my ride in, about Masri, about my block-out-the-sun roommate.

"Yeah, yeah, that's great," he said. "Glad you're the popular girl. Just don't get so busy making friends you forget to call me if you happen to hear about the location of any prime hunting cabins, okay?"

I assured him I wouldn't, then ended the call.

When I returned to my room, I busied myself by putting my meager belongings in my locker, all while keeping an eye out for Dupree through my narrow window. Then I made my bed and, not knowing what else to do, lay on top of it for a while.

My gaze went upward. There was no drop ceiling here, just wood planks supported by exposed steel beams. There were probably hipsters from Brooklyn who would have paid extra for it.

Idly, I wondered how many inmates had whiled away how many

hours doing just this—staring up at the ceiling—during the half century of Morgantown's existence.

Then I thought about Amanda. I wondered how her meeting with the Van Buren Gallery had gone. I savored our final good-bye just a little bit, both the kiss we had in the morning and the love we made the evening before. I closed my eyes and pictured her naked, her face the picture of concentration as she built toward climax.

It was going to be a long six months without her.

But that and other thoughts were soon interrupted by a tinny, metallic voice that came piped in from somewhere in the common room: "Raddah, propree pra pra daha."

Instantly, there was a scurrying of men on the move, of bedsprings creaking and steel-toed shoes scuffling. I sat up. The voice must have said: "Randolph, proceed to the dining hall."

I swung my legs off my bunk and made the short drop to the floor. My delay in understanding put me toward the back of a long line of men walking in twos and threes. Some were still dressed in their khakis. Others had changed into commissary-purchased workout clothes: white T-shirts and gray shorts, or one or both halves of a gray sweat suit.

It was difficult to tell from behind if one of them was Dupree. The only person I could see for sure up ahead was my new roommate, mostly because he was too huge to miss.

Then I heard, "Hey, Pete Goodrich."

Coming up from behind me was Masri.

"Hey," I said, like I was greeting an old friend. "You in Randolph?"

"Seems that way. How's your stay been so far?"

"Oh, it's better than the Ritz-Carlson," I said. "Only problem is I can't find the bar."

He immediately got this smug little grin and spoke out of the side of his mouth. "Then you probably haven't been looking hard enough."

"Huh?" I said.

"You jonesing for a little prison home brew, Goodrich?"

I must have still looked perplexed, because he took a quick glance around, then lowered his voice more. "I forget, you're new."

"So are you."

"To Morgantown, yeah. But not to institutional living. Just because you're in prison doesn't mean you have to go without all of life's comforts. You know that, right? If booze is your thing, that's pretty easy. There are probably two dozen guys in here who can hook you up. More if you don't mind the taste of rancid orange juice. You want pot? No problem. There are another dozen guys who can get you that. If it's coke or heroin or crank, that's a little harder, but not impossible. You just need to be patient and know who to ask."

"Oh," I said.

"I'm still figuring out that last part. But when I do, I'll let you know. Shouldn't take long."

"Thanks. Though I'm not . . . Drugs aren't really my thing," I said. Then, feeling my Pete Goodrich–ness, I added: "When I was a student teacher, I co-taught a unit on drug addiction in health class. Not sure if it had any impact on my students, but it sure scared me straight."

He laughed. "I hear you. But if you want some free advice? Find something to get addicted to. It'll make your time go by quicker."

"What d'ya mean?"

"I'm not into drugs, either," Masri said. "But you know what my thing is? Caramel M&M'S."

"The candy?"

"Yeah, the candy. It sounds stupid, I know. But when I was on the outside, there was a convenience store down the street from my office, and sometimes I'd sneak out midway through the afternoon and get myself a bag of them when I needed a little pick-me-up. So inside they've become my thing. They're not on the commissary list, so they're technically contraband. Things taste better when you know you're not allowed to have them."

"I thought they check pretty regularly for contraband," I said as we neared the dining hall.

"And they do," Masri said. "So make sure they don't find anything. Look, the COs aren't stupid. They know what's going on. And they care, but only when they think they're being watched. The rest of the time, they're just trying to get to the end of their shifts with a minimum of hassle. It's all about the *appearance* of following the rules. So if you've got your equivalent of caramel M&M'S, the absolute last place you want to put it is in your locker. Because, yeah, if they find them there, they'll have to bust you. So find a stash spot. Got it?"

I thought about the lack of a drop ceiling in my room. It wasn't about pleasing the hipsters. It was so we couldn't hide things up there.

But FCI Morgantown was a big place. There were surely other possibilities.

"Yeah," I said. "Got it."

"Pretty much everyone here has a hustle. If you find yours, it'll give you something else to focus on other than how much time you have left. That's Prison Survival 101."

He winked. We had entered the dining hall. Following the herd, I was soon shuffling along a stainless steel serving area, receiving my meal: pork chops, mashed potatoes, green beans, a small carton of milk, all of it steam warmed, FDA approved, and cooked to within half a degree of tasteless.

Then I sat down next to Rob at a long row that consisted of several rectangular tables stacked end to end. No one seemed concerned about who sat with whom, nor with any segregation. Black and white and brown mixed together. The Aryan Brotherhood couldn't be bothered with Camp Cupcake.

There was little conversation. The men ate with their heads down. Taking that as the local custom, I did the same.

But as I began sawing through a time-toughened pork chop with a plastic knife, I caught a glimpse of a guy sitting one table over.

A guy with a hangdog look on his face.

And receded brown hair.

And a goatee.

It was, unquestionably, Mitchell Dupree. I had finally found my mark.

Or, to use Masri's word, my hustle.

But I may have been enjoying this next victory a little too much, because I had allowed my eyes to lock on Dupree.

He looked up. Straight at me. Like he knew someone was watching him.

CHAPTER 16

Having witnessed the cost of failure, Herrera adopted a more pro-active management style in his new role as director of security for the New Colima cartel.

Especially before there was another surprise inspection.

And so, once he had the operation at Rosario No. 2 running to his liking, he traveled north until he reached one of the tunnels New Colima had taken from Sinaloa. It had been dug into the bedrock deep under the Rio Grande and was wide enough to drive a truck through. At the midpoint of the tunnel, there was a farcical "border crossing." It consisted of a large and thoroughly defaced photograph of the United States president.

The tunnel outlet was near El Paso, Texas, in a warehouse that also operated as a very legitimate produce-distribution center. It was owned by a Texas-based corporation that was a subsidiary of a Delaware-based corporation, and it was all perfectly legal, apart from being a front for New Colima. American law enforcement had no clue.

From El Paso, Herrera caught a plane to Pittsburgh and rented a car with a driver's license and Mastercard that identified him as Hector Jacinto. Herrera did not bear much resemblance to the man, other than the Mesoamerican set to their eyes and brown skin. But in the Pittsburghs of the world, that was more than enough.

He then drove to West Virginia, toward the prison where the banker was locked up.

Herrera understood the rules of engagement: The banker had documents; the documents would be released if anything happened to the banker or his family; therefore, the banker was untouchable.

It was a stalemate.

But El Vio didn't tolerate stalemates. And Herrera believed that he could find a way to break it.

New Colima had contractors in America who had been keeping watch over the banker and his family—listening in on their conversations, following the wife in case she slipped up and went to the document hiding spot, that sort of thing. The contractors had been briefing Herrera regularly. Still, Herrera suspected they did not feel the same urgency to close this operation that he did.

According to the contractors, the American prison backed up against a city park known as Dorsey's Knob. Incredibly, there were no fences separating the park from the prison. The Americans wanted to build a wall on their southern border but couldn't be bothered to enclose their own prisons.

Herrera parked his car in a lot near a picnic area, then picked his way through the woods, up the hill, until he reached the top of Dorsey's Knob. There, a high ridge provided an unfettered view down on the prison. He adjusted his binoculars and soon was seeing men in khaki uniforms, trudging through the neatly manicured grounds.

Then he pulled out his phone and called one of the contractors.

"I'm here," he said in Spanish. Herrera's English was fine. But cartel business was done in Spanish unless they were dealing with some monolingual American.

"Where?" the contractor asked, also in Spanish.

"Visiting our friend in West Virginia," he said.

Herrera could hear the sharp intake of breath on the other end. This was not what the contractor expected.

Be unpredictable, Herrera thought. The wisdom of El Vio.

"What?" the contractor finally spat, his alarm apparent. "Why?"

"Because I work for an impatient man."

They never said El Vio's name over the phone.

"I understand that," the contractor said. "We're doing everything we can on the outside. And we have a man on the inside. It's all in place."

"Who is this man?"

"He's someone who will get the job done."

"I want to talk to him."

"Are you crazy?" the contractor said. "We can't get him to you without running the risk he'd be caught and sent to a higher-security prison, where he'd be no use to us. And we're sure not going to take the chance of getting you to him. You'd compromise everything, and for what?"

I get to stay alive, Herrera thought.

"I need to be able to say I've inspected this matter personally," he said instead.

"And now you can. But you have to stop there. Our man has worked hard to get close to our friend. If our friend caught wind that our man was working for us, that would be over. You'd be setting us back months. You think the impatient man you work for would like that?"

The contractor was right. Herrera knew that. But he hadn't come all this way to have nothing to tell El Vio the next time they spoke.

"Tell me who your man is," Herrera said. "That will suffice for now."

"And you promise you won't approach him?"

"Yes."

The line was silent for a few seconds.

"Fine," the contractor said. "You say you're there right now?"

"Yes."

"Where?"

"On the hill above it."

"Which means you can see into our friend's residence?"

"That's correct."

"Then our man should be easy to spot," the contractor said. "You can't miss him. Just look for the biggest, blackest hombre in there."

CHAPTER 17

The next morning, Frank Thacker delivered on his promise to tutor me on the finer points of prison bed making.

He was a patient teacher, speaking to me in that bottom-dwelling voice, calling me "sir" the whole time. I was a dutiful student—not because I naturally was but because Pete Goodrich, the teacher, would have been. It was almost funny to see a man Frank's size, with hands that could crush rocks, get fussy about smoothing a blanket.

At breakfast, I thought about trying to engineer sitting with—or at least near—Dupree, but I couldn't pull it off without making it seem forced. And after getting caught staring at him the night before, I didn't want to push too hard. Dupree had to think the new guy was just another inmate.

So I hung out with Masri, my new best friend, and quietly plotted ways I might be able to get closer to Dupree in the future.

After the meal, I met with my unit manager. He was a ruddy-faced heart-attack-in-waiting named Mr. Munn, who noted that I was a history teacher and treated me to a long description of his passion for World War II reenactment. His "character" was a marine corporal whose greatest glory was that he pretended to fight at Guadalcanal, fake-winning a Silver Star for gallantry in imaginary action. Mr. Munn clearly had studied the battle in some detail. He also clearly had a social IQ of eleven.

I must not have responded enthusiastically enough to his fantasy life, because he assigned me to work in the laundry room.

This didn't turn out to be a bad thing. As soon as I reported for duty, it was explained to me that this job, like most at Morgantown, was more make-work than actual work. We had fifty men to do what could have been accomplished by seven. So there was a little bit of loading machines, unloading machines, and folding what came out. There was a lot more goofing off.

Some of the guys had invented a game, "wad," that involved flicking wadded-up paper balls against the back of a desk partition and scoring points based on where they landed. The competition was spirited, especially because they were in the midst of a tournament—"the Wadley Cup"—that involved best-of-seven game matches set up in bracket style. Naturally, there was wagering involved. Both participants and spectators were betting what they called "cans."

The amounts were low, usually one or two cans. One of the matches was for five cans, and it got a little heated. At the end of the match, I sidled up to one of the spectators, an older guy with smallish glasses that gave him an intellectual air.

"I'm new," I said. "What's with the cans?"

"Mackerel," he said.

"What about it?"

"They're betting packets of mackerel."

"I don't understand."

The next match had already started, and his attention was now riveted to the action.

"They're like currency around here," he said. "We're not allowed to have real money. The COs would confiscate it. We used to use tuna fish cans. But then they came out with the packets and those became the thing. We still call them 'cans.' They show up on the commissary list as 'fillets of mackerel' and they go for a buck twenty a packet. One packet is commonly understood to be a dollar. It's how we pay each other. You want a guy to clean your room for you? The going rate is four cans a month. You want a haircut? Two cans. You want a guy to change the channel in the TV room because all the TVs are taken and you really want to watch a certain program? One can. You want a joint or a pack of cigarettes? That's going to cost you ten cans."

"Mackerel packets," I said again. "That's crazy."

"Except you'll never hear anyone call them packets. Just cans. Chicken of the Sea is the brand, for what it's worth. And it's not so crazy if you think about it. They're so loaded with preservatives they probably last longer than your typical paper dollar. And unlike paper dollars, they have an intrinsic value, because you can eat them if you want to."

"Do people do that?"

"Some guys, yeah," he said, making a face. "Mostly the weight lifters, who need the protein. They smell terrible, if you ask me. But to each his own. Really, they're like any currency, in that they have value primarily because we've all agreed they have value."

Around us, a large cheer erupted as one of the guys won his match. He celebrated with a round of high fives.

"So that five-can match I just watched . . ."

"Yeah, that was pretty heavy. I was a financial planner on the outside, so I speak with authority when I say the mackerel economy is remarkably stable and well regulated. We only get three hundred bucks' worth of commissary a month, and we're only allowed to keep three hundred bucks' worth of commissary in our lockers. And if you read your handbook carefully, you'll see you're limited to thirty-five cans of any type of meat product at a time. So there are some rigid checks on inflation. The Brazilians should do so well. It means that five-can match you saw was worth, what, one-seventh of our available funds? Now, those can be replenished at the commissary, but even those five little cans represent roughly three percent of our monthly commissary allowance. Think of a man betting three percent of his monthly income on something."

"I hear you," I said.

"As you become familiar with the price structure, you'll find that the market for services is on the low side, because all of us have too much time on our hands. On the flip side, the market for goods is higher, because we can't exactly run to Walmart. You'll figure it out. You need something in here, you pay for it with cans."

Then he added, "Cans make the world go round."

The next match was already concluding. Everyone was buzzing about cans being won and lost.

Watching the excitement, I knew I had found my next hustle.

E ating was definitely not a leisure activity at FCI Morgantown, nor did it invite casual conversation, so I had to wait until after shoveling down lunch to approach Masri, my new guru for all things illicit.

I caught him about halfway back from the dining hall, sauntering along at an unhurried pace.

"Hey," I said, approaching him from behind.

"Hey," he replied.

As I drew even with him, I saw he had his eyes closed.

"Whatchya doing?"

"Just breathing," he said. "You can actually breathe here. Like real, fresh air that hasn't already been in someone else's lungs. It's nice. You couldn't do that at Hazelton."

"Should I come back some other time?"

"No, no," he said, opening his eyes. "What's up?"

"I think I've found what my caramel M&M'S are," I said.

The right side of his face pulled the rest of it into a grin. "Ahh, Grasshopper is growing up quickly."

"Have you heard about cans yet?"

He tilted his head, so I filled him in on what I had learned about the mackerel economy.

"I love it," he said. "So what's your hustle?"

"Let's smuggle in mackerel packets."

He smiled even broader.

"It's the perfect hustle," he said. "Contraband that isn't actually contraband."

"Exactly. Long as we keep it quiet and no one knows that we're flooding Morgantown with cheap currency, we'll live like kings."

And win friends. And influence people. Which was my real purpose. I don't care where you went in this world—the theater, the boardroom, the laundry at FCI Morgantown—money was power. Whether that money came in the form of green dollars or silver fish packets didn't matter at all.

"I like it," he said. "Partners?"

He stuck out his right hand. I shook it.

"Partners," I said.

"What's our first step?"

"Well, that's where I'm hoping that, no offense, a more seasoned convict like you might be able to help me. How *do* people get stuff in here?"

"Oh, there's a million ways. Obviously, this is a larger item, so some of the more, uh, bodily methods of smuggling aren't going to work."

I grimaced.

"Oh, don't get all prudish on me," he said. "As long as you wrap it in plastic, it washes right off."

I shivered as he continued.

"There was actually a guy at Hazelton who used to smuggle in joints in a hollowed-out callus on the bottom of his foot. His girlfriend would bring them in every Saturday. He got the cavity so big he could fit like three or four in there. The COs stripped-searched him thoroughly every time he returned from the visitors' area, and he just stood there flat-footed and grinning."

"Okay, stop. You're grossing me out."

"The other way you do it is you bribe a CO. But it takes time to develop that kind of relationship. And you can't do it with fish packets. You need someone on the outside with real cash."

"I don't think we need to go there," I said. "Look around. This place doesn't have fences. I'm sure there are guys in here who have figured out how to exploit that."

"I'm sure you're right."

"You think some of your new friends might be willing to share the acquired local wisdom on this subject?"

"I'll work on it."

"The other issue is: Where do we stash it once we get it in? We're only allowed to have thirty-five cans in our room at a time. I'm thinking on a bigger scale than that."

"And I like how you're thinking," he said. "But don't worry where to store it. My work assignment is in maintenance. We have access to this warehouse. That place is like a stashing wonderland. There's a chance of someone stumbling on it, but that's the price of doing business sometimes."

"True."

"Do you have someone out there who can get us enough product to make our efforts worthwhile? I don't want to do this for a grocery bag full of cans. I want, like, a whole flat of them."

"I can handle that part," I said, thinking of how receipts for a flat of mackerel packets would look in the FBI's asset seizure fund. "You just worry about how to get them in here without being caught."

CHAPTER 18

It didn't take long for me to slip into the rhythm of life at FCI Morgantown, a place governed by its routines.

Wake-up was at six. They began calling breakfast at 6:10, with the units going in order of how they had performed at the last inspection. At seven or so, that inspection actually occurred. At seven thirty, I went off to the laundry for a few hours of barely working. Lunch call commenced at ten forty-five.

After lunch and until the four P.M. standing count, I had free time, though Mr. Munn was already starting to get on me about taking vocational classes, which were offered in the afternoon. After dinner, which started at five, there was more free time until the final standing count at nine. We were confined to our housing unit after that. Lights-out was at ten. And, to be clear, "lights-out" was not a figure of speech when you were in prison. One moment you were sitting there, bathed in artificial illumination. The next moment, you were plunged into darkness. Some guys stayed in the television room or the card room until midnight or later. Not me. I needed my sleep.

Then I woke up. And did the same thing all over again.

My third day there, I was permitted my first commissary visit. I bought a lock for my locker; a Timex Ironman watch so I could stop asking other guys what time it was; a radio and earbuds so I could

watch television; and, of course, mackerel packets, so I could participate in the informal economy.

My fifth day there, I finally received my formal orientation, a long
day of meeting various members of the prison administration. They
talked a lot about reentry. "The day you get here, we want you to
start getting prepared for the day you leave," was something all of
them said in one form or another. They also harped on contraband,
as if I hadn't heard enough about that. Drugs were a concern, of
course. Cell phones—and, in particular, smartphones—were considered an even greater scourge, because they could be used by inmates
who might be tempted to continue the very criminal ways they were
being sent to prison to be cured of. If ever our eyes wandered across
one, we were to turn in the offender immediately, or risk the awful
wrath of prison administration.

Noted.

I usually talked to Amanda immediately after dinner. Though, to
be honest, what should have been the highlight of my day was often
a letdown. Our conversations were awkward, stilted, constrained by
having to maintain the pretense of being Pete and Kelly, on the off
chance someone was listening. Only in the vaguest terms could she
tell me that her visit to Van Buren Gallery hadn't gone as she hoped,
but she couldn't say why. It sounded like she wasn't painting anything new. She was just trying to adjust to life "in California."

It's not like I had much to contribute to the conversation. The
prison laundry was only so interesting. When I wanted to know how
her pregnancy was going, I had to ask her how my cousin Amanda
was doing. She answered in the third person.

We actually talked about the weather a couple of times. So little
of our two-year relationship had happened over the phone, it's like
we didn't know how to make a meaningful connection without eye
contact.

So even with the "I miss yous" and the "I love yous" that ended
the calls, I usually hung up filled with melancholy, despairing that we

were already growing apart. And if that was happening after a few days, what would six months do to us? Would we be recognizable to each other after it was over? Would her heart have wandered to some tall guy who wasn't currently incarcerated and whose long-term prospects were more promising?

It made me want to get out of Morgantown that much faster. Toward that end, I continued stalking Dupree from a distance in an effort to learn his patterns and preferences.

His job was in food service, which was a prized gig at FCI Morgantown, because it inexplicably paid better than the other jobs, even though it didn't seem to require any more work. (Plus some of the guys made extra money stealing food and reselling it. It had been explained to me there hadn't been a chicken soup in years at Morgantown that actually had meat in it, because chicken was such a popular black market food.)

He liked bocce, whose rules I was at least three decades too young to know, though there was no set time he played. He just showed up sometimes and joined whoever was there.

His idea of exercise was sitting on one of the stationary bikes in the cardio gym and pedaling while he read a magazine. From what I could tell, the magazine got as much of a workout as he did. Unsurprisingly, his commitment to it was sporadic.

He read books, sometimes out in the recreation area, when the weather was nice. But so far the only thing I had seen in his hands were military histories, which stopped me from trying to strike up a conversation. Fact was, *I* didn't know much about the pivotal battles of World War I, but Pete Goodrich should have.

I kept hoping to discover he was a fan of a certain genre of television, which would allow me to get close to him by feigning enthusiasm for the same reality show, news program, or family-oriented situational comedy. But he wasn't a regular viewer of anything, as far as I could tell.

The only thing he did reliably and predictably, besides report to work, was participate in a hold 'em poker game in the Randolph card room. It commenced at seven o'clock each day: he and three other guys—always the same three, always at the table farthest from the entrance. With the way they huddled around it, they didn't appear keen to invite anyone else to join.

No matter where I spotted him, I immediately shifted him into my peripheral vision, lest he become aware I was looking at him. Once or twice, I could have sworn he was staring at me. But that was probably just my overactive imagination.

I kept hoping for natural opportunities to approach him, but none presented themselves. And after a week of watching, I was getting impatient. I hadn't gotten myself tossed in prison just to gaze at him furtively from afar like some unrequited lover. If I was going to get him to whisper the location of that cabin, I needed to find a way to force contact.

My first tack was to see Mr. Munn and ask about getting switched onto food service. His reply was to show me the waiting list of inmates who had made that request already. When I asked how long he suspected the wait would be, he said, "Oh, you'll be there in no time. Six months, maybe a year."

So that was out.

Really, my best shot was probably the poker game. If I could somehow get a spot at the table, I could foster a relationship.

Most of what I knew about hold 'em poker came from a run as Nicely-Nicely Johnson in a regional production of *Guys and Dolls.* The cast decided it would be good character development to learn how to play craps and poker. Within a week, we all became sharks.

Asking Dupree to join the game felt too direct, too risky. If he said no, where would it leave me the next time I tried to talk to him? He'd start wondering why this Goodrich kid kept pestering him.

Of the three other guys, there was a tall one who I often saw going off to food service with Dupree. I also noticed them hanging out in the rec yard. He seemed to be Dupree's closest friend.

Then there was a guy with a ponytail, whom I saw only at the poker table or fleetingly at meals—when all we did was shovel food in our faces and leave.

But there was one of them I saw every day in the laundry. His name, I soon learned, was Bobby Harrison. He was a big guy, about six feet tall and pushing three hundred pounds, only some of it sloppy. He had a round, pinkish face. I put his age around forty-five.

It wasn't exactly difficult to find downtime on laundry duty. So one morning about a week into my stay, I walked up to him during the lull that always came after we got the first loads started in the washers. He had sequestered himself in the corner with a paperback, which he read through granny glasses.

"Hey," I said. "I'm Pete."

He looked up from the book and said, "Bobby."

"Noticed you in the card room in Randolph, playing hold 'em."

"Yeah," he said.

"Can I join you guys sometime?"

He weighed this for a moment, then said, "Probably not."

"Why not?"

He shrugged. "Table only sits four."

"I'll sit at the next table over and lean in."

He shook his head. "Nah, that's okay."

"Why not? Don't you want to take my money?"

"It's not that."

"What is it, then?"

He closed the book, keeping place with his finger. "We don't cheat. We're just a bunch of crooks playing a nice honest game of cards. But every time we've let a new guy in, he cheats."

"I don't cheat."

"That's what cheaters always say."

"I'll roll up my sleeves. Nowhere to hide any cards."

"No, thanks," he said. "But thanks for asking."

He went back to reading. My polite brush-off was complete.

Except I wasn't giving up that easily.

"I'll pay you for your spot," I said.

He looked back up. "How much?" he asked.

I thought back to what I had learned during wad. Goods were more valuable than services. This was a service. If a haircut was two cans . . .

"Five cans," I said.

"No, thanks."

"Ten."

"Fifteen," he said.

"Fifteen? For one night? That's outrageous."

"No, it's not," he said. "The buy-in for our game is five cans each, for a total pot of twenty. It's winner take all, and I win a lot. So you're costing me a chance to win, *plus* I lose out on the enjoyment of the game. That, to me, is worth fifteen cans."

Nearly half my monthly allowance. Including the five-can buy-in to the game, it was twenty cans total. I wouldn't be able to afford a second game until I went to commissary next week. Playing one game a week would hardly foster the closeness I needed with Dupree.

Unless, of course, Masri and I could get our can-smuggling operation going. Then I could play every night. Which is what I needed to arrange with Harrison.

"I want a volume discount," I said. "I'm not going to be able to make this worth my while unless I can play with these guys all the time, so I can learn their tells. I want to know I can buy your spot every night. And if I do that, I think you ought to knock your price down a little. Ten cans."

"Ten cans," he said. "Every night."

"That's right."

"Can you afford that?"

"I can make arrangements," I said. "And, of course, you can't tell the other guys I'm doing this."

He narrowed his eyes. "Now you're making me think you're cheating."

"Not cheating. I'm just that good. Ten cans a night for your spot in the game. Let's agree to doing it for at least a full month."

"A month!" he said.

"That's right. Ten cans a day for a month."

Bobby got this faraway look. For that kind of money, he could buy himself a drinking problem. Or a pot habit. Or whatever he wanted.

"All right," he said. "You got a deal."

"Okay," I said. "Let me make some funding arrangements and get back to you."

B efore dinner, I found Masri in the television room, watching *SportsCenter* with his ears encased in headphones.

I touched his shoulder to get his attention. He stayed tuned to highlights of a nicely executed six-four-three double play, then lifted a headphone flap.

"What's up?" he asked.

"You got a second to step into my office?"

He stood, and I led him back down the hall to my room. My mountain of a roommate, who had continued to be polite but quiet, was elsewhere. At an institution that housed nine hundred men, Masri and I had what passed for privacy.

"I was hoping for a status update on our hustle," I said.

"Funny you should ask. I actually have developed some intel that may be of assistance. I don't have it totally nailed down yet. But what I know is encouraging."

"Go ahead."

"This comes courtesy of one of my former associates from Hazelton, who came here about six months ago. We had done some business over there, so there was a trust factor. He explained how things work here. From what he tells me, the common method of getting things in here is what is known as 'running the hill.'"

"Running the hill," I repeated.

"According to my source, there is one CO assigned to watch over the five cottages each night. He's supposed to make the rounds between them. But usually he makes the midnight count and then he picks one cottage and hunkers down there until the three A.M. count. And that's if the staffing levels are what they're supposed to be. If they're short-staffed, which they often are, they skip out on having a man in the cottages altogether."

"God bless federal budget cuts," I said.

"Exactly. Once you figure out your cottage is empty, you slip out. Remember to prop open the door with a rock or something, so you don't get locked out. A cloudy night or foggy night is preferred, but the overhead lighting is pretty crappy here, so you can move in the shadows most of the way. The only really dangerous part is between the rec area and the woods, when you're in the open. At that point, you just have to haul ass. That's why they call it running the hill. But a young buck like you should be able to do that no problem. Once you're in the woods, you're safe. You do your business, then reverse operations for your return."

"What about cameras?"

"Well, yeah. They have them. But apparently there are some blind spots. That, and this is too big a place for the COs to watch everywhere at once. I think the general feeling is that it would cost millions of dollars to staff this place well enough to make it airtight, and the BOP just doesn't think it's worth that to stop some low-level cons from sneaking in a few joints."

"Okay," I said. "Still, sounds risky."

"Well, it's interesting you should say that, because I responded the same way. That's when my guy told me about the unicorn."

I am sure my expression reflected my dubiousness. Masri was enjoying himself.

"The unicorn," I said.

"Yeah," he said, and now his voice was even lower. "'The unicorn' is the code name for one of the most prized possessions here at Morgantown. It's, get this, a full guard's uniform. The shirt. The pants. The belt. The radio. Everything. The sizes are all medium, so if you're too big, you're out of luck. But you should be fine. Just roll the pants a bit. Once you put that thing on, you don't even have to run the hill. You can stroll up it, as easy as you please. It's the hottest of hot contraband."

"How do we get our hands on it?"

"There's a guy who rents it out. I haven't talked to him yet. He's pretty picky about who he lets have it. And apparently he's been getting more picky lately. If he meets you and suspects a village is missing its idiot, you're shut out. And the price is pretty steep. Thirty cans a night."

"Just made my commissary run. I'll put up fifteen if you put up fifteen."

"Deal," he said. "The other thing is, if you get caught, you have to agree to take a hundred percent of the heat yourself."

"What do you think that would consist of?"

"If they catch you running the hill without the unicorn, it's a month in the SHU. But with it?"

He shook his head as he considered it. "I don't see how they'd let you stay here. They'd ship you off to Hazelton or worse. They might even hit you with charges of impersonating a federal officer."

Which wasn't covered in my exoneration agreement. I could end up with real time to go with my fake time. I wondered if Danny would cover for me, or if he'd be so pissed off he'd let me rot.

"But we don't need to worry about that," Masri said. "There's a reason the unicorn has been passed here for years. This thing is a hundred percent authentic down to the last button. No one has gotten busted with it."

It was like some kind of crazy exercise in game theory. Should the inmate take a twenty percent chance of a tough (but survivable) penalty that would keep the game alive? Or accept a much smaller chance—one percent? five percent?—of a catastrophic penalty that would end the game permanently?

"Okay," I said. "So who is this guy?"

CHAPTER 19

Amanda had not painted since leaving Hudson van Buren's office. Every time she even thought about doing so, she found herself reliving the humiliation of that meeting; of allowing herself to be manhandled and half undressed while semisloshed on champagne; of having him casually dismiss her in that patronizing, paternalistic way.

Mostly, she was furious. At him for being a pig. At herself—for drinking the champagne, for not wearing something more prim, for sitting on the couch when she should have selected a chair, for being too stunned and drunk to slap his smarmy face the moment he touched her, for all the things she should have done differently but hadn't.

Between the self-blame, the shame, the embarrassment, the fear of what a Hudson van Buren blackball would do to her career, and the simple worry that no one would believe her anyway—ultimately, it was her word against his, and who was she?—she hadn't told anyone what had happened.

Even Tommy and Barb. Especially Tommy and Barb. To them, Amanda had related the part about her work needing more maturity and left it at that. She said she hadn't been painting because she wanted to reflect on that.

But, really, enough. It was time to get back to work. For her own self-esteem—and sanity—as much as anything.

She set up the easel by the window in Tommy's old bedroom, positioning a drop cloth underneath to protect the carpet.

The curtains were open wide. There was just no substitute for natural light when it came to revealing a painting. The canvas could look so different in the long red hues of early evening than it had in the direct white blare of noon.

Amanda's gift, if she had one, was that she could close her eyes and imagine what she wanted to paint. She knew exactly what image she was trying to create. Whether or not a painting succeeded was in how closely it hewed to that vision.

Her subjects were always personal, things she had seen. Many of the images came from her childhood in Mississippi. Her mother—or a woman like her mother—was a frequent subject. The woman scrubbed toilets. Or she cooked boxed mac 'n' cheese, the store brand because it was cheaper than the name brand. Or she smoked a cigarette while looking anxiously out the window of a double-wide trailer.

They were common scenes, depicting the people Amanda had grown up with, the white working poor of the rural South, the forgotten underclass of American life. Amanda brought empathy and understanding to them because, despite whatever refinement distance may have given her, she still was one of them. You could see it in every line and shading, in expressions that were grim or determined or focused or joyful or pained.

There were other subjects too. Some from her time in New York. Some from other places she had been. Traveling with Tommy had helped her see an America that was bigger and more varied than she previously understood.

Still, what Amanda had really discovered through her art and her travels was that people everywhere, of every age and shade, were basically alike. How they styled their hair or what clothes they chose, those superficial choices, were really secondary. What mattered to them were their own stories. The things they wanted. The people they loved. The goals they felt they still needed to accomplish. If you could capture that, you weren't really painting poor white house cleaners in Mississippi or wealthy Saudi expatriates in Manhattan. You were representing something far more universal.

Art journalists had labeled her work postfauvist, said she was influenced by Matisse. She understood they had to come up with something. The absence of real knowledge never stopped any critic.

She just didn't want to be defined by any labels. When Amanda Porter was painting, she wasn't trying to be pre-something or post–anything else. She was just copying the image that was most prominent in her mind.

What was in there now wasn't her mother or anyone like her mother.

It was a man.

Without overthinking what she was doing, she had loaded her pallet with blues and purples, like she was preparing to paint a three-day-old bruise. She might add other colors later, to provide accent or contrast. But that initial palette usually defined the work.

She started slowly, but her left hand—like a lot of artists, Amanda was a southpaw—quickly picked up its pace, as often happened once she hit her stride with a piece. This was pretty much the only area in her life where she could let go of the caution that otherwise defined her. When she painted, she allowed herself to be totally uninhibited. Her strokes were bold and unafraid. They lived, they breathed.

The critics might call this genius. Amanda called it practice.

Entering a kind of artistic trance, she could knock out a rough draft of a work in just a few hours. Later, she went back and added details. But by that point, shape and form and theme had basically been decided.

As this one leapt off her brush, what appeared was a man, peeking out from behind a curtain. There was darkness behind him, light ahead. He was about to go somewhere.

Half his face was visible, and perhaps a quarter of his body. He was not a tall man. But he was handsome. Dark hair. Dark eyes. His curled arm was thick with muscles. He was leaning toward something, about to propel himself forward. His momentum was undeniable.

What she had really captured was his yearning. This was a man who wanted something. It was in front of him, not behind him.

She worked into the afternoon. Then, gradually, the light changed. Amanda found herself looking at the painting in a different way.

Then she realized whom she had painted. And suddenly she couldn't bring herself to look at him. She knew what he wanted, and it scared her.

Removing the canvas from the easel, she wrapped it in two large garbage bags.

Then she walked outside and dropped it in the trash.

CHAPTER 20

The guy's name was Sal Skrobis. He was a former librarian, of all things.

According to the backstory Masri had gathered, he was originally from Wisconsin until life led him to North Carolina, then to the Shenandoah Valley in Virginia. There, he supplemented his meager librarian's salary with organic farming.

Which might have been well and good, except Sal Skrobis' most lucrative crop was marijuana.

He grew it on his property, wedged between his corn and his sunflowers, and some years it got higher than both. Putting his master's degree in library science to use, he exhaustively researched how to grow the sweetest, most mellow weed anywhere. And, after a time, he got quite good at it. Maybe too good. He began sharing it with friends, then neighbors, then friends of friends, then acquaintances. As word got out, people started coming from as far away as New York to buy his stuff.

Then, as happens, one of the customers got caught with it and ratted him out. Which likely explained why he was now so cautious renting out the unicorn.

With this in mind, I made a research trip to the library shortly after lunch the next day so I could prep myself for the role I needed to take on. Once properly educated, I went looking for him.

Masri had described him as "a Rip Van Winkle–looking sort." Skrobis had managed to convince the prison administration that his religious observance did not allow him to trim his beard. The religion primarily seemed to involve a stringent aversion to razors.

I found him at a picnic table under the pavilion next to the recreation area. His beard was, as advertised, long and white. What little hair he had on his head was tousled and windblown. The hair coming out of his ears was far thicker. He was so thin his uniform billowed on him.

He was sitting cross-legged on top of the table. As I neared, I realized he had his eyes closed. His palms were upturned in his lap, and his middle fingers were pressed against his thumbs.

Meditating. The guy was meditating right there next to the prison rec yard.

FCI Morgantown, meet Sal Skrobis.

I halted a few steps away, unsure if I should come back later or wait for him to descend from his higher state of consciousness. In my indecision, I was basically standing there, like a statue of a moron, until he opened his eyes.

"May I help you?" he asked in a placid voice.

"Mr. Skrobis?"

"I am."

"Pete Goodrich," I said, though I didn't feel like Pete Goodrich at the moment.

"What can I do for you today, Mr. Goodrich?"

I attempted to get back into character by using a trick one of my directors had taught me long ago. He called it "locking it down." It was based on the belief that in order to inhabit a character, you needed to start by feeling like that character physically. You took a deep breath while readjusting your shoulders toward whatever you were supposed to be facing: the audience, another character, whatever. That shoulder wiggle was when you took the opportunity to lock the character down. It was like a little do-over.

Which is what I did before saying, "I used to be a history teacher. I was hoping to offer you a history lesson."

I was still speaking too stiffly. But maybe it was okay for Mr. Goodrich, former history teacher, to be a little more formal around Mr. Skrobis, former librarian.

"Is that so?" he asked.

"World history was one of my favorite subjects," I said. "The first unit is on Mesopotamia, the Fertile Crescent, starting about ten thousand years ago. You can really blow kids' minds when you explain to them that what they know as Iraq, which they think of as one big sandbox, was once productive enough land to give birth to human civilization. Many of the plants and animals we still eat today were first domesticated there. It's where humans developed writing, which most people know. But did you also know there were many great artists?"

"Can't say I did," he said.

"Yep," I said. And it was the "yep" that made me start to feel more like Pete Goodrich again. I gave him my best folksy smile as I hit him with the next line.

"Matter of fact, did you know Mesopotamian artists were the first people to depict unicorns?"

"Ahh, I see," he said.

There was no return smile. But there was interest.

"Yes, sir. Unicorns later spread all over—China, India, Greece, you name it. Just about every culture has a mythology about a one-horned horse. But it started with the Mesopotamians. They believed the only people who could capture unicorns were virgins."

"Hmm," he said. "And I suppose now you're going to tell me you're a virgin?"

"I am, sir. Blushing and chaste and unspoiled."

"Mr. Goodrich, is that what you said?"

"Yes, sir."

"I appreciate the history lesson. Now I'm going to give you one on astronomy."

"Oh?"

"Tomorrow night is a new moon."

A new moon. As in, dark. As in, a good night to run the hill.

"I understand. That is a good lesson."

"It's the kind of night a virgin just *might* be able to capture a unicorn."

"Well, I sure would appreciate—"

"However, there is the matter of compensation."

"Of course. Thirty cans, right?"

"That's what it used to be," he said. "Not anymore."

"Sir?"

"I don't need cans," he said. "I've got more than I know what to do with already. What I really need are seeds."

Seeds? As in . . .

And then I got it. He missed being able to grow—and smoke—his favorite type of plant.

Just to make sure I hadn't misunderstood, I asked, "What kind of seeds?"

"You seem to know a lot about me," he said.

"I know what I've heard."

"Then you know what kind of seeds. I don't need many. A dozen would do fine."

And there it was. Sal Skrobis wanted me to smuggle marijuana seeds into a federal prison.

"You really . . . You got a place around here to plant them?"

"Let me worry about that. Your only concern is getting the seeds."

"I'll need the unicorn to be able to smuggle them in," I said. "You know that, right?"

"I'll allow payment to be made after the rental is completed."

"Okay," I said. "But for twelve seeds, I don't want to just rent the unicorn. I think that should be enough to purchase it."

His bushy white eyebrows raised.

"You want your seeds? This is how it's going to be," I said. "And, look, if you're able to start cultivating a cash crop like that, you won't need the unicorn for income anymore."

His wizened face squeezed, then released.

"Okay," he said. "This can be a purchase, not a rental. Are we agreed on our price?"

"Let me make a phone call first."

"To the Mesopotamians?" he asked, smiling for the first time.

"Something like that."

"Very well," he said. "I'll be here again tomorrow at this time. You let me know then."

He closed his eyes and resumed meditating.

T aking that as my cue to exit, I walked back toward Randolph and went straight for the phone. If this needed to happen during the new moon, I had to get my request to Ruiz and Gilmartin quickly.

I plugged in my TRULINCS account number, then dialed Danny. A recording informed him he was receiving a call from an inmate at a federal correctional institution.

As soon as the announcement ended, he unleashed a cheerful, "Slugbomb! How's it going in there?"

I felt my teeth jam together. I had been so careful to maintain my Pete Goodrich–ness, it galled me to have him make a reference to my old life so casually. Even if the chances of this conversation being monitored were slim, it was still careless of him.

"I don't know who Slugbomb is," I said tersely. "This is Pete Goodrich."

"Oh, right. Sorry. How's it going?"

"I had a hunch about some lottery numbers," I said. "I was hoping you could buy some tickets for my mom."

"You got it, pal. Hang on. Let me get a pen and paper."

He rummaged around in his desk, or went into the glove box of his car, or did whatever he had to do. I was resentful of the time. Every second he spent screwing around was one less second I would be able to talk to Amanda or my mother that month.

"Okay," he said, finally. "Shoot."

"Thirteen, five, forty-seven, five, sixty-one, twenty . . . ," I began, and kept going until I had spelled out my message:

M-E-E-T M-E-T-M-R-W N-T D-O-R-S-E-Y-S K-N-O-B P-I-C-N-I-C A-R-E-A O-N-E A-M.

As soon as I finished, I said, "Did you get all that? I know it was a lot of tickets."

"I did. Anything else?"

"I'm hungry. Really, really hungry. Especially when I wake up at one o'clock in the morning. I get these strange cravings."

"I understand. What for?"

"Chicken of the Sea fillet of mackerel packets," I said.

"Uh, okay. Really?"

"They're delicious. I swear I could eat hundreds of them. I bet I could eat more than I could even carry. And I'm lifting these days. So I could carry a lot."

"Hey, when you're hungry, you're hungry."

"Starving," I confirmed. "But I almost forgot. I think Kelly needs some lottery tickets, too. I'm just feeling really lucky today."

"Go ahead with those numbers."

This time, I spelled out: B-R-I-N-G T-W-E-L-V-E M-A-R-I-J-U-A-N-A S-E-E-D-S, again including enough numbers above twenty-six to throw off anyone listening.

"Oh my," he said when I finished.

"Is that a problem?"

"No, no," he said, chuckling a little. "I'm sure I can get my hands on some. I'll just . . . Well, whatever. I'll find some."

"Good. So are we on, then? You're going to buy all those tickets?"

"Yeah, although there's maybe one more set of numbers you should think about."

"All right," I said.

"Nineteen, sixty-two, five, five, forty-eight, twenty-seven . . ."

He continued until he had spelled out, S-E-E Y-O-U A-T O-N-E T-M-R-W.

"Got it," I said.

"Hey, one more question before you go."

"Shoot."

"How many phones do you have there in Randolph?"

I looked at the line of phones, each separated by a small partition that gave the appearance of privacy, but no actual privacy.

"Four. Why?"

"Just wondering. Talk to you soon."

CHAPTER 21

I was all jitters throughout the remainder of that day and the beginning of the next. Pete Goodrich may have been in federal prison for bank robbery, but Tommy Jump's most serious offenses were limited to parking violations.

And now I knew why: I didn't have the stomach for lawbreaking.

Masri probably didn't help matters much, because while he had solved one of our problems—he had managed to secure a key to the maintenance warehouse and told me where to store our cans temporarily—he pointed out another that we hadn't really addressed yet: Once the unicorn was ours, we needed to find a place to hide it.

Obviously, it wasn't impossible. Skrobis had been stashing it successfully for years. Still, we needed to come up with something more secure than wherever Masri planned to scatter the cans. Those were expendable to a certain extent, and if a CO came across them, it wouldn't raise much concern. The same could not be said of the unicorn.

Masri said he'd work on it. My first job after lunch was to let Skrobis know I'd be able to deliver on our deal.

I practically burst out of the dining hall, walking as fast as I could toward the pavilion without looking like a man in a hurry. Skrobis wasn't there yet. It was possible his unit was still at lunch.

Rather than sit there and be nervous, I took a lap around the jogging track. Then another. When I returned from the second lap, with a light sweat popping on my brow, Skrobis was there, having already assumed his meditative pose.

I walked up to him silently.

"Greetings, my friend," he said, opening his eyes. "Any news?"

"Yes. We're on."

"I figured as much."

"How did you know?"

"Your aura is very yellow," he said, as if that made perfect sense.

"I'm sure it is. So how are you going to get this to me?"

"Pull up your shirt," he said.

"Huh?"

He was already yanking up the hem of his own shirt.

"Be quick about it," he urged.

Then I understood: He had the unicorn on him. He was off-loading it like it was the One Ring from *Lord of the Rings*, having already possessed it long past the point where its mere presence was driving him mad.

And now it was about to be mine. Its power. And its curse.

He reached under his shirt and pulled out a bulky, roughly rectangular package. It had been wrapped in a white plastic garbage bag that had telltale dirt stains on it, which was suggestive of where Skrobis had been hiding it.

I fumbled with my own outfit, my nervous hands moving more thickly than I would have liked. When he judged me ready, he slipped the unicorn out of his shirt and passed it to me. I tucked it under my T-shirt, then retucked my shirt.

"Excellent," Skrobis said. "And you'll have my payment ready at this time tomorrow?"

"Sure hope so," I said. "If I don't, it's because I got caught and the COs are busy fitting me for a noose."

"If that's the case, you don't know me."

"Of course not," I said.

I gave him a solemn nod, then retreated. It was maybe 150 yards between Randolph and the pavilion. Five steps into the journey, I could already tell the return trip was going to feel twice as long. My T-shirt flattened out the package a little, but otherwise the bulge in my midsection made me look more pregnant than Amanda probably did at the moment. The lump for the radio was particularly unwieldy, like a tumor growing out of my large intestine.

There were other inmates coming my way in ones and twos from their dorms, ready to take advantage of a fine fall afternoon in the rec yard. It may have been my imagination, but I swore they were staring at me like my stomach was a glowing neon sign pointing the way to beer and naked ladies.

Then, to my increasing horror, a small, brown-haired woman emerged from around the corner. It was Karen Lembo, one of the prison social workers, and the moment she saw me, she made a direct line toward me.

I had met her during my orientation, and she was what you'd expect from someone in that role: high-energy, perpetually up in people's business, convinced she could save every lost little soul in her care. She had gone out of her way to assure us that just because we were incarcerated didn't mean we weren't still one of God's special creatures in her eyes.

Which was the last thing I needed right now. Forget my precious snowflake individuality. I yearned to be indistinct.

She was wearing black pants and sensible flats, and I was trying to keep my attention trained on the area near her shoes so we could just pass by without an exchange of any sort. Except even in my peripheral vision, I was aware she was making very direct, very intentional eye contact.

I was already sweating from the jog. And the tension. But now there was an extra burst of perspiration coming from my too-hot face and my belly, which was smothered by that plastic bag.

If I could just slip by her, this would be—

"Hello, Peter," she said.

She had stopped in front of me, blocking my path. She wore a knowing smile, like she could tell I was up to something.

"Hi, Mrs. Lembo," I said.

It immediately sounded wrong. Too high-pitched. No, wait: I had let my accent slip.

Quickly, I added a twangy, "How're you today, ma'am?"

"I'm doing fine, thank you," she said. "Are you feeling okay?"

"Great, thanks."

"You look hot."

"Jogging," I said. "They serve us all those carbs at lunch. If I don't get the blood moving a bit soon as I get out, I'll fall right asleep."

"Ah," she said. "Well, I had a conversation about you with Mr. Munn yesterday."

"Oh yeah?"

I shifted my weight and subtly—God, I hoped it was subtle—crossed my arms over my stomach. It was an entirely unnatural thing for a man in a full lather to do. And it only made me hotter.

"He says you haven't signed up for any vocational classes yet. Is that true?"

"Yes, ma'am, it is."

"I know things can feel pretty bleak at first, when you think your sentence will never end," she said gently. "But this really is the best time to get on the right path, when you're still new and still forming your habits here. It's like we said at orientation: You need to start preparing for the day you get out on the day you get in. Remind me, what kind of job did you have before you came here?"

"I was a teacher."

"That's right. History?"

"Yes, ma'am."

"You know you're not going to be able to teach again when you get out, right? School systems do background checks."

"Yes, ma'am."

"But that's no reason to give up on life. You'll still be a young man when you get out of here. This is a great opportunity to try something new."

"Yeah, I've been meaning to get on that."

"We've found educated inmates like yourself often really enjoy working with their hands. Carpentry, perhaps. There's always going to be a need for carpenters, and the industry tends to be forgiving to those with criminal records. We've placed a number of inmates directly with jobs as soon as they're released. Our instructor in the woodshop is excellent. I bet he'd take you under his wing."

"I'd like that."

"You should go see him right now. I'll walk you there if you like."

I'd like nothing less.

"That's real, real kind of you," I said, desperately trying to deflect her. "But I wouldn't want to meet him like this. I'm pretty sweaty."

She appraised me with suspicion. "Well. Okay. But I'm going to check with the woodshop later. I hope I hear you went there."

"Yes, ma'am," I said. "Right after I change my shirt."

She studied me again, her smile remaining unconvinced. I swear, the moment lasted longer than "City on Fire/Final Sequence" from *Sweeney Todd*—and that's a thirteen-minute song.

"Thanks, Mrs. Lembo, appreciate the talk," I said, then sidestepped her and continued toward Randolph.

I didn't dare turn around to see if she was still watching me. I just walked straight back to my room and—not knowing what else to do with it—stashed the unicorn under the plastic sheet that covered my mattress, closing up the hole I created in the seam with the safety pins that had cinched my pants that first day. I don't think I breathed the entire time.

One Ring to rule them all.

One Ring to send them directly to maximum-security hell.

Time moved slowly after that, taking an hour or two to pass each five- or fifteen-minute increment. I went to the library, where I studied some topographical maps of Dorsey's Knob. Then I established contact with the prison woodshop so I could keep Karen Lembo off my case.

Before dinner, Masri and I huddled one more time to review plans. He also gave me the maintenance warehouse key—another item I really wasn't supposed to have.

Dinner was tasteless. I ate it strictly because I knew I'd need the energy later.

My conversation with Amanda after dinner was even flatter than usual. "Kelly" told me my cousin Amanda had gone to the obstetrician. She was describing some routine test they had performed, but I was having a hard time concentrating. At one point she even asked me if I was distracted by something. *Yeah, honey, it just so happens I'm breaking the law tonight. . . .*

The final thing I did before entering Randolph for the nine o'clock standing count was rustle up a stick so I could use it later as a prop for the front door.

By ten o'clock, I was settled into bed when the lights cut out. Under my feet was the small rise in the mattress from where I had hidden the unicorn. I was exhausted from the anxiety but couldn't have slept without the aid of a tranquilizer gun.

Other than underwear and socks, the only thing I wore was my Timex, whose tiny LED light allowed me to check the time under the covers. I had decided that twenty minutes was sufficient time to get up, get dressed, and climb the hill. A lifetime in the theater had made me proficient at both speedy costume changes and hasty exits.

In the bunk underneath me, big Frank Thacker's breathing became slow and steady. Outside our room, the noises of Randolph settling in for the evening—latecomers shuffling in from the television room, guys using the bathroom one last time—slowly dissipated. The heavy snorers, guys who could rattle the walls with their soft-palate vibrations, didn't usually get going until later. This was the quietest time of day at FCI Morgantown.

I swore the loudest sound in the whole dorm was the thunderous beating of my own heart as I waited to make my move.

CHAPTER 22

Herrera loved the new moon.

As a boy, he would slip out of the house and roam through neighbors' farms, enjoying liberties given to him by the cover of darkness, going places forbidden to him during the day.

Sometimes he'd spy into the windows of the homes. These were not the dusty Mexican farm shacks of gringo imagination. They were large, elegant homes faced in stucco or tile.

Herrera grew up in Jalisco, in an area renowned for growing the best blue agave in the world. His family and their neighbors had their battles like any farmers—with capricious weather, with rot and weevils and fungus—but as long as the world remained thirsty for tequila, they would remain prosperous.

In that way, Herrera was unlike so many of the men in the cartel, who were raised in poverty and were either forced to join or signed up because they had few other choices.

Herrera had options. He had gone to college. He could have stayed and made a fine living with his family. He could have gone to the city and found a job. He joined the cartel because he wanted the action. Because he loved the things that could happen in the dark.

So even though he was in a very foreign place—the suburbs of Atlanta, an American city whose humidity he found oppressive even in the middle of October—he was comfortable in the small hours of the morning, approaching a house whose owner was unaware of his presence.

His target was a small saltbox with drab gray siding. Herrera had driven by it in his rental car a few times, then parked down the street and traversed the cracked sidewalk until he was outside. He pulled on a ski mask and walked up the driveway.

To the left of the three front steps was a blue octagonal sign for a security system. Herrera smirked at it. He knew the company. It favored pressure sensors—easily defeated—for windows and doors.

He continued around to the back of the house, where there was a deck with a barbecue grill and a small dry bar with an umbrella over it. More important, the deck's elevation offered easy, waist-height access to two windows.

One of which had an air-conditioning unit stuck into it. Which meant the pressure sensors on that window weren't being monitored. The unit hadn't even been bolted into the window frame. It had simply been propped under the window, which had then been shut on top of it. The owner might as well have set out a welcome mat.

Working carefully, Herrera needed only a few minutes to negotiate the quiet removal of the unit. The gloves he wore slowed him a little, but he didn't dare take them off.

Never give the Americans evidence they could use to extradite you. One of El Vio's rules.

Once the air conditioner was resting on the deck, Herrera climbed through the open window and into the kitchen. Finding it unremarkable, he passed into the living room next. It was stuffed with furniture, like the occupants had once lived in a much larger house and were now cramming the same amount of stuff into a space a third of the size.

Herrera paused at one of the end tables. Cluttering the top of it were a number of photographs. Most of them featured one or both of a pair of children at awkward ages, with their braces and their fast-growing bodies. But there was one portrait of the whole family.

The woman was pretty. Blond and nicely dressed. Herrera did like blondes.

The banker was next to her, his arm around her, smiling like he knew he was punching above his weight class. Herrera picked up the frame and studied the man who created all this trouble. He didn't look like much.

Herrera set down the picture and, satisfied by all he had seen on this level, started climbing the stairs. They were old, like the rest of the house. After the second step creaked on him, he took the rest gingerly.

At the top of the stairs, he was confronted with four doors. One was open. The bathroom. That made the other three bedrooms. He selected the door to what appeared to be the largest of them, grabbed the handle, turned slowly, then poked his face in.

The air was warm and moist from human exhaust. A king-size bed took up most of the space. On the right side of it, nearest to the door, there was a woman.

The blond woman from the picture, the banker's wife. She had kicked off the covers and was sleeping on her back, her legs akimbo. She wore panties and a T-shirt, which had ridden up, exposing her midriff. Her thighs were pale, almost alabaster, and well toned.

He walked toward her until he was standing above her. In the faint glow of a nearby alarm clock, he could see the rise and fall to her chest. He bent low and, from a sheath strapped to his calf, removed a serrated hunting knife. It was designed to cut through the soft flesh of a mammal, to slash muscles and arteries, causing an animal to bleed out quickly.

In one quick movement, he sat down on the edge of the bed and clamped his hand down on her mouth. Her eyelids immediately opened. He brought the knife to her face.

"If you scream, I will kill you," he said softly, in accented English. "Do we understand each other? Blink twice for yes."

She blinked twice.

"Very good," he said. "I'm going to remove my hand now."

He kept the knife blade inches from her cheek.

"My husband has documents," she whispered. "If you hurt us, he'll turn them over to the FBI and all of you will—"

"I'm well aware of what your husband has," Herrera said. "And I don't care. If I don't recover those documents myself, I won't live long enough to be prosecuted. El Vio will kill me and send someone else to do this job. So. I am going to make this very simple: If you don't tell me where those documents are, I will kill you, then I will butcher your children. I will leave them alive but horribly disfigured, so they can live out the remainder of their lives as grotesque orphans. Is that what you want?"

"No. But I—"

"Then tell me where the documents are."

"*I. Don't. Know,*" she said. "If I did, I would have turned them over to the feds a long time ago and gone into witness protection. You have to believe that."

He did. He had heard the tapes.

"There is a hunting cabin," he said.

"They're not there. I looked already."

"Not as carefully as I will. Tell me where the cabin is."

"It doesn't have an address."

"But you know how to get there."

"Of course I do, I—"

"Then you'll tell me."

"I . . . I have GPS coordinates. That's what we give to guests who visit. You can enter the numbers into your phone, and it'll take you right there."

"That will suffice," he said.

She retrieved the numbers from her phone. Herrera wrote them on his arm in pen, then brandished the knife in her face again.

"If you are lying to me," he said, "I'll be back."

CHAPTER 23

At a few minutes after midnight, I heard the CO making his rounds, doing the count.

He was using a handheld counter. The sound of his double clicks grew closer as he did, then faded away, like some kind of snap-clacky Doppler effect.

Then there was more quiet.

At exactly 12:40, I eased myself into a sitting position. Putting to use all I had learned about body control from many years of dance training, I gradually slid toward the edge of the bed, going slow enough its calcified bedsprings didn't creak, then climbed down the ladder.

My socked feet were silent on the tile floor. Reversing what I had done earlier in the day, I eased up the fitted sheet, then located the seam on the plastic mattress cover. Working by feel, my fingers found the safety pins and unhooked them.

Then I slid out the package. The plastic bag rustled too loudly for my liking—the sighs of angels were too loud for my liking at the moment—but I slowly shifted it over to our desk, placing it lightly on top.

I reached inside. My hand hit rough fabric, and I pulled out the canvas pants. Then I eased into them, being careful not to let the fabric rustle. They were too large, of course, but I rolled cuffs and tightened the belt and judged them good enough. The shirt came next.

After putting on my own footwear—the black steel-toed boots issued to the COs were essentially indistinguishable from ours—the finishing touch was the radio, which I attached to my shirt, just like the COs I saw every day.

There was no mirror in the room to check that everything was squared away, but looking down, I judged myself to have passed muster. This getup only had to fool someone from a distance of twenty feet or more. If one of the nighttime staff members got closer to me than that, I'd probably be done for anyway.

I took a tentative step toward the door to my room, then I heard: "Sir?"

It had come from the lower bunk. I froze. The ambient light coming in from our small window was faint. Could Frank see me in it?

"What's up?" I whispered.

"Where you going?"

"The bathroom," I said.

"Why you all dressed up like that?"

Crap.

Frank and I still hadn't really talked. All I could say about him was that he was huge and black and that he had gone to church on Sunday and Bible study on Wednesday, the classic convict trying to get right—or stay right—with Jesus. I still didn't know why he was in here. I hadn't explored his feelings toward authority. I was uncertain if he'd snitch on me to curry favor with the administration.

"I'm just going out for a little errand," I said.

"You runnin' the hill?"

"That okay with you?"

I wished I could see his face so I could have some idea what he was thinking. He shifted position, rolling toward me.

"Could you get me some Slim Jims, sir?"

Feeling a rush of relief, I said, "You got it."

"Okay," he said. "You be careful, now. Them woods is dangerous. You never know what's out there."

I almost laughed. The incredible bulk was afraid of a few forest creatures?

"Thanks, Frank. I will be."

I took two steps toward our door and paused, acutely aware that one of the most treacherous moments of the mission would be the first. Fact was, I didn't know where the CO assigned to the cottages had chosen to spend his evening. There were five possibilities, which meant there was a one-in-five chance this was going to be an exceedingly brief exercise.

And I had no way of knowing. I had heard the CO leaving the cottage after the midnight count—the bar that opened the door from the inside made this metal-on-metal shriek from not having been oiled in an eternity. The problem was, the thumb button on the handle that let you back in was much quieter. He could have reentered silently.

With this in mind, I walked softly out of my room and up the corridor, passing the bathroom. The glass-enclosed office where the CO would most likely be hanging out was up front, by the entrance.

As soon as I turned into the hallway, I flattened myself against the wall, face-in, and edged slowly along. I was primed to bolt back toward my room the moment I saw anyone in the office. That's *if* the CO was actually in the office. If he was doing what he was supposed to do—stay moving in and around the cottages—he could show up anywhere, including behind me. I was mostly relying on institutionalized laziness for protection.

I eased slowly forward. With each incremental bit of progress, more of the office came into my view. It was dark, which was a good sign. As long as he wasn't hunkered down in there with the lights off.

Inch by inch, the office revealed itself: fifty percent, then seventy-five, then eighty-five. Still no one. When I got to the point where I could see it in its entirety—and it was entirely empty—I moved decisively toward the exit.

Speed was now my friend. The less time it took me to travel from Randolph to the safety of the woods, the better. I slowed momentarily at the door, pressing the bar gently so I wouldn't trigger a squeal as I opened it. I found my stick lying on the ground where I left it and wedged it in the door.

Then I scampered down the steps and slipped into the night.

The nearest light stanchion was several hundred yards away and behind me. Its output was meager enough I barely cast a shadow. The moonless sky above was dark, save for the stars, which twinkled like an array of tiny, distant LEDs.

I set off toward the rec area, trying not to appear in too much of a hurry. I reminded myself of the role I was taking on: FCI Morgantown corrections officer. I walked confidently, without fear of anyone or anything. I was a little bored, of course. I did this every night. Nothing ever happened.

The administration at FCI Morgantown did a fine job hiding its cameras, so I wasn't aware of when I was on video or when I was in a black zone. But that was the point of the unicorn. Even if someone was monitoring the feed, the grainy image of a CO walking along in a navy blue blur wouldn't appear unusual.

I slid past the handball wall, then the pavilion, keeping my head down. There was no one out. At least no one I could see.

The last buildings I passed were Alexander and Bates, where inmates slept barracks-style. Each one housed a few hundred men. I didn't know if they had one CO each at night, or if they shared one— who might therefore be passing between them.

That wasn't my concern. I was just a CO myself. If I saw anyone, I'd just nod and carry on. The captain who commanded the night shift had told me to go check out something he saw on the camera, so that's what I was doing.

It was now just upward-sloping open space between me and the forest. My roiled stomach flip-flopped a little extra as I crossed over the perimeter road, the ring of asphalt that formed the outermost boundary of our lives. Beyond it was no-man's-land.

I scuffled quickly across, then plunged into the trees, safe for the moment. In theory, I had until sometime before the three A.M. count to get back. I still elongated my strides to cover more ground. My thighs burned from the incline. Freshly fallen leaves rustled under my feet. It was nice not to worry about the noise they were making.

My breathing grew heavier as the slope increased. My eyes were getting better adjusted to the darkness as I got farther away from the facility. I purposefully did not look back at the light stanchions, so my pupils would stay as widely dilated as possible.

The canopy of trees above me was mature enough that the undergrowth was not too imposing. I stumbled now and then as my steel-toed boots hit a root or rock but otherwise had no trouble navigating the darkness.

After maybe four or five minutes of steady climbing, the slope abruptly leveled out. I had reached the ridge that ran atop Dorsey's Knob.

I quickly flashed the light on my Timex. 12:56. Perfect.

According to my map study, I would crest a ridge, then come to a clearing. Sure enough, I found it after a small descent. Once in the open, I took a right turn, pointing myself in the direction of the picnic area, and broke into a brisk jog.

There were no lights on. The park was closed. But I could soon see the shape of a man, sitting on one of the tables. He was dressed in black.

When I was maybe fifteen feet away, I realized it wasn't Danny Ruiz.

It was Rick Gilmartin. His black shirt had the letters FBI printed in gray.

"Good evening," he said.

"Where's Danny?" I asked.

"New York. We have other cases, you know."

"Right," I said. "Well, let's get on with it, then. I have to get back."

He stood and walked over to another picnic bench mounded with dark shapes that turned out to be a backpack and two duffel bags.

"Per your request, these are stuffed with Chicken of the Sea fillet of mackerel packets," he said, patting the backpack. "You're looking at more than three hundred pounds of fish here. I had to go to one of their distribution centers in Maryland to pick this up. They looked at me like there was something wrong with me even after I flashed my badge."

The backpack was a large, military-style item, and Gilmartin had expanded its zip-out compartments to their full size. It had been packed solid. I tentatively tried to lift one of the duffel bags by its strap. It barely budged. I had no idea mackerel packets weighed so much. I might as well have asked for sacks of bricks.

"This is great," I said, using my own voice for a change. Pete Goodrich needed a break.

"I suggest you take at least two trips. I used three to get them here from the parking lot."

"Good call," I said.

I could squat more than three hundred pounds. But that was in the controlled environment of a weight room. I didn't want to know what the compound fracture would look like if I took an awkward step with three hundred pounds on my back.

"And, of course, there's this," he said solemnly. He pulled a plastic bag out of his pocket and handed it to me.

Inside were a small handful of what I assumed were marijuana seeds. I stuffed them in my pocket.

"Those were about to be destroyed," he said. "As far as the United States government is concerned, they *have* been destroyed. So do everyone involved a favor and never discuss this again."

"You got it."

He looked down at the bags. "I'll help you carry those things as far as the tree line if you'd like. After that, I wouldn't want to have to explain to the BOP what I was doing in their facility at one o'clock in the morning with a bunch of fish."

"Actually, there's something else I'd rather you do, if you don't mind."

"What's that?"

"There's a GoMart right down the road from here," I said. "Would you mind picking up some caramel M&M'S and some Slim Jims?"

I took the backpack first. It easily weighed as much as I did and only became manageable—barely—when I got the weight balanced right.

Still, I was able to work my way down through the forest until I was as close as I could get to the maintenance warehouse, which was conveniently located near the perimeter road.

Masri's key worked fine, and I was soon inside, hiding the backpack under a tarp that was exactly where he said it would be.

Then it was back up the hill. Even though it was a cool night, I was sweating profusely. I wondered if I could get away with laundering the unicorn when this was over. Otherwise I feared the COs would find it based on odor alone.

Back up in the picnic area, Gilmartin was waiting for me with a plastic sack containing five bags of caramel M&M'S and a fistful of Slim Jims.

"Here you go," he said. "This was all they had."

"Thanks," I said, stuffing the sack in one of the duffel bags.

I checked my Timex: 1:48. I was doing fine, though I still couldn't dawdle. I shouldered the first of the two duffel bags, then balanced myself off with the second. Again, the load was awkward but doable.

"All right," I said, then summoned my best *Henry V.* "Once more unto the breach, dear friends."

"Wait, there's one more thing," Gilmartin said, reaching into his pocket and producing a small Ziploc bag. "I want you to install these in the phones at Randolph. There are instructions inside. I included some double-adhesive strips. All you have to do is unscrew the mouthpiece and attach them."

"What . . . what are they?" I said, setting the bags back down.

"Listening devices," he said.

Now I finally understood why Danny had asked how many phones there were.

"But the calls are monitored already," I said.

"By the BOP. Not by us. And the BOP doesn't share well. We gave them the we're-all-on-the-same-team-here argument, and they told us they could only let us listen if there was evidence of lawbreaking. Then they told us if we had a problem with that to talk to their lawyers. This way is a lot easier."

I still hadn't taken the bag from him. I thought about sneaking out to the phones, unscrewing them in the dark, fumbling around with adhesive strips. . . .

"Forget it," I said. "I'm taking enough risk for you guys already. If you can't get the BOP to play with you, that's not my problem."

"This is not a request," Gilmartin said.

"What, you're giving me orders now? I don't work for you."

"Yes, you do."

"I signed a contract where I agreed to perform a role for a specific length of time. This has nothing to do with that role."

"You signed a contract that says you are to perform the duties asked of you by bureau personnel. That's me. And I'll remind you we're paying you quite handsomely for that. As a matter of fact, if you'll recall, I went to bat for you when you wanted more money."

"That contract also says I can't break the law," I pointed out.

"This isn't breaking the law."

"Yeah? Then show me a warrant."

"We don't need one. This is no different than you tapping the phones in your own home. West Virginia is a one-party-consent state. That means you're the only one who needs to be aware of it."

I had no idea if that was true. Frankly, I didn't care if I was break-ing the law—and, obviously, neither did the FBI, since Gilmartin had just handed me a bunch of marijuana seeds. I just wasn't sure how much more danger my stomach could handle. This is why the bureau had sent Gilmartin to do this errand. Danny wouldn't have been able to bring himself to be this much of a prick.

Sensing he had gained the advantage, Gilmartin moved quickly to finish me off.

"If you don't want to fulfill the terms of your contract, that's fine," he said. "I'll pull you out tomorrow, if you like. Is that what you want?"

"Just give me the bag," I said.

I took it from him and stuffed it in my pocket. "If you guys hear Dupree say something on those phone calls that leads to indictments against New Colima, I get my bonus, right?"

"Of course," Gilmartin said.

"Great," I said, shouldering the duffel bags again. "Thanks for the fish."

Then I started back down the hill. I wasn't wild about implanting the devices; or the way I'd have to do it; or that the FBI was now going to be listening to everything I said, too.

But mostly I disliked the precedent it established.

What were they going to make me do next?

CHAPTER 24

C harlie had made jazz band. One of just three freshmen to be so honored.

Claire had been invited to *the* sleepover birthday party of the fall season and was eager to discuss pajama strategy.

It was, all in all, a banner day in the Dupree household. And Mitch was enjoying every trust-fund-limited second of it. For at least a short while, he could suspend disbelief, tell himself he was just on a business trip—a really, really long business trip to a convention without a hotel bar—and that he would not be returning to the bottom bunk of a two-man cell when this call was over.

Then Natalie got on the phone, interrupting Claire with an ominous, "Sorry, honey, I need some time with Daddy today."

Claire chirped out a sugar-sweet good-bye—"Okay! Love you, Daddy!"—that practically pureed Dupree's insides. Then he took a deep breath. Usually when Natalie needed time, it was something financial. Something bad.

"What's up?" Dupree asked.

Quietly and without indulging the hysteria she was feeling—because the kids would hear if she broke down sobbing—Natalie related how a Mexican man broke into the house and held a knife to her throat until she surrendered the GPS coordinates for the hunting cabin.

"Did you call the police?" Dupree asked.

"Of course I did," Natalie said. "They lectured me about the air conditioner. Like I needed that."

"Are they even going to try to figure out who did it?"

"Doesn't sound like it. They told me it was breaking and entering, which, duh, I knew already. They asked me if the guy took anything, and I said no, I didn't think so. Then it was like they washed their hands of it. They said the only way guys like that get caught is if they try to pawn something later."

Dupree nearly punched the wall. His wife was being threatened, and there he was, hundreds of miles away, totally worthless to her. If there was a more impotent feeling, he had yet to experience it.

"The cartel is just trying to scare us," Dupree said.

"Well, congratulations to them. It's working."

"They won't do anything," he said, which he had to believe, because he'd suffer a breakdown if he didn't.

She sighed loudly. "On top of that, I saw Jenny Reiner coming out of Nordstrom yesterday with two big shopping bags. To think her husband is free and you're . . ."

"We can't dwell on that. There's nothing we can do about that."

More impotence.

"I know," she said. She knew this phone call was already running out of time, so she blurted, "I want to move."

"We can't afford it. And it wouldn't matter where you went. They'd find you."

"Mitch, I can't live like this much longer. You have to do something."

"Let me think about it," he said.

"No. That's not good enough anymore. There was a man sitting on my bed with a knife. What are you waiting for? For him to actually use it?"

"Of course not, I just—"

"I can't take this anymore. I just can't. I'm done."

Then she hung up.

They still had a minute left.

CHAPTER 25

I dedicated most of the next day to rest and recovery, not trusting my sleep-deprived self to be quick enough in thought and speech to have my first encounter with Dupree.

The odds and ends of the previous night's errand were tidied up easily enough. I had quickly installed the bugs Gilmartin gave me, reasoning that it was better to get it over with—especially when I was out already, and I knew there had been no sign of a roaming CO.

After lunch, Masri let me know he had distributed the cans to a variety of hiding spots he had scoped out, then camouflaged them. If I needed to make a withdrawal, all I had to do was ask before work duty.

The other significant improvement on my circumstance was that I was able to find a tree near the perimeter road that had a decent-size knot in it—one that, conveniently, faced away from the facility—that I could cram the unicorn inside. I hid the telltale white plastic with leaves. For all I knew, it was the same place Skrobis had been hiding it.

It wasn't until the morning *after* the morning after that I tracked down Bobby Harrison and told him I was ready to take his place in the nightly Randolph poker game. He tried to haggle me up to fifteen cans again, but I insisted we stay with ten. We both knew he was being fairly compensated. I paid for the first two nights, both to establish my credibility as a dependable payer and so I wouldn't have to trouble Masri for another withdrawal.

That night at five minutes before seven o'clock, I walked into the card room and took my place at the table farthest from the door. I wanted to be early, in case there were any questions about my legitimacy in the game. I had five cans bulging in my pocket for the buy-in.

I was feeling loose, relaxed. It was just a friendly game of cards. Never mind the effort I had expended to join it.

Pete Goodrich would be chill about it. On the outside, he had played in a regular game with a fellow social studies teacher, two math teachers, a chemistry teacher, and the football coach—when it wasn't football season, anyway. They rotated houses. Low stakes, except if you went all in with three of a kind and got beaten by a flush you didn't see coming, you'd hear about it in the faculty lounge at school all week.

Three minutes later, one of the guys from the game, the tall one, walked into the room. He was at least six-four. Probably fifty, though his tawny hair showed no signs of gray. He had a hooked nose that the rest of him was just barely large enough to accommodate.

"Sorry, this table's reserved," he said agreeably.

"I'm taking Bobby Harrison's place," I said. "He sends his regrets."

The man took this in for a moment. He apparently decided it didn't bother him very much because he folded his long body into the seat across from me. "I'm Jim," he said, holding out his right hand. "Jim Madigan. But people call me 'Doc.'"

I shook his hand. "Pete Goodrich. People call me Pete Goodrich."

He smiled as another guy from the game walked in. It was the guy with the ponytail—really, just a scraggly assortment of gray hair that he tied back. He was a light-skinned black man and was older than Doc, though it was difficult for me to peg his age exactly, on account of the gray beard that covered his face.

"This is Jerry Strother," Doc said. "Jerry, this is Pete Goodrich. He's taking Bobby's place."

"You don't cheat, do you?" Jerry inquired.

He said the line straight, but it was still a line.

"Guess you'll find out," I replied with a half grin.

"Oh, he's gonna fit in fine around here," Jerry declared, punctuating it with a quick cackle before he took a seat.

Doc had brought two decks of cards and passed them to Jerry, who began shuffling them with an expert flair.

"Feeling lucky tonight," Jerry declared. "This is my night."

Doc turned to me. "You can feel free to ignore him. He says that every night."

Just then Mitchell Dupree entered the room, looking hangdog as ever.

This was the encounter I had been trying to arrange since the moment I set foot in FCI Morgantown—potentially the start of a three-hundred-thousand-dollar life-changing event—but Pete Goodrich was casual about it, paying no more or less attention to him than he did the other guys.

"Where's Bobby?" Dupree asked.

This was my first time hearing his voice. It was higher and softer than I thought it would be. His accent was upper-middle-class Atlanta, which meant it had been watered down with enough Yankee influence through the years that it wasn't very southern at all.

"This is Pete Goodrich," Doc said. "He's Bobby for the night. Pete, this is Mitch Dupree."

So he was Mitch. Not Mitchell.

We exchanged nods. He was staring at me, hard, just like he had that first night in the dining hall and a few times since then. I strained to remain nonchalant.

"Everything okay, Mitch?" Doc asked. "You look bothered."

Mitch sat down heavily next to me and said, "I'm fine. Let's just play cards."

He had been carrying a cardboard box with him. He reached into it and pulled out a handful of construction paper that had been cut into stamp-size bits. He began organizing them by color.

"Mitch was a banker," Doc said. "So he brings the chips and handles the money. He also keeps stats on winners and losers if you're ever curious about that."

"It passes the time," Mitch explained.

"Sort of anal, if you ask me," Jerry said.

"It's in a banker's nature to document things," Mitch shot back.

Just hearing him say the word "document" was thrilling.

Doc was already moving on: "The chips are the usual denominations. Blue is ten, red is five, white is one. Buy-in is one can."

"One," I blurted. "Bobby told me five."

Doc and Jerry busted up laughing. Even Dupree cracked a little smile.

I hadn't meant it to be funny. Bobby lied so he could extort more money out of me. Somehow, I was genuinely surprised that I had been conned by a con.

"No, no, just one," Doc said, still smiling. "You can re–buy in once for another can if you want, but that's it. This is paupers' poker. The maximum pot is eight cans."

"All right, well, I'm in," I said. I extracted a can from my pocket and slid it over to Dupree, who was still organizing slips of paper. The other guys handed over their cans as well. Dupree placed all of them in the cardboard box, which was now beneath his chair.

"The blinds start at two and one," Doc continued. "The big blind goes up by two every time we get around to the same dealer again. We do it that way instead of doubling it because it makes the game last a little longer. Other than that, it's just regular hold 'em."

"Nothing wild except the players," Jerry hooted.

"Sounds like my kind of game," I said.

And, at least at first, it was. I managed to win enough to stay in the game as the large blind increased to four, then six, then eight. The whole time, I felt like Mitch was trying to steal glances at me out of the corner of his eye. I pretended to ignore it, but it was still distinctly unsettling. Why did he keep looking at me like that? I might have told myself he was just trying to read me, learn my tells. Except he had been doing the same thing before we began playing.

At one point, when the blinds were at ten, I was dealer and was just about to look at my hold cards when Mitch flipped up his cards and said, "Re-deal, re-deal."

I had mistakenly given him three hold cards. Two cards must have gotten stuck together. I hadn't noticed. I don't think anyone else did, either. Mitch could have easily gotten away with taking the better of the two cards and sliding the third back into the deck when no one would notice.

But he wasn't that kind of guy.

Apparently, he cheated only when the stakes were in the millions.

After that, we settled back into the game. Doc eventually busted out. Then Jerry did, too, leaving only Mitch and me. With Doc acting as full-time dealer and Jerry shuffling for us, the blinds increased quickly until they reached what they had decided was the limit—a dollar. My first time as the large blind at that amount, I was dealt a pair of kings. If Mitch stayed in for fifty more cents, in addition to the fifty he had already put in as the small blind, I'd raise pre-flop and buy him out.

Except Mitch beat me to it, raising a dollar pre-flop. A bold move. And it set up a showdown, because I wasn't folding with pocket kings. I saw him. Doc and Jerry—who were serving as our peanut gallery at that point—made appropriate noises of appreciation and anticipation. This was looking like it would be the culminating hand of the night.

Out came the flop: a queen, an ace, and a king. Lots of pretty faces smiling back at us. Doc and Jerry ahhed some more.

Without hesitation, Mitch bet a dollar. Which told me he probably had an ace in the hole. But I had those kings, giving me three of a kind. I saw him again.

The turn: a three. Which probably didn't change anything for either of us. Mitch announced he was all in. My remaining chips just covered his bet, so I pushed them in the middle and said, "Okay, looks like we're both all in."

"All right, all right," Jerry said. "It's about to get real up in here!"

"Okay, fellas," Doc said. "Pot's right, so here goes."

Doc paused dramatically, then revealed the final card.

Another queen. Giving me a full house, kings over queens. Unless Mitch had pocket queens, I was unbeatable.

Mitch immediately hooted out a boisterous, "Ha!"

He flipped up his cards, an ace and a queen, and cooed, "Full boat. Queens over aces. Thing of beauty."

It sure was. It just didn't beat a full house with kings over queens.

I could have broken Mitch's heart simply by turning over my cards. But I hadn't come here to win. So I slid my cards under what remained of the deck next to Doc and said, "Nicely played, Mitch. You got me."

"Fine game, young man, fine game," Mitch said, beaming.

I acted properly dejected. But when he stuck out his right hand, I shook it like the good sport I was.

"Dang," Jerry said. "Felt like I was watching World Series of Poker just now."

Mitch raked the pot toward him with both hands—a grand show, even if it was just slips of construction paper. Then he brought up the cardboard box and dumped them inside, along with the mackerel packets he now got to take home with him.

"It was your night, Mitch," Doc said.

"Sure was," he agreed, though he was now looking at me again. "Plus, I finally figured out why you looked so familiar."

And then he said the last words I wanted to hear: "I saw you in a play once. It was about tomatoes, if you can believe that."

Over the next few seconds, I might have aged a few millennia. Acting is about mastering character and then not breaking it, no matter what. And it took every bit of my experience to maintain my Pete Goodrich as a sudden rush of stress hormones cranked up my inner furnace.

The other two men were now staring at me curiously. A fine layer of perspiration had popped on my forehead—what I would have called a flop sweat, except we had already had the final flop of the evening.

Cherokee Purples had folded after ten weeks—seventy-six shows, to be exact. It ran in a theater that sat seventeen hundred—but was often no more than three-quarters full—which meant less than a hundred thousand people in America could claim to have seen it. Out of 320-odd million residents. The chances Mitch Dupree would be one of them were too small for me to calculate without the aid of electronics.

He was looking at me pleasantly enough, with no suspicion or malice. But I had already been introduced to him as Pete Goodrich. How could I finesse a double life as Tommy Jump? Could I tell him that identity fraud was part of my crime? Claim I had a twin?

"Oh yeah?" was all I said, willing my body to cool down.

"Yeah. For our anniversary, my wife and I used to go up to New York and see a show. She loved the theater. She followed reviews and everything. We ended up going to this one that she was really high on because the *Times* raved about it. You're a lot more muscly, but otherwise you look just like the guy who played the kid."

I was suddenly thankful for every weight I had lifted since I was a spindly teenager. *You look just like the guy who* was subtly but importantly different from *You're the guy who*. I had to hope that remained a distinction for him.

"Huh," I said. "How 'bout that."

"Yeah, it's uncanny," he said. "I'm good with faces, and I swore the moment I saw you when you first got here that I had seen yours before. I just couldn't remember how."

"Well," I drawled a little extra. "Guess I got a long-lost cousin out there."

"He had a big voice," Mitch said enthusiastically. "He was a little guy, but when he opened his mouth, man, he could belt it out. I wish I could remember the name of the show. . . ."

As his voice trailed off, Jerry filled the silence.

"What do you say, Pete, you want to do a little *West Side Story* for us?" he asked. And then he broke into an off-key "Mah-reeeeeee-ah! I just met a girl named Mah-reeee-ah!"

"I only sing in the car," I said quickly. "And, believe me, no one wants to hear it."

Mitch continued: "Damn, it's on the tip of my tongue. It was an unusual name . . . Doc, you'll have to look it up for me."

My attention went to Doc, who immediately shot Mitch a scornful look and mumbled something under his breath. Then suddenly Doc was collecting his cards and standing up, like he couldn't wait to get away from the table and distance himself from what Mitch had just said. Which only made me want to examine it.

Look it up . . . how, exactly? I couldn't imagine the FCI Morgantown library kept *Playbill*s from long-extinct Broadway musicals. And we were strictly kept away from the Internet.

Unless . . .

And then I understood:

Doc had a smartphone hidden somewhere. That's why he was hurrying away. He didn't want to bring any more attention to the secret that Mitch, in his excitement, had inadvertently spilled around the new guy.

I stood too. And, wanting to pretend I hadn't heard or understood the implications of Mitch's final sentence, I blathered out, "If you read German folklore, they say we all have a doppelgänger out there somewhere. Nice to know mine does Broadway."

"Yeah," Mitch said uneasily, having realized his mistake. "I just got this mental block about the name of the show. Eh, it'll come to me."

"Anyway," I said, pivoting away from this line of conversation, "it was great playing with you guys. It sounds like Bobby wanted to take a little time off from the game, so I think you might be seeing more of me."

"Fine with me," Mitch said, also anxious to move on from his gaffe.

"Yeah, long as I get to take your money home tomorrow night," Jerry said.

"Nice playing with you, Pete," Doc said.

"You too," I said, stretching perhaps a bit too extravagantly. "Just about time for the count, I guess."

They agreed it was, in fact, about that time. We scurried toward our respective rooms.

All the while, I was thinking back to our orientation, where smartphones had been fingered as the ultimate evil. I had more or less ignored it as more droning from paranoid administrators. If a guy wanted a burner so he could have phone sex with his wife somewhere that wasn't the Randolph common area, it truly wasn't my concern.

Now? Doc's phone suddenly *was* my concern. If Mitch could remember the name *Cherokee Purples* and told Doc to google it; or even if they googled "broadway musical involving tomatoes" and it led them to it?

They would soon find pictures of a younger Tommy Jump, who would bear a more-than-coincidental resemblance to Pete Goodrich.

CHAPTER 26

With each passing mile, Natalie Dupree gripped the steering wheel fractionally harder. Why was this making her so nervous? She wasn't doing anything illegal.

It just felt that way.

Her destination was in Gwinnett County, Georgia. When she was a girl, this was considered country. It had since been consumed by Atlanta sprawl.

The address she had plugged into her GPS led to a warehouse set aside from a two-lane divided highway. A small white billboard had been wheeled next to the turn-in. Its plastic lettering told her she had found the right place.

The parking lot was filled with vehicles that belonged at a political rally. DON'T TREAD ON ME decals fought for attention with FREEDOM ISN'T FREE bumper stickers. Enthusiasm for hunting, the military, and *Duck Dynasty* were manifest. Proclamations of devotion to the US Constitution shared window space with Confederate flags, a pairing that surely would have bewildered the combatants of the Civil War.

She pulled next to a truck that had been covered in a camouflage wrap—wasn't it safer if the other drivers *could* see you?—and got out, shouldering the Fendi bag that Mitch had bought for her during happier times. Just inside the entrance to the warehouse, a man sat at a table with a cashbox in front of him, selling tickets. Admission was twelve dollars for adults and four dollars for kids, or fifteen dollars and six dollars for what was called VIP access.

"What does VIP get me?" Natalie asked.

"No wait," he said, tilting his head toward a line of roughly a dozen people whose discontent with their diminished status was plain. "I can only let in so many at a time."

Charlie and Claire were at school. She wasn't scheduled to work at Fancy Pants until the afternoon. She still wanted to get this over with as quickly as possible.

"I'll do VIP," she said, handing over a ten and a five.

"All right," he said, inking her hand with a stamp that read VIP and waving her through.

The interior of the building had no windows. The only light came from fluorescent bulbs attached to the ceiling that cast a yellow pall on the scene below. Folding tables ringed the outside of the space, with more tables arranged in rows in the middle of the floor.

And every table was covered with guns.

Handguns. Shotguns. Long guns. Semiautomatics with scopes. AR-15s with pistol grips. AK-47s with banana clips.

Guns for sport. Guns from the old west. Guns used in World War II. Even a few muzzleloaders for the nostalgic collector.

It was almost too much for Natalie to take in at once. She made one clockwise pass around the room, pointedly not making eye contact with any of the sellers. There were enough other patrons that she could pass through without anyone trying to talk to her. She was just trying to get her heart to start beating normally.

Was her anxiety because this made her think of waking up with that Mexican man's gloved hand clamped across her mouth? And how different that confrontation might be next time if she had a weapon within arm's reach?

Or was it because she knew the other thing she ached to do with one of those guns?

Because, sure, Natalie could have spared the long drive to the exurbs and patronized a local sporting goods store instead. It wasn't difficult to buy a firearm in the state of Georgia. There was no need for a permit, no waiting period.

But they'd still ask for ID. They'd still run a background check to make sure she wasn't a felon. There would be a paper trail.

Not so with gun shows. They were considered private sales. No different from your neighbor selling you a gun. There would be no legal scrutiny. No paperwork.

Which is how Natalie wanted it.

Midway through her second pass around the room, she stopped at a table that seemed to be a little more neatly arranged than the others. Her gaze fell on a pistol that was black on the bottom, gray on top. A price tag was attached to the barrel with a piece of string. It informed her that the quality of her life could be improved for a mere 425 dollars.

"That's a Colt Mustang," said an eager-looking older man with a gray beard and an ice-cream-scoop belly. "You looking for something for yourself? Your husband?"

"I'm divorced," she said curtly, aware she was wearing her engagement ring and her wedding ring.

Whatever. Let him wonder.

"Well, that Colt's a good choice for a lady living alone," the man said as his eyes traveled up and down her body. "It's perfect for personal protection. Plus you can slip it in your purse if you want to carry concealed. Looks like it fits you real nice. You can pick it up if you want."

Tentatively, Natalie wrapped her fingers around the handle and lifted it for the briefest moment before setting it back down.

"Bought it from a police officer last week," the man said proudly. "His wife wanted something a little bigger. It's been well cared for."

Natalie had read online that one was expected to barter at a gun show. So she said, "I'll give you four hundred for it."

"I can do that," he said. Then, as an afterthought, he asked, "You from Georgia?"

"Yes," she said.

If he requested ID, she was going to bolt.

But he just said, "All right. I gotta ask. I can't sell it to you if you're out of state."

"I live in Atlanta."

"Okay, then."

And that was it. He started removing the price tag. She reached into her purse and pulled out four crisp hundred-dollar bills, the proceeds from a few stray savings bonds she had found tucked away in a filing cabinet. She slid the money across the table. The man handed her the gun, now wrapped in a paper bag.

"You got a carry permit?" he asked.

"Yes," she lied.

"All right. That's a good gun right there. Hope it works out well for you."

Natalie smiled weakly and thanked him. The entire transaction took about sixty seconds. Another minute later, she was out the door and back in her car.

With her new gun, legally purchased—and completely untraceable—at her side.

CHAPTER 27

Sleep had been slow to arrive that night as I pondered my options. I could attempt to steal Doc's phone, but I didn't know where he kept it. And I doubted I could find it simply by sneaking into his room and looking around. It had to be well hidden—that's why he still had it.

Did I try to follow him around and hope he tipped off his hiding place somehow? Possibly.

Did I use my can bounty and try to buy the phone from Doc? Again, possible.

Except either of those solutions ran into the same problem: If he had successfully snuck in one phone—and found a good hiding spot for it—there was every reason to believe he could do it again. And then I'd be back in the same predicament.

All I could do, in the short term, was hope that the phone was stashed somewhere that he couldn't access immediately and pray Mitch wouldn't have a two A.M. epiphany about the name of the musical he and his wife had seen a decade earlier.

As for the long term? I was no nearer to any kind of idea by the next day after lunch. My plan had been to meander up toward the rec area in the hopes Mitch would be playing bocce, allowing me to use our newly established friendship as an excuse to let him teach me the rules.

Instead, I saw Doc, sitting on one of the benches that ringed the pond. Given that he and Mitch seemed to be best friends, it made sense to get friendly with him, too. So I changed direction, angling toward the pond.

He was staring down into that weirdly green water with his long legs stretched out in front of him. I stopped when I was five feet away. He still hadn't moved or acknowledged my presence, so I said, "Mind if I join you?"

He looked up, genuinely bewildered, like he hadn't been aware there was another human being on the planet, much less one who was close enough to reach out and touch him.

"Oh hey, yeah," he said.

I sat on the other end of his bench and nodded toward the viridescent surface in front of us. "You thinking about buying some waterfront property?" I asked. "I hear it gets crowded during tourist season, but May and September make it all worthwhile."

He smiled, though it was one of those sad, prison smiles.

"No, just thinking about the vagaries of life," he said, sighing.

"Like what?"

"Like how one day you're an internist, running a thriving little family practice, and then one thing leads to another and you're suddenly at a federal prison."

"Oh, so you really are a doctor?" I asked.

"I was," he said. "Then one of my nurses guessed my computer password and started forging prescriptions for painkillers. I was running one of the most notorious pill mills in the entire state of Delaware and I didn't even know it until the DEA showed up at my door with a warrant one day."

"Why didn't they send the nurse to prison?"

"Because I couldn't prove it," he said. "If I had been auditing my own prescriptions like I was supposed to, I would have caught it and I could have approached the authorities with, 'Hey, something isn't right here.' But when they caught it first, I lost any benefit of the doubt. By the time I figured out what was really going on, it was way too late. I had already been indicted, and at that point I sounded like just another crooked doctor, blaming everything on my nurse. They laid everything out and told me I'd get ten years if it went to trial, then offered me eighteen months if I took a deal. My lawyer told me I'd be a fool not to take it."

"Man, that's rough," I said. "How much time you got left?"

"Ten months. I know to some guys around here, that's nothing. But there are times when I swear I can't remember my life before I came here, and I can't picture what it'll be when I get out. It's like this is all there is."

"I know what you mean. I've only been here a week and a half and it already feels like a year. Morgantown is like a time warp."

"Mmm," he said in a way that sounded like agreement. "So what's your story?"

I didn't hesitate: "Robbed a bank."

"You don't seem like the type."

"Didn't think I was the type either. I was just a teacher, struggling along like everyone. We were living paycheck to paycheck, but we were getting by. Then my wife got injured on the job and still somehow didn't qualify for disability, so we started having to skip payments. The next thing I knew we were three months behind. I went to the bank and saw the residential loan guy, Mr. Solomon, and asked him to restructure the loan or accept interest-only payments for a while or something. I said, 'Mr. Solomon, please, I'm begging you here. I'm working three jobs to try to feed my kids and keep up with these payments.' And you know what he did?"

I balled my fist before continuing: "He plugged everything into a formula the bank developed. And he said, 'Sorry, you don't have enough equity in your home to qualify for that. We have to foreclose.' I'm sitting there in front of him, a man with his hat in his hand and tears in his eyes, working myself to the bone for that damn bank. And he's looking at me like I'm nothing. Nothing but a number to put into a damn computer. And after that I just . . . I snapped. I was barely sleeping, and I lost my mind. I thought robbing that bank would solve all my problems and get me a measure of revenge to boot. Obviously, it didn't work out too well."

Even as I kept my head down, appropriately forlorn, I was thrilled with myself. A seasoned actor knows how to read his audience, and Doc was hanging on every word. Pete Goodrich had totally nailed that soliloquy.

"This was how long ago?" he asked.

"'Bout four months ago. I was like you: They had me dead to rights, so I took a deal."

"You still hurting for money?"

Where was he going with this? I wondered. But I sighed and said, "Oh yeah."

"Then explain something to me."

"What's that?"

He looked directly at me for the first time. "Why did you throw the game last night?"

I sat very still for a moment, my mind devoid of cagey responses. All I could think was to play dumb.

"What are you talking about?"

"When I got back to my room, I looked at the cards you slid under the deck. I know that's not good etiquette, but I wanted to know who I was playing with. You had pocket kings."

"Did I?"

"Don't try the innocent act with me. You had full-boat kings over queens. That pot was yours. Why didn't you take it?"

Without meaning to, I squirmed in my seat, which had grown both harder and hotter.

Doc wasn't letting it go. "What are you playing at, Pete?"

"I don't know," I said at last. "Guess I worried if I won the first time, you guys wouldn't want me back and I . . . I need some friends in here. I had this game on the outside with a . . . a few teachers and . . . Playing with you guys just brought me back to that. For a little while last night, I wasn't a convicted bank robber anymore. I was just a guy playing cards, and I liked it, that's all."

He was studying me carefully the whole time, and he didn't stop when I was through. Miserably, I added, "It was only a few cans."

"Yeah, I guess," he said.

And then he gathered his long legs underneath him and stood up.

"But if you ask me, a guy who's broke wouldn't go throwing away a perfectly good poker pot."

H e walked away, leaving me with the pond to myself.

It was a stretch to say Doc was onto me. But I had this feeling he'd be watching me closely now. That alone made him a threat. The cell phone made him even more of one.

It was time to eliminate all those threats. And in one flash of inspiration, I already knew there was one sure way to do it.

Snitch.

The moment the thought occurred to me, I immediately recoiled at myself, which speaks to how thoroughly I had embraced the role of inmate. I had to remind myself that, thinking like a law-abiding citizen for a change, it actually was quite illegal for Doc to have a cell phone; and that, by snitching, I was furthering the public good.

No, the only real quandary here wasn't the moral, should-I-or-shouldn't-I issue. It was how to do it without getting caught. From what I had seen, Danny was right: Morgantown wasn't a snitches-get-stitches kind of joint. But I would still be socially ostracized if anyone figured out what I had done. I'd be booted out of the poker game for sure, whether I paid off Bobby Harrison or not. And my chances of befriending Mitch would be shot, too. I'd be serving out the remainder of my six months with no chance of success.

The most direct method of snitching would be to go through the unit manager, Mr. Munn.

Except I could easily envision Munn going straight to Doc's room and attacking it like it was a pretend Guadalcanal machine-gun nest. I worried Mitch would know that (a) he had slipped up and mentioned Doc's phone, (b) Doc's room had been raided, and (c) I was the new guy looking to get in good with my unit manager. It would be too easy to put *a*, *b*, and *c* together.

I sat on that bench, tossing around other possibilities in my mind. Then Karen Lembo walked across my sightline.

She wasn't coming to see me. She was just crossing the middle of campus, on her way to another special snowflake in need of motherly love.

But it was all the prodding I needed. Mrs. Lembo was the perfect emissary for my snitching. There was nothing that tied the two of us together. And—unlike a socially inept, heart-disease-prone World War II reenactor—she would be prudent with the information.

I lifted myself off the bench and walked toward her office, which was in the education building, a safe space. I wasn't creating any rumors by going there.

There was a secretary in the office suite when I entered. With a friendly smile, I borrowed a pen and a piece of paper and wrote in neat block letters:

> JIM MADIGAN HAS A CELL PHONE. BUT PLEASE BE
> SMART ABOUT HOW YOU GO AFTER IT. I DON'T WANT
> ANYONE TO KNOW SOMEONE SNITCHED ON HIM.

Folding it once, I handed it to the secretary, who promised she'd make sure the note got to Mrs. Lembo. Then I walked out, headed back toward Randolph.

I shoved my hands in my pockets and began whistling, like a man without a care in the world, all the while lobbing prayers into the universe.

CHAPTER 28

Over the past few weeks, Amanda had come to dread 4:09 P.M. Or sometimes 4:07. Or sometimes 4:13.

That was when Barb, who worked from seven thirty A.M. to four P.M. each day, got home from work, usually full of pep and sass from a long and energizing day of extroverting. She would then scrutinize her future daughter-in-law for flecks of paint on her hands or sniff the air for turpentine.

Then, already knowing the answer, she'd ask the same blasted question.

Did you paint today?

And, no, she hadn't. At least not anything worth keeping. The truth was, she didn't even try to paint most days. And on days when she did? Goop. Slop. Muck. College Pro Painters could have done better.

This day, like so many recently, had been another one of Those Days. And when Barb arrived home at 4:10 P.M., Amanda was on the couch, cozied up with *Mansfield Park*, because lately she much preferred the early nineteenth century to the early twenty-first.

Barb took one look at her and didn't even bother asking the question. Instead she said, "Okay, that's enough."

Amanda looked up.

"You're not moping around here anymore," Barb announced.

"You miss Tommy. I know. I miss him too. But guess what? He's gone for a little while longer. You can't just spend all day in the house. You're an artist. You need to be creating. It's in your blood. But you can't put anything out if nothing is coming in. I get that. Art's not so different from comedy, you know. So you're going out tonight."

"Excuse me?" Amanda said, purely horrified.

"I said you're going out. Tommy has a friend, Brock DeAngelis. Lovely boy. He did all the musicals at Hackensack, so he and Tommy became buddies. Brock was always the leading man. I'm telling you, he should have been on a soap opera by now. He certainly had the looks for it. And the name. Brock DeAngelis. Is that a soap opera name or what? Anyhow, I'm going to call him up, and he's taking you out. It's not natural, a young woman like you, just staying around the house all the time."

"Barb, that's very nice, but I—"

"Yeah, yeah. That's enough out of you. If I wanted your opinion I would have given it to you. Get in the shower. Get a dress on. You're going out."

Amanda didn't move. Barb walked up to her, removed the book from her lap, and pulled her up with both hands.

"Let's go. You're getting in the shower, young lady. If you don't go by yourself, I'm getting in there with you. And, believe me, you don't want to see what you're going to look like thirty years from now. I could practically wear my boobs as a belt. Now go."

With that image searing her brain, Amanda stumbled off toward the shower. She washed herself, took extra time blow-drying her hair. As a kind of reflex, she added a dab of perfume behind each ear. Then she put on her face, as her Mississippi-born mother liked to say, and donned a dress, as Barb had ordered.

She studied herself in the mirror. Fine. Good enough. Whatever. This whole thing was ridiculous. She didn't want to go anywhere. Except maybe to a place where Barb wasn't riding her like a sad county-fair pony.

Perhaps an hour later, the doorbell rang. Amanda was back to her Jane Austen, without harassment this time, and Barb answered the door. Amanda finished the paragraph she was reading, then looked up.

What filled her vision was a solidly constructed young man whose upper parts were somewhere in that stratosphere above six feet. His shoulders extended out from his neck for a considerable distance. His skin had a hint of olive. His hair was dark and just long enough that it got a little kinky at the ends.

He was wearing a blazer, jeans, a white button-down shirt, and a contrite smile.

"Hi, I'm Brock," he said, his hands shoved in his pockets.

"Yeah, yeah, yeah, move it out, you two," Barb said. "I feel a hot flash coming on. Get lost so I can strip."

Neither needed further motivation. They were soon out the door.

"Sorry about Barb," Amanda began as they descended the front steps. "She's a little—"

"If you start apologizing for Ms. Jump, we're going to be here all night. I learned a long time ago it's better to just go along with whatever she says."

He opened the passenger-side door of his Mini Cooper for Amanda, and soon they were off. Brock recounted his friendship with Tommy. They ran with the same crowd, the basically good kids who were all going somewhere and doing something with their lives, even if their high school ideas about what those things were now struck him as comical.

"Tommy was the only one who really knew what he wanted," Brock said. "What's he up to these days, anyway? Ms. Jump just said he was out of town."

Amanda delivered the lie she and Barb had manufactured for everyone in Hackensack: Tommy was with a national touring company doing *Mamma Mia!* and wouldn't be back until April. They kept the story consistent because Barb, of all people, knew how the gossip went.

Brock accepted it without question. Before long, they were in

Tenafly, an upscale suburb, and he was escorting her into a restaurant called Axia, a place with swank to spare. There was a fireplace going; live guitar music, soft and unobtrusive. They were greeted warmly by a maître d', who knew Brock's name, and then escorted them to a corner table.

The menu was Greek. Brock ordered without looking at it. Amanda concentrated on selecting something that would neither harm her fetus nor make her throw up.

They kept talking. Yes, he had done some acting in high school. But Barb was barking mad if she thought he was going to make a career out of it. His family owned DeAngelis Jewelers. His father, Angelo DeAngelis, was a classic immigrant success story, having come to America with nothing more than a work ethic and his skills with precious metals. He had started with one store that then became two, then three. It had since turned it into a thriving chain across New Jersey, New York, and Connecticut.

Brock's mother, Mrs. DeAngelis No. 3, was a former fashion model who gave Brock his long limbs and some important portion of her striking good looks. Brock's half siblings—there were four of them— had no interest in the family business. That left Brock to take over for his aging father. The younger DeAngelis was now more or less running the show. He traveled to Europe and Africa half a dozen times a year to make buys.

They shifted to talking about art next. He was surprisingly literate on the subject but also deferential to her expertise.

Before she knew it, she was enjoying herself for the first time since Tommy had gone to prison. His incarceration was this fog that Brock cleared without even being aware of it. She was free to laugh, which she never felt like she could do around Barb, whose son was in prison. She didn't realize how much she missed being able to be twenty-seven and—at least for a little while—frivolous again. Things didn't have to matter quite so much.

They could talk about their shared affinity for Olivia Newton-

John. Or how they were quietly mortified by people who described things as being "very unique." Or how they hated roller coasters with the white-hot passion of a thousand exploded suns and truly did not understand people who enjoyed the sickening lurch of having the bottom drop out from underneath them.

They even shared a birth month and, very nearly, a birthday. He was November 9. She was November 11.

After he insisted on paying for dinner—"It's *seriously* no big deal," he said—she was quite sure they were done for the evening. Then he proposed they go out dancing. It was Thursday, the *perfect* night for dancing, he insisted, because it wouldn't be too crowded, and there wouldn't be too many drunks out. And he knew just the place. They danced until their legs ached, laughing and talking and generally having a fantastic time.

During the slow songs he danced with her too. But there was nothing indecorous about it, no below-the-waist involvement. It was just dancing.

By the time he dropped her off, it was past midnight.

"I haven't had fun like this in ages," he said. "Let's do this again soon."

CHAPTER 29

The noise and the lights came simultaneously, assaulting more than just the senses ordinarily assigned to them. The lights tasted like battery acid. The noise felt like a blow to the head.

It was early, though I couldn't guess the time. I just knew one moment I had been in the trenches of a deep and edifying sleep, and the next moment Randolph was under attack by an army of corrections officers.

They came into our wing, shouting orders, aiming for shock and awe and, from my standpoint, achieving it quite fully. Even as someone who theoretically should have been expecting some kind of offensive—since it was my snitching that generated it—I was completely disoriented.

"Everyone out, everyone out, everyone out," I heard from the common area.

"What's . . . what's going on?" I asked. Under the circumstances, I didn't have to get into character to act confused.

"Inspection, sir," Frank said, struggling to extract his bulk from the bottom bunk.

Before I had done much more than prop myself up in bed, a corrections officer I didn't recognize—meaning he wasn't normally assigned to Randolph—burst into our room.

"Let's go, you two. Out, out," he barked.

Frank was already on his feet, walking toward the door. The CO stomped toward me so aggressively I thought he was going to hit me.

"All right, inmate, you got a point," he said, grabbing the bed frame and shaking it. "You want more? Keep lying there."

With my motivation now in less need of assistance, I swung my legs around and dropped to the floor. Soon, I was out in the common area with the other men, all of us bedraggled and grumpy. A CO ordered me not to talk and to place my hands, palms down, on the mattress of one of the empty beds in the middle of the room.

From the shouts down the hallway, I could tell a similar scene was transpiring in the other two wings as well. The coordination was impressive, even ruthless; a consonance of action well beyond what I had so far seen from FCI Morgantown personnel.

I knew I had nothing to worry about. My contraband was safe, well off-dorm. I was still scared stupid.

Then I realized that was half the point. They wanted us to feel terrorized. This was our forceful reminder that we were not free men; that they could do this at any time they wanted, whether we liked it or not; that they were in control, not us.

I looked around the room. The men who weren't scared like me were straight-up pissed off. There was a lot of under-the-breath grumbling, most of it profane descriptions of the COs' sexual preferences. Still, everyone kept their hands on the beds. That was the other point of the shock-and-awe routine: to convince us resistance was futile.

It took about a minute to remember the raid was actually a positive turn of events for me. Mrs. Lembo had done well. A dorm-wide inspection—with no specific room or wing being targeted—would undoubtedly prompt speculation about what had triggered it. But there would be as many theories as there were men in Randolph.

Once we were all accounted for in the middle of the room, the COs plowed through the rooms one by one, in teams of two. Some of the teams were decent about it, showing a modicum of respect for our belongings. Others were almost gleefully malicious.

When contraband was discovered, they would shout out the item, document it, then toss it in a large black plastic garbage bag. There were times they'd speculate how many points an inmate might be receiving when it came time to mete out discipline.

Most of what was being stumbled upon was innocent. Food that had been stolen from the kitchen. Chewing gum, which wasn't sold in the commissary and therefore wasn't allowed. A pair of pliers purloined from a work crew. That sort of thing.

When the team hit our room, it wasn't long before I heard, "Got some Slim Jims here!"

Frank's face fell. I couldn't see where they had found his treasure, but the disposal of it happened within our view: Frank's precious Slim Jims, thrown in the trash.

I wondered how the inspection was going over in Doc's wing. All throughout the poker game that previous night, he hadn't made mention of our pondside conversation, nor of his suspicions about me. At least he couldn't accuse me of throwing the game: Jerry had gotten all the cards from start to finish, cleaning us out in relatively short order.

The only big find on our wing came out of one of the corner rooms about fifteen minutes later, when one of the COs was suddenly crowing, "Suboxone, I got Suboxone!"

I had heard about this stuff. It was an opioid that came in paper-thin sheets, allowing you to hide it pretty much anywhere. And it was powerful. Even a tiny little piece could keep you high for hours.

The COs had determined that this particular sample had belonged to an inmate named Murphy, and they were saying things like, "Murphy's heading to the SHU now. Think he'll get one month or two?"

Having chatted with Murphy a few times, I felt a twinge of guilt. He was a nice enough guy from Philly who had told me about his plan to turn his life around when he got out. He had a baby daughter he hadn't met yet, which had made me think about Amanda and our baby, whom I looked forward to meeting on delivery day.

"Tough break, Murph," I said softly.

"No talking, inmate," barked the CO who had already given me a point.

I glared back at him. In my mind, it was a defiant gesture. Although I did keep my mouth shut from there on out.

Maybe ten tense minutes later, the teams had completed their sweep and I thought we were going to be sent back into our rooms to clean up the mess they had made.

Instead, that's when they brought in the dog.

It was the dog, a German shepherd mix, that proved to be Doc's undoing.

I got this all during and after breakfast from Masri, who was in Doc's wing and watched everything up close. I had assumed the dog—one of the COs said he had been brought in from Allenwood—was for drug detection. But he had been trained to sniff out cell phone batteries, and his nose was sharp enough to smell them through concrete.

Which is where he found Doc's phone. In the wall. Apparently, Doc had worked free the edges of one of the blocks in his room. With enough wiggling, he could slide it out, like a cabinet drawer, and store things inside.

When he was done, he'd shove it back in place, then artfully seal the cracks with toothpaste, which blended nicely into the whitewash paint. When he wanted to access it again, he'd just clean away the toothpaste with water.

Inside Doc's little stash box, the COs found several bags of pills, three jars of clean urine—which he had been using to beat drug tests—and the phone. It was current generation, and it contained ample evidence that not only was Doc using it to smuggle pills inside Morgantown, but he had been continuing his pill-mill operation on the outside, hooking up his old customers with a new doctor who had taken over the prescribing.

I thought about Doc's tale of woe, about the alleged nurse who did him wrong, and wondered if any of it was true. Gilmartin's admonishment—*everything your fellow inmates tell you will likely be a lie*—had seemed so cynical. But I guess there was something to be said for the instincts of an FBI agent who had spent a career listening to criminals prevaricate.

Masri said Doc cried when they led him out. He wasn't heading for the SHU. He was going from Club Fed to hell: a high-security facility out in Indiana. There, he would serve out the rest of his sentence and whatever else they were going to tack on for this new offense—which would no doubt be substantial, now that he was a two-time loser.

And whereas I had felt bad for Murphy, I didn't feel any regret about Doc.

Murphy was a guy with a problem. Doc *was* the problem.

As the day unfolded, there was a lot of buzz about what had triggered the raid. But Karen Lembo had brilliantly covered for me there, too. Word soon got out that a BOP muckety-muck—a regional director or something like that—was scheduled to be visiting Morgantown. The brass had wanted to show him Randolph, which therefore had to be squeaky-clean.

Whether this was true or a rumor Mrs. Lembo had skillfully planted, I couldn't say. I just knew I was safe.

This allowed me to move onto more pressing matters. Like the new opening in the Randolph poker game.

During laundry duty, I found Bobby Harrison and laid everything out for him: He had lied to me with the five-can buy-in thing and was therefore screwing me over with the ten-can payment, but I would forgive him, and continue the payments—ten cans a week, not ten a day—if he would come to the game that night and recommend I take Doc's place.

After some negotiation, he agreed. We both knew he was getting a fine deal.

That was the first of two financial arrangements I made that day.

The second came after lunch. Doc's departure hadn't just cleared a place at the poker table. It had also opened up the job of Mitch Dupree's best friend at Morgantown. And I was determined to start filling that void—with a little help from my massive (and massively intimidating) roommate.

Nothing cemented a friendship faster than facing adversity together and finding out you had each other's backs. And, with the proper motivation, Frank Thacker was adversity personified.

I was sitting on top of my bunk when he came into our room.

"Hey, Frank," I said.

"Sir," he replied. I was starting to think Frank didn't actually know my name.

"Sorry about the Slim Jims."

"Not your fault. I shoulda hid them better."

"You going to get in trouble?"

"They gave me a point, sir," he said morosely. "First I've gotten since I come to Morgantown."

"Aw, man, that's terrible," I said. "You going to be able to get more?"

"Suppose I could. There's a man who will sell them to me. 'Cept I don't got no cans right now."

Perfect.

"What if I told you there was a way you could earn some by doing me a favor?"

"What kind of favor?"

"Do you know Mitch Dupree?"

The name didn't appear to mean anything to him, but he said, "Yes, sir. I think I do."

"I want you to pick a fight with him."

Frank's expression shifted a little. He had probably been the biggest kid in his neighborhood, and nothing had changed since. A man his size didn't need to fight, and he certainly didn't go looking for one.

"Ain't got no quarrel with Dupree," he said.

"I know you don't. Doesn't matter. He'll be playing poker with me tonight at seven o'clock in the card room. Give us about thirty minutes to get going, then come in and accuse him of being the snitch. Say you heard he's the reason we had that raid, and you're pissed off because you lost your Slim Jims, and now you're going to make him pay."

He was already shaking his head. "Already got one point today. Don't want to get another for fighting."

"You won't. I'll come to Dupree's defense, and you'll back down. I'm trying to get into that poker game full-time, and I want him to feel like I've done him a solid. You just have to scare him a little. The card room is all the way down at the end. The COs almost never go in there. It'll be over so quickly, they'll never even know about it."

Then I got to the interesting part of the proposition: "And I'll pay you twenty cans."

The entirety of his huge forehead lifted in surprise. "Twenty cans?"

"Yes, sir," I said, giving him a dose of "sir" for a change. "You have to make it good, though. Make him think he's going to get his ass kicked."

"Okay," he said, before his crazy roommate could change his mind. "Twenty cans."

CHAPTER 30

The first part of my plan went perfectly.

Bobby showed up, followed by Mitch and Jerry. We shared some somber reflections about Doc, gone but not forgotten. All three knew about the cell phone, of course. They professed total ignorance about the pills, the pee, and the rest of the things that seemed so at odds with the cheerful, kind, affable guy we knew.

"Guess you never know what a man's really doing with himself when you're not around to see it," Jerry opined.

No, Jerry, you sure don't. . . .

Once we had eulogized Doc to what felt like an appropriate degree, we moved onto the business of the game. Just like I had paid him to do, Bobby proposed me as Doc's permanent replacement. Actually, he laid it out like it was a foregone conclusion. Mitch and Jerry acceded to it with polite murmurs. Ultimately, my cans would spend as well as anyone else's.

Then we started playing. As in the first two nights, my only real goals were to stay in the game as long as possible and to continue neighborly relations with Mitch. When I lost, I did so good-naturedly. When I won, I did so without gloating.

I was in the midst of trying to draw an inside straight—odds of success: roughly one in thirteen, but what the hell—when Frank rounded the corner and entered the card room. His proportions were such that he changed the air pressure when he entered a room. Even Bobby, no dainty flower, glanced Frank's way.

Frank lumbered over to Mitch, who was on the other side of the table from me, and loomed above him.

Well above him.

"I got a problem with you, Mr. Dupree," Frank said.

The words themselves were not especially intimidating, particularly with the courteous title thrown in. And, speaking strictly as a thespian, his inflection was a little flat. But being as it came from a mouth surrounded by 350 pounds, it was effective enough.

"And what's that?" Mitch asked. He was trying not to show fear, but his already high voice had climbed another half an octave, bringing it into alto territory.

"I'm hearing you a snitch," Frank said. "That inspection was because of you."

Jerry and I put our cards down on the table. Mitch was still clutching his. Bobby sat up like a rod had been inserted into his back. These were fighting words, except no sane non-colossus would take on Frank.

"Well, now, people hear all kinds of things," Mitch said. "That doesn't make them true."

"Lost my Slim Jims because of you," Frank continued.

"I'm sorry to hear that. But I had nothing to do with it. I lost a pair of socks my missus knit for me. Why would I bring that on myself?"

Bobby interjected: "Yeah, didn't you hear? The inspection was just because there's some kind of big cheese from the BOP coming in."

"Don't know when I'm going to get Slim Jims again," Frank said, ignoring them both. "They was a special occasion. Afraid I'm going to have to beat you up now."

Again, Frank's delivery left a lot to be desired. And, again, it didn't matter.

"Now what's that going to solve?" Mitch asked.

"Make me feel better about losing my Slim Jims," Frank said.

"I didn't have anything to do with you losing your—"

Frank interrupted whatever Mitch was about to say by grabbing his neck. I sprang to my feet, rounding the table, ready to begin my intervention.

"I could tear your throat out right now," Frank growled. "That way you couldn't snitch no more."

Mitch's eyes flared with fear. Frank leaned into him a little, increasing the pressure. The other guys at the table were simply frozen. Only in action movies do people react to unexpected conflict with instant heroism. In real life, they need a little time to figure out what's even happening.

"Okay, that's enough, Frank," I said in a stentorian voice.

But Frank wasn't paying me any attention. His hubcap-size hand was covering the entire front of Mitch's fleshy neck, with the thumb and fingers wrapping around to the back.

"Don't like no snitch," he said, with his teeth bared.

This time it actually was theatrically convincing. But I had this sudden fear he wasn't acting. It was like I was seeing a different side to Frank, a savage side that was only coming out now that he quite literally held a man's life in his huge hand. Morgantown was supposed to be reserved for nonviolent offenders, but had Frank slipped through the cracks somehow?

I spoke with renewed force: "I said that's enough, Frank. Knock it off."

Mitch wasn't speaking. It wasn't clear to me if that was from fear or from being physically incapable of getting air into his lungs.

Whatever the case, this had gone on long enough.

"Stop it!" I said. "Now!"

I pushed Frank with both hands. He didn't budge.

"They gave me a point," Frank said. "Never got no points before."

Mitch was clutching at Frank's hand, trying desperately to rip it off. His efforts to move Frank were as successful as mine.

This had to end. Immediately. But I couldn't even seem to get

Frank's attention, much less stop his behavior. Not knowing what else to do, I gathered my legs underneath me and, with every bit of strength I could summon, launched myself into Frank's midsection.

This finally staggered him. A little. He took two steps backward, releasing his grip in the process.

Mitch gasped for air.

"I'm no snitch," he choked out. "What's wrong with you?"

I wished he'd shut his face. If Frank—in whatever state of mind he now found himself—decided he was going to finish this job and crush Mitch's windpipe once and for all, there was nothing I could do to stop him.

Yet somehow I was able to use the momentum I had gathered to keep herding him out of the room. It took all my might, because Frank was battling against me. But my lower center of gravity kept him off-balance.

Then, once we were out of sight of the poker table, Frank grabbed both my shoulders and set me upright, like he was playing with a particularly animated doll.

I was still so wound up I thought this was just the next round. Then I looked at his face. He was smiling at me. Gentle Frank had returned. Maybe he had never really left. I bent over and put my hands on my knees.

"Good God, Frank. I was worried about you there for a second," I said, still breathing heavily from the effort I had just expended.

He wasn't even winded. "Just wanted to make sure you got your money's worth, sir."

W hen I returned to the game, the guys were already in the midst of convincing Mitch the incident wasn't worth reporting. Fights were rare at Morgantown, and unless there was physical evidence—a bruise, a cut, something like that—the administration wasn't likely to pursue discipline.

Bobby also proposed, and I seconded, the notion that telling a CO would only reinforce Frank's strange assumption that Mitch had been the snitch. Better to de-escalate the situation, leave it be, and hope Big Frank forgot about his suspicions.

"He's my roommate," I said. "I'll talk to him later. I think I can get this whole thing to blow over. He trusts me."

"All right, all right," Jerry said. "Can we play cards now?"

At that point everyone else folded. Only a guy sitting on trip jacks was that eager to get back to the game.

The incident wasn't mentioned the rest of the evening. And I thought it had been only a moderate success—worth the twenty cans, but ultimately just another small step in my journey—until the next morning on the way to breakfast.

It was one of those misty mountain mornings, with a late-fall chill in the air. I had my hands shoved in my pockets and was hurrying toward the dining hall when I heard Mitch's voice from behind me.

"Hey, Pete," he said. "Wait up a second."

I turned to see Mitch double-timing. I stopped on the side of the path and resumed walking only when he had caught up to me.

"I owe you an apology," he said. "I was so shaken up last night, I realized later I never thanked you for saving my ass."

"Oh, no big deal, really."

"Hell it wasn't. That guy—Frank is his name? That's one big son of a bitch right there. It was pretty brave of you to throw yourself at him. No way I'd have the stones to do something like that."

I just gave him a modest little shrug. "Big guys never expect a little guy is going to go after them. And when you do, they think you must be nuts, so they back off pretty fast. How you feeling this morning?"

"I'm okay," he said, rubbing his neck. "A little sore, but it could have been worse. I got the sense from the way he was squeezing that he wasn't even trying that hard. Don't want to know what he could do if he really put his mind to it."

He looked appropriately haunted.

"I wouldn't worry too much about that," I said. "I talked to him last night and convinced him you had nothing to do with the inspection. Then I told him if he wanted to get to Mr. Dupree, he was going to have to go through me first. That scared him off good."

I smiled. Mitch laughed and clapped me on the shoulder. Just like good buddies do.

"Well, I thought about it, and I wanted to give you a little thank-you," he said. "Can you meet me in the card room at one o'clock?"

"Let me consult my calendar. Oh, I happen to have an opening then, yes."

"Good," he said, then added, "Come hungry."

Three minutes before the appointed hour, I walked into the empty Randolph card room and took a seat at our regular table.

Mitch wasn't there, nor did he show up at one o'clock, nor at five after. I hung out anyway. It wasn't like I had pressing engagements elsewhere.

Finally, at about ten after one, he came hurrying around the corner.

"Sorry I'm late," he said. "A damn CO came into the kitchen and wouldn't leave, so I had to wait before I could sneak out with this."

He unzipped his jacket and pulled out a rectangular silver-colored tin, then slid the lid off and set it in front of me. There was parchment paper on top. But my nose told me what was inside before my eyes did.

Freshly baked chocolate chip cookies.

I lifted the paper to reveal the bounty. There were six of them, baked to a perfect golden brown. The chocolate glistened, still gooey from the oven. My mouth flooded with saliva.

It wasn't that the food at Morgantown was bad. It was edible enough. But this? I breathed in the delectable odor again and may have moaned a little.

"We cooked up a batch for that VIP who's coming in," Mitch said. "Wouldn't you know a few just wouldn't fit on the platter they asked for? One of the guys in the kitchen worked in a bakery as a kid. He won't share the recipe, but it's pretty dynamite."

I was about to dive in. And then I remembered I wasn't Tommy Jump.

I was Pete Goodrich, who was torn up from being away from his family, just like Mitch; Pete Goodrich, a husband and father whose greatest ambition in life had been to make a happy home for his wife and children; Pete Goodrich, who missed the simple pleasures of life on the outside, pleasures he wouldn't get to experience for another eight long years.

Pleasures like chocolate chip cookies.

I can cry on command. Most experienced actors can. In a perfect world, when you cry onstage you're doing so because you've become enmeshed in the character you're playing and alive in the world being created. Depending on how good the writing is, I can *sometimes* summon that kind of emotion for a part.

And maybe Meryl Streep can do that all the time. As for the rest of us? Summoning tears eight times a week can require a little method acting.

So call me a hack, but I had a pet hamster, Mudpie, who was my best little buddy for four years before he went off to that big running wheel in the sky. I was nine, and it was my first experience of death. I cried for an entire day.

And even now, when I think about poor little Mudpie . . .

"Sorry," I said, the tears already starting to roll down my cheeks.

"You okay?" Mitch said, alarmed. "You're not allergic to chocolate, are you?"

"No, no. I just . . . my wife, Kelly, she used to make me chocolate chip cookies for my birthday. She'd serve them to me all warm like this. And I . . . You know, you try to just hunker down and forget everything and get into the routine around here, and most of the time I can do it. But then . . . Sometimes, it's the little things, you know?"

I dabbed my sleeves against my face.

"I'm so sorry," Mitch said. "We've all been there, friend. I keep hearing about how much better this place is than real prison. But it's still prison."

"Damn right," I said, making a show of trying to compose myself.

Then, like I was embarrassed about having wept and was trying to deflect attention from myself, I said, "So what about you? What's the thing you miss the most?"

"You mean besides the obvious?" he said with a grin.

"Yeah, besides that."

He got a faraway look. "This is going to sound strange, but I miss, just, driving somewhere with my family."

"Driving."

"Yeah. Having the four of us together in the car. Maybe we're planning to stop somewhere along the way and grab a meal. Maybe we're traveling late at night, trying to get somewhere for the holidays. It didn't really matter. There was just something about it. You know everyone's okay, because they're right there. You could reach out and touch them if you wanted to. You have kids?"

"Three of them," I said reflexively.

"Yeah, so you know. You spend so much of your time as a family being pulled in this direction or that. One person's over there and another person's over there and you're always worried about what might be happening to them, or worried they might be worried about you, or I don't know. When you're not with each other, a part of you is in the wrong place. But then finally you're in the car, and you're all going somewhere together so you know you're where you're supposed to be. It's like you're this perfect little unit and nothing in the whole world can stop you."

I took in a deep breath and let it go. I was thinking about Amanda and the family she was growing, projecting to the life we would soon have.

"Yeah, I know what you mean," I said. "Mine are little, five, three, and one, so—"

"So even getting them in the car is a triumph. I remember those years."

"Well, right," I said. "But once they're all in? And you get them all buckled? And then you get on the way, and you turn the heat up a little, and you get some soft music playing, and they all fall asleep?"

"Ohhh. Best feeling ever."

"You know it."

And there we were, two dads sharing the small joys of fatherhood. Mitch touched the corners of his eyes with his palms, stopping tears I couldn't yet see, then gave his head a shake.

"Speaking of the best feeling ever," he said, "warm chocolate chip cookies have to rank in there somewhere, so let's dig in before they get cold, what do you say?"

"Great idea."

"Good man. Show me how it's done."

I reached into the tin and lifted out the one closest to me. It was heavy for its size, always a promising sign for a cookie—weight being a proxy for butter saturation. Then I slid it into my mouth and felt a minor explosion as the bitterness of the chocolate collided with the sweetness of the sugar.

"Oh my God," I gushed, my eyes closed.

"Not bad, huh?"

"Amazing."

He grabbed one. We chewed in silence, each of us savoring this small escape from the dreariness of incarceration. I might have been imagining it, but I swear Mitch was enjoying my delight as much as he was his own.

It was a rare trait to find in any man, much less one you had met in prison. And it was difficult to square the man contentedly munching cookies, talking about how much he loved family road trips, with a guy who could do the bidding of one of the most barbaric criminal syndicates on earth. I knew it was possible for both to coexist. Human beings are nothing if not complex monkeys.

Still, I had to admit—for whoever he was before he arrived here—I actually liked the Mitch Dupree who was now at FCI Morgantown. Which was nice.

One less thing I had to pretend.

CHAPTER 31

B rock texted two days later, on a Saturday morning. There was a
new Korean fusion restaurant in Fort Lee that was supposedly
out-of-this-world dynamite. Was Amanda free?

And, well, of course she was.

They didn't finish it off with dancing this time. He took her down
to a park in Edgewater, where they enjoyed a walk along the Hudson
River, gabbing as they took in the New York skyline.

On Sunday, he proposed they go to El Museo del Barrio in Har-
lem. Amanda was so happy to have something to do—and so enjoying Brock's company—she pretended like she hadn't already seen the
new exhibit there.

Before long, they were spending all kinds of time with each other.
It was one of those friendships that went from zero to besties in five
seconds flat, as sometimes happened when two people just clicked.

If it was a weekend, they'd plan a full day—breakfast at a bakery
in Wayne, followed by a stop at a gallery in the city, followed by a
drive up to an out-of-the-way restaurant in Connecticut that was reported to be a foodie paradise. Other times it was more spontaneous.
He had heard about a local band that was playing somewhere that
night. Or they'd go dancing. Or do karaoke. He couldn't make a
whole room swoon like Tommy, but he could hit enough high notes
that most pop songs were in his range.

They celebrated their birthdays together, turning it into a three-day extravaganza: November 9 was his birthday; November 11 was her birthday; and November 10 was what they called interbirthday, a day of joint merrymaking.

When they didn't go out, they'd stay in. She'd drive to his loft apartment and cook dinner with him. Or he'd come over to Barb's place and they'd watch a movie.

Or—and this was quickly becoming one of Amanda's favorite things to do—they'd go to his family's jewelry studio, which was seldom used after hours. It had all the equipment needed to create new pieces. Once Amanda mastered a few basic techniques, her artistic talents quickly took over. She worked exclusively with silver and cheap gems, even as Brock pushed her to toy around with more expensive materials. He even made noises about having DeAngelis Jewelers commission her to create custom pieces, perhaps even a line of them.

The Amanda Porter Collection. It had a nice sound to it.

And, sure, Brock's family thought they were together. So did Amanda's art friends, on the rare occasions when she and Brock would hang out with them in the city. They'd wait until Brock was out of the room, shoot her sly grins, and ask what was *really* going on with her and this tall, totally gorgeous guy.

Whatever. Amanda didn't let it bother her. She knew the truth: They were just friends.

Brock never acted like he was interested in anything else. He didn't make veiled passes at her or get handsy when he had been drinking. Sure, he'd sometimes kiss her on the cheek when they greeted each other. But only in the same way you'd kiss your favorite aunt. And he'd hug her when they said good-bye. But only in the same way you'd hug your sister.

Because not only were Brock and Amanda friends, Brock and *Tommy* were friends. Brock would never two-time his buddy like that.

Also, Brock knew she was pregnant. She had to explain why she never drank with him. And, the first trimester being what it was, she'd sometimes fall asleep fifteen minutes after they started watching television. She'd wake up three hours later to find Brock had draped a blanket over her.

Barb didn't seem to care when Amanda came home late from her time with Brock. Nor did she comment that Amanda was sleeping until eleven almost every day to make up for the late nights. Nor did she remark on the dearth of painting that was happening. Barb was giving Amanda space for a change.

And Tommy? When she—or, rather, "Kelly"—explained that she and Brock had started hanging out a lot, he said he was happy she was making a new friend, like it was no big deal at all.

Because it wasn't.

CHAPTER 32

For the next few weeks, in this place governed by routines, all I did was slip into a new, comfortable one—with Mitch Dupree at the center of it.

It was like some kind of weird buddy flick where everyone wore khaki. We played cards at night. During the afternoon, we'd wander out to the bocce court, or head to the gym, or find a movie on TV. We ate our meals together more often than we didn't.

Mitch seemed to enjoy mentoring me, so I allowed him to. If nothing else, it was improving my financial literacy. He also liked to tell stories, which worked for me, because I liked to listen to them. You never knew when he might spill some useful detail about, say, the best place to hide valuables. I even feigned interest when he talked about golf—and, believe me, there are few things less interesting than listening to a man talk about his struggles to conquer his putting yips.

Whatever he felt like discussing, I was there to listen. I was just good ol' Pete, the best pal any guy could want, having slid seamlessly into the void that Doc's departure had created. Mitch and Rob Masri were starting to become friends as well, which was convenient. We were one contented little prison family.

Meanwhile, my family outside prison was struggling. Amanda had proposed that we give up trying to talk every day, because that was leading to nothing but a string of short, futile conversations. Our new thing was that we have a weekly call every Friday afternoon, so we could have a longer, more meaningful dialogue.

Except that wasn't working either. We'd run through the usual topics—how my cousin Amanda was doing with the baby (fine), how her painting was going (poorly), what she was reading or what movie she and my high school buddy Brock DeAngelis had watched most recently (whatever)—and then we'd run out of steam. I could tell myself it was because we were worried about who was listening, now that I had both the Bureau of Prisons *and* the Federal Bureau of Investigation potentially eavesdropping on us. But the truth was, neither of us had much to say. There were these long pauses where I could practically feel us becoming more estranged.

I didn't share my concerns with Masri or anyone else, because I knew they would just tell me to get used to it—and that it would likely get worse. Morgantown was rife with stories of guys who had gone in with what they thought were solid relationships, only to become disabused of that notion.

Jerry Strother was one of them. He made a nasty, offhanded comment one night at poker about his wife. Only later did Mitch provide context. About three months after Jerry arrived, his wife rather unapologetically began cheating on him with his best friend. She told Jerry she had needs, and if she had to go elsewhere to meet them, it was his fault for getting locked up.

Amanda would never do that me. Still, there was no question that if being long-distance was our first true test, we were struggling along with a D-minus.

I was just coming out of another dissatisfying Friday afternoon call when I bumped into Mitch, coming back from the library for the three P.M. count with a stack of books under his arm.

"Damn," I said, nodding at his collection. "You leave any for the rest of us?"

"Just trying to keep my mind off what I'd normally be doing this weekend."

"What's that?" I asked, because my policy since we started becoming friends was that if Mitch ever opened the smallest conversational door, I was going to attempt to enter it.

And then he said something that made me instantly forget my struggles with Amanda.

"A hunting trip with some buddies."

A hunting trip. The words gave me a tingle. I may not have known much about hunting, but I did know hunters often hunted near their hunting cabins.

Their secluded, illicit-document-laden hunting cabins.

This was what I had been waiting more than a month for; what I had been wheeling and dealing and wheedling to arrange ever since I entered through that split-log fence at the front entrance: for Mitch to mention hunting in my presence.

Without sounding too overenthusiastic, I said, "Oh yeah?"

"Yeah, some college buddies and I went every year the weekend before Thanksgiving. We told our wives not to buy turkeys because we might get ourselves one. We drank a lot more Wild Turkey than we ever shot, but whatever. You a hunter?"

"Sure," I said. Then I modified it with, "A bit."

I did the so-so shake with my hand. I didn't want to overcommit, lest I get trapped into a detailed conversation about barrel-twist rates. The closest a kid from Hackensack, New Jersey, came to shooting anything was when we played *Big Buck Hunter* at the local arcade.

Still, West Virginia Pete would never be antihunting, so I added, "Less so after the kids were born. It just didn't seem fair to Kelly to leave her on a Saturday or Sunday morning when I had already been working all week."

"I hear you," he said.

"What kind of hunting did you do?" I asked, hoping that was the correct formulation of that question.

"Bowhunting. No offense to rifle hunters, but if you ask me, that's not really much of a sport. That's practically a trip to the grocery store. With the scopes they got, they can put down a deer at a hundred fifty, two hundred yards. Where's the sport in that? The animal doesn't even have a chance to know you're there. It's not fair."

Tommy Jump would have pointed out that hunting would never be truly fair until the animals got rifles, too.

"I hear you. Anyone can do this," I said, mimicking a trigger pull.

"Well, exactly. On the other hand, you get a bow with a fifty-pound draw on it, and you know you got to get within thirty yards to get a kill shot, and you better damn well be downwind, and if you so much as think too loud you know that deer is going to take off? Now you're talking *hunting*."

He got a dreamy, far-off look. "Last year when we went out, I was going out to one of my usual spots, making way too much noise, just checking out the property, when I caught sight of this big, mature buck, a twelve-pointer at least, biggest spread I ever saw. I usually don't go for bucks because we have a rule: You gotta eat what you shoot. A young doe tastes way better. But this guy, he was magnificent. I just had to have him. I'd battle my way through a tough venison steak if it meant having his head on my wall. And I swear when I first saw him, he turned, and he looked at me and he stared me down for a moment, like, 'Oh yeah? You think you can take *me* down? It's on.'

"Then he took off. I tracked him a little bit, and I got the sense of where he had been hanging out. There were some droppings I thought were his. I told the guys I was with, 'Okay, that one's mine.' The next morning, I was up at three A.M. I wanted to get up in a blind while he was still sleeping. So there I was, waiting for him, freezing my nuts off, because you got to stay real still if you're going to have a chance."

He set down the books so he could demonstrate the position he was in, as if the story wouldn't be complete without visuals.

"Well, two hours later, it's starting to get light, and along comes Mr. Buck. He's coming down the hill toward me. At that time of the morning, you're still getting cold air settling from the top of the hill down into the hollows, so he can't smell me yet. All I'm doing is waiting for him to get a little closer, a little closer, a little closer. He's so damn big, the last thing I want to do is try to take him from too far out, because if all I did was wound him, that'd be a damn shame for everyone involved. As I'm waiting, the sun is getting closer to the horizon and there's getting to be this orange glow coming over the next hill, and I know I'm running out of time, because he's going to bed down again soon. So I draw my bow and I get him lined up. I mean, I've got the most perfect shot of the most gorgeous buck I've ever seen."

He cocked his elbow and pulled back an imaginary bowstring while keeping his other arm straight.

"And then," he said, and I waited for him to narrate the bloody conclusion to this story.

But he just relaxed his arms.

"You didn't shoot?" I asked.

"I couldn't. That big boy had been out in those hills for a long time. He was probably a great-great-great-granddaddy, and I just thought, 'You know, he's been on one hell of a run.' I couldn't bring myself to end it for him. All I did was stand up in the blind and yell, 'Gotcha!' Just so he knew who had won."

"Ha!" I said.

"I swear, he looked up at me, like, 'Yeah, you got me.' And then he tore ass off through the brush. Just seeing him run made it all worth it. Magnificent."

"Did you ever see him again?"

"Nope. That was last year. Back then I would have told you I'd be out again this year looking for him. Never knew this was going to happen."

"Well, yeah," I said, again trying to be as casual as I could be. "You and your buddies go to the same place every year?"

"Uh-huh. I got a cabin up in Chattahoochee National Forest. Been in my family for a long time."

"Chattahoochee?" I said, now pouring on the enthusiasm. "Get out! My uncle has a place there. I used to go there as a kid. That's where I learned to hunt. My dad and I would go out with my uncle. He was a big bowhunter, just like you."

Because of course he was. Uncle . . . Burt.

Burt Goodrich. Bowhunter. Friend to all. Except deer.

"Huh, small world," Mitch said.

"Real small," I said. Then, ever so smoothly, I asked, "Where's your place, anyhow?"

"We're way in the eastern part. Up twenty-three, just past Tallu-lah Falls."

"Dang! That's where Uncle Burt's place is. We weren't but a few miles from Tallulah Falls."

"We're on the east side of twenty-three, maybe a mile or two as the crow flies from the Chattooga River. That's where they filmed *Deliverance,* you know. They called it the Cahulawassee in the movie, but everyone up there jokes about it. You see a stranger when you're out hunting, and you know one of your buddies is going to go, 'Squeal like a pig, squeal like a pig.'"

He chuckled at this. I wanted to get us away from discussions of classic movies and back into geography.

"Yeah, I think Uncle Burt was right off twenty-three," I said, like I was now traveling it in my mind's eye. "It's been a while, though. I can't remember the name of the road. I want to say it was a left turn. We'd be coming from up north, so we'd be traveling south."

"Was he north or south of Tallulah Falls?"

"North," I said, gambling. "What about you?"

"Same thing. Jeez, what are the chances?" he said, getting excited. "He's not on Camp Creek Road, is he?"

"No, that's not it," I said, because the last thing I needed was to get pinned down on the exact location of my fictional uncle's fictional cabin. I deflected the question back at him with: "That's where your place is?"

"Uh-huh," he said. "We'd be traveling north, so it was a right turn for us. Just past Tallulah Falls."

"Camp Creek Road," I said. "I feel like I've seen the sign. Are you directly on Camp Creek Road? I'll have to tell Uncle Burt. He goes down to his cabin all the time and he's always rambling around the back roads. Maybe he's passed your place?"

"I doubt it. We're one of the turns off Camp Creek Road, maybe a mile or so down. It's just a little dirt road, and it's got a PRIVATE PROPERTY sign, so people tend not to go down it unless they know it."

"If you want, I could tell Uncle Burt to check out your place, make sure it's holding up okay."

I held my breath, silently praying I'd hear, *Sure, that'd be nice. Let me give you the address.*

What I got was: "That's real kind of you. We got neighbors who check on it. There are only a few houses up our road, and we're all part-timers. We kind of all keep an eye on each other's places."

"Oh, yeah, sure," I said.

I didn't want to push my questioning—or my luck—too much further, lest it raise any alarm bells. This had to seem natural. I could always have "Uncle Burt," aka Danny Ruiz, just happen to be down that way, then ask more questions based on specific knowledge. I was only one month in. With five months to go, I could be patient.

So I lobbed out a breezy, "Sure is beautiful in those parts."

"God's country. We have five acres that back up against US Forest Service land, so you feel like you own the whole world."

"That sounds just like Uncle Burt's place," I said. "He's got this little stream running through it. We used to catch crawfish in there. Just heaven."

"Mmm. One of the first things I'm going to do when I get out of here is go back up there for a visit," he said. "Maybe you can come by if you're out too. I'll teach you to bowhunt for real."

"I'd like that," I said.

Then, as gracefully as I could, I extricated myself from the conversation.

I couldn't wait to get to a phone.

I didn't reach Danny on any of my first three attempts, but on the fourth he answered with a testy, "I'm in a meeting. Would you stop blowing up my phone?"

"This is worth ducking out of a meeting," I said.

"You better not just be calling me because you've gone through all that fish."

"No. But I do need a favor. A buddy of mine here needs someone to check in on his family's hunting cabin."

"Really?" he said, and from the way his voice was climbing the ladder, I knew he understood what I was really saying.

"Yeah. He's worried about it being empty now that he's here."

"I got you," Danny said. "What's the address?"

"It's not that simple. My buddy doesn't know the actual address. He said he always got there by feel. But based on what he told me about it, I think maybe you can find it."

Then I talked him through what I knew: Chattahoochee National Forest. North of Tallulah Falls. Off Route 23. Down Camp Creek Road. After a mile look for a dirt road guarded by a PRIVATE PROPERTY sign. The parcel in question would be roughly five acres and back up against USFS land.

"Okay. Let me start digging. Call back in two hours."

Over the next two hours, I entered the fantasy where Danny found that property . . . obtained a search warrant . . . uncovered those documents.

And the whole thing would take, what, a few days? A week, max?

I wasn't sure what I was more excited about: collecting the money, returning to normalcy with Amanda, or not having to share a roof with ninety criminals every night.

To burn off extra energy, I went to the gym and tossed the medicine balls around for a while. Then I pounded the track. As I washed off the sweat afterward, I was already counting the remaining number of times I'd have to use that soap-scum-encrusted shower.

They would start calling dinner at five o'clock. But Danny's two-hour deadline was just before that. So with ten minutes to spare, I called him.

"Hey, got anything?" I asked hurriedly, after the recording that informed him he was receiving a call from a federal correctional institution.

"We think so," Danny said. "We used satellite imagery to find a dirt road that fit your buddy's description. This is the high-quality USGS stuff, not the junk you get from Google Maps. Then we matched it with local property tax records. There are six properties down that road. Four of them were smaller than five acres. Of the two remaining, one is registered to a guy from South Carolina. The other is registered to a family trust. It looks like the place: five point one acres backing up against US Forest Service land."

There was no one milling near the phones, so I punched the air a couple of times in celebration.

"How soon do you think you can check it out?" I asked.

"Well, it's a funny coincidence. I just so happen to be going down to Georgia this weekend."

CHAPTER 33

They took Delta to Atlanta. Didn't *everyone*—FBI agents, crooks, and everyone in between—take Delta to Atlanta?

Gilmartin wanted to rush out Friday night. Ruiz argued that it didn't make sense to try to find a remote cabin at night. They could wait until the morning.

They hopped on the first flight out. Because it was a Saturday, and because they anticipated a day of tromping around in the Georgia wilderness, they dressed casually. No suits. No FBI logos. Straight-up civilian clothes.

They didn't even bring their weapons with them. Too much hassle.

Once they landed, they hustled to the rental car center and asked for a truck with four-wheel drive. Before long, they were on their way out of Atlanta in a green Jeep—a very non-FBI vehicle—angling northeast on Interstate 85.

The morning was dark gray, fifty-four degrees. Georgia in November. Other than when Gilmartin gave Ruiz directions, they talked little. The route was straightforward enough. It was divided highway, except for when the roads briefly merged for the town of Tallulah Falls.

After they got back out into the countryside, it wasn't too much longer before Gilmartin called out, "Okay. This is it. Camp Creek Road."

Ruiz slowed and took the short exit ramp. They reached a T in the road.

"Take a right to stay on Camp Creek," Gilmartin said, his vanilla accent sounding more like a GPS than most GPSs.

Then, before too much longer, he ordered, "Slow up here."

There was a small dirt road, jutting off to the left at an obtuse angle. At the mouth of the road was a black sign with orange lettering that warned, PRIVATE PROPERTY.

"This is it," Ruiz said. "This is exactly like Tommy said it would be."

Ruiz turned, and they departed the asphalt. The Jeep's tires spun slightly, finding the remnants of loose gravel buried under the dirt. The road tilted upward. Trees hung over them, growing together as they reached for the sky, turning that little rutted track into an arboreal tunnel.

They passed a house on the left. Then one on the right. They were simple getaways. Neither appeared to be currently occupied.

Then Gilmartin pointed and said, "Turn here."

There was a narrower path off to the left, one that had been even less frequently traveled. The ruts were deep enough Ruiz was glad for the Jeep's higher wheel clearance. Dry yellow grass clogged the middle of the track.

Finally the driveway flattened out. They entered a small clearing, just like they had seen in the satellite picture. They looked for the cabin, the garage, the shed.

Except where the satellite photo had showed the three structures should be, there was nothing.

Not a wall. Not a roof. Not a foundation.

Nothing but three empty patches of dirt and some scattered debris.

Ruiz muttered, "What the—"

"Someone beat us here," Gilmartin said.

"Who?"

"I don't know. But whoever it was, they cleaned the place out."

CHAPTER 34

Herrera had found the cabin, broken into it, and, after a thorough ransacking, found nothing.

Just like the banker's wife.

Unlike the banker's wife, he hadn't stopped there. Because, really, if you were Mitchell Dupree, and you had the FBI and a cartel after you, and you had something that bulky you absolutely had to stick somewhere, and you had a tucked-away hunting cabin no one knew about, isn't that where you would hide it?

The documents simply had to be somewhere in, around, or under that cabin. By Herrera's estimation, they consisted of nearly four thousand pieces of paper. Plus whatever folders or partitions were needed to organize them. Herrera was thinking a banker would use banker's boxes.

Herrera just needed to be methodical about finding them. He also needed reinforcements.

It had taken him a few days to get a crew up from Mexico, through the tunnel; and then a few more days to arrange the proper equipment for them.

Sledgehammers. Pry bars. Drills. Saws. A jackhammer. A backhoe. A dump truck.

The larger equipment was rented. Herrera didn't worry about anyone noticing or asking questions. For one thing, the cabin was so remote. For another, who would pay attention to half a dozen Hispanic construction workers? There were few parts of America anymore where that was an unusual sight.

Once Herrera got his team in place, he set it into a controlled destructive fury. The men started in the attic and worked their way down. And they were thorough: ripping out walls, removing insulation, exposing the bare bones of the cabin to make sure they had missed nothing. They carted the place out, one chunk at a time, to the dump truck.

Herrera inspected every scrap before it got tossed. Anything larger than a cardboard box got broken down into smaller pieces. Even the appliances were dismantled.

It was slow going. When the first day was over and they still hadn't found anything, they slept in the partially deconstructed cabin. Same thing with the second day. Herrera was a patient man. He had time, if only because if he didn't find those documents, he would soon be out of it.

Once the house was gutted down to the studs, Herrera had them take it apart, board by board. There would be literally no place left where the documents could hide. They filled the dump truck, emptied it, then filled it again.

When they were done with the cabin, they took apart its cinderblock foundation and the small poured-concrete patio that surrounded it. Herrera thought there might be a trap door leading to a cellar of some sort. Or a hidden lockbox. Something.

But no. Nothing. Herrera was starting to get frustrated.

He still didn't quit. When the men were done with the house, having reduced it to a patch of bare dirt amidst the weeds of the clearing, they moved onto the outbuildings, a shed and a detached garage.

They did the same thing. They got the same result. They were staying at a local hotel by that point, having demolished any structure that might have given them shelter.

Herrera kept sending them back to work. When they were done

with the buildings, Herrera had them start walking the property in a grid pattern. All five acres of it.

Those documents had to be somewhere. In a lean-to. A shack. A tree house. A hole in the ground. *Somewhere.*

Except if they weren't. After two weeks, having made the men walk the search grid three times, Herrera finally ended the operation.

He was satisfied what he was looking for was nowhere on that property. In every other way, he was distinctly unsatisfied.

CHAPTER 35

My giddiness over Mitch revealing the location of the cabin lasted until Danny told me what was actually there.

He speculated that the cartel's people had reached it first, and also that they hadn't found anything.

After all, if they had, Mitch Dupree would already be dead.

To Danny and Rick, it was a minor setback. To me, it was a catastrophe, and I spent the next few days stewing in disappointment. I had done everything I was supposed to do: insinuated myself into life at Morgantown, become friends with Mitch, gotten him to tell me where the cabin was.

By now I should have been back with my lovely, pregnant fiancée, wealthy enough to start a new life with her.

Now everything felt off the rails. If the documents weren't at the cabin, where were they? And how was I supposed to get Mitch to tell me?

With no other real plan, I continued palling around with Mitch, hoping something he said—about another hunting cabin his family owned, or about his favorite fishing spot, or about his condo in the Bahamas, or whatever—might be revelatory.

Thanksgiving was on us before I knew it. As you might expect, Thanksgiving in prison was not easily confused with the version of the holiday celebrated elsewhere. You get the day off, but that only made things worse, because you had more time for absence pangs.

I tried to console myself that, unlike some of the guys at Morgantown, this would be my only Thanksgiving away from my family, and that by this time next year, Amanda and I would be celebrating our first Thanksgiving as newlyweds, joined at a festive table by a baby in a high chair. But that only worked so much. The COs were in crappy moods, because they didn't want to be working, and they took it out on us in vindictive fashion, with a contraband search that succeeded in grinding whatever joy out of the day I might have been able to falsely manufacture.

At lunch, we were served a meal that appeared on the menu as "Thanksgiving Dinner." It included processed, pressed-meat turkey; a light-brown mound of something that looked like mashed potatoes and tasted like sawdust; and an assortment of bland, wilted steamed vegetables. It was all covered in a cold, gelatinous substance that, by process of elimination, must have been the item called "gravy" on the menu.

The phones were busy most of the day, crammed with morose guys pretending to sound upbeat as they called home to talk with second cousins and great-aunts. By the time I finally waited my turn, I reached Amanda on her cell with what sounded like a stadium full of people behind her, laughing and talking boisterously. She spoke circuitously, in case anyone was listening, but I was able to gather that she and my mother had gone over to Brock DeAngelis' parents' house, where Brock's extended family was nearing the end of a multihour, eight-course Italian Thanksgiving dinner.

She was clearly having a great time, and she seemed to want assurances that I wasn't perfectly miserable. So I told her a local Quaker meeting group had come in and served a sumptuous meal of fresh turkey. I stopped just short of saying they served it to us wearing buckled shoes.

Amanda then passed the phone to my slightly drunk mother, who was gushy enough that I rushed her off the phone before she slipped up and said something she shouldn't. As she hung up, I heard another burst of laughter and happy shouting that reverberated in my thoughts throughout the lonely evening that followed.

Come Friday, it was back to the usual grind. Wake up. Work. Find a way to fill the afternoon. Play poker at night. According to Mitch's stats, I had gotten on a hot streak.

Being Pete Goodrich—thinking like him, talking like him, acting like him—was becoming second nature. It was Tommy Jump who didn't know where he was sometimes.

Through it all, Mitch and I continued to build our friendship. It sounds funny—given how mercenary my ultimate goals for our interaction were—but I was starting to care for the guy.

I was particularly struck by his devotion to his kids. He was trying hard as a father, limited though his opportunities were, and he was constantly sharing his hard-won wisdom. About how what kids wanted more than anything was just your attention. About how sometimes you had to shut up and listen, resisting the urge to give them advice. About their constant need for reassurance ("You'll never find someone on the therapist's couch, complaining that their dad said 'I love you' too often," was his memorable line).

None of it quite applied yet. I stored it away all the same.

Still, nothing we talked about was otherwise noteworthy until the Thursday after Thanksgiving, when the deputy warden—for no apparent reason—canceled morning work duty and ordered us to stay confined to our dorms.

I certainly didn't mind missing a day of doing other people's laundry. A cold fog had settled into the tiny bowl where our prison sat and was refusing to budge. A good morning to stay inside.

After room inspection, I spied Mitch's roommate wandering toward the televisions and took that as an opportunity to visit Mitch. I found him in his bunk, reading *Time* magazine.

"Hey, what's up," I said. It wasn't exactly difficult to affect a listless tone to my voice.

"Unbelievable, what they're letting these banks get away with," he said, shaking his head. "It's like they learned nothing from 2008."

The moment he said "banks," I sensed an opening. We had yet to broach the subject of why either of us was incarcerated. It was a threshold we needed to cross—the next step in our relationship, such as it was.

But, of course, Pete Goodrich wasn't going to let on that he was any more or less interested in this observation than he was in That Time I Almost Broke 90 at Pinehurst. It was just another thing to pass the time.

"Oh, that's right, you worked for a bank, didn't you?" I said casually.

"Sure did. Union South Bank. 'A bank designed around you,'" he said, serving up its longtime advertising slogan with a side of sarcasm. "Or, as we liked to say, 'A bank designed around fools.'"

Taking a seat on the top of his desk like I was still properly bored, I asked, "Would a lowly history teacher even understand what you did there?"

"I was director of compliance for our Latin American division," he said, then forced out a grim chuckle. "That means I was responsible for making sure the bank followed the law. Pretty ironic I ended up in here, huh?"

"What do you mean?"

He rested the magazine on his chest and stared up at the underside of the top bunk.

"This may sound like another convict spouting a line of bull, but in a way I was sent here for doing my job *too* well."

"How so?"

"Aw, it's not worth going into. It'd just sound like sour grapes."

"What's the point of prison if you can't take sour grapes and make some whine?"

"Yeah, I guess," he said, then glanced over my way. "You sure you want to hear this?"

"Got nothing better to do," I said, with just the right degree of nonchalance.

"All right," he said, and tilted himself toward me.

And just like that, it was confession time.

I leaned my back against the cold cinder-block wall and put my feet up on the bolted-in chair, as indifferent as could be, so Mitch wouldn't feel like he was being studied too carefully.

Isn't that why the Catholics put up that screen in their confessionals? No one wanted to be scrutinized while unburdening their soul.

"To begin with, one of the really stupid things about federal banking regulations is that they rely on the banks to regulate themselves," he said. "They take for granted that a banker is the honest one and that it's the customer who will commit fraud at the expense of the unwitting bank. If a bank is willfully breaking the law, they're going to get away with it. It's only the people who are trying to follow the law who get screwed."

He paused. "Told you this would sound bitter."

"Sounds like honesty to me," I said.

"Well, so, anyway, one of my jobs as compliance director was to fill out what were called suspicious activity reports, known as SARs. If I saw something that didn't look right, I filled out a SAR and sent it up the food chain at the bank, which then electronically submitted it to FinCEN, which is the Financial Crimes something-something . . . Uhh, Enforcement Network. Lord, how could I forget that? Anyhow, FinCEN was founded to combat money laundering, the financing of terror networks, all that happy stuff. It's part of the Treasury Department. So is the IRS, if that gives you an idea about who you're dealing with."

"Real sweethearts," I interjected.

"Exactly. Now, the first rule of compliance is: Know Your Customer. We like that rule so much we even give it an acronym. KYC. The banking industry talks all the time about KYC guidelines, KYC procedures, KYC checks. You could spend the next month of your life doing nothing but study KYC regulations twenty-four hours a day and you'd probably still only know half of it. Am I boring you yet?"

"Not at all."

"Don't worry, I will be soon. Anyhow, I started this job about five years ago. I was USB's director of compliance for Latin America. It was sort of a dream job for me. I had worked in Latin and South America before I got into banking, and I had majored in Spanish and international relations in college. It just felt like this is what I had been building toward all along. And I was getting into it at a pretty exciting time. Coming out of the financial crisis, FinCEN was really tightening up its KYC requirements. There had been some decent-size fines for banks that hadn't been on the up-and-up with this stuff. This is the kind of thing that keeps a banker up at night, you know what I'm saying?"

"I hear you," I said.

"So there I am, starting a big new job, and I'm all gung-ho. And I immediately trip across this relationship the bank had in Mexico with these *casas de cambio,* money exchange houses. It was a damn KYC nightmare. My predecessor, the guy who had allowed this, was completely asleep at the wheel. Literally anyone could walk in off the street in Mexico with a big wad of cash or traveler's checks, deposit it at a *casa de cambio,* and tell them to route it to a certain account number at USB. There was no check on it. There was no 'show me your driver's license.' There was no automatic reporting of transactions ten thousand dollars or higher, like there would be if you did the same thing in America. And once that money was in an account at USB, it was clean as a whistle. You could do anything with it: transfer it to another bank, buy an airplane, whatever you wanted."

"Are you serious?" I said. It sounded way too easy.

"As a heart attack. I took everything to my boss, the vice president for the Latin American division, this guy named Thad Reiner. I laid this out for him, then told him we either needed to clean it up or shut it down. I thought he would freak out and immediately start fixing it. Instead, he laid out his side for me. There were billions of dollars flowing back and forth through these *casas de cambio,* and USB was reaping transaction fees on all of it. It was a huge portion of the division's profits, and he wasn't going to jeopardize it because of a few transactions that might or might not have been legitimate. He gave me this whole sad song about how it was mostly being used by poor laborers who were sending money to their families, and vice versa, and how if we cracked down by insisting on documentation, we'd be starving them to death, because a lot of them didn't have paperwork. He said it was up to the *casas de cambio* to know the customers and that therefore we didn't have to."

Mitch rolled his eyes at this.

"I was the new guy, so I kind of went along with it. But the closer I got to it, the worse it looked. I'd take trips down to Mexico and I'd ask the *casas de cambio* to show me the original deposit slips. You couldn't even read the signatures on the things. It was a total joke. Some of these deposits were a million pesos, two million pesos. Depending on the exchange rate, that was fifty grand, a hundred grand in US dollars. That's not a huge number in the grand scheme of international money laundering, except if you're doing it every day, at dozens of locations around Mexico. Some of the deposits were traveler's checks that were already in American dollars or straight-up US greenbacks. So not only were they doing this with pesos, it looked like they were hauling money down from America and depositing it at these *casas de cambio,* rather than doing it at a US bank where someone would insist on seeing ID.

"Basically, USB had created the perfect vehicle for someone to launder money and move it across international borders without any legal friction whatsoever. And it was clear when I looked at the pattern of these large, suspicious deposits that one cartel in particular had figured this out, because a lot of them were coming from the Colima state or nearby. That's the power base for a cartel called New Colima."

He didn't even flinch as he said the name. And the way he was laying everything out for me, I could tell he didn't suspect I had any idea what he was talking about.

"From a compliance standpoint, this was like a bundle of TNT that could explode any second," he continued. "All it would take was someone from the FBI or DEA poking around a little and deciding to follow the money. Thad Reiner had already told me to shut up about it. So I just said to myself, 'All right, he's not shutting this down like he should, I'm just going to SAR this puppy until the feds start banging down the door, then we'll see how he feels.' At least I knew my butt would be covered, right? I made it my goal to write at least one SAR a day. I knew what I was looking for: large transactions of cash or traveler's checks with a *casa de cambio* in or near the Colima state. When I found one, I'd call up the *casa de cambio* in question and make them send me the deposit slip, which I would then scan and include in the SAR. The crazy thing is, I started to be able to recognize the different signatures on the deposit slips. Even though the names were changed, the handwriting would be the same. It was clear there were about a dozen guys who were trusted by the cartel to handle the money, and they were making all these deposits among a rotating set of *casas de cambio*. I thought it would make for a great case when the feds finally came knocking."

"And when did that happen?"

"Well, that's the thing. It didn't. I hadn't expected anything immediately. FinCEN gets about a million SARs filed every year. That's, what, three thousand every business day? And that's just the banks. Insurance companies file SARs. So do investment companies. Even casinos. Anyone who deals in large amounts of money. I know how slow the government can be. Plus, the regulatory environment had changed with the new administration. It had a bit of a Wild West feel. I just kept sending in my stinky transaction du jour, dotting my i's and crossing my t's, thinking maybe they were so backlogged they hadn't gotten to me yet.

"After four years of doing this, I finally said, 'What the hell? Are they really just ignoring this?' I mentioned FinCEN had this electronic filing system, right? Every financial institution gets an ID and a password, and the rule at USB was that only someone at the vice president level or above had the password. I had been relying on Thad Reiner to submit my SARs for me. And finally I asked him, point-blank, 'Thad, have you been filing all those SARs I sent?'

"He starts giving me this stuff about needing to see the bigger picture and thinking about the division as a whole. He kept saying, 'We're a family here, Mitch. A family. Let's not rock the boat.' Which is what he had said to me four years earlier when I first started talking about the lack of KYC material. And I was like, 'Thad, did you file the damn SARs or not?' He said he had, but I knew he was lying. At that point, he reminded me I was being very well compensated and lived a very comfortable life. And without actually coming out and threatening it, he made it clear I would lose my job if I pushed this any further. I still went away from that meeting thinking to myself, 'I don't care what he says, this boat is about to get rocked.'"

"And did you?" I asked.

"Not as quickly as I should have. I was no babe in the woods with all this stuff, but I was in Atlanta. FinCEN is in DC or Virginia or wherever. I couldn't just knock on their door and be like, 'Hey, so, my boss is committing this massive fraud, want to come investigate?' I needed to proceed cautiously. I was looking up whistle-blower laws, trying to find an attorney I could trust who *wasn't* connected to USB but who still understood the regulations. Just getting my ducks in a row. And that's when the FBI swooped in with warrants and raided my house, my office, everything. I was like, 'What the . . . Wait, guys, you got it all wrong.'

"But when I tried to tell them what had been going on, they didn't want to hear it. It wasn't until I got in a room with them and my lawyer that I understood why. There's something known in legal circles as a Bank of Nova Scotia subpoena and . . . anyway, not worth going into the details. Point is, Thad 'found' a piece of paper that I supposedly left in the trash at work, which is so preposterous that . . . sorry, I keep interrupting myself. Anyway, it contained information that led to an account in Jersey—not the state, the island in the English Channel—that had my name and what looked like my signature, which Reiner had obviously lifted off one of my SARs. It also had more than four million bucks in it, thanks to a wire transfer from an account in the Caymans that was known to be linked to New Colima. The Jersey account had been opened the day after I confronted Thad Reiner."

"He was setting you up," I said.

"Exactly. And I tried to explain this to the feds, but they mostly wanted to know how a guy who had never claimed a net income above two hundred grand on his taxes had managed to amass this huge fortune. Reiner had told the feds *he* had confronted *me* at that meeting with what he termed to be *my* total lack of KYC oversight. And he told them he suspected I was working with New Colima and was taking a kickback on everything I helped them launder. I kept telling them, 'But that account's not mine, I don't know how it got there.' Which only made me look more guilty. Finally my lawyer told me to stop talking. The feds weren't listening anyway."

Sitting up a little straighter, I said, "So let me get this straight: Reiner made it look like you were taking payouts from the cartel in exchange for setting up the money-laundering scheme, then looking the other way?"

"That's about the size of it, yeah."

"But where did Reiner get that kind of money?"

"From the cartel, of course. I can't prove this, but he was the one who established that relationship with the *casas de cambio*. And not only was he getting bonuses because his division was making such nice profits, I'm sure he was getting paid by the cartel. He probably just went to the cartel and said, 'Hey, we have a problem here, but toss a few million bucks at it and I can make it go away.' Four million bucks is nothing to New Colima."

"And just when you were about to blow the whistle on him, he scapegoated you."

"That's right."

"So you're . . . you're actually innocent," I said.

"Sure am."

Gilmartin's warning—*everything your fellow inmates tell you will likely be a lie*—was now returning to me with a force not found in nature. I knew I shouldn't have believed a word Mitch was saying.

Just like I shouldn't have bought Bobby Harrison's line about a five-can buy-in. Or Doc's whopper about a prescription-forging nurse.

But what if this really was the truth?

CHAPTER 36

It speaks to my torpid mental processor, and my genuine lack of a criminal mind, that I spent the rest of the day wandering around in a daze.

At poker that night, I was still so distracted, I actually folded before the river on a large pot that I would have won because I didn't recognize the two hearts in my hand plus the three already on the table made for a flush.

But slowly, after a good night's sleep and a solid morning folding laundry, I put things together. In some ways, Mitch's confession changed nothing. I had been sent to prison to cozy up to a felon. That he was possibly innocent didn't alter my mission.

All it had really done was provide more information I could use. Once I got over my surprise and played the whole conversation over in my mind enough times, I arrived at the real takeaway:

I now knew what he was hiding. It was those four years' worth of suspicious activity reports and deposit slips. Mitch must have kept copies.

The deposit slips were the smoking gun. Assuming he kept the originals. They had signatures on them, and I was sure a competent handwriting analyst could prove they had come from the same roughly dozen men, no doubt top players in the New Colima cartel. More important, at least a few of those deposit slips had fingerprints on them.

Sure, they were a few years old by now, but I once watched a cold case show where fifty-year-old prints had been used to catch a killer. Once you had a print on one deposit slip, you could match it to the signature, which would then allow you to match it to hundreds of others.

Put it all together—a documented record of hundreds of fraudulent transactions, involving millions of dollars, with the beyond-a-reasonable-doubt certainty of fingerprints—and you had a package that was a game ender for the cartel and a career maker for any FBI agent and US Attorney who put it all together.

Now that I understood what I was looking for, I still had to decide what to do about it. I had my usual frustrating Friday afternoon conversation with Amanda, where neither of us could say what was really going on in our lives. I ended the call after just a few minutes, because I wasn't able to concentrate, and for some reason hearing her say she loved me just made my heart hurt more.

It wasn't until after the four P.M. standing count that I managed to get my head fully straight, having figured out how I was going to try to turn this into a win-win-win: a win for me, my bank account, and my future family's prosperity; a win for the FBI and its efforts to fight a nefarious cartel; and even a win for a man who shouldn't have been in prison after all.

And I was going to accomplish all this by telling Mitch the truth. Sort of.

"Hey, you got a second?" I said, intercepting him on his way out of his room after the count.

"What's up?"

"I wanted to talk about something. Not here."

"Okay," he said agreeably. "Where?"

"Let's take a predinner walk. I hear that's good for digestion anyway."

"Sure, hang on," he said. He disappeared back into his room and reemerged zipping up his jacket.

We strolled out of Randolph, into an afternoon that was seasonably brisk, with a fast-sinking sun, and pointed ourselves toward the jogging path.

"Been thinking about what you said yesterday morning," I began. "It seems horribly wrong that you're here and that Reiner guy has gotten away with everything."

"You sound like my wife," he said. "I keep telling her there's not much I can do about it now."

"What if I could?"

He stopped walking and jerked his head toward me. "How?"

Here came my half-truth:

"I have a friend who works for the FBI," I said. "I grew up with him. His name is Danny Ruiz. The last time I talked with him, he told me he was working in a unit that handles money laundering. And when you said 'New Colima,' it sparked a dead brain cell. I'm pretty sure that's who he's been trying to nail."

"Jesus. He could be one of the guys who showed up at my house with that search warrant. There were a bunch of them."

"Danny is a good guy. He really is. I know you might not believe that given what you've been through, but he's got his heart in the right place and he's really motivated by some personal things that have happened to him," I said, thinking of those Kris Langetieg photos. "If I told him about your case, I bet he'd be really interested in talking to you."

Mitch started walking again. I followed.

"Why would he want to do that?" Mitch asked. "I'm just another convict."

That's when I hit him with: "Because you're a convict who kept copies of all those SARs and the deposit slips that went with them."

This stopped him. Under his jacket, I could tell his breathing had changed.

"What makes you think that?"

"Because you keep stats on a prison poker game. Because it's in a banker's nature to document things," I said, echoing some of the first words he ever said to me. "You were dotting your i's, crossing your t's, covering your butt. In the back of your mind, you knew it was prudent to save everything you could."

"And what if I did?" he asked. He was giving me a look that was as hard as any of the hills that surrounded us.

"If you turn them over to the FBI, they'll get your sentence reduced. I bet if you played things right, they'd let you out with time served. They'd probably even pay you for it. From what my friend Danny tells me, you'd be surprised at the amount of money the FBI would be willing to throw at you."

He shook head. "I'd never live to spend it. These cartels can get you anywhere. Even in prison. Hell, especially in prison. They probably have a man here already, waiting for the order to slit my throat."

"Just give me a chance to talk to my friend Danny," I said. "At the very least, you could see what kind of deal they'd be willing to offer you."

"They already offered me a deal," he said. "In exchange for giving them documents and admitting I was the mastermind of everything, they'd put my family in witness protection, change my identity, and have me serve a mere four years. They said they couldn't let someone who had played such a central role and had profited so handsomely get away with less time. It was a joke. And the joke was actually on them in at least a couple of ways. One, they wanted me to testify against my quote-unquote 'contact' with the cartel, which would have been impossible, because I didn't have one. Two, they wanted me to surrender the money in the Jersey account, which I couldn't do, because I didn't have the code that went with it. I tried to explain this to them, but they had such tunnel vision, they couldn't see me as anything but a cartel guy. Oh, and I guess I might as well add joke number three: The cartel would have killed me long before I ever got to testify. Those documents are the only thing keeping me alive."

"Look, maybe the deal will improve," I said. "Some time has passed. They're coming to grips with the fact that they aren't going to have anything against New Colima unless they get those documents from you. Danny won't have the same tunnel vision. He can talk some sense into them. I bet once the cartel members were arrested, they would even turn on Thad Reiner. He'd end up taking your place in here."

This brought a grim smile to his face.

"I wouldn't let him into the poker game if I were you," he said.

"Definitely not. Anyhow, let me talk to Danny. He's been my friend since kindergarten. He can help you. I'll tell him he has to get you out of here before you hand over those documents. Same with your wife and kids. The cartel wouldn't be able to touch any of you. What's the harm of seeing what they come up with? If it all works out, you'd be out of here by Christmas, taking nice long drives with your family again, probably out west somewhere."

He looked in that direction and squinted. A weak autumn sun in the final throes of setting lit his face. I studied those sad eyes of his for some hint of what he was thinking. It wasn't hard to guess his calculus featured more thoughts about his family's well-being than his own.

Beyond that, it was difficult to speculate. If Mitchell Dupree was to be believed, he was an honest, ethical man—with enough personal conviction that not only had he tried to do the right thing, he had stood up to others who didn't. For all his efforts, he still ended up in prison, professionally disgraced and personally ruined. Along the way, he had surely developed a strong skepticism toward the institutions I was now calling on him to trust with his life.

And yet the call of freedom, of reuniting with family, had to be just as strong.

Finally, he allowed: "I guess it couldn't hurt to see what they have to say."

W ithout further discussion, we went to dinner. As I shoved some overcooked ham steak into my mouth, I thought about my impending phone call with Danny.

There was no way I could impart all the information I needed to in code. I had too much to say. I needed to be able to talk normally.

If a CO happened to be listening, it would be pretty clear Inmate Peter Lenfest Goodrich was not what he seemed to be. If that somehow got out, it could have disastrous consequences.

Then I thought about the odds. Nine hundred and something guys were each bestowed 300 phone minutes a month. Some inmates didn't use all their minutes, so let's say the average was 200. That was still 180,000 total minutes, or three thousand hours of "I love you too" and "How's the weather in Cincinnati?"

Even if they had one CO whose only job was monitoring phone calls—and I'm pretty sure the budget-strapped administration at FCI Morgantown didn't dedicate nearly that much time to the task—that was still less than two hundred hours of listening capacity a month to spread out over those three thousand hours. A one-in-fifteen chance of being overheard. Probably far less.

So it was still a risk.

But it was one I felt like I could accept.

I finished dinner even more hurriedly than usual, then went straight to the Randolph phones and dialed Danny's cell number. When he picked up, I could hear loud music playing in the background.

"Hey, where are you?" I asked.

"Just out with some colleagues, having a Friday afternoon beer. What's up?"

"I had an interesting conversation with our friend today."

"Oh yeah? What about?"

"About—"

I realized I was yelling into the phone. I didn't want Mitch—or any of my other fellow convicts—to be able to overhear this.

"Actually, can you go outside?" I asked. "You're making me feel like I have to scream to be heard."

"Yeah, sure. Hang on," he said.

I looked around. The hallway was still empty. Most of the guys were at the dining hall. That ham steak was a tough chew.

The music coming through the earpiece actually got louder before it quieted. Then it was replaced by street noise.

"This better?" Danny asked.

"A little," I said. "So I got some stuff to tell you. And I'm not going to bother with the lottery tickets."

"Go ahead."

"For starters, our friend admitted he has what I came here for."

"Really?" Danny said, now yelling himself. "That's great!"

"You were right about what he hung on to. You'll be able to shut down the whole operation."

"Fantastic. Did he give you any hint about where?"

"Well, hang on, it's more complicated than that."

"Complicated how?"

"What if I told you our friend is innocent? He didn't do what he was accused of. He was set up to take the fall by his boss. He was actually going to be a whistle-blower."

"Yeah? And you believe that?"

After all my tortured pondering of that question, the answer came to me quickly.

"I do, actually," I said. "What he described seems too elaborate to have been made up. And I've gotten to know this guy. He's . . . Look, I know you might think I'm being a sucker here, but he's a good guy. He's . . . he's a good dad. He doesn't even cheat at cards when given the chance. He's got this ethical core to him."

"The people who convicted him didn't agree. You remember that, right?"

"I do. I just think he got railroaded."

"Okay. Fine. Even if that's true, it doesn't change anything."

"Maybe it does."

"How so?"

"Because if he's actually innocent, what I'm about to ask you to do should be a little easier for everyone to swallow."

"And what's that?"

"I want you to negotiate a deal for him," I said. "The honest-to-goodness best deal you can. Acting like he's innocent. Acting like he's gone to prison for something someone else has done, and you ought to be treating him that way. Can you do that?"

"That depends. What kind of deal are we talking about?"

"First, you've got to get him off with time served. He shouldn't have to spend one more day in this place. Then I want you to get him out of here and into witness protection. Like, the kind where they change your name and your face and send you and your family somewhere they can't possibly be found. And you guys can't tip your hand in any way that this is happening until he is already out of here. Hell, until both of us are out of here. No filing for extraditions, no indictments, nothing the bad guys would see. This is his life we're talking about, not to mention the lives of his wife and kids."

"Right, of course."

"Then offer him enough money so he can't say no."

"How much?"

"I don't know. But dig deep."

"Okay," Danny said. "And if I can arrange all this, do you have his assurance he'll take the deal?"

"Not yet."

"But he was interested?"

"He was. Look, if you want what he has, you're going to have to think big picture here."

"I hear you. Let me run this up the flagpole. Call me back at noon tomorrow."

"I will," I said.

Then I hung up, hoping we were the only ones who had heard the conversation.

CHAPTER 37

Herrera's eyes scanned the horizon again, looking for that large, telltale swirl of dust approaching Rosario No. 2 that told him a phalanx of Range Rovers was bearing down.

Even a beater pickup truck, poking along at thirty miles an hour, barely kicking up any dirt at all, could trigger a minor panic attack in him. Or the glinting windshield of an aging Datsun. Anything, really. Herrera had taken to keeping binoculars around his neck, just so he could rule out non-threats more quickly.

He just never knew when El Vio might be coming. *Be unpredictable.*

This sense of dread had followed Herrera ever since he had returned to Mexico. El Vio had known about the operation in Georgia, of course. Herrera had required too many men and too much money for El Vio not to know about it.

And, therefore, Herrera had no choice but to inform El Vio about his failure. New Colima had a private-key encrypted e-mail server where messages permanently erased themselves after forty-eight hours. It was as secure as could be, so Herrera had written out a detailed description of his efforts in Georgia to El Vio's account.

His reply, which came back fourteen minutes later, was simply: "Okay."

And it left Herrera wondering: Was that "okay," as in, "I applaud your initiative and *atrevido,* even though the results weren't what we wanted"? Or would El Vio soon be making one of his inspections, ready to promote someone else into Herrera's position?

There were times when Herrera swore that if he saw one of those long plumes traveling his way, he'd flee.

But where would he go? Where could he hide?

No. He would simply hold his chin high, meet El Vio's gaze, and tell him, *I am still your man. I will get this done.*

Still, the anticipation was brutal. And that's why he was at the edge of Rosario No. 2, his eyes scanning the distance, when one of the lieutenants called to him.

"General," he said.

Herrera turned as the lieutenant continued, "There's something that requires your attention in the bunker immediately. It's regarding West Virginia."

Herrera didn't need to hear more. He dropped his gaze and walked across the hardscrabble soil and into the reinforced concrete structure. The lieutenant led him to one of several computer terminals, where an audio file was cued up.

The United States government wasn't the only entity with its ears trained on the phone traffic coming out of FCI Morgantown.

Herrera listened to the conversation regarding the banker three times. He knew who the recipient of the call was, of course. But who was this man initiating the call? How did he factor in? And how had he gotten close to the banker?

So many unanswered questions. Herrera dragged the audio file to a place where he could listen to it again if needed.

Then he pulled out his phone and called one of the contractors in America to demand answers.

CHAPTER 38

After dinner and before the card game that night, I relayed to Mitch an edited version of my conversation with Danny. I played up Danny's side of it, to make it seem like my FBI buddy had been more enthusiastic. But Mitch remained noncommittal.

"You'll talk to your friend at noon tomorrow?" he asked.

"That's right."

"Then I guess we'll just have to wait and see."

And wait I did. I waited all through the card game. Then I waited through a long night, made longer because Frank had a cold and was snoring like a one-man thunderflash.

When Saturday morning came, there was the usual excitement of visiting hours, which was not something that ever applied to me. I avoided the chatter about it—*Hey, Pete, how come no one ever visits you?*—in my usual way, by burying myself in a book. It was a thriller called *Say Nothing*, by an author I had never heard of.

I probably averaged a peek at my watch every six minutes or so, which is not a recommended technique for making time go by faster.

At quarter of noon, I went over to the phone bank, ready to wait on line and establish a position at one of them. But that didn't prove necessary. There was no one else around.

When my watch hit 11:59:40, I started dialing Danny's number, punching the buttons slowly enough to fill those final, plodding twenty seconds.

After the usual delays and recordings, I heard, "Hey, how's it going?"

I took a breath, thought about my less-than-one-in-fifteen odds, and decided to roll the dice with uncoded speech again.

"Talk to me," I said. "What did your boss say?"

"We got a deal."

I wasn't celebrating yet. "What kind of deal?"

"Everything you asked for. We talked with David Drayer, and he's willing to recommend to the judge that Dupree be let off with time served on account of his extraordinary cooperation."

"Good. You told him to keep this zipped, right? Don't file anything yet?"

"Of course."

"Okay. Go on."

"So, time served. Full entry into WITSEC, which means a new identity, relocation, a salary, and a place to live until he finds a job and becomes self-sufficient. Plus we'll give him a million dollars, conditional upon indictments. However, and my SAC was very explicit about this, we need the documents first. Nothing happens—and I mean *nothing*—until we have our hands on those documents and have our attorneys verify that they're legit."

"What if he wants to do it the other way around? What if he wants to be out first and *then* tell you where the documents are?"

"No can do. This is a hundred percent bureau policy. We've been burned too many times. Think what you want about your friend's innocence, he's still a convicted felon. You seem to have forgotten that, but we sure haven't."

"I understand," I said. "But are you sure your attorneys can be quiet about this? These documents are the only thing keeping him alive."

"You'd have my personal assurance that nothing would be filed until both of you are out of there. Same with his family. The FBI isn't perfect, but we aren't in the business of letting civilians get slaughtered."

"Okay," I said. "Anything else?"

"Not that I can think of."

"Great. Keep your phone close. Let me see what our friend has to say."

A Get Out of Jail Free card. A new life under the protection of the world's most powerful government. A million dollars—seven fat figures with a dollar sign at the front—with which to start it.

Mitch couldn't say no to all that, right?

CHAPTER 39

It had been a long week for Amanda.

Her art had been a struggle, as usual. There were too many days when she got a brush in her hand, ready to paint whatever came into her mind, only to find an image of Hudson van Buren, leering at her crotch. And then the day was ruined.

She still forced herself to paint. Even when it just meant giving the garbage truck more to haul. It was a matter of self-image. An artist without discipline is an unemployed person *telling* people she's an artist.

But the greater struggle, she could admit, was that her good friend—and great distraction—had been out of town. Brock was on a cruise in the Caribbean. He had asked her if she wanted to come at the last minute. He even offered to treat.

She declined, telling him she was concerned about the Zika virus.

And that was true. But the larger truth was that it didn't feel right to do something like that while Tommy was in prison. Even if Tommy would have implored her to go and have a blast, she wouldn't have been able to enjoy herself. The guilt alone would have destroyed the trip.

She missed Brock all the same. And she was thrilled when her phone, which had been so silent all week, buzzed with an incoming text early Saturday afternoon. The message itself, however, was puzzling:

Dinner tonight? Pick you up at 7? I need to tell you something.
Then I need to ask you something.

She didn't immediately answer. He wanted to tell her . . . what? And ask her . . . what else? It wasn't like Brock to be so cryptic. She tried to keep herself from conjecturing.

Yet she worried. She knew enough about guys and how their minds worked. Brock had been away for a week, allowing him to think. A guy like Brock—so decent, so gentlemanly, so far above making a sleazy move on his friend's fiancée—would need that kind of time to summon his courage.

And now he was going to lay his feelings out for her in the most mature, aboveboard way possible. He wanted more from their relationship. More than friendship. More than quick hugs and brotherly pecks on the cheek. He didn't care that she was pregnant with his friend's child. He would raise the baby as his own, and then they'd have their own kid together. Maybe two. Blended families were so common now, what did it matter?

Amanda could see it all coming so easily.

But what should she do about it? She couldn't actually consider that proposition, could she?

Yet the moment she asked the question, her gut answered it for her. Brock was beautiful, sophisticated, smart, rich, and fun; he was the scion of a thriving jewelry business that could launch the Amanda Porter Collection and give her an artistic alternative to her sputtering career as a painter; he had that and a thousand other things going for him that any woman would be lucky to find in a mate.

But he wasn't Tommy. She had never once felt that Rice Krispies *snap, crackle, pop* around him.

Damn. She missed that sound, that sensation. Missed it like a limb that had been amputated.

And, yes, things with Tommy were rocky at the moment. Of course they were. She still hadn't told him about Hudson van Buren.

In that respect, they hadn't had a fully honest conversation in months. Plus he was in *prison*. What did she expect their relationship to be like?

When he got out, it would probably take six seconds for them to be back to normal. And normal with Tommy was what she wanted. Now and forever.

She texted Brock back:

Sounds great. See you tonight at 7.

She'd just have to let him down easy.

CHAPTER 40

A cold rain was coming down hard enough to make the puddles bounce, which made me think I would find Mitch holed up in Randolph somewhere.

But he was neither in his room nor in any of the common areas.

More eager to get his answer than I was to stay dry, I plunged into the elements. I jogged over to the education building, flinching against hydraulic assault the whole way. Except I didn't find him in the library. Ditto with the cardio gym, the basketball gym, or any of the classrooms.

It was times like this that I missed my phone sorely. A simple where-are-you text would have solved everything.

I ran to the dining hall next, to see if he was working an extra shift. But he was not among the postlunch cleanup crew. Then I tried Health Services. By that point, I was wet and chilled enough that the nurse looked at me like she was going to be treating me for pneumonia soon.

The very last spot I thought he might be was the chapel. Our conversations had covered a wide range of subjects. And yet even though our prison, like most, was a hotbed of spirituality—there are probably more Bible-thumpers per capita in prison than anywhere else in America—Mitch and I had never discussed God, religion, the afterlife, any of it.

Since I was out of other options, I ran over there anyway. The chapel was supposed to be nondenominational, but it still looked more than vaguely Christian. There were pews and stained glass and an altarish slab of wood at the front of the room with an understated pulpit off to the side. The only thing that kept it from being certifiably Presbyterian was that I don't think anyone served coffee after the services.

By the time I entered the building, having completed my third dash across campus, my shirt was soaked through at the shoulders, my pants at the thighs. Wetness was rolling off my head down into my T-shirt. I clomped heavily through the entryway door into the main area of the chapel, my boots making sloshy noises.

I expected I'd turn right around after taking a brief glance at the place, because it would be empty on a Saturday afternoon. Except there was one guy, sitting in the front pew with his shoulders hunched. He turned around.

Mitch.

"Hey," I said, walking between the pews toward him. "What are you doing here?"

"Praying."

"You pray?"

"Every day."

"But you never go to chapel."

"Praying is about having a personal relationship with God," he said. "I'm not always sure what going to chapel is about, especially around here."

Fair point. I had reached the front of the room, where I was dripping on the thin carpet. Everything about the setting—the pews, the altar, his unexpected piety—had distracted me from what I had come there to do.

"Anyhow, what's up?" he asked.

"I was hoping we could talk, actually. But if I'm interrupting . . ."

"Take a seat," he suggested.

I lowered myself onto the edge of a pew and wiped my face with my damp sleeve before I began.

"I chatted with my FBI buddy," I said.

"I figured. And?"

"And I don't think . . . I don't think it should be a difficult decision, to be honest. The deal they're offering is very, very generous. They've agreed to letting you out with time served, putting you in WITSEC, and paying you one million dollars."

I emphasized the last three words, to make sure they had the proper impact, then continued: "Plus, I've received assurances they won't make any moves that will tip off the cartel until you and your family are a long, long way from here. It's really pretty perfect."

"And all I have to do is tell them where the documents are, is that right?"

"Yep," I said.

He closed his eyes. The bags underneath them seemed particularly heavy today. I wasn't the only one in Randolph who hadn't slept well the previous night. His breathing was slow. He sat perfectly still, consulting whatever higher authority he thought might put some wisdom into his head.

Then he brought his hands to his temples, massaging them as he opened his eyes. He let out a large breath.

Then he said, "I'm sorry, Pete. Tell your friend I can't."

I felt something detonate behind my eyeballs. "Why not?"

"It's complicated."

"No, Mitch. Quantum physics is complicated. This is easy. It's a million bucks, tax-free. It's getting to be with your wife and kids again."

"It's not that simple."

"Sure it is. Look, I know life has dealt you a crappy hand, but there's nothing you can do to get back that American dream life you had. This is as close as you're going to get. This is like having to go all in with a seven and a three and winding up with a straight flush.

Think about what you can do with a million dollars. You can send your kids to whatever college they want to go to, with plenty left over. You can go on vacations where you and your wife can rent a private little bungalow by the beach and have sex to the sound of crashing waves. You can get a big RV and drive anywhere you want with your family, and it doesn't matter that you're getting eight miles to the gallon. You can do anything."

He shook his head. "You wouldn't understand."

"You're right. I wouldn't. So help me. Why would you possibly say no to this?"

"Why do you care so much?"

Because this isn't just your happy future, I thought, picturing Amanda, our baby, getting out of this wretched place, and everything else that hung on his giving the right answer.

Then, with my character wandering, I scolded myself. *Lock it down, Goodrich. Lock it down.*

I squared my shoulders to him and said, "Because you're my friend. And I want what's best for you, and I'm . . . Look, I'm stuck in here. We've never talked about what I did to get here, and it's kind of embarrassing, because it was no big, grand conspiracy. I'm just a broke dumbass who got really frustrated one day and robbed a bank. That's right, Mitch. You worked for a bank, and I robbed one. And I was too stupid to know they put tracking devices in the money, so you can guess how long it took for me to get caught.

"Point is, there's no one coming along to offer me a million bucks or my freedom. I'm stuck here for eight years. You want to pray about something? Pray my wife doesn't leave me between now and then. Pray my five-year-old has some dim shred of a memory of what Daddy looks like by the time I get out, because you can be damn sure the three-year-old and the one-year-old won't. Pray I'll be able to find some way to support my family or find my dignity again when I get out, and that having to check 'yes' on every employment application that asks if I'm a felon won't doom me to working at a Popeyes chicken until I die.

"And that's what you would be facing too. Except now someone is coming along and giving you a chance to not miss your kids growing up, and to have some semblance of a life worth living, and I . . . I just can't stand to see you throw that away. So, yeah, take the deal. If not for you, then for me. Knowing you're out there somewhere will make me feel a little bit freer."

It was a lovely monologue, beautifully delivered. And late in the last act of every stage show ever written, it would have won the day.

But Mitch was just sitting there, shaking his head. "Sorry," he said again. "I really appreciate you going to your friend for me. I just can't."

I sat there in my puddle on the pew, the wet clothes almost as heavy as my incredulity. First the hunting cabin debacle, now this. Why wasn't he taking this sweetheart of a deal? What was he waiting for? Two million dollars? A ride out of prison on a white steed? It made no sense.

"All right," I said.

And then, because I wasn't ready to give up on a hundred and fifty grand without more of a fight, I said, "I'm going to tell my friend you need some time to think about it. That way the deal will stay open in case you change your mind."

CHAPTER 41

The kids were out.

Charlie was at a friend's house, blissfully stoning himself on video games. Claire had a dance rehearsal.

So it was just Natalie, which meant that after the "hellos" and the "how are yous," Mitch could get right to the news:

"The FBI came at me today," he said, like this was something as mundane as changing his socks.

"They came to the prison?"

"Not exactly. There's this kid, Pete Goodrich. At least that's what he says his name is. He's an inmate. Allegedly. I'm pretty sure he works for the FBI. I think they sent him here."

"Why?"

"To win me over, gain my trust."

"What makes you think that?"

"He's been trying to get close to me ever since he got here. Bobby Harrison told me he paid him to get into the poker game. Ten cans! Who pays ten cans to get into a penny-ante poker game?"

"Maybe he just likes poker," Natalie suggested.

"That's not all. I mentioned the cabin at one point, just telling a hunting story—"

"About the big fifty-seven-point buck you, the ultimate humanitarian, didn't shoot?"

"Yeah, that one. He gave me this whole song and dance about an uncle who just so happened to have a hunting cabin in Chattahoochee. And where was my cabin? And, oh my goodness, what a coincidence, his uncle's cabin was near Tallulah Falls, too. Because doesn't everyone in the whole world have a cabin near Tallulah Falls, Georgia?"

"Well, it's possible he—"

"Just wait. I wasn't totally sure myself he was FBI at that point. But then, lo and behold, the moment I tell him about what I'm in here for, he just so happens to have a quote-unquote friend who is an FBI agent, and maybe, just maybe, he could broker a deal for me. Don't get me wrong, the kid is good. Real good. Like I said, I didn't suspect him for a while. But whatever."

"So what's the deal?"

"Time served. Plus WITSEC. Plus a million bucks."

All he heard on the end of the line was a sharp intake of breath. Then a soft moan. Then: "Oh, Mitch, a million dollars."

"The only thing I have to do is tell them where the documents are," he said.

She had no response. There was no point in rehashing it.

"You haven't changed my will, have you?" he asked.

"No. Why would I?"

"So it still has the same verbiage about how in the event of my death, no matter the circumstances, the SARs and the deposit slips get sent to the US Attorneys Office, with copies sent to *The Washington Post*."

"Of course, dear," Natalie assured him.

"Good. I'm going to hang up now. We might as well bank some minutes. Love you."

CHAPTER 42

Amanda had picked out a gray cowl-neck sweater and black pants, the least sexy outfit she could find that was still appropriate for a restaurant.

She had spent the afternoon rehearsing lines designed to spare Brock's feelings as much as possible, about how great a guy he was, about how lucky any woman would be to have him, about how much she loved him and cared about him as a friend.

All the while she knew how much those last three words would kill him. Ultimately, it didn't matter that your heart was being shattered by a rubber mallet instead of an ice pick. Rejection was still rejection.

When Brock's Mini Cooper pulled up to the curb, she walked quickly down the front steps, wanting to get the whole uncomfortable thing over with. He was wearing his usual jeans and blazer and met her with a quick peck on the cheek. Then he held the door for her, like usual.

On the way to the restaurant, they small-talked stiffly. The cruise had been great. He had gone scuba diving at every place the boat had stopped. He had done time on the treadmill so he could work off at least some of all the amazing food the ship served. She should really have come with him because he didn't see a mosquito the whole time.

Amanda wasn't going to push him on his agenda—it was his thing to tell, his thing to ask—and he didn't mention anything until they were seated at the restaurant and he had a glass of wine in front of him.

He took a long gulp, then set down the glass and said, "Sorry for the mysterious text earlier."

"Oh, right," Amanda said, like she hadn't been thinking about it. "What did you want to tell me, anyway?"

She braced herself. And then he came out with:

"I met someone on the cruise."

"Oh," she said, trying to sound more excited than surprised. "That's great, Brock. Who is she?"

"His name is Jonathan."

Amanda felt at once relieved and incredibly stupid. Of course Brock was gay. She should have known from the way he danced during those slow songs. The Mississippi girl's gaydar had epic-failed once again.

"He lives in Baltimore, so I don't know how much of a chance I'll get to see him," Brock continued. "But we had a really amazing time. He kind of reminds me of you, in that he's quiet at first, but he can really talk once he trusts you. We didn't hook up a lot—that sort of didn't happen until the end. But when we did . . ."

"Baltimore isn't that far away, you know," Amanda said.

"I know, I know. Look, you can't tell anyone, okay? My mom knows and doesn't care. But my dad is just so old-school. His idea of manhood is three wives and five kids, and I don't think he's even considered that there's any other way. He's always on me about why I don't find a nice girl and settle down. Sometimes I bring women like you around just to make him happy. I swear, I'll come out after he dies. But for now . . . He just wouldn't understand. Half the reason I travel so much is so I can be with guys without worrying about my father finding out."

"Sorry," Amanda said. "That has to be hard."

"Oh, it's fine. I think some people around Hackensack have probably figured it out. I'm pretty sure Ms. Jump knows."

Which explained why her future mother-in-law had no compunction about setting them up on a quasi date and why she hadn't objected to them spending so much time together since.

He continued: "I've gotten so used to living in the closet I practically have hangers imprinted in my back. I just, I felt strange not telling *you*. We've been spending so much time together and have gotten so close, not telling you felt like lying."

"Well, I won't tell anyone," she said, reaching across the table and patting his hand. "And I'm glad you trusted me enough to tell me."

"You're welcome. And now that I've told you my truth, I'm hoping you can tell me yours."

Amanda stiffened. What was he talking about?

"I was thinking about you while I was away, worrying about you, actually," he said. "So I googled '*Mamma Mia!* touring company' to see where Tommy was going to be around Christmas. I was thinking your Christmas present would be flying out to see him somewhere."

She shifted her gaze down and was now staring at the tablecloth.

"Honey, there *is* no touring company of *Mamma Mia!* There hasn't been for a few years now. It's none of my business if you don't want to tell me, but . . . what's Tommy *really* up to?"

Amanda reached for a strawberry-blond curl near her shoulder and twisted it around her finger. What was she supposed to say? She had seen the nondisclosure agreement Tommy had signed. It was explicit about the consequences of Tommy's arrangement with the FBI becoming public.

But Brock had plenty of practice keeping secrets. And who was he going to tell? So, after swearing him to silence, she gave him the brief rundown: how Tommy had been approached by Danny Ruiz to take an unusual kind of acting job for the FBI.

Brock listened, clearly puzzled.

"Danny Ruiz?" he said. "Like, *our* Danny Ruiz? The Danny Ruiz who grew up in Hackensack?"

"Yeah, why?"

"That . . . that doesn't make sense."

"Why not?"

"There's no way Danny works for the FBI," he said.

"What are you talking about?"

"As I understand it, he really ought to be in prison right now," Brock said.

Amanda's stomach lurched beyond even the usual bounds of morning sickness. She had to hold the sides of the table just to steady herself.

"Could you please start making sense?" she asked.

Brock leaned forward. "I was at a party in the city, maybe two, three years ago and I randomly bumped into this guy I hadn't seen since graduation. His parents had moved out of town, so he never really had a reason to come back to the old neighborhood. Anyway, he had just graduated law school and was now clerking for a federal judge. I asked him if he kept in touch with anyone from high school, and he said, 'You'll never guess who was a defendant in my courtroom last month.' And I was like, 'Who?' And he said, 'You remember Danny Ruiz?'"

Amanda was too stunned to say anything. She was losing her grip on the table, on reality itself.

"I was like, 'Yeah, of course I remember Danny. Danny Danger.' And then he told me this whole big story. The feds had Danny nailed dead to rights for trafficking some huge amount of crystal meth. He wasn't just the supplier. He was the supplier of the suppliers. And my buddy said he had obviously been doing pretty well with it, because he showed up in court with three lawyers in really, really nice suits. It was obvious to my buddy that Danny was guilty as hell, but he was just sitting there with this Cheshire cat smile the whole time. Sure enough, the lawyers got him off on some kind of technicality. They poked a hole in the search warrant or something like that, and it blew up the whole case. Danny just waltzed out of the courtroom, free as a bird."

Amanda's hand had gone over her mouth. She was shaking. Tears were pouring from her eyes, snot from her nose. It was every fear she had about this whole stupid thing, amplified, multiplied, and intensified.

"So Danny Ruiz is not working for the FBI," Brock finished. "Sounds like he's working for a cartel."

ACT THREE

Death doesn't discriminate between the sinners and the saints.

—Aaron Burr, from *Hamilton*

CHAPTER 43

The gun was never far from her reach.

When Natalie Dupree went out, she snuck it in her purse. When she was at Fancy Pants, she stashed it on a shelf under the cash register. When she slept, it was nestled beneath a nearby pillow. Just let that Mexican guy *try* to come at her again.

And so, as she drove aimlessly that Saturday night, with the Kia making an ominous rattling sound somewhere near the transmission, it was not at all unusual that the Colt was in the Fendi handbag, which was in the passenger seat next to her—riding shotgun, so to speak.

She had gone out simply because she couldn't sit around that dingy gray house anymore. Too depressing. Too empty.

Claire was at a sleepover. Charlie was at a movie with the same friend from before. It had left Natalie alone with her thoughts.

A million dollars.

One. Million. Dollars.

What would she do with that kind of money?

There was a time, before Mitch went away, when she barely gave a thought to sudden financial windfalls. Even when she passed one of those lottery billboards, announcing some obscene jackpot, all she'd think about is how the money wouldn't change her life that much. She would have stayed in the same house—she loved that house— hung out with the same friends, sent the kids to the same schools, kept the same routine. Oh, maybe they'd take nicer vacations or buy new cars. But when it came down to what actually mattered? She was set.

I don't need to win the lottery, she'd think. *I've won it already.*

It pained her to think of how much that had changed. And now here was Mitch, calling her and telling her the FBI had dangled a million bucks and his freedom in front of him and . . .

She cringed. She had passed one of her old haunts, an upscale restaurant in Buckhead where she and her girlfriends had gone to drink thirteen-dollar appletinis and share seventeen-dollar appetizers that contained no more than four bites of food. They'd run up a tab, slap down their credit cards, and never once worry if there'd be enough money at the end of the month to cover it.

What a life.

Natalie slowed further as she neared another favorite spot. It was packed with a Saturday night crowd full of women who didn't have to work at Fancy Pants, who considered mani-pedis a basic human right, who thought drugstore hair dye was for sex workers and refugees.

She sped up again. For a moment, she swore she was being tailed. By Mexicans? By the government? She wasn't going anywhere in particular, and she certainly wasn't following a straight path to get there, yet this one pair of headlights seemed to be going everywhere she did.

Then they were gone, and she decided the only thing that had really been following her was her own paranoia.

Before she really knew what she was doing, she was gliding by her former house, gazing at it longingly, remembering all the wonderful times her family had there. The new owners hadn't changed a thing. It really had been perfect.

Then she drove by that neoclassical eyesore with those stupid lions.

She went down a few houses more, turned around in a driveway, then came to a stop on the opposite side of the street from the Reiner residence. She killed the engine and hunkered down, as if lowering her profile made her invisible.

The neighborhood was quiet. The house was dark. The only nearby illumination came from the faux gaslights that lined the street.

And, really, she was just going to sit there, let herself fill with righteous anger, treat herself to her recurring revenge fantasy—the one that involved Thad Reiner's shocked countenance shortly before his brain exploded out the back of his head—and leave it at that.

Five minutes passed. Natalie stewed on Reiner's incredible mendacity, about that day when Mitch came home and said Reiner hadn't been submitting those SARs, about how methodical Mitch had been as he considered the right way to proceed, about the shock when the FBI came with search warrants and tore apart her cherished home.

Ten minutes. She was really burning now. At how skillful Reiner had been pinning his crime on Mitch. At how Mitch had been presumed guilty by pretty much everyone. At how quickly people turned on him. And her. Even her parents, who never should have doubted Mitch, took her aside to ask if she knew *for sure* he hadn't been working for the cartel. It was so infuriating.

And that's where she was stuck—at infuriated—when a pair of headlights came her way. Not the same headlights as before. They were a different shape. Natalie slumped lower. The headlights slowed.

Then a BMW 5 Series turned into the Reiner driveway.

Thad Reiner drove a BMW 5 Series.

The vehicle stopped at the top of the driveway. A light set to a motion detector above the garage came on, so Natalie had a good view of Reiner getting out, then entering the front door of his house.

Alone.

Natalie's face was flushed. This was as good an opportunity as she would ever have to do what she ached to do without any collateral damage. She could go in, shoot him, take some stuff to make it look like a robbery.

No, better: pull his pants down, staging it like some kind of lover's tryst gone wrong, so Reiner's family could experience some slice of the shame hers had.

Then she would flee. No one would suspect the suburban housewife. And the gun was untraceable.

She reached into her handbag and felt its handle. She was certain it had a full cartridge, but she pulled it out anyway. Just to check.

Yes. Fully loaded. She shoved the cartridge back in, then felt the weight of the gun. It was heavier than it looked. In so many ways. She slid it back into her bag. She put the bag over her shoulder.

She would shoot him once. Maybe twice. Enough to get the job done. Not so much to make it look like the shooter had been filled with righteous rage.

One deep breath to steady herself. Another. She could do this.

She opened the car door and was soon outside. Now that she was going, there would be no stopping her.

The Reiner household had a slate walkway coming off the sidewalk. It was guarded by a decorative wrought-iron gate, painted a glistening black. Natalie reached around, unfastened the clasp that held it, and swung it open.

With one last glance over her shoulder, to make sure no one was driving past, she walked through it. Her low heels clicked on the stone path. She had no doubt Reiner would open the door for her. He undressed her with his eyes every time he looked at her.

What a pig. Still, that would be her way in. She would tell him she needed money. She would say she was desperate. She would hint she was willing to do anything.

And then?

Vengeance. Justice. Would it feel empty, or would it fulfill her the way she had always hoped? She looked forward to having the chance to find out.

Now nearing the front porch, she opened her jacket and undid one of the buttons on her blouse. Then another. She wasn't wearing the right bra for maximum cleavage, but this would have to do.

She was ready. Maybe eight steps to go and she'd be knocking on the front door.

Then her phone bleeped.

She stopped.

The ringtone. It was the one she assigned to texts from Charlie. She was sure he was just messaging to say the movie was over and he needed to be picked up. He could wait a few extra minutes for her to finish this. She just had to get her legs moving again.

But by that point, her momentum was already gone. So was her nerve. Whatever spell she had been under was broken.

Fantasies aside, Natalie Dupree was no assassin. She was a mother. A mother who didn't want to do something that would send her to jail and make orphans of her children.

Still, she hadn't come this far not to get any satisfaction at all.

She pulled out the gun, took aim at one of the lions, and shot it in the face.

CHAPTER 44

There was no dust plume, no glinting windshield, nothing that alerted Herrera or anyone else to El Vio's impending arrival.

That's because he had come in the dark of night. El Vio and his motorcade of Range Rovers were at the gates of Rosario No. 2 before anyone could sound the alarm, before Herrera was even out of bed, and certainly before he could gather his wits about him enough to run.

Unpredictable. Always.

Herrera was still shoving his hand through his sleep-matted hair and hoping he had managed to button his shirt properly as he stumbled into the bunker. El Vio was standing there, perfectly alert, perfectly impatient, perfectly dressed in black, still wearing his mirrored sunglasses. His utility belt had two pistols strapped to it instead of the usual one.

"Where have you been?" he demanded.

There was no point in lying. "Sleeping," he said.

"Do you think the *federales* are sleeping right now? Do you think the Zetas are sleeping?"

Yes, actually, Herrera thought.

"We have a night watch, El Vio," Herrera said. "I have trained them to be on the lookout for any large threats. If Sinaloa made a move against us, we would be ready for them, and they would pay a terrible price. We had three rocket launchers trained on your vehicles as you approached. It's a good thing our men recognized your motorcade and eased off their triggers. Next time, you might want to let us know you're coming."

That was a lie, though El Vio accepted the bluff thoroughly enough that he shifted his weight, momentarily uncomfortable, like he was imagining the cabin of his Range Rover engulfed in flames. He turned his head to the side for a moment, exposing a momentary flash of white from his right eye.

"Very well," El Vio said, turning back. "What's the latest with our friend in West Virginia?"

Herrera suppressed the urge to twitch. There couldn't have been a worse time for El Vio to be here or to ask that question. Herrera had listened to the phone call between the banker and his wife four times. It didn't sound like the banker was going to take the FBI's deal, but if El Vio heard the same phone call and thought otherwise . . .

It could be a disaster. The kind that would have El Vio deciding he needed a new director of security.

"We have two contractors in America," Herrera said. "They are very good. Our friend is their sole concern. They are monitoring the situation closely."

"I want more than monitoring. I want results. I am tired of this remaining unresolved. You're not being aggressive enough."

"We're doing everything we can."

"What are the contractors' names?"

"Ruiz and Gilmartin."

"I want to speak to them. Now," El Vio said.

What choice did Herrera have? At least it was possible El Vio's ire might be redirected toward the contractors. Herrera pulled out his phone and called Ruiz, so they could talk in Spanish. When Ruiz answered, mumbling about how it was three o'clock in the morning, Herrera pressed the button for speakerphone.

"It is time to wake up," Herrera announced. "I have El Vio on the phone."

"El Vio!" Ruiz said, now awake. "This is an honor, sir!"

"What is the news from West Virginia?" El Vio asked.

"We are there now," Ruiz said. "We have a man inside the prison. He has gotten close to our friend."

"This is the large black man the General has told me about?"

"Not exactly, El Vio."

"Explain yourself."

"I told the General we had a man inside. I just misled him about which one," Ruiz said. "Forgive me for lying, El Vio. I didn't want anyone fouling up our operation and approaching our asset. We worked too hard to develop him. Our man is not a large black man. He is a small white man. And he's not an assassin. He's an actor."

"An actor!" El Vio said.

Was Herrera mistaken? Or did El Vio actually sound . . . pleased?

"Yes, El Vio. And he doesn't know who he's really working for. He thinks we are with the FBI. Right now, the actor has made our friend a very generous offer—a million dollars in exchange for the documents."

"But the offer is really coming from us," El Vio said, actually smiling. Herrera had never seen El Vio smile before.

Now Herrera doubly didn't want El Vio hearing the phone call between the banker and his wife. Nothing would erase the smile from El Vio's face faster if he understood how unlikely it was the banker would take this deal.

"That's right," Ruiz said. "We feel confident our friend will accept the offer. He's thinking it over right now."

"Very good. Offer two million if you like. Three million. Whatever it takes. The money is not important."

"Yes, El Vio."

"And the actor is unaware who he's really working for?"

"I assure you, El Vio, he has no idea."

CHAPTER 45

I skipped the poker game that Saturday night.

My official excuse was that I had been running around in the rain and now I was coming down with something. I sent Masri as my replacement. I'm sure the guys didn't care too much.

I then filled the night by brooding. I had called Danny and told him Dupree needed time to think about it. It was a simple enough message to convey that I used our code. There was no point in taking that one-in-fifteen chance unnecessarily.

Danny replied, also in code, that he would talk to his SAC about keeping the deal open for a week.

Which gave me a week to get Mitch to change his mind. There had to be a way.

The alternative was that I just stick it out for the next four-plus months, hoping he inadvertently slipped up and gave me a lead I could have Danny and Rick chase down—a lead that worked out better than the cabin.

Whatever the case, I wasn't going to give up. I had already decided that. I was closing in on two months inside. I could make it another four. Even if I didn't get the big bonus, seventy-five grand was more than I'd be able to make between now and April 9 doing anything else. I just had to grit it out.

When I woke up the next morning, that cold rain was still falling.

It made me feel like maybe I *was* coming down with something. There's no inspection on Sundays, so after breakfast I climbed back into my unmade bed. Frank had already gone off to church, giving me the room to myself. I had my book. My hope was to stay there and do nothing but read it until at least lunch, a plan that was going perfectly until one of the Randolph COs came into my room shortly after eight o'clock.

"Goodrich," he said. "You've got a visitor."

"I do?" I said, genuinely confused. "Who?"

"Your cousin."

That barely seemed possible. I had two cousins. They grew up in Yonkers. Even when I wasn't in prison, I barely—

Then I realized which "cousin" he meant. It had to be Amanda. She was the only nonfictitious person on my visitors list.

But what was she doing here? And without notice? We had talked on Friday, like usual. Trying to get a conversation going had been another exercise in dental extraction. There had been no mention of coming to see me. Not even a hint it was something she was thinking about.

I kicked off my blankets and hopped down to the ground. My fingers trembled as I tied the laces on my boots. I was already making guesses as to why my fiancée had felt compelled to make the five-hour drive down to West Virginia and take the risk of seeing me.

None of them were good. My first thought went to the baby. She had lost it. Or there was something wrong with the fetus. Or there was something wrong with her.

Then there were other possibilities. My mother was sick. My mother was hurt. Someone in the family had died. Whatever the case, it was devastating enough she didn't want to tell me over the phone and pressing enough that it couldn't wait.

The CO had already moved on, leaving me to escort myself up to the administration building, which housed the visitors' center. I ran there. A CO just inside the door logged me in and reminded me I wasn't allowed to accept any items from my visitor and that I would be searched on the way back out. I could barely bring myself to pay attention.

Then I was let into the visiting room, a large, cafeteria-like space with vending machines against the wall and tables and chairs set up throughout. Only a few of the tables had people sitting at them.

Amanda was in one of the corners and stood when she saw me. She was wearing a cowl-neck sweater she thought wasn't sexy on her. Naturally, I disagreed. The last time she wore it, we had gone out to a party, then come home and made love, then fallen asleep together in a naked tangle.

But I could tell right away the next memory associated with that sweater wasn't going to be nearly as happy. She looked tired, empty. Like she had been crying a lot.

My head, already spinning with awful thoughts, rotated even faster. My heart was throwing itself against the inside of my rib cage. Seeing her was at once joyous and agonizing. Something terrible had happened. Something that had already gutted her and was now going to take its turn with my insides.

I walked over to her and, without a word—and without worrying about what the COs might think if any of them realized Amanda was listed as my cousin—kissed her softly on the mouth. Then I embraced her. FCI Morgantown regulations permit one hug and one kiss at the start and end of a visit—yes, the Bureau of Prisons even rations how much affection an inmate can receive. I was going to make the most of mine.

Despite the circumstances, despite the surroundings, despite my fears about the terrible news I was about to hear, it felt incredible just to be near her. Incarceration divests you of so many liberties and material comforts, from something as consequential as the freedom of movement to something as simple as what brand of toothpaste you use. But the most powerful of all the deprivations is loving human contact. I missed it more than I had realized, on both a deep emotional level and a more immediate physical level: Within a second and a half, I had an erection. I pressed myself against her. She pulled herself even tighter, reaching around to grip my ass with both hands. I inhaled her scent, a smell I missed more than I realized.

I could have spent the entire day like that. Not talking. Not moving. Just holding her, feeling her heat, feeling the curves of her body. For all the times I had sung about characters who didn't want to let go, this was the first time I had truly felt it myself.

But, finally, a CO who had been hanging out near one of the vending machines walked up and gently said, "Okay, inmate. That's enough."

We released each other, then sat down. She scooted as close to me as she could. I was desperate to hold her hand, just so we could keep touching. But no one else seemed to be doing it, and I didn't need the CO hovering over us anymore.

I began with, "I've missed you so, so—"

"And I've missed you, too. But we can't start with that now. There's something really important I have to tell you."

Okay, here goes. I braced myself and said, "What's that?"

And then she said among the last things I ever expected to hear:

"Danny Ruiz doesn't work for the FBI."

I felt my brow wrinkle. "What are you talking about? Of course he does."

Amanda proceeded to tell me about how Brock had figured out I wasn't on tour. She then related a story Brock had heard from a high school friend of ours. It involved Danny Ruiz appearing in federal court.

As a defendant, not as a prosecuting witness.

"That's . . . I'm sure there's some kind of misunderstanding," I said. "You've seen him. He has that FBI car. And that FBI shield. And that FBI business card. And that FBI helpline. And that FBI money. And those FBI documents . . . I mean, those were—"

"Fakes. All of it was fake," she said quietly.

"No. I'm sure Brock just got it mixed up. There's got to be some kind of explanation—"

"I just spent all night in the car with Brock," she said. "He drove me down here late because he knew I wasn't in any shape to drive myself. I was on the Internet most of the way. Daniel Ruiz is a pretty common name, but Brock remembered that Danny's birthday was November 10, the day after his."

"Yeah. We'd get cupcakes on back-to-back days in homeroom."

"Well, anyway, I paid for full access to one of those public record search sites. I found a Daniel Roberto Ruiz who matched that birthday who was indicted on drug-trafficking charges in federal court. And there was a judge's order to dismiss the charges. It was a *sua sponte* dismissal, whatever that means. Southern District of New York. Dated two years ago."

I thought back to the quick bio Danny had given me as we were walking away from the Morgenthau back on Labor Day weekend. He mentioned the army, college, and being recruited by the FBI. Then he talked about having worked there for three years.

Three years, yeah. Hard to believe. It's been a good ride, though.

There wasn't any space in that timeline for facing federal drug charges, much less room in the FBI for someone who was a legal glitch away from being a convicted felon. Maybe as an informant. But not as an agent.

"Oh my God," I said.

I looked up at the ceiling, already blinking back tears. But I couldn't hold them. They were soon streaming down my face as the enormity of my blunder surrounded me.

"Oh, Amanda," I groaned, then repeated, "Oh my God."

"Shh, honey. Shh."

But there was no consoling me. Not immediately. She had to know that. So she just let me spout for a while.

Bizarrely, I found myself thinking of something I learned in science class many years earlier. At any given moment of any given day, we are carrying around a column of air that's as tall as the atmosphere itself. It's a massive weight: something approaching forty thousand pounds for a full-size adult, the equivalent of thirteen Honda Civics. We don't feel it, though, because just as that pushes down on us from above, an equal force supports us from below, and all is well.

Or at least that's how it's supposed to go. It just wasn't working for me anymore. The entire weight of that column was crushing me with nothing to counterbalance it. It was like I was never going to be able to get out of that chair or take another step.

I had covered my face with my hands and was drawing in labored breaths. My first intelligible words, after a string of unintelligible ones, were: "I am such a fool. I am *such* a fool."

"We were all fooled."

"But I'm the bigger fool. The much, much bigger fool. I was just . . . I was blinded. By the money. By my friendship with Danny. By . . ."

By wanting so badly to be with you, Amanda. But I didn't say that part. I didn't want to sound like I was blaming her for my own stupidity.

And there was lots of it, now that I looked back. I thought of the morning after they first approached me, when we returned to the diner. When Danny suggested I ask for more money, I took it as a sign he was looking out for me. Because I wanted to believe it. The whole thing was just a gambit, designed to set the hook, then reel me in. When I asked Gilmartin about taking the contract to a lawyer, he probably already knew I couldn't afford one.

And on it went. They cautioned me against speeding because they couldn't risk the scrutiny of real law enforcement. They wouldn't go anywhere near the federal courthouse in Morgantown for the same reason. They paid for everything in cash, even the things they bought for themselves, because not even they could fake an FBI credit card.

I removed my hands and looked at her. "And I'm sorry. I'm so sorry. This is all my fault. And I haven't just ruined my life. I've ruined yours, too. I've ruined the baby's life. I've ruined everything."

"Just try to get ahold of yourself," Amanda said.

Glancing at the CO, who was watching me carefully from about fifty feet away—because I was clearly in the middle of a breakdown—I lowered my voice to a fierce whisper. "Get ahold of myself? Don't you get it? I pleaded guilty. Freely and voluntarily. In an actual court of law. In front of an actual judge. And the FBI isn't going to be able to come get me out anytime I want, because the real FBI has no idea I'm even here. I'm stuck here for the next eight years of my life. *Eight. Years.*"

"Shh," Amanda said again.

"This is *for real*. What am I supposed to do? Go to the actual FBI and be like, 'Yeah, so, there's been this little mix-up. . . .' The administration here won't even let me talk to the FBI. It's very clear in the handbook that I'm not allowed to initiate contact with law enforcement. Only with the courts. And the courts would look back at my sentencing and be like, 'Uhh, sorry, pal, you pleaded guilty. Nothing we can do.' That's if I could even get them to pay attention. And I probably couldn't. Chances are they'd just ignore me, because I'm nothing more than another crazy convict who has become unhinged in prison and is now telling wild stories that no one would possibly believe.

"And it's not even like I can say, 'Ha-ha! That was Pete Goodrich who pleaded guilty, not Tommy Jump. So you can keep Pete Goodrich, but Tommy Jump is leaving now.' I gave them my fingerprints. So, sure, I could waltz out of here and they might not notice for a few hours. But you can be damn sure they'd start looking after that. And when they caught me, they wouldn't care if I was Tommy Jump or Pete Goodrich. As far as they would be concerned, my fingerprints belong to a guy who is supposed to be in prison. All I would have done by running away is added five years to my sentence for attempted escape. And I would serve it in a place a lot worse than this."

I finished that long rant with: "I am totally and completely screwed."

And then Amanda, who had apparently not just driven all this way to watch her fiancé have a mental breakdown, got this look of determination and, in her most proper Mississippi way, said, "Well, maybe not."

She made me compose myself before she told me what she meant. For at least a little while, this involved treating me like the large toddler I had become. She bought me a bottle of water and a cookie from the vending machine. She made me take deep breaths. She told me to walk a few laps around the room.

This, naturally, brought an inquiry from the CO. But Amanda was ready for that and fended the guy off with: "His meemaw died. It was very sudden. She had been in good health."

After my tears stopped and my respiration had returned to nearly normal—I was still taking these sharp, involuntarily gasps now and then—she sat me back down. We talked in low voices, our heads close.

"Feeling better?" she asked.

"A little. How are you so calm?"

"Oh, believe me, I wasn't at first. I went through everything you just did and worse when Brock told me about Danny. We were at a restaurant. I was so mortified by the scene I was making, I actually ran out. But I've had twelve hours to process this. Brock and I talked a lot on the way down here. He's been a prince."

"Please thank him for me."

"I will. But first things first. David Drayer."

The assistant US Attorney who, at least technically, convicted me. "What about him?"

"He's in on it. He has to be. He's the link between the very fake FBI of Danny Ruiz and the very real justice system that put you in here. He was the one who put in all the paperwork, who made it look like you were confessing to a real crime. Without a David Drayer who knows how to work the system, none of this happens."

"Okay, assuming you're right, how does that help us?"

"I don't think he wants to be in on it," Amanda said. "Do you remember what he was like when he came to see us at the Holiday Inn? He was really uncomfortable the whole time. He kept looking at Danny and Gilmartin like, 'Am I doing this right?' He knew they were frauds. Looking back on it, I think he was afraid of them."

"Oh my God. Kris Langetieg," I said.

"Who's that?"

"Remember when Danny asked you to leave the room so he could show us some super–top secret classified documents?"

"Uh-huh."

"It wasn't documents. It was a photograph of a murdered assistant US Attorney named Kris Langetieg. They had obviously tortured the guy before they killed him. It was . . . horrible. Indescribably horrible. Danny presented it like this was his motivation for being such a dedicated agent, like he was somehow Kris Langetieg's avenging angel. But he was actually sending a message to Drayer: Keep your damn mouth shut, or this is what you'll get."

"Why didn't you tell me about that?"

"It sounds stupid now, but I didn't want you to worry. Maybe I . . . I also didn't want you talking me out of doing this."

She frowned just slightly. "Okay. I understand. But from now on, we have to be a thousand percent honest with each other. About everything. No more holding back, okay? As a matter of fact, I have something I need to confess to you. Remember your friend from Arkansas?"

"Sure," I said.

"On Labor Day, while you were out on the deck chatting with your mother, he called to see if you were interested in taking that job with the Arkansas Repertory Theatre. I told him you had taken another job, which was technically true. Then I pretended like it never happened, because the truth was I didn't want you changing your mind. I was just as blinded by the money as you were. So when you say you're sorry and you ruined our lives, you can give yourself a break. I'm just as responsible for all this as you are. And if you want to be mad at me, you're certainly entitled to be."

I wasn't. Not even close. I looked into her eyes and the only thing I felt was extreme gratitude for whatever luck, fate, or happenstance had brought me into contact with this remarkable woman. Here I was at the lowest moment of my life, a wreck of a man, and she could have easily walked away from me. Yet she wasn't merely sticking by me. She was lifting me up, putting half of those Honda Civics on her own back.

Amanda had talked in the past about how she worried that our relationship had never been tested. It was being sorely tested now. And she was absolutely passing.

"You have no idea how much I love you right now," I blurted.

"Don't make me cry. We need to focus. David Drayer."

"Okay," I said.

"What you're saying about Kris Langetieg only confirms Drayer wanted no part of this. My guess is the cartel first approached Langetieg, who was Drayer's colleague. Maybe Langetieg went along with them for a while and then pulled out, or maybe he told them right away to go to hell. Either way, they killed him and then confronted Drayer with a combination of incentive and coercion."

"So it was 'take this bribe or we'll give you the Langetieg treatment'?"

"Something like that, yes," Amanda said. "My point is, he's not truly working for the cartel. What he does for them, he does only reluctantly. I have to go to Martinsburg and try to talk to him."

"What if he runs straight to Danny?"

"I don't think he will. In his heart, David Drayer is still one of the good guys."

"And you're thinking that if he's been coerced into cooperating with the cartel, we can get him to uncooperate somehow?"

"Or he'll know a way out of this," Amanda said. "He seemed like a man who had been backed into a corner. Maybe he'll know where there's a window you can climb out of."

"It's possible. And maybe there's room for Mitch to crawl out, too," I said, then proceeded to tell her about the whistle-blowing, the SARs, the deposit slips, and the duplicity of Thad Reiner.

As the visitors' room continued filling up, I kept having to talk louder to be heard. Before long, it was getting difficult for us to say anything that wasn't potentially going to be overheard by someone else.

And so, while it was painful, we agreed we should part ways rather than run the risk of something we said falling into the wrong ears. I had to go back to being Pete Goodrich, committing myself to a character who now had the extra burden of pretending he didn't know anything more than he had when he first walked into the room.

What's more—and I reminded Amanda about this—Pete couldn't even talk honestly over the phone with his wife, Kelly, because I had bugged those phones for the cartel. We would have to wait until Friday for our usual call, and even then we would have to converse as if nothing had changed.

To say anything or do anything differently, including destroying the listening devices, might tip off the cartel that I was onto them. In case David Drayer really did have an escape hatch for us, we would be giving away one of the few advantages we had over the cartel: the element of surprise.

After our one sanctioned kiss and hug, both of them far too brief, I had to whisper my final words: "Promise me you'll be safe. If you get the slightest hint Drayer is taking this to the cartel, run like hell and don't stop. You can leave me in here. I'll be fine. The last thing I want is for you to be seen as a threat by the cartel."

Then I added, "I've seen what they do to threats."

CHAPTER 46

Amanda had two conversations on the way to Martinsburg, one of which went much more smoothly than the other.

The easy one was with Brock, whom she briefed on what she had learned from Tommy.

Then there was what happened when Barb—who had made waffles for Amanda, thinking that would be a nice Sunday morning treat—discovered that her future daughter-in-law wasn't just sleeping in. Barb called, frantically certain that Amanda was "lying in a ditch somewhere."

It didn't help when Amanda attempted to reassure her by saying she wasn't in a ditch, she was in West Virginia. After that, Barb wasn't going to be satisfied with vague answers and half explanations.

"That's it," she announced when she had finally wrested the truth from Amanda. "I'm coming down. I'll see you in a few hours."

Amanda tried to protest, saying there was nothing Barb could do to help.

To which Barb replied, "I'd agree with you, but then we'd both be wrong."

Then she hung up.

Before long, Brock had delivered Amanda back to exit 13. A few hours later, Barb joined them. They didn't stay at the Holiday Inn. Amanda would have spent the whole time worrying she was going to round the corner and bump into Rick Gilmartin. They chose the Days Inn instead.

On Monday morning, they crammed into Brock's Mini Cooper for the short drive down the street to the W. Craig Broadwater Federal Building and United States Courthouse. Brock let the women off in front. They had agreed he would stay outside. If Drayer did something unexpected—had the women arrested? had the cartel come grab them?—Brock was their only backup.

They entered the same glass doors that Tommy had when he surrendered himself and were met by the same blue-blazered court security officers. Amanda said they were there to see David Drayer. One of the CSOs asked for their identification. Amanda couldn't be Kelly Goodrich, of course. So she handed him her Amanda Porter license.

The name would likely mean nothing to Drayer. But that was a good thing.

"Do you have an appointment?" he asked.

"No," she said curtly.

"Can I say what this is regarding?"

"No," she said again. "That's between me and Mr. Drayer."

The guy studied her for a moment. She was ready to tell him she wasn't going away until she talked to Drayer. She would stand in that lobby all day, stalk Drayer if he tried to leave for lunch, follow him as he walked out to his car, whatever it took. She was practically spoiling for a fight.

Something had finally clicked back into place in Amanda's mind, perhaps on the ride down from New Jersey, perhaps while talking with Tommy, perhaps during the trip to Martinsburg. Sometime during the last few months—more than likely during that horrible half hour in Hudson van Buren's office—she had forgotten herself. She had stopped being that scrappy girl from Mississippi. She had allowed herself to wallow, to feel sorry for herself, to let her obstacles define her.

To hell with that. Amanda was done being the victim. She was done with Hudson van Buren's leering face. She was the five-foot-two strawberry blonde with the adorable freckles who was ready to kick some ass.

It was possible she had managed to convey that to the guy in the blue blazer with one steely glance. Because after some back-and-forth on his walkie-talkie, he said, "Okay. Fourth floor."

They rode up the elevator in silence. A secretary greeted them and ushered them to Drayer's office. He was sitting behind a desk, staring at his computer screen through his rimless glasses. His fine white hair was more unkempt than it had been the first time Amanda saw him.

The moment he recognized Amanda and placed her—she was the woman from the hotel room, the woman whose husband he had sent to prison—his face went almost as white as his hair.

"Barb, close the door, please," Amanda said with quiet firmness, the voice of a woman who wasn't going to be disputed.

Barb did as she was told, then took a seat. Amanda stood in front of Drayer's desk with her arms crossed.

"You remember me. I can tell," Amanda said, keeping that deadly serious tone. "My fiancé, the man you sent to prison in October, isn't really named Pete Goodrich. His name is Tommy Jump. And he didn't rob a bank. But I think you knew that already."

Drayer either couldn't—or wouldn't—respond.

"The men in that hotel room weren't FBI agents," Amanda continued. "They work for the New Colima cartel. But you knew that, too."

"I don't . . . I don't know what you're talking about," he said.

The sentence limped out of his mouth, then died before it got much farther than the desk. No one in the room believed it, least of all Drayer.

He shifted his glance from Amanda, with her disbelieving scowl, to Barb, who looked ready to claw out his throat. His right leg started bouncing nervously. He simply couldn't maintain the guise of ignorance. He was a man who had built a career constructing castles of truth with boulders of incontrovertible evidence.

Finally, he gave up his attempt at artifice.

"You don't understand, I . . . I didn't have a choice," he whispered through clenched teeth. "They came to my house and told me exactly what happened with Langetieg. They made him an offer, he refused, and they killed him. Just like that. They said they'd do the same and worse to me and my whole family. By that point, we all knew Langetieg had been murdered. And we knew the body had been mutilated and that he had probably been tortured before he died. What was I supposed to do? Test them to see if they'd do it to me, too? I just—"

"So you sent an innocent man to prison?" Amanda snapped.

"Look, I didn't know anything about him. He's your fiancé? I still don't know anything about anything," Drayer protested. "I assumed he was working for the cartel too. I just thought . . . Well, I don't know what I thought. I was following orders. That's it. Those cartel guys told me to write up charging documents, and I did. They told me this guy would go along with whatever I came up with and plead guilty, and he did. I just wanted the whole thing to go away."

"But you still took their money," Amanda said. "You took money from them the same way we took money from them. The difference is, Tommy believed they were FBI agents. You knew better."

"I gave the money to charity," Drayer said. "My daughter works for a nonprofit, the Virginia Institute of Autism. I gave all the money to them."

"I'm sure that makes you feel a lot better about yourself. My fiancé is still in prison."

Drayer shook his head and reiterated, "I didn't have a choice."

"Well, you have a choice now," Amanda said. "You can do the right thing. My fiancé isn't a criminal. He's an actor. That's why New Colima hired him. They told him they wanted him to play a role that involved going to prison for them. I know it sounds crazy, but he went along with it. He's totally innocent in this. He doesn't belong behind bars."

"And what do you think I can do about that?"

"You got him in there. There's got to be a way you can get him out."

"How?" Drayer asked. "I'm just a prosecutor here. I'm not God. I don't get to tell the federal judiciary or the Bureau of Prisons what to do. Even if I did take this to a judge and say, 'Your Honor, this inmate has been cooperating with federal authorities and I'd like you to reduce his sentence,' there would need to be a hearing. The judge would expect testimony from the FBI. I can't invent cooperation that doesn't exist. I'm sorry. I wish I could help you here, but I can't."

Then Barb, who had managed to stay silent, finally couldn't contain herself any longer.

"You can't, huh?" she said. "You know, that's too bad. Because I noticed something on the way in here. There's a newspaper office next door to the courthouse. And you know something about newspapers? They love pretty young white girls with names like Amanda.

"And you know what they love more than their names? Their pictures. Newspapers *love* printing pictures of pretty young white girls in trouble. It doesn't even matter what the story is, whether they have something to say, or whether they're lost in Aruba, or what. The paper will run the story on the cover just so horny old men will walk by the newsstand and say, 'Hey! I wonder what's wrong with that pretty young white girl? I think I better buy the paper to find out.' Do we have to go that route? Do we have to march her into that newspaper office and tell her to start talking and posing for pictures?"

If it was possible for Drayer to shrink any further, he did.

"Please don't," he said in a barely audible voice.

"All right, then I think you need to be a little more creative in your thinking here. Tommy Jump, the man you sent to prison, is my son. And once the paper was done with her, they could talk to me. Newspapers might not love wrinkled old women as much as they love pretty young girls, but scorned mothers make for pretty good copy too."

"Okay, okay," Drayer said, breathing out heavily. "I want to help you. I do. I just don't know . . ."

He shook his head. "There are only two options that I can think of. Number one would be if we got him a new trial. The problem there is, I'm not sure how to do it. You can only get a new trial if there is genuinely new evidence that comes out, something that couldn't possibly have been discovered at the time of his conviction. It's a high bar. Especially when you're talking about disproving an event that was completely fabricated in the first place. It's not like we're going to find someone who will say, 'Oh yeah, that was actually me who robbed that bank.' There was no bank robbery."

"What about an alibi?" Barb suggested. "I don't know when this fictional bank robbery was, but I'm sure Tommy was hundreds of miles away, doing a show somewhere."

"Again, that's going to be very difficult, because the question the court will ask is, 'Well, wait a second, if this guy had such a solid alibi, why wasn't this presented during the first go-around? And why did he plead guilty?' It just raises too many questions we can't answer. So, really, I think we have to go with our second option."

"What's that?" Amanda asked.

"We get him resentenced based on his extraordinary cooperation with law enforcement. That's a somewhat easier route, and it happens more often. The question there is, on what issue is he cooperating? It has to be something real, something that will get the FBI excited when I take it to them."

Barb presented it like it should have been obvious to all: "He can testify against Danny Ruiz and Rick Gilmartin for impersonating federal law enforcement officers."

Drayer was already shaking his head before Barb could finish. "I'm sorry, but I doubt that's going to move the needle. When judges weigh cooperation, one of the things they're asking is how important the cooperation actually is. How much public good was done here? Impersonating a federal law enforcement officer would be seen as a less serious crime than robbing a bank. So a judge might shave a year off Tommy's sentence, which would be nice. But I'm guessing that's not what you have in mind here."

There was silence in the room. Frustrated, stymied silence.

"This is madness," Barb said. "He didn't actually rob a bank! How can he be in jail for something he didn't do?"

"I'm sorry, ma'am, but you've got to put that thought out of your mind," Drayer said gently. "As far as the courts are concerned, he's had his bite at the apple. They bend over backwards to make sure that first bite is as fair as it can be. That's what the presumption of innocence is all about. But once he's had that, it's very, very difficult to get him a second bite. Plus, if we tried to reopen the case, he'd have to admit that he lied to the court the first time by pleading guilty. That's called perjury. And he'd have to acknowledge he took money from the cartel in exchange for breaking the law. That's called criminal conspiracy. Both carry their own penalties. That's why I think cooperation is the way to go. But it has to be big. Does he have something on the cartel itself?"

"No," Amanda said immediately. "But the man he went to prison to get close to sure does."

Amanda talked Drayer through what Tommy had told her, about Dupree and the smoking-gun evidence he was harboring.

"Would that be enough?" she asked when she was done.

"Sure would," Drayer said. "If your fiancé can play a role in bringing down the most notorious drug lord in the Western Hemisphere? I think any judge would go for that."

"Okay, so what do we do next?" Amanda asked.

"We talk to the FBI," Drayer said. "The *real* FBI."

CHAPTER 47

Herrera had waited until El Vio departed Rosario No. 2.

Then he called back the contractors and demanded to know everything—*everything*—about this actor they had hired. How had they found him? Had they needed to convince him to do this job, or had he been eager? Was there any chance this "actor" wasn't really an actor and was in fact working for someone else?

After all, the actor was now a subcontractor for New Colima—acting, even if he wasn't aware of it, on the cartel's behalf. Which meant the director of security needed to give him a thorough vetting.

Ruiz assured Herrera all was as it seemed. Still, Herrera knew he could never be too careful. Law enforcement was more cunning than ever. Especially when it came to high-level targets like New Colima.

This actor could actually be some kind of sleeper agent. Herrera had heard devastating stories about such people. These were law enforcement officials who spent years establishing their credentials as criminals and worked their way deep into the organizations they would someday destroy, even committing illegal acts in order to improve their cover.

They would then wait until the most critical moment—like, say, when the criminal syndicate in question was about to recover some vital documents—to reveal themselves.

Another scary scenario: that the actor was working not for law enforcement but rather for a rival cartel. One of their enemies could use those documents to extort New Colima out of hard-won territory and supply lines.

Anything was possible. There was something about this whole setup that smelled wrong to Herrera. He didn't like that the contractor had lied about who his asset had been. Herrera was also nervous about the personal history between Ruiz and the actor.

Who was this actor, *really*?

This was what led, two days later, to Herrera making another journey through the tunnel, past the border checkpoint—to which several new insults had been added—and into America. As Hector Jacinto, he caught a flight to Newark, then rented a car.

He made a quick stop at a New Colima safe house in Newark's North Ward, arming himself courtesy of two associates who were thrilled to be able to help such a high-ranking member of the cartel. Then he continued farther north.

The actor grew up with Ruiz in a town called Hackensack. According to the contractor, the actor had a mother and a fiancée. This delighted Herrera. They were potential leverage.

Before long, Herrera found himself once again in the knotty tangle of suburban America. Shortly after ten P.M.—earlier than was probably wise, but Herrera was tired—he turned onto the actor's street and drove past his house. Just once. It was small, like all the others on the street. There were no lights on. Its short driveway was empty, and it had no garage. So no cars. Which suggested no one was home. That was the extent of what Herrera could distinguish at twenty-five miles an hour.

He parked around the corner and was soon on foot. Just a guy going for a walk. It wasn't a new moon, which he would have preferred. And there were streetlights. Still, he felt less conspicuous than he had in Atlanta. There were more Mexicans here.

After one walk-by, he allowed himself another, looking for signs of habitation. During that second pass, the exterior lights on the house next door turned on. A tall, dark-skinned man in a turban emerged from the front door and stood on the porch.

His intent was unmistakable. *I see you. I know my neighbors. You don't belong here.*

Herrera hurried along, retreating back into his car, scolding himself for being sloppy, impatient. He drove to a Marriott two towns away and checked in under the name Hector Jacinto. Then he waited.

At two A.M., he returned to the neighborhood. Surely, the man in the turban was asleep by now. Just in case, Herrera approached the actor's house from the opposite direction. He was no longer some amiable ambler, out for a stroll. He was moving with purpose.

When he was two doors away, he pulled on his ski mask. His gloves were already on. He turned quickly into the actor's driveway and then skirted around the right side of the house. There was a narrow gap between two fences—one belonging to the actor's house, one belonging to the neighbor's. Herrera scaled the one to his left and was soon in the actor's backyard.

There wasn't much to it. Just a small patch of grass, now dormant in winter. It was dark back there, shaded from the streetlights by the house. Finally, Herrera felt like he could take his time and look around without worrying about being spotted.

The house was simple. Just a plain white box, not like the gracious homes Herrera had grown up around in Jalisco. There was a deck with a cheap patio set, its umbrella tightly wrapped. The only other structure was a shed in the far corner.

No lights were on inside the house. Not even a nightlight in a hallway. Herrera climbed the three steps up to the deck and peered into one of the windows. He tried it, just to see if he could get lucky. But no. Locked.

The only door was sliding glass. He checked to see if it was reinforced by a bar. It wasn't. He had found his way in.

He descended the steps back into the yard, then opened the shed. He wasn't expecting a full lockpick set, but with what he was able to rummage—screwdrivers, some twelve-gauge wire, a gardening fork, and whatnot—he was confident he had everything he needed. It wasn't like he had to worry about the noise he was making.

Fifteen minutes later, he was inside the house. Whoever had been there last had left in a hurry. There were dishes in the sink. A plate full of waffles, now partially desiccated, had been abandoned out on the table.

Herrera treated himself to a full tour of the house, learning everything he could. There were pictures of a small woman, likely the actor's mother, and a small boy who resembled her. That had to be the actor. He had been scrawny as a teenager and as a young adult. Only in his later pictures had he added some muscle.

There was one picture of the actor with his arm wrapped around the waist of a beautiful young blond woman. The fiancée, obviously. She was wearing a sweater that hugged her upper half, a skirt that showed off her legs. He allowed his eyes to linger on her. His thing for blondes again.

With his phone camera, Herrera snapped a picture of the picture, then continued on. Nothing in the house triggered Herrera's alarm. No pictures of the young man graduating from a police academy or a diploma from a criminal justice college. No indications any of them had traveled to Mexico. No conspicuous signs of new wealth that may have come courtesy of a rival cartel.

The last room Herrera entered was the second bedroom. It was ringed with glass-covered framed snapshots from Broadway musicals. The actor was featured in all of them. When he wasn't onstage, he was posed with other people who must have also been actors. They had that glossy glow about them.

Herrera brought his face close to the glass. The pictures were authentic, not photoshopped. And, really, even the FBI or Sinaloa wouldn't have gone through the trouble of making that many fakes. The actor had, in fact, been an actor.

He continued into the bathroom, which was connected to the

bedroom. As he had done in the other bathrooms, he opened every door and drawer. He only slowed down when he got to the medicine cabinet. On the second shelf up, next to some tweezers, there was a jar of vitamins.

But not just any vitamins. Prenatal vitamins.

The fiancée was pregnant.

Interesting.

CHAPTER 48

For three days, I lived in a kind of suspended animation.

My body kept operating, because it had to. My mind was working through the very real possibility I would have to spend the next eight years serving time for an invented crime; and while I could rail against Danny Ruiz or the New Colima cartel, I ultimately had nothing to blame but my own gullibility.

The dread of that came at me in waves. At times, I almost convinced myself I could handle it. I had made a colossal mistake for which I would pay dearly, but others in this world had made worse mistakes or had worse things happen to them. They had survived. So would I.

Eight years wasn't a life sentence. It just felt that way.

At other times, the awfulness of it all hit me so hard I could barely breathe. Eight years of soul-deadening monotony, of time thrown away, of pain for people I loved.

Eight years was the remainder of my late twenties and the entirety of my early thirties, prime years of my life. It also encompassed the first seven years and three months of existence for my son or daughter, who would have scant to no relationship with Daddy, not to mention being saddled with the confusion and shame of Daddy's incarceration. Some huge portion of the child's personality—basically all of it, right?—would be formed, with barely any help or input from me.

All the while, Amanda would be struggling along as a single parent. I didn't want to think about what kind of resentment she would have built for me or what our relationship would look like by the time I got out.

It was thoughts like this that made me wish there was someplace I could just hide. But the federal prison system doesn't allow inmates vacation days.

So I kept going through the motions, there but not there. I trudged off to the laundry each morning, played in the poker game each night—why not?—and maintained the guise that nothing had really changed for Pete Goodrich, that there was no before/after schism in his life that had started the moment he learned he had been duped.

Despite my efforts at projecting normalcy, I swear Mitch was acting differently toward me. The first few times, I thought maybe I was just imagining it. But after several days of it, there was no question: Mitch's behavior had changed. He was guarded. There were no stories about hunting. There was no more talk about his days at USB.

Not that it really mattered. My mission had changed. It was no longer about Mitch.

It was about getting the hell out of there.

Not being able to talk to Amanda only made it harder. Was she making progress? Had Drayer shut her down? Had she given up and gone back to New Jersey? Was she leaving me to rot? I could only guess.

Perhaps the strangest thing about those three days was that, in some ways, nothing else had really changed. To me, the earth shifted on Sunday morning. To FCI Morgantown, it was right where it had been all along.

It wasn't until Wednesday morning, when I was coming out of laundry duty, that Karen Lembo flagged me down.

She gently grabbed my arm and steered me to a place where no one would be able to hear us. And then, softly, she said, "The warden sent me to get you. Two FBI agents are here. They're waiting for you in a conference room up in the administration building. Will you come with me, please?"

My first reaction was that Ruiz and Gilmartin had a lot of nerve, fake-badging their way into FCI Morgantown. Shouldn't they have treated a federal prison like the one patch of turf they didn't dare tread on?

My second reaction was fear. This was a bold move on their part, bordering on reckless. And they wouldn't have made it for no reason. Amanda's maneuvering must have triggered some chain reaction. Drayer ran straight to them and now they were coming here, to tell me they were onto me being onto them. They would deliver that news alongside some kind of threat against me. Or, worse, against Amanda.

My third reaction—and this one began forming as I walked up to the administration building with Mrs. Lembo—was that maybe I could turn this around on Ruiz and Gilmartin. Could I, without alerting my fake FBI friends, signal to Mrs. Lembo or someone else high up at FCI Morgantown that these so-called FBI agents were really cartel henchmen? Had they, in fact, made a massive mistake that I could turn into my advantage?

These were among the many thoughts making waves in my brain as I walked up the hill toward the administration building.

Mrs. Lembo led me inside, then took me to a part of the building I had never been in, down a carpeted corridor. Without a word of explanation, she opened a door to a conference room, where two people were waiting.

Not Ruiz and Gilmartin.

It was man and a woman, both in suits. The woman had a no-nonsense air about her and shoulder-length brown hair that was starting to get streaks of gray. The man was blond and square-jawed. I had never seen either before.

They invited me to sit down, which I did. I was still trying to process what was happening when the door opened again.

And in walked Mitch Dupree.

H e didn't look at me or at the two strangers in suits. He seemed mostly interested in the table.

"My name is Special Agent Lia Hines," the woman said to me. She had a warm, earthy voice that would have sounded at home on an elementary school teacher. She gestured toward the guy. "This is Special Agent Chris Hall."

He made brief eye contact with me but otherwise sat stone-faced. There weren't going to be any five-paragraph essays coming from him.

"We work in white-collar crime for the Federal Bureau of Investigation," Agent Hines continued. "Mr. Dupree is already quite familiar with us. It's nice to see you again, Mr. Dupree."

She glanced serenely toward Mitch, who was still furiously studying the table. She slid business cards toward both of us, which triggered in me a strong sense of déjà vu. Danny Ruiz had done the same thing. Except this time it was real, right? Dupree knew them.

I looked at her card:

LIA HINES
SPECIAL AGENT
FEDERAL BUREAU OF INVESTIGATION
ATLANTA FIELD OFFICE
3000 FLOWERS ROAD S.
ATLANTA, GA 30341

It looked legit. But then again so had the one Danny gave me.

Once bitten, twice shy, I asked Mrs. Lembo to go to the FBI's website, look up the number for the Atlanta Field Office, and verify Lia Hines' employment. It took Mrs. Lembo a few minutes to accomplish this, but she was soon giving me a thumbs-up and saying, "Thank you," to whomever she had talked to.

Hines sat patiently through this exercise, then began.

"Mr. Goodrich, you obviously don't trust me, and that's fine. I understand. Mr. Dupree can tell you I'm a pretty straight shooter. I believe you lay things on the table and then see where that leaves you. You're either going to love it or hate it, but I won't be apologizing either way. How does that sound to you?"

"Fine, I guess," I said, still mystified as to what was going on.

"What brings us here today is a little unusual," she said. "We were contacted by an AUSA from the Northern District of West Virginia named David Drayer. He said you had a conversation with your fiancée, who then relayed the conversation to Mr. Drayer in the hopes of getting a sentence reduction in exchange for cooperation with us. Now, before we get into the details, I want you to understand that the FBI is not the federal judiciary. We do not have the power to shorten or commute your sentence. At most we can make a recommendation to a judge, and then it's out of our hands. Is that clear to you?"

"Yes," I said.

"Okay, good. Moving on, the story that came through to us was . . . Well, it's certainly a different version of events than we're familiar with. And it included some new details about the documents Mr. Dupree has been withholding from us. I assume you know what I'm talking about?"

"Yes," I said earnestly.

"Would you mind repeating what you told your fiancée, just so I make sure I've gotten this all correct?"

Mitch glanced at me, his annoyance plain. This was a betrayal of the time-honored no-snitch code. I didn't care. If it got me even three inches closer to walking out that front gate at FCI Morgantown, I was going to throw him under the bus and run over him until his face had tread marks on it.

I reiterated for the agents a condensed version of what Mitch had told me. As the amateur lawyer in me suspected, Agent Hines was particularly interested in the deposit slips. I told her what I could.

When I was done, she turned to Mitch.

"Well, Mr. Dupree. That is certainly more detail than we were ever able to get out of you. Do you care to confirm what Mr. Good-rich has told us?"

Mitch had an ugly set to his jaw. His bottom teeth were showing, clenched against his top lip. When he spoke, it was with venom in his voice.

"Oh, so *now* you want to talk to me?" he said. "You people. You didn't want to hear a thing I had to say when I tried to tell you what was really going on at USB. But *now* you're interested? After you've thrown me in jail and ruined my life? Forget it. Forget it now. Forget it later. I have nothing to say to you."

Agent Hines took this in placidly. The elementary schoolteacher had dealt with petulant third graders before.

But she could be as calm as she wanted, and it wouldn't placate Mitch, who was beyond fuming. I suppose I would be too, were I in his situation: wrongfully convicted of a crime that I had actually tried to prevent from happening.

The problem was now, his rage had made him myopic. He was so dug in against the FBI—so insistent he didn't give them any kind of victory—he couldn't recognize what was truly in his best interests.

I had to get him to see that by turning over these documents, he would really be helping himself and his family.

And mine.

I wasn't going to stress that part, of course. But I still suddenly felt like I couldn't properly say what I needed to as Pete Goodrich.

He needed to hear it from Tommy Jump. Agent Hines had already started in on her next angle of attack, but I interrupted her. "Actually, Agent Hines, would you give me a moment to talk to Mitch? I need to be honest with him about some things."

Straight-shooting Lia appraised me with curiosity but simply said, "Sure, go ahead."

I turned myself to Mitch and began, "The first thing you need to know is . . ."

And then I dropped the Pete Goodrich West Virginia mountain lilt.

"My name isn't Pete Goodrich," I said in my normal voice. "I'm not a history teacher. I didn't rob a bank. I don't have a wife and three kids. More or less everything I've ever said to you about myself is a lie."

I paused there, to see how he was taking this. He was giving no indication of having a reaction to it either way, so I continued:

"My name is Tommy Jump. I'm an actor from New Jersey. I have a pregnant fiancée and a worried mother, and that's about it. I was hired by the FBI to come here and see if I could figure out where you stashed those documents. They paid me seventy-five thousand dollars, with the promise of more if I was successful. Except the guy who I thought worked for the FBI, because he was a childhood friend of mine and because I trusted him, turned out to actually be working for the cartel. Obviously, I didn't know that when I first came here. I really did think I was working for the right side."

An actor knows few things better than how to read an audience, and none of them had expected this twist. David Drayer must not have mentioned this part. Which made sense, because that would have been admitting his own underhanded role.

"This past weekend, my fiancée figured out the truth and came here to warn me. Then she went and spoke to this prosecutor, and here we all are. The point of all this is not merely that I'm an idiot and that I've been lying to you this whole time—I'm sorry for that, by the way. The point is that this cartel isn't going to stop looking for those deposit slips. They'll throw as much money and as many people at it as they need to. And they're only going to get more creative and more ruthless about how they do it. They failed with me, obviously. But they're going to try and try and try again until they succeed.

"The moment they find what they're looking for—and someday, they will—it would be over for you. That scenario ends the same way every time. So let's think about a different scenario, one where you turn the documents over to the FBI. I know you don't like the FBI, and I don't blame you. But think about what they'll do with the deposit slips. They'll use them to destroy the cartel. Destroy it. Completely. El Vio would either be dead, because he didn't allow himself to be taken alive, or in a supermax prison, where he'd be shut off from the rest of the world. His employees would either be dead, in prison themselves, or working for whatever pestilence arises to take New Colima's place. It would take some time, obviously, but eventually there wouldn't be anyone left with both the will and the means to kill you. You wouldn't have to look over your shoulder anymore. You'd be free. Truly free. So come on, just give them the documents and let's go back to our families."

I looked at Mitch hopefully. My words had swayed him. There was no question. He wasn't as angry.

At the very least, he seemed to be thinking it through. His banker's brain was trained in risk assessment and loss prevention. What I had just laid out appealed to those disciplines.

After a pause, he looked at Agent Hines and asked, "Are you recording this?"

"No," she said.

"I think maybe you should start," he said.

She reached into her suit pocket, pulled out her phone, tapped it a few times, then set it on the table. To make things official, she announced the date and setting, then introduced herself and the other people in the room.

"Okay, Mr. Dupree," she said. "You are now on the record with the Federal Bureau of Investigation. Go ahead."

"All right. I just want to make sure I understand this properly. If I hand over these documents, I will be considered a cooperating witness, is that right?"

"Yes," Hines said.

"And what would the FBI be prepared to do for me?"

"We could probably improve the last offer we made you."

"Improve it how?" Mitch demanded.

"Well, now that we understand just how potentially valuable this evidence is, I think we could see clear to recommending you be released with time served. From there, I assume you would want WITSEC for you and your family, and we would enter you in that program if you wished."

"That would be a start," Mitch said. "But that's not good enough. I'd want you to promise that you intend to pursue a case against Thad Reiner and seek the harshest possible penalties for him and any others at USB who knew about his scheme. I'd want a written apology from the FBI, saying it was wrong to prosecute me, acknowledging that I was a hundred percent innocent, admitting that you were totally and completely incompetent."

Agent Hines briefly pursed her lips—the only show of emotion she had yet allowed herself—then shifted her face back to neutral.

"If your evidence corroborates what you're saying, we would acknowledge any mistakes we may have made," she said.

"In writing."

"In writing," she repeated.

Mitch sat there, staring her down, enjoying this small moment of vindication, anticipating the larger one that was to come.

"So, time served, WITSEC, a case against Reiner, and a letter of apology in exchange for the documents," he said. "Do I have that all right?"

"With the aforementioned caveats, yes," Hines said.

I was holding my breath and thinking of Amanda. Of our baby. Of no longer having to wash convicts' undergarments. Of getting on with a quiet, ordinary, blissfully boring life.

And then Mitch smiled maliciously and said, "Yeah, go to hell, it's still not happening."

The bastard. That whole setup was just his way of twisting the knife after he plunged it into all of us.

Mitch Dupree wasn't giving up anything. Which meant I was going to lose nearly a decade of my life before I was again a free man. I actually moaned.

"I'm glad we could get that on the record," he said, enjoying himself. "Now, if you'll excuse me, I have time to serve."

He shoved his chair back at an odd angle and stood up. He was making for the door, leaving us all a little stunned.

Then Chris Hall, the blond agent, opened his mouth for the first time.

"Mr. Dupree, you might want to wait a moment," he said.

Mitch wasn't slowing down. He already had his hand on the door handle. Hall was pulling a piece of photographic paper out of a folder and placing it on the table. It was glossy eight-by-ten picture of a petite woman with frosted blond hair.

Dupree's wife.

And she had a gun in her hand.

CHAPTER 49

Mitch still had his hand on the door, but he was no longer moving in the direction of the hallway. He had turned his body back toward the table.

"What . . . what's this about?" he asked.

"Why don't you have a seat," Hall suggested.

"Why don't you tell me what the hell is going on."

"Well, Mr. Dupree, that's your wife—"

"I know that, asshole." Mitch bristled, then looked at Hines. "Stop the damn recording."

Then he turned his gaze on me. "Do you know anything about this?"

"Not a thing," I said. "I swear."

Mitch was still near the door. He had yet to take a step back in our direction.

"Have a seat, sir," Hall said, this time more firmly.

Whatever brief argument Mitch was having with himself soon ended. He walked back to his still-warm chair. He sat.

"Okay," he said. "Start talking."

"I think you're aware we've been keeping an eye on your wife," Hall said. "Not all the time. We don't have the staffing for that. But we occasionally go by her new house and point a parabolic her way.

And we've had a sporadic tail on her in the hopes that she leads us somewhere we don't know about yet."

Mitch's jaw muscles flexed as his back molars ground together.

"A few days ago, on Saturday night, we had an agent on her. We often find that subjects who suspect they may be followed are a little more careless on weekends, because they think we're not going to be working. Anyhow, we captured an interesting series of photographs. To be honest, we weren't really sure what to do about them. Especially once Mr. Drayer approached us on Monday. They were . . . an inconvenience, really. Maybe you'd like to have a look."

Hall began placing glossies on the table. They were all this odd shade of green, like they had been shot in the dark by a night-vision camera. But they were plenty clear. The first showed Natalie Dupree in the driver's seat of a Kia, parked in front of a vast brick house adorned with white columns.

"I believe you're aware that's Thad Reiner's residence," Hall said.

Mitch didn't reply. In the next photos Hall placed down, Natalie had the gun in her hand. Then she was returning the gun to the bag.

"She's about to break the law for the first time right here," Hall said. "In the state of Georgia, you're allowed to carry a handgun in your residence or your vehicle. But the moment she steps out of the vehicle with the handgun on her person, she needs a carry permit—which, according to records, she doesn't have. It's only a misdemeanor. But it's a start. So here we go."

Another photo. Natalie was now out of the car, her hand on the front gate of that big brick house, her head turned back toward the street, checking one last time to see if anyone was watching. I didn't know what was going to come next, but if I was on a jury, I would have been ready to convict. It was like a director had told her, "Actually, could you try to look a little more guilty, please?"

Hall was clearly enjoying himself. "So now we've got her for criminal trespassing, because she's entering someone's property uninvited, with the intent to break the law. We got prints off that gate, by the way. It was high-gloss paint, so she left some nice fat ones for us."

In the next shot, she was striding up the front walkway. The angle was such that you could only half see her face. Her determination was still unmistakable.

"And now we get to the felony," Hall said, placing down four photos in rapid succession.

Natalie Dupree aiming the gun at the house. Natalie depressing the trigger. Then Natalie with her eyes half-closed and the barrel of the gun raised slightly from the kickback. The final one was a close-up of a stone lion that had stood guard next to the front entrance of the house. It had been taken sometime later, in daylight. A small chunk of the lion's face was missing.

"We found the bullet, in case you're wondering," Hall said. "It was a little deformed, but our forensics people are good. They'll be able to match it to the gun that fired it, no problem."

Mitch had been braced like he was expecting more, like this was going to end with blood-and-gore crime scene shots or Thad Reiner's autopsy photos. Now that it had turned out to be benign—at least relative to that—he was on the attack.

"She shot the lion," Mitch said. "So what? Half the people in that neighborhood probably wanted to shoot those stupid lions."

Hall shook his head, like this somehow saddened him. "In the state of Georgia, the threatening of a witness is a serious matter."

"You've got to be kidding me," Mitch said.

"There are two parts of the statute," Hall said, ignoring him. "One deals with the attempted murder or threatening of a witness. It's punishable by ten to twenty years. Was this attempted murder? There is case law where discharging a weapon at someone's domicile can be considered an attempt on their life. It would be up to the prosecutor how to charge it, of course. Given the enmity Mrs. Dupree clearly has for Mr. Reiner, I could certainly make the case."

"She shot the damn lion," Mitch repeated, practically shouting now.

"Ah, but then we get to the other part of the statute, which deals explicitly with what we're looking at here. It talks about a person who threatens to damage or damages the property or household of a witness. The property *or* the household, Mr. Dupree. In this case, we'd be talking about both. The mandatory minimum listed in this part of the statute is two years. Plus, there would be enhancements to the sentencing because she used a firearm in the commission of a crime. The statute allows for up to ten years.

"Whatever the number, your wife would be a convicted felon. She'd be heading for the state penitentiary. We understand her parents are disabled, so Social Services would be unlikely to consider them appropriate caregivers. And according to your presentencing report, you have no other family members in the state of Georgia. Your kids would go into foster care. Children older than five are notoriously tough to place. Yours would end up in a group home."

"Okay, I get it, I get it, stop," Mitch said. "Why are you telling me all this?"

Agent Hines stepped back in. "It's really pretty simple, Mr. Dupree. Part of our deal would be that we'd forget we have these pictures. Right now, Thad Reiner suspects your wife is the one who shot his lion, but he doesn't have any evidence. We'd make sure it stayed that way. The last thing we'd want is a cooperating witness who was worried about his wife's prosecution. Plus, once Mrs. Dupree entered WITSEC and established a new identity, it would be impractical to have her returning to Georgia to face criminal charges. It would be much easier for us if this never happened."

Mitch put it all together: "So basically, you're offering me not only my freedom but my wife's freedom as well."

He shook his head. His body rocked slightly with each breath he took.

"You people are scum, you know that?" he said. "Following around my wife and then using these photos to extort me. I really don't know how you sleep at night."

"I don't like to play it this way, Mr. Dupree," Hines said. "But it doesn't compare to what this cartel has done. And by withholding those documents from us, you are enabling them to continue their operation. The murder, the terror, the drugs, all of it. I'll do anything within my legal power to stop them, and I sleep just fine, thank you."

"Just hand over the documents, Dupree," Hall said acidly. "It's time."

Mitch actually laughed, then shook his head, a sound and a gesture as sardonic as it was resentful. He looked down at the table, shook his head a few more times, like he couldn't believe this was happening. Then he brought his gaze up again.

"You're right," he said. "It's time. It's time I tell you the truth."

He stopped. For a moment, he was a man whose finger was hovering above a detonator. Then he pressed the button:

"The truth is, I don't have any documents."

L ike any good performer would, Mitch followed that utterly staggering bit of dialogue—*I don't have any documents*—with another pregnant pause.

He wanted to give his audience a beat to absorb this information in their own fashion. No-nonsense Lia Hines had adopted a look of fastidious concern. Tough-guy Chris Hall's square jaw had suddenly gone asymmetrical, as if this revelation may have been too much for even his composure to handle.

It was certainly too much for mine. I had confessed to an invented crime so I could go to prison at the behest of impostors to uncover the location of something that existed only in a fabrication. The whole thing was a series of frauds stacked on top of each other like layer cake, then iced with irony.

"I'd love to turn over the documents, but I can't turn over something I don't have," Mitch said. "What I told Pete here—or whatever his name is—was true. I was a very dutiful little compliance director.

I put together those SARs, which included scanned versions of the deposit slips, for years and years. I sent them along to Thad Reiner, thinking he was forwarding them to FinCEN. But it was all on computer. I destroyed those deposit slips. Every single damn time. I can't tell you how often I've wished I saved even one of them, because I'm pretty sure I wouldn't be here right now. But, no, I shredded them. It just never occurred to me I was going to be double-crossed by my boss. I thought eventually FinCEN was going to come in, do a lookback, then shut down the whole thing. I thought worst-case scenario for me was that I'd be looking for a new job, because my relationship with Reiner and the people above him would have become too toxic. But I'd be doing that job search as the hero who saved his bank a huge fine because he had been self-reporting the whole thing.

"When I finally realized Reiner hadn't been submitting those SARs, I thought I was going to have time to assemble more examples of illicit transactions and collect more deposit slips. But the next thing I knew, the morning after we had that confrontation in his office, I was followed to work by these Mexican guys. I thought I had to be imagining it at first—like, this couldn't be real, right?—but, yeah, they were following me. So I was pretty spooked. And then, as I'm still trying to get things in order so I can blow the whistle, Reiner beat me to it and you guys rode in with your badges and your warrants and arrested me."

He gave a derisive eye roll, then continued: "You obviously had the black hats and the white hats confused, but there was no way I was going to convince you of that. Objectively, the evidence against me was pretty overwhelming, and I knew I was going down no matter what. Especially once I figured out that the SARs no longer existed, that Thad not only hadn't filed them, he had been using his VP access to erase them from the server. He was covering his tracks well. And I knew eventually I was going to be just another liability and that the cartel was going to eliminate me—one less loose end. I worried about my family, too, because those Mexican guys knew where

I lived. So I made up the story about having kept the SARs and the deposit slips and blabbed about them whenever I suspected there was an open microphone nearby. It was the only way I could keep myself and my family safe.

"My wife and I developed this whole routine about how she wanted to go into WITSEC and I didn't, and how I knew where the documents were and she didn't, and how I had put this codicil in my will. But it was all an act. So you can try to blackmail me into turning everything over, but I have nothing to give. All you'd be doing is compounding the error you've already made and punishing a family that has been through more than enough pain."

He leaned back in his chair and crossed his arms. Agent Hines still looked like she had swallowed something that tasted bad. It was Agent Hall who spoke first.

"I don't believe you," he said. "You're just trying to save your wife's skin."

"Would you get your head out of your ass for just one second?" Mitch said. "Think about it: If I *actually* had the SARs and the deposit slips, don't you think I would have used them at trial to prove my innocence?"

"No, because you wanted to cover for the cartel, just like you're continuing to do now," Hall shot back. "You're going to serve your time and follow your orders, knowing they'll reward you for it in the end."

Mitch threw up his hands. "I don't know how many times I have to tell you: I don't work for the—"

"Sure you don't," Hall spat. "You have the language skills. You had the access. You had the contacts. There were all those trips down to Mexico—"

"All of which were legitimate bank business," Mitch protested. "I was in the Latin American division. Where was I supposed to go? Australia?"

"And then I suppose you've come up with a new explanation for the account in Jersey? Let me guess. You inherited the money."

"Would you listen to me for once? I didn't know *anything* about that stupid account. That was Thad Reiner. It was all—"

Mitch interrupted himself with an exasperated sigh before resuming: "Never mind. This is pointless. You want to prosecute my wife for shooting a statue? Go ahead. Make my kids orphans. If that's what it takes to move your career forward, I hope you're real, real proud of your next promotion, you heartless son of a bitch."

"I'm not the one who pulled the trigger," Hall said superciliously. "I'm not the one who—"

Agent Hines placed a hand on Hall's arm for a moment, stopping him midscreed.

"Okay, gentlemen. I think we're done here," she said. "Mr. Dupree, if you change your mind, talk to Mrs. Lembo. She knows how to reach us."

"It's not about changing my—"

Ignoring him, she turned to Hall and said, "Let's go."

Hines stood, bringing up a briefcase from under the table and opening it. Hall began collecting photographs.

This meeting was over. The rest of my incarceration, all eight years' worth, would now commence. I knew, in a very sure place in my heart, that Mitch didn't have any documents. The Mitch Dupree I had come to know so well over the last two months would have done anything to save his wife from prison and his kids from foster care.

But whether or not the agents ultimately believed Mitch had already become a fringe issue, at least where my reality was concerned. If Mitch didn't have any documents, I was simply stuck here. I could wail and moan about being tricked by Ruiz and Gilmartin, I could make accusations about David Drayer, I could try to get the courts to pay attention to my plight.

None of it would matter. It would always come back to the same thing: I had pleaded guilty, ergo I belonged here.

Mitch was watching the agents with a forlorn expression, the kind he had mastered thoroughly during a life that had been so unfairly sideswiped off its chosen road. His anger was fading fast, rapidly swapping out for desperation.

"What are you going to do with my wife?" he asked.

The agents kept packing up their things.

"What's going to happen to Natalie?" Mitch asked again.

Hines had snapped the briefcase closed. Hall was buttoning his jacket.

"Please," Mitch said pathetically. "She's all my kids have. You've already taken their father from them. Don't take their mother, too. I swear to you, I don't have any documents. If I did, I would have surrendered them a long, long time ago. Please believe me. I can't create something that doesn't exist. *Please.*"

His voice was trembling. And I was so absorbed in his drama, I almost didn't hear the most important sentence he had spoken all day:

I can't create something that doesn't exist.

It was giving me an idea. Not a well-formed one. It was lumpy, misshapen—wet clay, at best. Were this any other kind of meeting, I would have just kept my mouth shut until I could think it through.

But I didn't have that kind of time. These FBI agents from Atlanta weren't going to come running back to West Virginia simply because a lowly convict declared he had fully concocted a marvelous scheme. Half-cocked was going to have to do.

I can't create something that doesn't exist.

The idea was in my brain, somewhere. If only I could wrestle it more fully from all the folds and wrinkles in which it was currently trapped.

I can't create something that doesn't exist.

And then I finally asked myself the right question: *But what if we could?*

The agents were rounding the table, heading for the door. They had said good-bye to Mrs. Lembo and thanked her for her hospitality. She had returned their courtesy. In five more steps, maybe less, they were going to be out the door and forever out of my life.

If I was going to speak, now was the time.

"Wait," I said. "I think we're all missing a golden opportunity here."

That was enough to halt the agents. They had turned their heads toward me. My words came out in a rush.

"I believe Mitch when he says the documents don't exist anymore. But it actually doesn't matter whether you do or not. The important thing is that *New Colima* believes they exist. Mitch has done a brilliant job making them believe it. Let's use that against them."

I had everyone's attention. I kept going.

"I assume the FBI would be interested in arresting two cartel members who have been posing as FBI agents and are responsible for killing an assistant US Attorney named Kris Langetieg. They admitted as much to David Drayer. I'm sure he would testify to that."

"I'm listening," Agent Hines said.

"Good. Because right now, my fake FBI agents think Mitch is currently weighing an offer from them: a million bucks, plus witness protection and blah-blah-blah in return for the location of the documents. They have no idea I've met with you. I can call them and say something like, 'Hey, guys, the jig is up. I figured out you're not real FBI. But Mitch is willing to play ball anyway. He wants five million dollars in exchange for the documents. And I want five million for brokering the deal.' They'll want to see the documents first, of course. And we're going to give them what they want, because Mitch is going to forge some SARs and some deposit slips. You could do that, right?"

Mitch didn't have to think about it. "If I had access to a computer? Sure. I spent four years filling those things out every day. I could do it in my sleep."

He then turned to Hines. "Actually, if you could have someone go to some *casas de cambio* in Mexico and get some blank deposit slips, I could really make it look good. The signatures were all fake anyway. It was like they had a random Spanish name generator. Juan Carlos Pablo José whatever. Some of them would come in a little wrinkled, like they had spent time in someone's pocket, but that would be easy enough to simulate."

Mitch was now back to me. "The only problem is, I was submitting these SARs for four years, pretty much every day. I even invented the number of them I supposedly had: nine hundred and fifty-one. So they'd be expecting to retrieve nine hundred and fifty-one SARs. That's going to take a long, long time to fake. It's a three-page form. I could probably fake one in about twenty minutes. But even if that's all I did, it would still take months to—"

"You don't need to do that," I said. "The SARs are worthless without the deposit slips. We can tell Danny you only kept the deposit slips and you brought them with you to prison. It's believable enough. We're allowed to bring legal documents in with us. Nine hundred and fifty-one deposit slips could probably fit in a shoebox."

"So we use the fake deposit slips as the bait, then swoop in and arrest these guys?" Hines said.

"Exactly," I said. "What do you think?"

No one spoke for maybe ten seconds, until Mitch doused my enthusiasm with a cold bucket of his reality.

"Sorry, I just don't see what's in it for me," he said, then nodded toward the agents. "They get a couple of cartel members. You get some help proving you didn't belong here in the first place, which maybe sways a judge somewhere. What do I get, exactly? I'd just be poking the bear. You may have noticed I have enough problems without doing that."

"But if you cooperated in this, it would prove you weren't working for the cartel," I said.

"Yeah? So what? They name me Citizen of the Year and give me a bright blue ribbon? It's too big a risk for zero payout."

"Not zero," I said. "I'm sure these agents would graciously promise to deep-six those photos of your wife."

Mitch grimaced at the mere mention of that evidence. But Hall said, "I think we could agree to that."

More deliberative silence followed. We didn't absolutely need Mitch for this plan to work. We could fake deposit slips without his help. They might not be quite as good, but they'd be good enough.

But I could tell this plan wasn't really exciting anyone very much. Ruiz and Gilmartin may have been everything to me. To New Colima, they were little more than midlevel foot soldiers. Cartels were designed to be able to lose guys like them and keep right on ticking. Hines and Hall would get a nice little pat on the back from their supervisors. I might or might not get out of here. It was all relentlessly small-time.

I needed to think bigger. A lot bigger.

This was when that wet clay I had been playing with transformed into the *David*.

"What if I tell Ruiz that Mitch will only turn the deposit slips over to El Vio himself?" I said. "So the story becomes: Mitch is demanding five million bucks *and* a meeting, because he wants El Vio's personal assurance that if he gives up the deposit slips, he and his family won't be immediately killed. We could tell them we want the exchange to happen at Dorsey's Knob Park in the middle of the night. Gilmartin is familiar with it. We made an exchange there before."

It was fair to say this electrified the agents. As it should have. To be the agents who captured El Vio? That was fame everlasting, both inside and outside the bureau.

Books would be written.

Movies would be made.

Glory would be achieved.

Hall was acting like someone had put tacks in his shoes. Hines had just barely managed to wipe the dreamy look off her face.

"So you arrange for El Vio to come here to West Virginia," she said. "We lie in wait and grab him when he shows up."

"That's right. Though you'd have to be damn careful. El Vio

would be looking for a trap. If he got even the slightest suspicion you were hanging around . . ."

"Forget about us," Hall said. "We know how to do this. You really think you can pull off your end? You think you can convince them to get El Vio to come here?"

"Yes," I said, sounding more filled with brio than I perhaps felt.

And then I added: "However."

Hines focused on me. Hall stopped his tack dance.

"I would need an ironclad assurance from you," I said.

"What's that?" Hines asked.

"We both go free," I said. "It wouldn't be safe for Mitch to be here any longer once word got out he double-crossed El Vio. And I never should have been here in the first place."

The agents conferred through brief eye contact. Then Hines spoke:

"If you can deliver us El Vio? I'll personally see to it you're taken out of here in limousines."

CHAPTER 50

We spent the next few hours getting granular with the details. By the time we had something workable, it was three o'clock in the afternoon. I felt ready to confront Danny Ruiz. Or as ready as I could be.

We had decided I would make the call from a burner phone. If I used the Randolph phones, the Bureau of Prisons would be listening—which, if nothing else, would prevent Danny from being able to talk freely. With Mrs. Lembo's blessing, Agent Hall went out and procured a flip phone that, by appearances, had not set the FBI back much.

I told them I didn't want to make the call in front of them, which Hines had originally fought against. But I convinced her my job was already difficult enough, without the added pressure of performing for a live audience. I won the argument when I pointed out that we were each going to have to trust each other a lot in the coming days if this plan was ever going to succeed.

Eventually, she acquiesced. They set me up in an empty office down the hall from the conference room. It was strange—strange and powerful—being gifted with cellular technology again after two months in the dark ages. In my hands, that cheap burner phone felt like Excalibur.

Now sitting at a desk, like some midlevel BOP bureaucrat, I took a few deep breaths to mentally prepare myself. I had to be the same actor Ruiz and Gilmartin had hired. They couldn't suspect I had switched roles behind their backs.

I dialed Danny's number. After three rings, he answered with a cautious, "Hello?"

This was the first time I had actually talked to him since learning what he really was. His treachery, the ease with which he had manipulated me—and the unwitting guilelessness I had shown throughout most of it—was coming back to me as both humiliation and anger.

But I swallowed the bile rising in my throat and, in my regular voice—not my Pete Goodrich accent—said, "Hey. It's Tommy."

"Slugbomb? What's this number you're calling me on?"

"It's a burner phone. I had a CO smuggle it in for me. I wanted us to be able to talk without the Bureau of Prisons listening in."

"Oh, right. Smart. So what's up? Did Mitch finally make up his mind?"

"Yeah, he did."

"What did he say?"

"Not yet. We've got some business to discuss first," I said, then presented my newfound knowledge without adornment: "I know what you really are, Danny. I know who you really work for."

"I'm sorry, what?"

"I know you're not an FBI agent."

"I'm not?" And then, in typical smooth-Danny fashion, he tried to made a joke out of it: "Then why am I wearing this suit right now?"

"Knock it off, Danny. I know about the drug charges you faced. I know you killed Kris Langetieg. I know you threatened David Drayer into cooperating. I know you have been lying to me about everything."

"Slow down, slow down. I have no idea what you're talking about. Did someone . . . Did you hear something that got you upset? Help me out here. I'm confused about where this is coming from."

"Stop it. Stop pretending. It's over."

"There's nothing to pretend, I'm—"

"Great. Then prove it. Come to FCI Morgantown. Bring Rick Gilmartin, or whatever his name really is. Tell the warden here you're FBI and that you want to speak to an inmate. Present him with that big fake gold badge of yours, and let's see if your credentials hold up for more than about five minutes."

"Whoa, take it easy, Slugbomb. I'm . . . I'm actually in the middle of some things right now. I can't just drop everything because you have some wild hunch about—"

"This isn't a hunch," I said, then lied a bit, so I could cover for Amanda. "Just stop, Danny. I hired a lawyer to do a records search. He found documents from your trial. There was a *sua sponte* dismissal in the Southern District of New York. It was dated two years ago, when you told me you were already working for the FBI. Now, are you going to stop lying to me so we can get on with the rest of this conversation? Or are you going to keep wasting my time? Because Mitch Dupree has made up his mind about taking the deal, but we're not going to get to that until you stop playing dumb."

There were certain phrases that a career actor simply wouldn't know. "*Sua sponte* dismissal" was one of them. And I suspect Danny was working through his very limited set of possible responses now that I had him verbally cornered.

The only thing I heard for the next ten seconds or so was an open cell line, clicking and hissing through that burner phone's earpiece.

"Okay. Fine. I'm not FBI," he said at last.

"You work for New Colima cartel."

"Yes and no. I got into mercenary work after the army, and one thing led to another. I made some contacts down there. I was distributing for them when I got arrested, and they paid for the lawyers who got me off. After that, they decided I shouldn't handle product anymore. I'm now an independent contractor. But, yes, I am currently working for New Colima exclusively."

"Okay. Great," I spat, and had to tamp down my anger again.

I wanted recriminations and explanations. I wanted him to be contrite about having lied so blithely to me and genuinely sorry that his scheme involved leaving me to fester in prison with no hope of escape. I wanted, in other words, for him to be human.

Then I reminded myself I was never going to get those things and that they no longer mattered anyway. The actor had to leave his feelings out of this and stay on task.

"So what's up with Mitch Dupree?" Danny asked.

"He knows what you are, too. And what I am. And he's willing to deal."

"He'll tell us where the documents are?"

"Better than that, he has the documents with him," I said. "Once I finally told him what was going on, he admitted he never kept the SARs, just the deposit slips. Which is all that really ties the cartel to the money laundering anyway. They're stored in a shoebox, if you can believe that. All nine hundred and fifty-one of them. They're safely locked away here at Morgantown, and he gets full access to them because they're considered legal documents. He can bring them up to Dorsey's Knob Park, same place I met Gilmartin with the mackerel. He'll know where it is. But the price has changed."

"To what?"

"Five million bucks. Each. Since you're not really FBI, and therefore you can't get us out of here, we figure that's adequate compensation for the time we're going to have to spend locked up. We'll set up overseas accounts. The money will have to be in there before Mitch so much as turns over his pocket lint for you. Plus . . ."

I let the "plus" dangle out there before getting to the important part.

". . . Mitch will only hand the deposit slips to El Vio himself."

Danny's response was immediate: "Ha. No chance."

"Sorry. That's how it's going to have to be. Mitch wants a personal, face-to-face, eyeball-to-eyeball promise from El Vio that when this transaction is over, they'll go their separate ways with no bad blood whatsoever. El Vio returns to being an international drug lord, knowing he won't have extradition hanging over his head. And Mitch returns to being a convict, knowing neither he nor his family will be harmed, and he'll have five million bucks to spend when he gets out. That's the deal."

"You don't understand. El Vio isn't some clown you can call in to tie balloons at your kid's birthday party. He doesn't make scheduled appearances. Even his own people don't know when he's going to show up. He just does."

"Fine. Then you can tell your bosses that Mitch will be turning the deposit slips over to the FBI. The real FBI."

The line crackled some more, the uninterrupted static telling me I had just articulated El Vio's idea of the apocalypse.

"Well, I'm sure he wouldn't want that," Danny said.

"That's what I thought. And one more thing."

This was the part I wasn't sure about. But Hines, citing several white papers from FBI psychologists, had insisted that speed was vital.

"You've got exactly twenty-four hours to decide," I said. "If the answer is no, the documents go to the FBI. If the answer is yes, we make the exchange tomorrow night. I'll call you back at this time tomorrow to get your answer."

CHAPTER 51

Herrera had sent the e-mail as soon as Ruiz was done relaying the actor's offer.

El Vio replied four minutes later with three words: "Where are you?"

Herrera wrote back that he was at a Marriott hotel in Saddle Brook, New Jersey, performing his due diligence regarding the actor.

El Vio's answer contained two words: "Stay there."

Soon it was four o'clock in the afternoon. Then seven in the evening. Then nine at night.

Herrera grew agitated. He had spent his day staking out the actor's house. "Hector Jacinto" had rented three more cars so that nosy man in the turban wouldn't see the same one driving past.

The house had stayed quiet through the morning. Shortly after one o'clock in the afternoon, two cars appeared in the driveway. He drove past again, perhaps half an hour later, and spotted the actor's fiancée removing a duffel bag from the back hatch of her SUV.

His plan was to return when it was dark so he could watch her more. But now he was stuck in this hotel room. Herrera couldn't even guess what was happening. It wasn't like it was taking El Vio this long to get the money together. Ten million dollars was milk money to El Vio. He was obviously weighing the other half of the deal, the risk versus the reward.

The delay was worrisome. El Vio was the personification of action. He never took this long to do anything. He surely understood the time constraint here. The actor's threat to go to the FBI was possibly a bluff. But the price of calling it was far too high.

Herrera kept watching the clock. He didn't dare go to sleep, lest he miss a message.

One finally came in at quarter to midnight. Again, two words: "What room?"

What did that matter? Herrera thought. But he replied all the same. When El Vio asked a question, he got an answer.

Four minutes later, there was a knock at the door. Herrera looked through the peephole and blinked three times to make sure his eyes weren't deceiving him.

It was El Vio. The man himself. Flanked by two bodyguards. In the hallway of an American Marriott.

Be unpredictable.

Herrera was both thrilled and terrified. Perhaps more of the latter. El Vio didn't kill people in upscale chain hotels, did he?

There was no more time to ponder the possibility. Herrera just opened the door wide, forced cheer into his face, and said, "El Vio! This is an unexpected surprise."

"Yes," El Vio said. "I'm sure it is."

El Vio turned to the bodyguards and said, "Stay here."

He entered the room. Herrera stood to the side, allowing El Vio to walk past. He was wearing his black clothes, his sunglasses, his utility belt, though it was devoid of weapons for once. Not that it gave Herrera much reassurance. The men outside could be called in to handle matters if El Vio decided he needed a new director of security.

Not knowing what to expect, Herrera stood there, his every sense alert for whatever El Vio was going to do next.

Then, in the most unguarded gesture Herrera had seen from the man, El Vio sank into a chair on the far side of the room. He removed his sunglasses, setting them on the small end table next to the chair. He rubbed his eyes, the good and the bad.

Whatever El Vio had been up to—traveling here from . . . where? Mexico? Europe? it could have been anywhere—he was actually fatigued.

"I need something to drink," he said in a cracked voice.

Herrera paused. Surely El Vio didn't mean a *real* drink? There was no minibar in the room. Herrera tensed.

Then El Vio clarified: "Some water."

"Would you like ice?" Herrera asked.

"Please."

Herrera grabbed the ice bin and walked into the hallway, past the bodyguards, toward the elevator, where he had seen an ice maker. It was almost surreal. Arguably the most powerful man in Mexico, and there was Herrera, fetching him a cool beverage.

Herrera returned to the room, filled a glass, and handed it to El Vio. He drank it in one long gulp and said, "More, please."

Two refills later, he said, "Thank you." He already sounded stronger. He took in one long breath and released it slowly. Herrera was making an effort not to stare at El Vio's white eye, which was atrophied and did not move in concert with the dark one.

"The contractors in America have done well," El Vio said. "This is quite an opportunity."

"Yes. Though I worry it could be a trap."

Herrera had thought of little else during the last few hours.

"From law enforcement or from one of our rivals?" El Vio asked.

"Either. We must be vigilant for both."

"I agree," El Vio said. "I don't think the banker is working with American law enforcement. He has had that opportunity in the past, and he has never taken advantage of it. And it seems unlikely he would have come across another cartel at a minimum-security prison. But the actor is a new presence. What do we know about him?"

Herrera's confidence surged. This was a question he could answer with certainty.

"He is what he appears to be," Herrera said. "Ruiz grew up with him. He truly has been working as an actor. I broke into his house early this morning. There were pictures of him appearing in many musicals. I don't think it would be possible to fake what I saw."

"What is his name?"

"Pete Goodrich. Peter Lenfest Goodrich."

El Vio bobbed his head, storing away that information before asking, "Did you see any evidence he had spent time in Mexico?"

"No."

"Then our chief worry is that this Peter Lenfest Goodrich is work-ing with American law enforcement. Is that possible?"

"Possible, but unlikely. There is nothing that makes me suspect that."

El Vio closed his eyes. Apparently, both eyelids worked fine. This was a side of El Vio that Herrera had never seen. The uncertainty. The hesitance. The doubt.

"We could use a body double," Herrera suggested.

"Who looks like this?" El Vio said, opening his eyes and staring rather pointedly, managing to get the bad one directed at Herrera along with the good one. "There are pictures of me on the Internet without my glasses. If we lost the documents because we decided to play games . . ."

El Vio didn't finish the thought. He just shook his head and said: "I want this to be over."

So do I. Even more than you, Herrera thought. And it was that thought—being free of the constant threat of death—that motivated his next utterance.

"I think we need to be daring," he said. "For ten million dollars and one evening of your life, we can end this for good."

El Vio narrowed his eyes as soon as Herrera said *atrevido.*

"And if the actor springs some kind of trap?" El Vio asked.

"I have something in mind."

"What's that?"

"We take out an insurance policy," Herrera said, producing his phone, showing El Vio the picture of the actor with his beautiful fiancée.

"She's pregnant," Herrera added.

El Vio studied the photo for a beat, then nodded. "Call Ruiz. Tell him we'll take the deal."

CHAPTER 52

My first stirrings the next morning came before the wake-up call.

Two months in Randolph had habituated me to sleeping through all kinds of noise, but there was something different about what I was hearing: the repeated opening of a squeaky metal door, the scuffling of bare feet around the room, the apian buzz of a zipper making its way up the tracks.

It sounded like someone packing. I opened my eyes to see Frank, already fully dressed in his khakis, bustling about our room. I reached for my digital watch, which I had strapped to the bed's metal crossbeam.

Five thirty-eight. My long wait until three o'clock was beginning earlier than I would have liked.

"Sorry to wake you, sir," Frank said. "I was too excited to sleep."

All his belongings—which, admittedly, wasn't much—had been removed from his locker and were stacked on our desk.

"You going somewhere?" I asked, my throat still thick with morning sludge.

"Yes, sir," he said, drawing up his already massive body just a little more. "It's my last day. Going home."

A smile broke across my face. "Hey, that's great, Frank. Really great. How long you been here?"

"My sentence was eighteen months, but I got me some good-time credit. Going home about two months early."

"Well, congratulations," I said.

I might have lain back down, but I knew my own efforts to get home—albeit less conventional than Frank's—already had me too keyed up. I propped myself up on my elbow and watched him continue his preparations.

Other than when I bribed him to attack Mitch, my interaction with Frank had been limited. He had his church. I had my schemes. We had remained polite but distant. It seemed to suit both of us.

But now I wanted to know:

"What were you in here for anyway, if you don't mind my asking?"

He turned his huge head toward me. Being on the top bunk had brought me closer than normal to eye level. Only the whites really showed. The rest blurred into the darkness of the room.

"My little girl got sick," he said. "It was this thing with her kidneys. I never could pronounce it. She needed medicine that cost twenty-two thousand dollars a year. I had a business mowing lawns, sir. My wife does people's hair. We got by, but we didn't have no insurance, and we didn't have no twenty-two thousand dollars. The government said we couldn't get free insurance for our little one. They said we made too much money. So I stole another family's card and used it to take my little girl to the doctor, then to get her that medicine."

"Medicaid fraud?" I said. "You committed Medicaid fraud?"

"Did it for years. That's why I'm in here. The government said if I hadn't done it so bad, I could have just gotten me a big fine. But they said I stole more than a hundred fifty thousand dollars from them, so I had to go to jail."

"Because you wanted your little girl to get better," I said.

"Yes, sir. They say my time in here was supposed to make me learn better, but I'd do it again if I had to."

What little light came into our room was now reflecting off his glistening eyes.

"My little girl," he said. "I'd do anything for her."

"Yeah, I know," I said, understanding that urge all too well. "How is she doing now?"

"She's fine, long as she gets her medicine. When I got thrown in here, we were finally poor enough to get government insurance. God provides. Sometimes he just do it in strange ways."

He hefted the bag, which looked small against his giant shoulder.

"I got to get going," he said. "They said if I get up to administration by six, they got a van going out that I can hitch a ride on."

"Good luck, Frank," I said.

"You too, sir."

We shook hands one last time. Then he was gone.

CHAPTER 53

Amanda swore she had never been this tired in her life. And it wasn't even like she had been that active. Not physically, anyway.

All she, Barb, and Brock had done the day before was drive back from West Virginia, caravanning it in their two cars. Amanda's body felt like she had walked the entire way.

By eight o'clock at night, she succumbed from the effort of keeping her eyes open and declared she was going to bed. Her obstetrician warned her she would need more sleep during the first trimester as the tiny life inside her formed its vital structures. Amanda just didn't realize this would hit her like advanced narcolepsy.

Even now, twelve hours later, she was still in bed, convinced she needed the strength of ten Herculeses just to get out of it.

The trip to West Virginia had taxed her in ways she hadn't quite recognized while she was in the midst of it. First there was watching Tommy have a near mental breakdown in that visiting room. Then there was having to convince/cajole David Drayer into cooperation. Then there were the meetings with the FBI agents, Hines and Hall, who started out as plainly disbelieving and had to be worked hard just to get up to circumspect.

Each step was its own wrenching challenge, requiring her to summon skills she hadn't exactly been taught at art school. Thank goodness for Brock. And for Barb. Even the scrappy girl from Mississippi needed backup.

Amanda had wanted to stay in West Virginia, to be closer to Tommy. But Drayer and the agents said it would likely take several weeks to put together any kind of operation, and perhaps several more before Tommy had a hearing that might—even under a best-case scenario—lead to a reduction of his sentence.

Therefore, it was better if they all went home. Amanda reluctantly agreed, even if she wondered if the agents weren't just coming up with an excuse to get her, Brock, and Barb out of the way.

Now here she was, back in her own bed. Or Tommy's bed. Or whatever. She blinked a few times, then, with great effort, got her feet down to the floor.

She stood, looking at herself in the mirror over Tommy's dresser. She was wearing the nightgown Tommy loved, mostly because it was easy to remove. As had become her custom of late, she briefly lifted its hem to study her stomach.

It was perhaps a little rounder than normal. But it could have just been bloating. She yawned, stretched, then walked down the hall toward the kitchen. Sometimes, if she ate something small before the nausea hit, she could stay on top of it.

The first thing that struck her as out of place was that Barb was sitting on the couch. Just sitting. Barb was not a sitter. She was a woman of action. And shouldn't she have been at work?

The next thing that registered as being off was Barb's cheeks. They were stretched tight, but not in a smile. There was strain Amanda had never seen before.

Amanda had stepped fully into the room when the final and most significant incongruity filled her ears.

A man's voice, coming from behind her.

"Good morning," he said pleasantly. "My name is Herrera. I hope you had a nice sleep. I didn't want to have to wake you."

"What's going on?" Amanda said, turning to see three men, all of whom appeared to be Mexican, standing behind her.

The one who called himself Herrera stepped forward. His eyes traced up and down her body three times.

"I'm afraid you're going to have to come with us," he said.

She didn't look at him as he spoke. She was too focused on his gun.

CHAPTER 54

B y three o'clock, I had returned to the administration building, in that empty middle manager's office, with that six-ounce burner phone heavy in my hand.

Agents Hines and Hall had been making their necessary preparations, calling in enough personnel from surrounding field offices that they could overwhelm whatever forces New Colima brought along. Their assumption was that El Vio would have several armed bodyguards and an advance team that would inspect all of Dorsey's Knob Park before they would allow their boss to approach.

Concealment was therefore critical. As Hall had put it to me, "Our job is to make sure that any of our people who are within a mile of that park look like a local, a log, or a tree."

Mitch had been busy as well. A parcel with a thousand empty deposit slips from Mexico had arrived that morning, having been priority overnighted the previous day. He had recruited Jerry Strother, Bobby Harrison, and Rob Masri; swore them to secrecy; and then inducted them into what he called "the Fake Squad." Equipped with more than a dozen pens of varying color, width, and ink type, they had been holed up in a room with a large whiteboard. It was covered with all the Spanish names, first and last, that Mitch could remember the cartel using.

Each deposit slip was filled out with a different combination of names and a random amount of money, per Mitch's instruction. A few were placed directly in the shoebox, remaining crisp and pristine. The rest were distressed to varying degrees—sat on, folded, stuffed in a pocket, and so on—before going in. Once they got the hang of it, each man was averaging a fully forged deposit slip roughly every minute. At that rate, they were expecting to be done with all 951 anytime now.

The plan was that Mitch would march up the hill with me, receive his assurances that he would be allowed to live a long and happy life, then hand the box to El Vio. Neither Mitch nor I would be wearing a wire—it was too risky, we all agreed—but the FBI had already planted enough listening devices nearby that a cricket wouldn't be able to fart without them hearing it.

The FBI was hoping that El Vio might say something incriminating to Mitch. But even if he didn't, the moment Mitch and I were clear, they would swoop in and make the arrest. The initial charge would be obstruction of justice—for receiving stolen evidence. It was a bit like getting Al Capone for tax evasion, but whatever.

Hines and Hall would then work on flipping Ruiz and Gilmartin, getting them to admit that they were operating under orders from El Vio when they murdered Kris Langetieg. The killing of a federal prosecutor would earn El Vio, and anyone else in the chain of command, a life sentence with no possibility of parole.

It was all in place. I just needed to confirm we had a deal.

Ruiz answered my call on the first ring with a brusque, "Hello."

I didn't waste time with niceties. "Are you in?"

"Yes," he said.

I balled my fist and squeezed. "Good. Meet us up there at one A.M. sharp. I'll be wearing the same CO's uniform Gilmartin saw me in last time. I'll have Dupree with me, obviously. And he'll have all nine hundred and fifty-one deposit slips. Are you ready to take the routing and account numbers for the five million?"

"Go ahead," he said.

I read off the numbers that Hines had given me. She had ex-plained that the money would eventually be seized by the FBI as part of a larger legal action against New Colima. That was fine by me. I was done worshipping at the altar of cash.

"Got it," he said when I was done.

"The bank has a customer service line for high-net-worth individ-uals that's staffed twenty-four/seven. I've told them I'm expecting two large deposits. I'm going to call them at twelve thirty A.M. If the money isn't there, we'll go straight to the FBI."

"Understood."

"Also, just so you don't get any ideas about shooting us the mo-ment Mitch hands over those deposit slips, my roommate knows I'm running the hill," I said, even though my roommate was hopefully in South Carolina by now. "I've told him if I'm not back by one thirty, he's supposed to sound the alarm. He'll tell everyone at FCI Morgantown that the New Colima cartel helped me escape. It'll take about five minutes for your boss to become the subject of a major manhunt. They'll be closing roads, closing airports, sending up chop-pers, the whole thing. Cops live for stuff like that."

"Okay," Ruiz said. "And just so *you* don't get any ideas, we'll be checking that shoebox for tracking devices. If there's anything metal, electronic, or emitting some kind of signal in that box, we'll know it. It had better be clean. Oh and one more thing."

He left some dead air, so I said, "What's that?"

"I want you to hang up your phone and keep the line clear for the next two minutes. Someone is going to call you and have a brief chat with you. Then I'm going to call you back."

"Okay, who?"

I waited for a response. None came. He had hung up.

It took thirty seconds for my phone to ring again. The number was one I didn't recognize from the 973 area code, which was north-ern New Jersey.

"Hello?" I said.

"Hi, honey, it's me," said Amanda. Hearing her mellifluous Mississippi accent should have been a sweet treat. But there was quaver in it that didn't belong.

"Hey, love, what's going on?"

In a surprisingly calm voice, she said, "I'm supposed to tell you that your mother and I have been kidnapped. We're fine. They're treating us fine. We're being held at a—"

And that's all I got.

"Amanda!" I shrieked. "Amanda!"

She was gone. I reeled, sickness and panic slamming into me. No discernible thoughts were forming in my head. It was filled with a terror that was like loud white noise, blocking out everything else. It took most of my concentration not to fall out of the chair.

Then the phone rang again.

Ruiz.

I cursed him, his mother, his whole rotten genome going back to when his ancestors crawled out of the primordial slime.

He waited until I was done, then said, "Just so we're perfectly clear: If there is any trap here—any trace of law enforcement, any rival cartel, anything other than this exchange going exactly as you've described—they will be dead, got it? We're going to hold on to them as long as we feel like it. If you have us followed in any way, if El Vio doesn't make it safely all the way back to Mexico, they will be dead. If El Vio is not a hundred percent satisfied by the documents he received, they will be dead. If we get wind there's any kind of effort to rescue them, either by the cops or by someone else you're working with, they will be dead. They are our ultimate insurance policy. Do you understand all this?"

I was hearing the words. I was quite sure if I fully understood them—if I grasped how much danger my future wife and my mother were now in—I would have passed out from the shock. Already, I was dizzy from all the extra blood my supercharged heart had sent racing around my veins.

"And you . . . you won't hurt them?" I managed to say.

"We don't plan to," he replied, which wasn't what I wanted to hear.

"But how do I know you won't just kill them once the deal is done?"

"You don't," he said. "See you tonight."

I staggered out of the office and down the hall to the conference room where Hines, Hall, and their colleagues were bent over laptops and mumbling into mobile phones.

The door was open, which was fortuitous. I wasn't sure I had the strength to open it. It was all I could do to fall back on my voice training and remember how to draw enough breath into my lungs to make myself heard.

"The operation is over," I said, interrupting at least three different conversations. "It's over. I want everyone except Mitch and me to be as far away from that stupid park as humanly possible."

There were half a dozen agents in the room. They had all stopped talking but were eyeing me blankly.

Men in khaki uniforms didn't tell them what to do.

"You want to tell us what's going on?" Hines asked.

In a brisk staccato, I recounted my exchange with Ruiz and my brief conversation with Amanda. Hines' face darkened as she listened.

"We should have anticipated the cartel would make a move like that and sent a protective detail," she said. "That's our fault."

"You're goddamn right it is," I snarled.

"Call the Newark Field Office and let them know what they have going on," Hall said to one of his fellow agents, then turned to another and added, "And call down to Atlanta. Let's get a detail on Dupree's family a-sap."

It was like they hadn't been listening.

"No, no, no," I said. "You're missing the point. There is no Newark. There is no Atlanta. You guys are going home now. You effed up. They win. We lose. Good-bye. This is over."

Hall already had his hackles up and was ready for a good old-fashioned cockfight.

"I'm sorry, Mr. Jump, I am. I hate to be blunt about it, but having a chance to capture the head of the New Colima cartel is a lot bigger than your family. El Vio has killed thousands of people's family members, and he's going to kill thousands more if we don't stop him. Do you understand that?"

"And you're just ready to add two lives onto his tally, just like that?" I said. "You're a cold son of a bitch, you know that?"

"I can live with that," he said stiffly.

"Well, I can't. So let me make this really, really simple for you: You're going to cease and desist right now because I'm not walking up that hill tonight until I am utterly convinced that everyone with a badge in the state of West Virginia is well clear of that park. There's no threat you can make, no payment you can promise me, no torture you can devise that will make me change my mind. Do *you* understand *that*?"

Hines put on her schoolteacher voice. "Everyone just take a deep breath for a moment, okay?"

I couldn't have if I wanted to. I was too furious. But I at least stopped talking as I glowered at Hall as Hines spoke.

"To begin with, Mr. Jump, you don't give the orders around here. I do. So we're not ending this operation because you said so. We're ending this operation because I said so. Are we clear on that?"

Hall was readying a counterargument, but Hines cut him off before he could spit out the first syllable of it.

"Chris, I'm sorry, but our guidelines are very clear here. The bureau doesn't get to play Machiavelli. That's not my opinion. That's policy. We can't knowingly go through an operation that will directly lead to the extermination of two civilians. It would give Mr. Jump a wrongful death suit against the bureau that would have the director looking to fire anyone who came near it. So perhaps that's the big picture you want to focus on. I'm afraid Mr. Jump is right. The cartel outmaneuvered us. They win this round. Our only goal now is to make sure everyone gets out of this alive. And the best way to do that is for us to stand down."

For the first time since I heard Amanda's voice, I felt like I could breathe just slightly.

"Thank you," I said. "Thank you so much."

"You realize without us capturing El Vio, there's nothing we can do to help you long term," Hines said. "We'll still be putting Mr. Dupree in witness protection. It's the right thing to do for his safety, and we probably need to keep that promise just to get him to cooperate tonight. But there's nothing we can do to help you. You're free to take your case to the courts and I certainly hope they give you a hearing. But there's a very real chance you'll have to stay in prison and serve your sentence."

"That's fine," I said. "Absolutely fine."

It was a blessing to have the chance to make that sacrifice.

"Okay," she said. "You can go ahead with the exchange tonight as planned. We'll let you keep the burner phone so you can check to make sure the money has been deposited, but don't get any cute ideas about moving it somewhere else. We've put a no-withdrawal block on the accounts and will be changing the passwords in the morning."

"Right."

"I'll brief the warden about what's happening so he doesn't interfere. Hall and I will be here, because we have to take Dupree away as soon as this is over. Otherwise, I'll have everyone clear out. You realize, of course, this means you'll be going up there naked, no backup. If the cartel decides to make a move against you . . ."

"I'll take my chances," I said.

"Well, then I guess we're done here. You can go back to your dorm now."

"Thank you," I said.

And then she made the grand pronouncement: "All right, people. Let's pack up and get out of here."

CHAPTER 55

If time onstage always went too fast for me, flowing so blissfully I barely felt its passage, the time after I left the administration building dragged to a near-frozen halt.

All I could think about were Amanda, my mother, my unborn child, and the extraordinary peril they were in. As far as I was concerned, nothing in the universe—not space, not time, not the most distant matter in the farthest galaxy—would move normally again until I knew they were safe.

I pictured Amanda, now perhaps starting to show just slightly, bravely looking for any opportunity to improve her chances of survival. She and my mother would be strong, neither wanting to give in to the fear they surely felt, because they would be worried about the other. But they had to be beyond terrified.

Had a cartel goon tied them up? Were they stashed away in a basement somewhere? Had they been beaten, tortured, or broken in some way to make them more compliant? I didn't even want to ponder any of it, and yet I couldn't help it.

The harrowing fact was that their continued survival was reliant upon the basic decency of the world's most violent criminal syndicate. The knowledge of that was so oppressive I thought it might cripple me. I swore the only reason my body kept working is because the basic functions that kept it going—respiration, circulation, that sort of thing—were automated, and therefore too stupid to know they probably should have stopped.

At least a dozen times, when I knew I was alone, I pulled out my burner phone and called Amanda, my mother, our home line. All three went to voice mail. I listened each time, just to hear them talk to me.

After dinner, and after the sun went down, I snuck out to the tree where I had hidden the unicorn. I was relieved to find it still there, unbothered.

When I returned to my room, I stuffed the package under Frank's bare mattress, which remained unoccupied. Mr. Munn had told me it might remain so for a while. To say the room felt emptier without him was a Frank-size understatement.

After lights-out, I lay on top of my bunk, not bothering with getting under the covers, staring at the wooden planks above me, just like I had on my first day at Morgantown. It seemed impossible that had been only two months ago. It seemed equally impossible how many months I still had left to contemplate that ceiling.

This was around the time that my thoughts naturally turned dark. The horrific image of Kris Langetieg's carved-up death mask kept visiting me, like a sick song that was stuck in my head.

Did a similar fate await the people I loved most? Was that the only way the cartel knew how to conduct its business? Could I ever survive their loss?

There was no need to ponder that last question. I already knew I couldn't.

It went to something I had slowly figured out sometime during my early twenties: that for as hard as we have searched for them through-out the ages, there are no all-encompassing epistemologies, no meta-narratives that elucidate the real truth, no Rosetta stone that translates our baffling existence into a more readily understood tongue. Human beings are basically bumbling along, each of us constructing these self-contained dramas so we can offer ourselves some reasonable explanation of what would otherwise be a bunch of random, chaotic interactions.

In short, we're telling ourselves stories in which we conveniently happen to be the protagonists. And while that is true, so is this seemingly paradoxical fact: People who put other people at the middle of their stories lead the most rewarding lives. If all you live for is yourself, it's pretty damn lonely out there.

So what would I be without Amanda and my mother?

That was a story I didn't want to contemplate, a door behind which lay only the most unimaginable pain.

I made myself stay in bed with my terrible thoughts until 12:25 A.M., at which point I shucked off my prison khakis and donned the unicorn, rolling and cinching as needed.

Then I strolled out of my room, down the hall, and past the empty CO's office, not caring whether anyone was in there.

Once outside, I powered up my burner phone and called the customer service line for the bank. After I recited the proper numbers and the soon-to-be-changed pass code, a young woman with a friendly Caribbean cadence informed me five million dollars had been wired to the account earlier that evening. I repeated the same procedure for the second account and got the same answer.

We were a go. This was happening.

Since a 12:40 launch had worked for me the last time I ran the hill, I decided to make that the appointed minute again. I would be a little faster, since I didn't need to bother with as much stealth. However, I would also be a little slower, with Mitch in tow. It averaged out.

I loitered outside until 12:38, then went to fetch Mitch. He was dressed and waiting for me at his door. We made brief eye contact. Under his arm, he carried a shoebox and 951 of what I hoped were the most exquisite counterfeits ever created.

We exchanged no words. I simply turned back toward the front entrance, and he followed. Back outside, I let him take the lead. We had decided to do it that way in case any of El Vio's goons were watching from afar. It would look more like a CO escorting a prisoner, which was the general effect we were going for.

"Thanks for doing this," I said as we marched through the rec area. "I know this is going to be pretty disruptive for your family."

"It's better this way. You were right about the cartel. They were never going to stop coming after me. Hopefully this makes them happy."

"What happens to you after this?"

"They haven't told me exactly. I just hope we go somewhere warm. Arizona, maybe. You know I've never seen the Grand Canyon?"

"Good luck with that," I said.

"Yeah, we'll see."

We walked a few more feet before he added, "Sorry about, uh, your family. Hines told me."

"Let's just get this over with," I said. "I'll fall apart if I think about it too much."

We reached the tree line quickly enough, then started the serious part of the climb. As I suspected, it was slower with Mitch.

I remained vigilant for signs that Hines hadn't kept her word to keep herself and her people scarce. I could still abort at any time. The FBI wouldn't have probable cause to make an arrest until El Vio actually took possession of the evidence. I had watched enough cop shows to know an unrighteous arrest could screw up everything that followed. If I saw anything that made me nervous, I was going to tackle Mitch and beat him until he was either senseless or surrendered the box voluntarily.

But there was nothing in the forest except forest. Every indication was that the FBI had left Dorsey's Knob Park to the criminals.

We reached the ridge, then, a short time later, the clearing. I had charted a better course this time, such that we came out closer to the picnic area, near the parking lot.

There were three vehicles, all black SUVs. A group of men was milling around the tables. I counted eight of them. One of them was theoretically El Vio. Ruiz and Gilmartin were surely there as well. That left five men who were there as extras—lookouts, muscle, body-guards, whatever you wanted to call them.

"Okay, there they are," I said to Mitch, as if he somehow couldn't see them.

As soon as the men became aware of our presence, they shined flash-lights in our direction, trying to get the beams to land on our faces.

"That's close enough," Danny called out. "One at a time now. With your hands up."

I went first. With the flashlights having now found my eyes, it was difficult to make out who or what was coming my way. All I knew was there were a lot of paws all over me. It was like being groped by an octopus. One of them pulled up my shirt. Another yanked down my pants. A third passed a wand over my front and back. It didn't squelch at my belt or my steel-toe boots, so it must have been looking for radio waves, not metal. A bug detector. There were flashlights scanning up and down my body the entire time.

"Hurry up," I said. "Both of us have to be back at one thirty or all hell is going to break loose."

"Sorry, Slugbomb," said Danny, and at that point I realized he had been the guy with the wand. "We do things a certain way here."

I subjected myself to their prodding until one of my octopi mut-tered something in Spanish and it stopped.

"Okay, Mitchell, you're next," Danny said.

As I put my clothes back in order, Mitch received the same treat-ment. He kept the shoebox clutched in both hands over his head. Again, the inspection ended with a gruff half sentence of Spanish. Mitch put himself hastily back together, tucking the shoebox under his arm as he did so.

Then a hooded figure walked toward us from the gloom. From

the way the other men reacted to his presence—with large shows of respect and smaller shows of fear—I could deduce this was El Vio.

He was smaller than I thought he'd be, perhaps only a few inches taller than me. It was too dark to see him all that well, but I could make out the basics: He was brown-skinned; he had a full head of hair, also dark, peeking out from under his hood; he was certainly from somewhere in Latin America. He was wearing mirrored sunglasses. I didn't know how he could see a thing through them.

Apparently, neither did he. Because as he got closer to us, he removed them. His white eye, the one Danny had told me about in that long-ago diner meeting, blazed in the darkness.

But the sense I really got, and it radiated from him powerfully, was this aura of evil. Just looking at him gave me the feeling you might get when an ominous cloud passes over just after sunset, blotting out what little light remains; and the wind chooses that moment to pick up; and all you're wearing is a thin T-shirt and flip-flops, so the cold instantly soaks you even though you swear you're not wet.

He had walked up to Mitch and stopped.

"I am El Vio," he said in accented English. "What is it you feel you need to say to me?"

Mitch had obviously been rehearsing this, because his response came without hesitation. "I just wanted to meet with you, man to man, and hear directly from you that we have no more beef with each other. You're getting what you want. So I want to make sure I get what I want, which is to be left alone. I want you to promise you won't come after me, my wife, or my kids."

"I'm a peaceful businessman," El Vio said smoothly. "I have never 'gone after' anyone. I wish you and your family a long and prosperous life."

"I'd like to shake on that," Mitch said.

He held out a hand. El Vio let it hang there for a moment, like maybe he was expecting fire to burst from it.

"Where I'm from, a man shakes another man's hand when he makes a promise," Mitch said.

His hand was still outstretched. When nothing happened after another beat or two, El Vio said, "Okay."

They shook hands. It lasted maybe a second.

"Good," Mitch said, then looked in my direction, like it was now my turn.

"And you'll release my family once you're back to Mexico," I said, the nerves rocketing around in my stomach.

"I don't know what you're talking about," El Vio said smugly.

His nonchalance infuriated me. Instinct took hold, and I rushed forward, grabbing him by the sweatshirt and pulling him toward me. The men near El Vio were momentarily caught flat-footed. They hadn't expected me—a small man with no weapons—to make this kind of move.

"The hell you don't," I growled, getting so close to his face I could see him flinch as my spittle landed on his cheeks. "If you hurt them, I swear I will make it my life's work to put you in the ground."

I managed to get the sentence out. Then one of the bodyguards reached me. With one hand, he ripped me off El Vio, throwing me toward another bodyguard—the biggest one, probably a foot taller than me—who put me in a chokehold. I grasped his forearm and attempted to pry it off, but his free hand had already grasped the other one, adding more strength to the hold. He lifted me off the ground, using my own bodyweight to further constrict my windpipe.

El Vio calmly straightened his clothes. Just as pinpricks of light started popping in my vision, he said, "Let him go."

The bodyguard dropped me. I fell on all fours. Another body-guard kicked me in the ribs. Maybe not as hard as he could have. But he made his point. Whatever wind was left in my lungs was knocked out.

Still gasping for breath, determined to show I was tougher than any of them thought, I got back to my feet. Mitch was looking at me, wondering if I was going to give it another go. But I had made my point too.

"Go ahead," I said to Mitch, my voice coming out in a ragged wheeze. "Give the man what he came for."

Mitch extended the box. El Vio took it with both hands.

All that maneuvering, all those machinations, all that money, and in the end it was that simple. A Mexican drug lord had just paid ten million dollars for 951 meaningless scraps of paper.

"Thank you, Mr. Dupree," El Vio said.

"Right, then," Mitch said.

El Vio said something in Spanish. The group formed a shell around him and moved as one toward the parking lot.

I wasn't waiting around for anyone to engrave invitations for us to make our own departure. Neither was Mitch. He pivoted toward the trees. I was right behind him. The forest meant safety.

We had taken perhaps ten or fifteen steps. We still had roughly another fifty yards to cover. My wind was coming back to me. I never thought I could be so eager to get back to prison.

And then, quite suddenly, the silent night was torn open by three explosions.

At first, I couldn't hear. The detonations had rendered my ears worthless.

But I could see. At least a little. And it was like the air was spontaneously producing people in gas masks and black tactical gear.

They were pouring in from all angles. They even seemed to be coming up from the ground itself. They were holding AR-15s and running fast toward the clump of men that had formed around El Vio, though I could no longer make them out. They had disappeared in a cloud of white smoke.

The first sound to penetrate my concussed skull was the popping of gunfire. It was impossible to tell whether it was coming from the Mexicans or from the people in the gas masks. I suppose I should have thrown myself on the ground, but I couldn't make myself move.

Rick Gilmartin emerged from the cloud of smoke. He was just a contractor. He wanted no part of defending El Vio to the death. He was running low, angling toward the woods, except he was holding a pistol and sprinting straight toward a phalanx of soldiers. They had no choice but to take him down. His arms flew in the air as he fell.

Danny Ruiz was also trying to flee, also armed. He didn't make it far. A short burst of fire spun him, then a few more rounds buried themselves in his back. He arched, then crumpled, facedown. It hardly seemed real. This was something we might have done back on the playground in Hackensack, where we shot each other with sticks we pretended were *Star Wars* blasters. Except Danny Danger wasn't wearing his camo pants. And he wasn't getting back up to keep playing.

Then, finally, beneath the booming report of all that weaponry, I heard the words being shouted:

"FBI! FBI! Get down! Get down!"

What came out of me next was a primal scream that surged up from my diaphragm.

"No!" I roared. "No! No! No!"

Heedless of the bullets whizzing through the air around me, I ran toward the first gas-masked person I could catch up to, a man who was advancing slowly in a low crouch, with his AR-15 swiveling, waiting to take aim at whoever materialized from the smoke cloud next. I seized him by his body armor, like stopping him would somehow stop this whole horrible scene.

"You idiots," I bellowed. "You're killing them. Don't you know you're killing them?"

But of course he didn't care. None of them did. Lia Hines' talk about bureau policy and wrongful death suits had been a total con, a deception designed to gain the cooperation she would have otherwise never gotten from me. And I had been fooled by her elementary school teacher act enough to believe her.

She had even made a show of pulling out. And that's all it had been. A show. For my benefit. She probably never even considered canceling the operation.

Repugnant Chris Hall had been the one telling the ugly truth: The bureau wasn't going to pass up a chance to collar El Vio. Maybe it believed it could rescue the civilians in time. Maybe it really had made the icy calculation that a pregnant woman and some guy's mom were just collateral damage. To some suit in Washington, their lives didn't mean much.

The agent I had grabbed was trying to twist himself free of my grasp. In a rage, I reached for his gun. I was going to rip it out of his hands, then shoot every damn last one of those agents. Maybe if El Vio saw me fighting for him, he would know I hadn't been the one who betrayed him. Maybe he would spare my family.

That plan lasted for exactly two seconds before another agent tackled me. Then two more agents leapt on me. As I thrashed and swore and spit and howled and fought with everything I had, they kept me pinned to the ground, easily subdued.

I wished they had just shot me. It would be far less painful than what was coming next.

Because with sickening certainty, I knew:

If Amanda and my mother weren't already dead, they would be soon.

CHAPTER 56

The women were bound, gagged, and blindfolded, quite nearly as incapacitated as a human being could be. Still, Herrera had not left the room for hours. He had barely even taken his eyes off them. He was leaving nothing to chance.

They were on the second floor of New Colima's Newark safe house, in a room whose windows had been covered over with cardboard. The panel van they had been transported in—another Hector Jacinto rental—was parked outside.

The older woman was dressed for work, as she had been earlier in the day when Herrera had entered her house through the sliding glass door that he had left open for himself. The younger woman was still in her nightgown. She used what little freedom she had with her hands to continually tug it down.

Herrera had made the older one call into work and tell them she would be out a few more days. She had already taken off the first three days of the week, so this was not unexpected. The other woman, the blonde, was simpler. She didn't have a job to call into.

There would be no one looking for them. And, even if there were, they wouldn't know where to start.

Herrera was joined in the room by the associates who ran the safe house, the two men who had helped arm him two days earlier. They were locals, ordinarily far down in the cartel pecking order. Their lives otherwise consisted of counting inventory and helping to settle the occasional turf dispute. This was the most exciting thing that had ever happened to them.

Every hour or two, Herrera removed the women's gags and poured water down their throats. It was important to keep the hostages alive for now, in case the actor demanded proof of life.

The older woman swore profusely and spat the liquid back at him. The blonde, likely mindful of her baby, accepted the hydration without resistance.

Herrera's orders from El Vio were . . . Well, actually El Vio didn't need to bother, since it was Herrera's plan all along. Herrera knew exactly what he was doing. He had prepared a long time for this. He just had to wait until the time was right, until he got the call.

Other than the swearing of the older woman and the occasional grunt from one of the associates, the room remained quiet.

Then, finally, Herrera's phone rang.

It was someone in West Virginia.

"Yes?" he said in Spanish.

He walked into the hallway and listened for a while. Then he said, "I understand. Thank you. I'll take care of everything."

Herrera reentered the room.

"Is it time?" one of the associates asked.

"Yes. Stand over there," Herrera ordered, pointing toward the corner to his right, the one opposite where the women were crumpled. "Unless you want to get blood all over you."

Herrera pulled the pistol from his waistband. Its fifteen-round clip was fully loaded. He had cleaned the gun, dry-fired it, made sure it was in perfect working order. He didn't want any mistakes.

"We should have some fun with the little blonde first," the other associate said.

"Yes, you're right," Herrera said. "Let's have some fun."

And then he pointed the gun at the associates.

"Lace your hands behind your head," he said. "You're under arrest."

The associates looked at him like he was joking. From downstairs, there were two distinct noises. First a loud thud, then the sound of splintering wood as the front door was broken down.

"FBI, FBI!" yelled several voices at once.

"Hands behind your head," Herrera said again more forcefully. "You are failing to comply with an order from a sworn law enforcement officer. I know you're armed. If you make a move toward your weapons, I am authorized by the laws of the state of New Jersey to use deadly force. Now, hands up."

One of the associates raised his arms. The other jerked his right hand toward his belt.

It didn't get far. Herrera shot him twice, center mass. The force of the bullets tilted him against the wall. His lifeless body left a bloody line as it slid down to a resting position.

One of the woman, the blond one, screamed into her gag.

From downstairs: "Shots fired, shots fired."

The other associate now had his hands locked behind his head. Several pairs of boots were clomping up the stairs toward them.

"We're in here," Herrera said calmly. "One man down. The other is complying."

Two body-armor-wearing FBI agents entered the room. In short order, they had the remaining associate handcuffed and escorted him from the room.

It was only then that the man who had been calling himself Herrera for years put away his gun and crossed the room. He knelt next to the women and gently tugged off their blindfolds and removed their gags.

"You can relax," he said. "You're perfectly safe."

He removed his jacket and placed it around the shoulders of the blond woman, who had started shaking.

"As you have perhaps figured out by now, I am not truly with the New Colima cartel," he said. "I'm with the Policía Federal Ministerial, the PFM, in Mexico. We are working in cooperation with the

Federal Bureau of Investigation. My name is really Sanchez. I'm what's known as a sleeper agent. I'm sorry to have put you through this ordeal, but it was important that El Vio, everyone in the cartel, Tommy, and even the two of you believed you were in great danger."

The older woman was working her jaw, still stiff from being gagged. The younger woman spoke first.

"Is Tommy okay?"

"He's fine," Sanchez assured her. "El Vio was arrested a short time ago in West Virginia and is now in custody, along with the men who were wise enough to surrender themselves without a fight. Tommy knows you're safe. He's being debriefed right now. I would expect he'll be able to call you shortly. He'll be in FBI custody until tomorrow, when he will be meeting with a federal judge in closed chambers for an emergency resentencing hearing. We fully expect at that time he will be set free."

"Except he won't be free," the blonde said. "The cartel is going to come after him, won't it?"

"They're about to have bigger problems on their hands than getting revenge against a person who probably won't be called to testify against them," Sanchez said. "But even if they wanted to, I don't know how they could. I was the only member of New Colima who ever heard the name Tommy Jump. The rest of them, from El Vio on down, are convinced they have been tricked by Peter Lenfest Goodrich. As we both know, they can search the world over for Mr. Goodrich. They'll never find a record of him that they themselves didn't create."

"What about Ruiz and Gilmartin?" the young woman asked.

Sanchez shook his head. "They were killed in the gun battle when we apprehended El Vio. They were the only ones who knew who Pete Goodrich really was.

"Tommy's secret died with them."

EPILOGUE

The seats were filling up before the show, and I was feeling the same rush as ever, even if I wasn't going to be the one who got to stride out onstage to romance this particular audience.

This was not the continuation of the career of Tommy Jump, actor.

It was the debut of Tommy Jump as director of the Hackensack High School spring musical.

We were doing *Anything Goes*. The name was probably perfect, given everything I had been through in the preceding months, though the show wasn't actually my choice. It had been selected by the previous director—who then had to quit early in the run due to an indiscretion that involved too many drinks and too much driving.

I was the understudy who stepped in, both as director and as his long-term sub at the high school. As a history teacher, of course. I passed the background check no problem. After all, Tommy Jump had never pleaded guilty to any felonies.

Early indications were that both positions would be mine permanently. The teacher had quietly retired to save his pension, and the principal—who lived in mortal fear of my mother's rapier tongue—had told me that if I could get my teaching certification by the time school started the next fall, I could have the job. It looked like between the credits I already had and the ones I could take online, I'd be able to get it done.

That was only one part of what had been some delightfully hectic months. Amanda and I had gotten married a week after I returned from Morgantown in a small ceremony at Hackensack City Hall. I used the *When Harry Met Sally* line in my vows. My mother and Brock DeAngelis were our only witnesses. His present to us was these gorgeous matching wedding bands.

Otherwise, we hadn't been seeing much of Brock. He spent most of his weekends in Baltimore.

We used the seventy-five thousand dollars I'd already been paid by Danny and Rick—which the FBI hadn't known *what* to do with, and therefore quietly left to us—for the down payment on a house. Serendipitously, a place around the corner from my mother had gone up for sale. The nursery was already painted and ready for action.

Outside our little world, things had been busy as well. El Vio had been indicted on a long list of charges, chief among them the murder of Kris Langetieg. Many, many more charges were expected. The New Colima cartel was in full collapse, with all of El Vio's top aides either extradited or in hiding. There was already speculation about which of several competing abominations would take its place.

The day of El Vio's arrest, Thad Reiner had been apprehended as well. He flipped faster than an Olympic gymnast and confessed to everything: the money laundering, the framing of Mitch Dupree, the totality of his years-long association with New Colima. He even admitted he had continued laundering money for the cartel after Mitch's arrest, using his high position at the bank to set up fake accounts. It was why the cartel had kept him alive.

He was now being held at an undisclosed location, segregated from the rest of the population for his own protection. Even with his cooperation, he would be in jail for many decades.

We mostly followed it through the news. The FBI didn't want to touch Peter Lenfest Goodrich, much less bring him near a courtroom. During my debriefing, it was explained to me that Pete's testimony was considered "legally problematic"—starting with the fact that he wasn't a real person and shouldn't have been in prison. Besides, most of what I had witnessed pertained to Ruiz and Gilmartin, who were now dead.

As far as I was concerned, the final word on the subject came not from the FBI but from Mitch Dupree. About three months after coming home, I received a postcard with the Grand Canyon on the front. On the back, there was no return address, just a two-sentence inscription: "Having a great drive. Enjoy your chocolate chip cookies."

We made a batch in his honor that evening. I still think of him every time I see one.

Amanda had returned to serious painting shortly after I got home, trying to get as much done as she could before the baby arrived and seriously curtailed her productivity. She entered a juried competition for artists under thirty and absolutely crushed it, which resulted in a small gallery on the Upper West Side getting interested in her. It wasn't instant stardom, but it was a great next step. Her first exhibit was scheduled for the fall.

As for Hudson van Buren, he finally received his well-deserved comeuppance. A dozen prominent female artists gave interviews to *The New York Times*, detailing decades of his abusive sexual behavior. The *Times* dubbed him the Harvey Weinstein of the art world.

We debated whether Amanda should come forward, taking a wait-and-see approach. If van Buren tried to deny the allegations, we agreed she would have to tell her own story, to support the other women. Then van Buren issued an apology to "all the women I've hurt with my reckless behavior" and announced he was permanently closing his gallery and withdrawing from public life. He accompanied this with a large donation to a nonprofit that assisted victims of sexual violence. It was enough that we considered the matter as settled as it could be.

Besides, we had other things to worry about. Amanda was now thirty-nine weeks along with a little girl who was, by all indications, as healthy as could be. We were in the phase of pregnancy her obstetrician called "late third trimester." I called it "pillow-arranging time"—because only with the artful placement of pillows could she get any sleep at all.

She was not in the audience for opening night of *Anything Goes*. There weren't enough pillows in the universe to make a high school auditorium seat comfortable for two-plus hours. My mother, who had staked out a spot in the front row, promised to give her a full review.

Me? I was backstage, where I was already starting to feel like I belonged. Teaching these kids all the tricks I had learned and watching them blossom was rewarding in ways I had never expected. My once-tentative Reno Sweeney just needed to learn to open her throat when she sang, and she transformed into this brassy alto whose fortissimo could knock over anyone who wasn't seated firmly in the back row. My Billy Crocker was this half-Mexican, half-Japanese kid who, once he was shown how to breathe properly, found one of the more beautiful tenor voices heard in recent memory on the Hackensack High stage.

It turns out applause can actually be more fulfilling when it's for someone else.

Already, some of the younger members of the cast were buzzing about what musical we'd do next spring. I was thinking *Pippin*. I would start rehearsals by telling them what it was like to find a new corner of the sky.

It wasn't that I had given up on acting forever. I was still tinkering with my own musical in my spare time, even if it was now about a former child Broadway star who found happiness directing high school kids. I might even go back to auditioning someday, when I got old enough for character roles, and when my life didn't have as many other demands.

But that was a long way off. The fact is, my own dreams and aspirations weren't as central as they once were. Actors have to be selfish to a certain degree. Dads can't be.

This show wasn't about me anymore.

As a result, the most important person in this particular production—to me, anyway—was a member of the stage crew, a highly responsible, bespectacled junior named Beth Flanders. She was the one I had assigned to monitor my phone. I told her I absolutely didn't want to be bothered by anything.

Unless it was Amanda, making The Call.

And so there was a fist-size flutter in my stomach when Beth came running up to me out of breath about an hour before the curtain was scheduled to go up.

"Mr. Jump, Mr. Jump," she said breathlessly. "It's your wife. She says it's time."

I grabbed the phone from her and said, "Thank you. I have to go now."

"But, Mr. Jump, what are we supposed to do without you?"

"You'll be fine," I assured her. "Hasn't anyone ever told you? The show must go on."

I assume it did. I couldn't say for sure. I was already speeding back to Amanda, to what really mattered. It was a much bigger, more important drama than anything I had ever experienced onstage. And it wasn't even close to the last act.

In truth, it was only the beginning.

ACKNOWLEDGMENTS

As a journalist turned novelist who endeavors to salt his fiction with large grains of truth, I am often the beneficiary of my former profession's work product.

I mean that in the small sense that the Fourth Estate provides a constant stream of insight, inspiration, and information on topics that might otherwise remain obscure to this struggling writer.

But I also mean it in a larger sense that seems to grow only more important. The defining conflict in our world today pits those who acknowledge the existence of objective fact against those who subvert it for their own purposes. Now more than ever, we need determined, honest journalists to shine lights in dark places and remind us how much the truth matters.

For this book, I am particularly indebted to *The Guardian*'s Ed Vulliamy, a man I've never met or spoken to but whose brilliant reporting about malfeasance at Wachovia Bank—and dispatches from the US-Mexico border—helped inform these pages.

That said, I also make up a lot of stuff. And you would never have the chance to read any of it were it not for the incredibly supportive team at Dutton. That starts with my editor, Jessica Renheim; her pinch-hitter for this novel, Stephanie Kelly; and their able helper, Marya Pasciuto. I'd also like to salute publicists Maria Whelan, Becky Odell, and Amanda Walker; marketeers Elina Vaysbeyn and Carrie Swetonic; jacket designer Christopher Lin; production editor LeeAnn Pemberton; paperback guru Benjamin Lee; and the triad of John Parsley, Christine Ball, and Ivan Held.

Thanks, gang. Truly, you're the best.

In addition, I'm thankful to the many foreign publishers who spread this book around the globe, including Angus Cargill at Faber & Faber, whose sharp edits I deeply appreciate; and Andrea Diederichs and the rest of the good folks at Fischer Scherz, whose success would have made my German ancestors proud. *Herzlichen dank.*

Then there's Alice Martell, who gets her own paragraph in these acknowledgments and in my grateful heart. Where would I be without you?

As always, the vast majority of this novel was written in the corner booth of a Hardee's restaurant, my home away from home wherever I happen to be. I'd like to especially call out Benji Frye, who recently celebrated twenty years of coming in every day with the best attitude imaginable.

I'd also like to thank:

Marilyn Veltri, Tim Thompkins, and the staff at FCI Morgantown, who let me in to tour their prison and, even better, let me out at the end of the day.

Joyce Flanagan, Pat DiMunzio, and the late Shirley Kibbe, who long ago helped instill my love for musical theater on the stage at Ridgefield High School.

Shevon Scarafile and Greg Parks, who should absolutely not be blamed for any legal mistakes I've made.

Rob Masri, whose wife, Natalie, made a generous donation to the Virginia Institute of Autism so I could malign her husband's good name.

Pete Goodrich, Amanda Porter, and the rest of our extended family at Christchurch School. It's great to be back.

Kris Langetieg and the wonderful people at Cardigan Mountain School, who make summers so magical.

Librarians everywhere, especially Sarah Skrobis of Staunton Public Library (who does not, for the record, have any issues with ear hair).

Booksellers like Veronica Vargas at the Springfield, New Jersey, Barnes & Noble, who has spent many years pushing my work on her customers.

And, finally: you, dear reader. I absolutely love being an author, and I remain forever cognizant that I only get to continue doing this job because of your support. Thank you for buying my books, attending my signings, and sending those e-mails saying you shirked your chores so you could continue reading. I cherish being the cause of undone laundry.

Finishing up where I probably should have started, I am blessed beyond measure by a wonderful family: my parents, Marilyn and Bob Parks, who continue to be my greatest cheerleaders; my in-laws, Joan and Allan Blakely, who are such terrific grandparents.

And, of course, my wife and children. There's a moment in this book when Tommy has this sudden revelation as to why he was put on this planet. I've known for a long time now. Thanks, guys, for being my reason.

ABOUT THE AUTHOR

International bestselling author Brad Parks is the only writer to have won the Shamus, Nero, and Lefty Awards, three of crime fiction's most prestigious prizes. A former reporter with *The Washington Post* and *The Star-Ledger* (Newark), he lives in Virginia with his wife and two children.

3-27-19
4-28-22
17
0